✠ ANCIENT ✠
SHORES

✠ ANCIENT ✠
SHORES

Jack McDevitt

HarperPrism
An Imprint of HarperPaperbacks

"Lightnings in the Sky," in Chapter 2, is quoted from *P–38 Lightning in Action*, by Larry Davis. Reprinted courtesy of Squadron/Signal Publications.

Native-American poetry epigraphs are from *American Poetry Volume Two: Melville to Stickney, American Indian Poetry, Folk Songs and Spirituals* (New York: Library of America, 1993); George Copway, *Life, History, and Travels of Kah-Ge-Ga-Gah-Bowh* (1847) (Chapter 25); John Mason Browne, "Indian Medicine," *Atlantic Monthly* (1866) (Chapter 26); Fannie Reed Giffen, *Oo-Mah-Ha-Ta-Wa-Tha* (1898) (Chapter 29); Don D. Fowler and Catherine S. Fowler, eds., *Anthropology of the Numa: John Wesley Powell's Manuscripts on the Numic Peoples of Western North America, 1868–1880* (Smithsonian Institution Press, 1971) (Chapter 33).

Excerpt from "Sonnet III," George Santayana, *The Complete Poems of George Santayana* (Bucknell University Press, 1979) (Chapter 22). Reprinted by permission.

HarperPaperbacks *A Division of* HarperCollins*Publishers*
10 East 53rd Street, New York, N.Y. 10022

HarperPaperbacks may be purchased for educational, business, or sales promotional use. For information please write: Special Markets Department, HarperCollins*Publishers*, 10 East 53rd Street, New York, N.Y. 10022.

Charts by Virginia L. Staples

First printing: April 1996

McDevitt, Jack.
   Ancient shores/ by Jack McDevitt.
     p. cm.
    ISBN 0-06-105207-8
    I. Title.
PS3563.C3556A8 1996
823'.954--dc20   95-26727
                               CIP

Printed in the United States of America

HarperPrism is an imprint of HarperPaperbacks.
HarperPaperbacks, HarperPrism, and colophon are trademarks of HarperCollins*Publishers*.

❖ 10 9 8 7 6 5 4 3 2 1

For Roseanne and Ed Garrity,
with whom I've always been able to think aloud.

ACKNOWLEDGMENTS

✠

I would like to express special appreciation to those who graciously allowed their fictional alter egos to be flown into a desperate situation during the closing chapters. Also, I am indebted to Galen Hall and Brian Cole for their comments on an early version of the manuscript; to Major Jim Clark, U.S. Air Force (retired), and John Goff, for technical advice; to Lorna Sharp, at the Devil's Lake Sioux reservation in North Dakota; to Christopher Schelling at HarperCollins, and Sue Warga for editorial assistance; to my wife and in-house editor Maureen, who maintains a sense of humor about it all. And to Jim Karas, who first called Lake Agassiz to my attention.

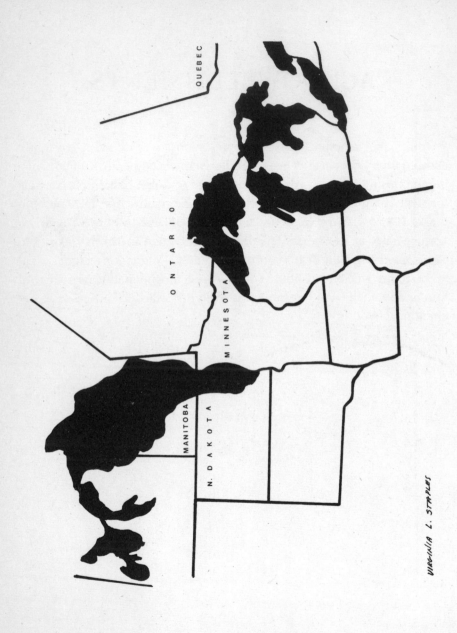

QUEBEC

ONTARIO

MINNESOTA

MANITOBA

N. DAKOTA

VIRGINIA L. STAPLES

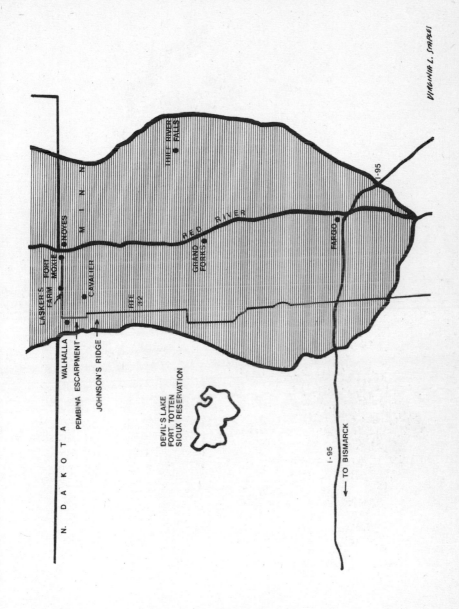

⊹ ANCIENT ⊹
SHORES

✠ 1 ✠

Pretty, in amber, to observe the forms
Of hairs, or straws, or dirt, or grubs, or worms;
The things, we know, are neither rich nor rare,
But wonder how the devil they got there.

—Alexander Pope, "An Epistle to Dr. Arbuthnot"

"If that ain't the damnedest thing." Tom Lasker had to raise his voice to be heard over the wind. Will paused with his spade full of black earth to see what had drawn his father's attention.

A triangular plate, not unlike a shark's fin, stuck out of the ground. It was tough. Metal, apparently, but not corroded.

They were on the low ridge that bordered the west side of the farm, working late under a string of lightbulbs, trying to put in a system that would pump water uphill from the well. Lasker played his flashlight over the object, and Will pushed at it with the tip of his boot. The night smelled of approaching winter. A cold wind chopped across the rise and shook the lights. Lasker knelt and brushed the soil away with gloved fingers. The object was bright red. Smooth and hard. When he pulled, it had no give.

1

The house was about a quarter-mile away, a two-story frame building set back in a thick growth of trees. Its lights were warm and cheerful.

The fin was attached to a rod of the same color and texture, all of a piece. It angled down into the soil at thirty degrees. Will wedged his spade under it, and they tried to lever it up. It wobbled but wouldn't come loose. "On three," said Lasker.

He did the count, and they yanked together, lost their balance, and fell laughing over each other. "That's enough for tonight, Pop," said Will. "Let's go eat."

The Pembina Escarpment was visible through the bedroom windows of Tom Lasker's house. The escarpment consisted of a line of rounded hills and ridges and jutting rocks, a fairly impressive feature on land that was otherwise pool-table flat. Ten thousand years ago it had been the western shore of an inland sea that covered large areas of the Dakotas, Minnesota, Manitoba, and Saskatchewan. The spot where the house now stood would have been several hundred feet underwater.

Lasker was a big man: awkward, with thinning brown hair and wide shoulders. His features were sharp, raw-edged, carved by too many unforgiving winters. He'd lived his entire life in the Fort Moxie area. He thought of himself as basically uninteresting, just a farmer who worked hard, didn't socialize too much, and took care of his family. He was happily married, his two sons seemed to be developing into reasonable adults, and he enjoyed flying. Like many of the local farmers, he had a pilot's license, and he owned a Katana DV–20. He also owned a World War II–era Navy Avenger and was a member of the Confederate Air Force— a group of enthusiasts dedicated to restoring antique warbirds.

ANCIENT SHORES

Shortly after dawn on the morning following the find, he and Will were back atop the slope. October on the northern plains tends to be bleak and cold. This day was typical. Lasker was half buried in his down jacket, not having yet worked up enough sweat to shed it.

The fin stuck several inches out of the ground, mounted on a support pole about two inches thick. Lasker was thinking about the damage it might have done had he run a tractor over it.

Will sank his spade into the earth. "Well," he said, "let's get rid of it." He turned the soil over, and even this late in the season it was heavy and sweet.

The air was still. A blue jay sat on a fence rail, watching, and Lasker felt good about the world. The shark fin interested him. Hard to imagine what it was or how it had come to be buried on land his family had owned for sixty years. More important, it provided a temporary puzzle that bound him a little closer to his son.

How deep did the pole go? He measured off a few feet in a straight line from its point of entry and began throwing up soil in his methodical way. Will joined in, and after a while they struck metal. The pole was at least six feet long. They continued digging until Will had to leave for school. Then Lasker went into the house, had some coffee and toast, and came back for another go. He was still working on it when Ginny called him for lunch.

She came back with him afterward to see what the fuss was about. Ginny was tall, clever, a product of Chicago who had come to North Dakota as a customs inspector, with the primary objective of getting away from urban life. She'd fallen in love quickly with this guy, who in turn had started making trips to Canada, hoping she would clear him when he returned. Sometimes he'd even bought things, stuff he could pay duty on. She

3

remembered the first time he'd tried that approach: He'd spent thirty dollars in a Winnipeg bookstore for a history of Canadian aviation and had clearly been disappointed when she'd waved him through because books were free of duty.

His friends had tried to warn him away from Ginny. *She'll get tired of the harsh winters,* they'd said. *And small-town life. Eventually she'll go back to Chicago.* They'd talked about Chicago more or less in the tone they'd have used for Pluto. But twenty years had passed, and she was still here. And she and Tom thrived on snowy nights and roaring fires.

"Is it creating a problem?" she asked, puzzled, standing over the trench that Lasker had dug around the thing. It was about six feet deep, and a ladder stuck out of it.

"Not really."

"Then why do we care? There isn't any reason to tear it out of the ground, is there? Just cut it off and don't worry about it."

"Where's your sense of romance?" he asked, playing back a line she used occasionally. "Don't you want to know what it is?"

She smiled. "I know what it is. It's a pole."

"How'd it get here?"

Ginny looked into the trench. "There's something down there," she said. "At the bottom."

It was a piece of cloth. Lasker climbed down and dug around the fabric. Tried to free it. "It's connected to the pole," he said.

"This seems like more trouble than it's worth."

"It shouldn't be here."

"Okay. But we've got other things to do today."

He scowled and chunked his spade into the soft earth.

It looked like a mast. Complete with sail.

Connected to a deck.

The Laskers invited their neighbors, and everybody dug.

The deck was part of a yacht. And the yacht was of not-inconsiderable size.

The revelation came gradually during a week's work by a growing force of friends and high-school kids and even passers-by. The shark's fin appeared to be a decorative piece atop one of two masts.

The yacht itself was a substantial piece of marine architecture, complete with pilothouse and cabins and full rigging. They hauled it out of the ground and laid it on its side, propping it up with stacks of cinder blocks. Lasker's younger son, Jerry, played a hose on it. And as the muck washed away they saw bright scarlet paint and creamy white inboard paneling and lush pine-colored decks. The water created a fine spray where it struck the hull. Cables dangled from the starboard side, front and rear. Mooring cables, probably.

With every hour the crowd grew.

Betty Kausner touched the keel once or twice, tentatively, as though it might be hot.

"It's fiberglass, I think," said her husband, Phil.

Jack Wendell stood off to one side, hands on his hips, staring. "I don't think so," Jack said. He'd been in the Navy once. "It doesn't *feel* like fiberglass," he said.

"Tom." Betty Kausner's eyes found Lasker. "Whose boat is it?"

Lasker had no idea. The boat was gorgeous. It gleamed in the shrunken Dakota sun.

At least once every few minutes, someone asked whether it was a joke.

Lasker could think of only one reason someone would

bury a boat like this, and that was that it had something to do with drugs. He fully expected to find bodies in it, and, when they went inside, he peeked reluctantly in each cabin.

He was gratified to find nothing amiss.

The boat looked different from anything Lasker had seen before, although he couldn't have said why. It might have been, that first morning, the shifting texture of the light beneath dark passing clouds. It might have been the proportion of bow to stern, of tiller to mainmast. It might have been some subtle set of numbers in the geometry of the craft.

Will glanced toward the east, in the general direction of the Red River of the North. "It's a long way to the water," he said.

"It looks in good shape." Ray Hammond, who owned the land to the east, along Route 11, scratched his head. "It looks like you could run her out tomorrow." He touched the sails with the tip of his boot. "These might need a little soap and water, though."

A car pulled into the driveway. Ed Patterson and his wife and five kids climbed out. Ed ran the Handy Hardware in Walhalla. He inspected the boat, shaking his head, and his wife looked at Lasker as if Lasker had family secrets that had just been exposed. The kids began chasing one another around the driveway.

Kausner had gone back to his station wagon. He returned with a tape measure. He made marks in the soil at stem and stern and measured it off. "Forty-seven feet, five inches," he announced.

Had anyone been there with a nautical background, that person would have recognized the craft as a ketch. It had a full keel, a wide beam (just under seventeen feet), a full underbody, and a graceful turn to the bilge. Waist-high bulwarks surrounded the deck, tapering toward the bow.

There were two steering stations, one in the cockpit and a secondary one inside the pilothouse, just aft of the beam. Air scoops opened out to port and starboard.

The only visible damage to the craft was a broken propeller shaft.

They took down the sails, washed them, and hung them in the basement to dry. Lasker removed the mooring cables, cleaned them, and put them in the barn.

It took two more days to clear out the belowdecks area.

There were two cabins, a galley, and a washroom.

The cabins were unremarkable. There was a table in each, a scattering of chairs, and two bunks. Several empty cabinets were built into rough-hewn bulkheads.

The galley had a refrigerator, a bank of devices that might have been microwave ovens, and liquid dispensers. But symbols on the microwaves and in the refrigerator were unfamiliar. The washroom had a shower and a washbasin and the oddest-looking toilet Lasker had ever seen: It was low and squat and had neither a seat nor a cover. Again, they found writing no one could identify.

"It's spooky," he told Ginny that first evening after they'd looked belowdecks. The small crowd had broken up after a while and drifted away, leaving Lasker wondering how the boat had got into the hillside. What had Will said? *It's a long way to the water.*

After dinner he looked at the yacht through the windows over the kitchen sink. It gleamed in the moonlight.

"You okay?" Ginny asked.

"I wish I knew what it was. Where it came from."

She offered him a piece of lemon meringue pie. "Must have been your father," she said. "Who else could it have been?"

Later, while she read, he put on his jacket and went out.

Fort Moxie lent itself to timelessness. There were no major renovation projects, no vast cultural shifts imposed by changing technology, no influxes of strangers, no social engineering. The town and the broad prairie in which it rested were caught in a kind of time warp. It was a place where Harry Truman was still President. Where people still liked one another, and crime was virtually unknown. The last felony in Fort Moxie had occurred in 1934, when Bugsy Moran shot his way through the border station.

In all, it was a stable place to live, a good place to rear kids.

The plain stretched out forever. It had been the basin for Lake Agassiz, the inland sea whose surface area had been broader than that of the modern Great Lakes combined.

Agassiz.

Long gone now. He looked west toward the ridge at its old coastline. Not much more than a wrinkle in the plain. An inglorious end. He'd flown over it many times, pointing it out to his boys. He wanted them to love the place as he did.

Ben at Ten, KLMR-TV, Grand Forks, 10:26 P.M., October 18.

Markey: We've got a strange story out of Fort Moxie tonight, Julie. They've found a yacht in a wheat patch.

Hawkins: (*Smiling*) A yacht in a wheat patch?

(Cut to long shot of Fort Moxie; pan out across prairie, close in on windbreak and farm buildings)

Markey: Anybody out there misplace a sailboat?

8

There's a farmer up near the border who's scratching his head tonight. Carole Jensen reports.

(Cut to long shot of yacht and spectators; close-up on Jensen)

Jensen: Ben, this is Carole Jensen at the Tom Lasker farm in Cavalier County.

(Cut to Lasker)

That is a beautiful yacht, Mr. Lasker. Are you really trying to tell us somebody *buried* this on your farm?
Lasker: Yes, I am, Carole. Right up there. *(Pointing)* That's land I'd held out through the last planting season. We're going to plant wheat in the spring. But I needed a system that would pump water uphill. So we were burying pipes, and there it was.
Jensen: The yacht?
Lasker: Yes.

(Angle shot to emphasize the dimensions of the boat)

Jensen: Was it all buried? Or just part of it?
Lasker: All of it.
Jensen: Mr. Lasker, who would leave something like this on your land?
Lasker: Carole, I haven't a clue.
Jensen: *(Turning full face)* Well, there you have it, Ben. I wonder what else is lying around the Red River Valley. We might want to pay a little more attention when we put the begonias in next spring. This is Carole Jensen reporting from the Lasker farm near Fort Moxie.

(Stage shot)

Markey: And that's a wrap for your news team. Good night, Julie.
Hawkins: Good night, Ben. *(Full face to camera)* Good night, folks. We'll see you tomorrow at ten. *Late Edition* is next.

The number of visitors swelled considerably the day after Lasker's boat made *Ben at Ten,* which is to say there were seldom fewer than a half-dozen people and sometimes as many as twenty. The kids took to selling coffee and sweet rolls and turned a nice profit right from the beginning.

Hal Riordan, who owned the Fort Moxie lumberyard, showed up. He wandered through the cabins, where the Laskers had installed a battery-powered heater. He peered closely at the hull and at the masts, and he finally arrived at Lasker's front door. "Something you got to see," he said, leading the way back to the boat. Hal had been old when Lasker was in school; his hair, gray in those days, was now silver. He was tall and methodical, a man who would not go to the bathroom without careful consideration. "This is very odd, Tom," he said.

"What's the matter?" asked Lasker.

"Take a look where the mast is joined to the cabin roof."

Lasker did. "What about it?"

"It's all one piece. The mast should have been manufactured separately, I would think. And then bolted down. Everything here looks as if it came out of a single mold."

Riordan was right: there were no fittings, no screws, nothing. Lasker grunted, not knowing what to say.

✠   ✠   ✠

In the morning Lasker leased a trailer and brought in a contractor from Grand Forks to lift the yacht onto it and move it close to the barn.

The crowd was growing every day. "You ought to charge admission," suggested Frank Moll, an ex-mayor and retired customs officer. "You got people coming in all the way from Fargo." Moll was easygoing, bearded, short, strongly built. He was one of Lasker's old drinking buddies.

"What do you make of it, Frank?" he asked. They were standing in the driveway, watching Ginny and Moll's wife, Peg, try to direct traffic.

Moll looked at him, looked at the boat. "You really don't know how this got here, Tom?" There was an accusation in his tone.

"No." With exasperation. "I really don't."

Moll shook his head. "Anybody else, Tom," he said, "I'd say it's a hoax."

"No hoax."

"Okay. I don't know where that leaves you. The boat looks to be in good shape. So it was buried recently. When could that have happened?"

"I don't know. They couldn't have done it without tearing up the area." He was squinting at the ridge, shielding his eyes. "I don't see how it could have happened."

"Thing that baffles me," said Moll, "is *why*. Why would anyone put a boat like this in the ground? That thing must be worth half a million dollars." He folded his arms and let his gaze rest on the yacht. It was close to the house now, just off the driveway, mounted on the trailer. "It's a homebuilt job, by the way."

"How do you know?"

11

"Easy." He pointed at the stern. "No hull identification number. It would be in raised lettering, like the VIN on your car." He shrugged. "It's not there."

"Maybe this was built before hull numbers were required."

"They've been mandatory for a long time."

They hosed off the sails, which now hung just inside the barn door. They were white, the kind of white that hurts your eyes when the sun hits it. They did not look as if they'd ever been in the ground.

Lasker stood inside, out of the wind, hands in his pockets, looking at them. And it struck him for the first time that he had a serviceable boat. He'd assumed all along that someone was going to step forward and claim the thing. But on that quiet, bleak, cold Sunday, almost two weeks since they'd pulled it out of the ground, it seemed to be his. For better or worse.

Lasker had never done any sailing, except once or twice with someone else at the tiller. He squeezed his eyes shut and saw himself and Ginny gliding past the low hills of Winnipeg's shoreline in summer, a dying sun streaking the sky.

But when he climbed the rise and looked down into the hole from which they'd taken it, peered into that open wound on the west side of his property and wondered who had put it there, a cold wind blew through his soul.

No use denying it. He was spooked.

The taffrail was supported by a series of stanchions. These also seemed not to be bolted or joined to the deck, but were rather an integral part of the whole. When, on the day before Halloween, a souvenir hunter decided to steal one,

12

he had to saw it off. Nobody saw it happen, but Lasker responded by moving the boat into the main barn after dark each night and padlocking the door.

In mid-November Lasker was scheduled to fly the Avenger to Oklahoma City for an air show. Ginny usually went along on these occasions, riding in the gunner's seat. But she'd had enough action for a while and announced her intention to stay home this time. Anyway, she knew the yacht was worth some money, and she didn't like just leaving it in the barn. "Everybody in the world knows it's here," she told her husband.

Lasker laughed and pointed out that yachts were parked in driveways all the time and nobody ever stole one. "It's not like a car, you know."

She watched him fly overhead Friday afternoon. He dipped his wings, and she waved (although she knew he couldn't see her) and went inside to tackle the laundry.

Six hours later she was relaxing in the den, watching an old *Columbo*, listening to the wind bleat around the house. Will was out, and Jerry was in his room playing with his computer. The occasional beeps and the rattling of the leaves were soothing, not unlike the sound of kids sleeping or the blender making milk shakes after school.

She got up during a commercial to get some popcorn. And looked out the window.

The night was moonless, but there was too much light in the curtains. She moved closer to the glass, which was permanently shut against the North Dakota climate and never opened, not even during the brief summer. The barn was slightly downhill from the house.

A soft green glow leaked through its weathered walls.

Someone was inside.

✠ 2 ✠

Oh, Hedy Lamarr is a beautiful gal,
And Madeleine Carroll is too.
But you'll find, if you query,
A different theory
Amongst any bomber crew.
For the loveliest thing
Of which one could sing
This side of the heavenly gates,
Is no blonde or brunette
Of the Hollywood set,
But an escort of P–38's.

—Author unknown, "Lightnings in the Sky"

The Lockheed Lightning gleamed in the late-afternoon sun. It was a living artifact, a part of the great effort against Hitler that could still take to the sky, that still looked deadly. The twin tail booms, the chiseled cockpit, the broad sleek wings all whispered of power. The machine guns and cannon concentrated in its nose had been abrupt and to the point. Its firepower was far more precise than the spread-wing guns of other aircraft of its time. You did not want to get caught in the sights of this aircraft.

"It's not an easy plane to fly," Max said. The P–38J had its own mind; it required a pilot willing to blend with its geometry. A pilot like Max, maybe. A pilot whose senses could flow into its struts and joints and cables and rudders.

"Doesn't matter," said Kerr. He took out his checkbook. "I don't intend to fly it." He threw the remark in Max's general direction.

Kerr was tall and imposing, good-looking in a used-up sort of way, rather like Bronco Adams, the barnstorming pilot-hero of his books. The fictional Bronco flew his trademark Lockheed Lightning in and around WWII China through a series of high-octane, high-sex thrillers. Kerr wrote in a style that he liked to describe as the one-damned-thing-after-another school of literature. It was not surprising that he wanted to own one of the few P–38's left in the world. "You're not going to fly it?" Max asked, not sure he had heard correctly. "It's in great condition."

Kerr looked bored. "I don't fly," he said.

Max had read three of the novels, *Yellow Storm, Night in Shanghai,* and *Burma Crossing.* He'd enjoyed them, had not been able to put them down, and had been impressed with the author's mastery of the details of flying.

"It's true," said Kerr. "I fake it. It's easy."

Max stared at him, outlined against the blue and white star on the nacelle. The plane wore a fresh coat of jungle-colored paint. Its K–9122 designation was stenciled in white on the fuselage, below the name *White Lightning* and the image of a whiskey jug. In 1943 it had operated from a field outside London, where it was part of a squadron cooperating with the RAF. Later it had escorted bombers on missions over Germany, a task for which its combination of range and fire-power were ideally suited. In 1944 it had gone to the Pacific.

White Lightning had a lot of history. Max had tracked it

down from Army Air Force records, had interviewed pilots and ground personnel, and now produced a computer disk. "Everything we could find is here. Pilots. Campaigns. Kills. Eight confirmed fighters, by the way. And two Hinkels. Bombers."

"Good." Kerr waved it away. "I won't need it." He uncapped a gold pen and glanced around for something to lean on. The port side tail boom. "You want this payable to you?"

"To Sundown Aviation." Max's company, which restored and traded in antique warbirds.

Kerr wrote the check. Four hundred thousand. The profit to the company would be a hundred and a quarter. Not bad.

The check was green, and the face contained a reproduction of Bronco's P–38 in flight. Max folded the check and put it in his breast pocket. "Are you going to put it in a museum?" he asked.

The question seemed to surprise Kerr. "No," he said. "No museum. I'm going to put it on my lawn."

Max felt a twinge in his stomach. "Your lawn? Mr. Kerr, there are *six* of these left in the world. It's fully functional. You can't just put it on a lawn."

Kerr looked genuinely amused. "I would think," he said, "that I can do damn near whatever I want with it. Now, I wonder whether we can get on with this." He glanced at the folder in Max's hand, which contained the title documents.

Kerr's pilot-hero was a congenial, witty, and very human protagonist. Millions of people loved him, and they agreed that his creator had raised the aviation thriller to a new level of sophistication. Yet it struck Max that that same creator was a jerk. How was that possible? "If you just leave it on the lawn," Max said, "it will get rained on. It will rust."

What he really meant was that this kind of aircraft deserved something far better than being installed as an ornament on a rich man's property.

"When it does," said Kerr, "I'll give you a call and you can come down and touch it up for me. Now, if you will, I have work to do."

A Brasilia commuter plane was circling the field, getting ready to land. It was red and white against a cloudless sky.

"No," said Max, retrieving the check. He held it out for Kerr. "I don't think so."

"Beg pardon?" Kerr frowned.

"I don't think we have a deal."

The two men looked at each other. Kerr shrugged. "Yeah, maybe you're right, Collingwood," he said. "Janie didn't much like the idea, anyway." He turned on his heel, crossed the gravel walkway into the terminal, and never looked back. Max could only guess who Janie was.

Max came from a family of combat pilots. Collingwoods had flown over Baghdad and Hanoi. They'd been with the USS *Hornet* in the Pacific and with the RAF in the spring of 1940. The family name appears on the 1918 roster of the Ringed Hat squadron.

Max was the exception. He had no taste for military life or for the prospect of getting shot at. His father, Colonel Maxwell E. Collingwood, USAF (retired), to his credit, tried to hide his disappointment in his only son. But it was there nonetheless, and Max had, on more than one occasion, overheard him wondering aloud to Max's mother whether there was anything at all to genetics.

The remark was prompted by the fact that young Max should have been loaded from both sides of the barrel, so to speak. His mother was Molly Gregory, a former Israeli helicopter pilot, who during the Six-Day War had earned her nickname, Molly Glory, by returning fire at shore batteries during the rescue of a crippled gunboat.

Molly had encouraged him to stay away from the military, and he could not help reading her satisfaction that her son would not deliberately put himself in harm's way. Her approval under those circumstances, ironically, had hurt him. But Max enjoyed being alive. He enjoyed the play of the senses, he loved the companionship of attractive women, and he had learned to appreciate the simpler pleasures of snowstorms and sunsets. He expected to have only one clear shot at the assorted joys of living, and he had no intention of risking it to meet someone else's misconceived expectations. Max would take care of Max.

If he'd had any doubts about his character, his suspicions had been confirmed by an incident at Fort Collins when he was twenty-two. He had taken a job flying cargo and passengers to Denver and Colorado Springs for Wildcat Airlines. On a cold mid-November afternoon he had been inspecting his twin-engine Arapaho, standing under one wing with a clipboard, when a commuter flight came in. He never knew what had drawn his attention to the flight, but he paused to watch the plane touch down. The sun was still well above the mountains, the plane a blue-and-white twin-engine Bolo. It rolled down the runway, and he saw the face of a little girl, brown curls, big smile, in the right-hand forward window. The plane slowed and was approaching the terminal when, with only a brief wisp of black smoke as a warning, the port engine burst into flames.

Horrified, Max had started forward. A fuel line must have burst, because the fire roared across the wing and engulfed the cockpit before the pilot had time to react. The little girl with the smile did not even seem to know what was happening.

Someone in a white shirt, with his tie loosened, burst from the terminal and charged the plane. But he was too far away. The fire roared over the fuel tanks. Max had taken only a few steps before he realized it was hopeless. He stopped, waiting for the explosion, knowing it was already too late, almost wishing the blast would come and end it.

The little girl had been watching him, and now she saw the fire. Her expression changed, and she looked back at Max.

Max never forgot those eyes. Then the man with the tie bolted past, his shoes making clacking sounds on the concrete, and Max called after him that he would get killed. He got to the plane, fought the door open, and went inside. Still the girl stared at Max. Then hands drew her away from the window.

And in that moment it went.

The aircraft erupted in a fireball. The blast of heat rolled over him as he fell face down on the apron.

Max had found out who he was.

People rarely recognize the significant moments of their lives without the assistance of hindsight. A trip downtown to buy a book results in a chance meeting that ends at the altar. A late taxi leaves one stranded with a fellow traveler who becomes a friend and who, two years later, offers a career move. You never know.

Max had experienced a turning point shortly after the incident at Fort Collins, when a weekend of planned seduction went wrong and he found himself with nothing to do on an otherwise pleasant spring Sunday. Friends persuaded him to attend a warbirds air show, and he met Tom Lasker and his Avenger torpedo bomber.

Lasker was a flying farmer with several thousand acres up on the border. He had just purchased the Avenger at an auction and was having second thoughts when Max, looking for a lunch partner, came upon him and saw first the plane and then the big weather-beaten man seated beside it, staring at it, his wooden chair turned backward, his rough features creased with concern.

The Avenger was battered; it sagged, and its paint was flaking off. But something about it touched Max. He was a romantic at heart, and the Avenger was pure history, lethal and lovely and in trouble. It was his first intersection with an antique warplane. And it changed his life forever.

"It could use some work," Max had told him.

Lasker spoke to the plane. "I think I got carried away," he said.

Which is how Max got into the antique plane business. He cut a deal and spent the next few weeks restoring the Avenger. He subcontracted to replace the engine and tighten up the hydraulics. He installed state-of-the-art electronics, applied fresh gray paint to the aircraft, and gave it a new set of insignia. Battle stars gleamed on its fuselage and wings, and he drew a crowd when he flew it into Fort Moxie to turn it over to its owner.

That had been a reluctant transfer. Lasker was pleased with the results and handed Max a generous bonus. His wife, Ginny, came with him, and she was ecstatic when she saw what he had done. That earned Ginny a permanent place in Max's affections. She posed in front of the plane and insisted on going for a ride. Lasker had taken her up and circled the town for a half-hour, buzzing the water tower, while Max waited in the office. When they came back, they all went out to the farm, and Ginny laid out a roast-beef dinner. They drank and talked long into the night, and Max slept in the guest room, as he would do many more times.

Max had been restoring antique warbirds ever since.

The colonel and Molly Glory had both approved.

ANCIENT SHORES

✠   ✠   ✠

Max cruised down through cloud decks in the early evening toward Chellis Field outside Fargo. The P–38 felt good, felt damn out of this world. But he had lost the high bid, and the company would have to begin the process of a sale all over again. It was unlikely he would do as well next time.

Still, Max thought of himself as more of an artist than a businessman. His art was incorporated with power and flight as well as with cockpit design and battle emblems. Sundown's warbirds were not intended to rust on someone's lawn. (He didn't even like museums very much, but at least there people could admire the old aircraft for what they had been.)

Well, what the hell. Maybe he would take a beating, but for tonight he was back at the controls of the Lightning.

He'd installed modern navigational systems, of course, and he rode his directional beam in and lined up with the runway. At the three-mile mark the aircraft was at five hundred feet. He reduced throttle and dropped flaps. Indicator lamps blinked on to signal that his wheels were down. The field lights rose toward him. Gently he pushed the yoke forward. Off to his left, ground traffic was moving along Plains Avenue. Just over the tarmac he cut throttle and pulled the nose up. The plane drifted in, and his wheels touched.

Sundown Aviation had its own hangar, which also housed its business offices. He brought the P–38 around, opened the doors with his remote, and rolled inside. There were a couple of other aircraft here that the company was currently working on: a North American P–51 Mustang, which was headed for the Smithsonian, and a Republic P–47 Thunderbolt. The Thunderbolt was owned by an Arizona TV executive.

He shut the Lightning down and climbed out, grinning, picturing how his mechanic would react in the morning when

21

he walked in and saw that the Lightning was back. Moments later he was in his office. Stell had left the coffee machine on. He poured a cup and eased himself down behind his desk.

There were a couple of calls on the machine. One was from a parts supplier; the other was from Ginny Lasker.

"Max," her recorded voice said, "please call when you can."

Her voice had a tightness to it. He could almost think she sounded frightened. He picked up the phone but put it down when he heard the outer door open.

Ceil Braddock smiled at him from the doorway. "Hi, Max." She looked at him curiously. "What happened? Deal fall through?"

Ceil was the owner and sole pilot of Thor Air Cargo, which was also based at Chellis. She had riveting blue eyes, lush brown hair, a wistful smile, and a TWA navigator in St. Paul. Max had tried his luck, but she'd kept him at arm's length. They were able to joke about it occasionally. "You don't love me," she told him, "you love *Betsy*." *Betsy* was a C–47 that Sundown had sold her three years earlier. It had become Thor's flagship, hauling freight around the United States and Canada. There were two other planes in the fleet now, and she was negotiating for a fourth.

Ceil flew *Betsy* occasionally at air shows, and she and Max had even used it to do a joint good deed. On this past New Year's Day a blizzard had buried the Fargo area. There had been more emergencies than there were medevac teams, and a boy who'd taken part of his hand off with an electric saw was in desperate shape on a remote farm. They had attached the skis and flown the C–47 to Pelican Rapids. They'd landed east of the town on a frozen lake, picked up the boy, and brought him back to Fargo, where doctors reattached the hand.

Max smiled. "She was too good for him," he said.

She looked pleased. Max knew that his tendency to be

protective of the planes was one of the features she most liked in him. "What happened?"

"I didn't like him much."

She picked up a cup and filled it. "We're talking a lot of money here. There must have been more to it than that."

"That's it," he said. "Listen, there are plenty of people out there who would kill to own that plane. I don't have to take the first offer."

"I doubt many of them will have Kerr's money to throw around."

There were times when Max almost thought he had a chance with her. He'd stopped beating himself up over her a year ago. "Maybe not." He shrugged. "Probably not."

She sat down across from him, tasted the coffee, and made a face. "You need some fresh brew."

He looked at her. "You're working late."

"Headed for Jacksonville tomorrow."

That would be the annual open house at Cecil Field air show. He understood she'd been inspecting the C–47. "Everything all right?" he asked.

"Five by." She got up, put the cup down. "Gotta go."

He nodded. "See you whenever."

She looked at him for a long moment and then withdrew. He listened to the outer door open, heard it close.

Damn.

He punched the speed-dial button for the Laskers and listened to the phone ring on the other end. Ginny picked it up. "Hello?"

"Hi, Ginny. What's wrong? You okay?"

"Yes. Thanks for calling, Max." The hint of unease was still there. "I'm alright." She hesitated. "But there's something strange happening."

"What?"

"I wouldn't have bothered you, but Tom's gone to Titusville and I haven't been able to contact him."

"Why do you need him? What's going on?"

"Do you know about the boat we found here?"

"Boat? No. Found where?"

"Here. On the farm."

Max visualized the big wheat farm, acres and acres of flat land. "I'm sorry, Ginny. I'm not sure I understand."

"We found a boat, Max. Dug it up. It was buried. Hidden."

"You're kidding."

"Max, I'm not talking about a rowboat here. This thing's a *yacht*. It's been on TV."

"I guess I haven't been paying much attention."

"Reason I called, I looked out the window earlier this evening and saw lights in the barn. It's the boat."

"The boat is lit up?"

"Yes. The boat is lit up."

"So somebody went in and turned the lights on? Is that what you're saying?"

"The barn's locked. I don't think the boat's been touched. I think the lights came on by themselves. They're running lights, long green lamps set in the bow."

Max still wasn't sure he understood. "Who buried the boat?"

"We don't know, Max. As far as we can tell, nobody. At least, nobody recently." Her voice shook.

"You want me to come out?" She hesitated, and that was enough. "I'm on my way," he said.

"Thanks." She sounded better already. "I'll have Will meet you at the airport."

✠ 3 ✠

Here at the quiet limit of the world . . .

—Alfred, Lord Tennyson, "Tithonus"

If nothing else, it was an excuse to take the Lightning out again.

Fort Moxie and the border are a hundred fifty miles north of Fargo. It was a starless night, and the landscape was dark, punctuated by occasional lights, farmhouses or lone cars on remote country roads.

When he was in a cockpit, Max felt disconnected from his own life. It was as if all the mundane events of daily existence were directed toward the single purpose of getting him off the ground. The steady roar of the twin engines filled the night, and he thought how it must have been, flying alongside the B–17's over Germany. He imagined himself strafing an ammunition train, watching it erupt into a ball of flame as he pulled up to engage two ME–109's.

He was grinning when he touched down at Fort Moxie International Airport. Will Lasker was waiting with a black Ford station wagon. The kid wore a jacket with a football letter, and he looked embarrassed. "I'm sorry you had to

25

come all this way, Max," he said. "I mean, we aren't really scared of a *light*, but you know how women are."

Max nodded and threw his bag in the trunk.

Will was full of information, describing how they had found the boat, what it looked like, how visitors were still showing up every day. "A lot of them think *we* put it in the hole."

"I can see," said Max, "why they might think that."

Will hunched over the wheel, and the car left the lights of Fort Moxie behind and rolled out onto the dark prairie. "You'd have to be crazy to think that," he said, as if Max hadn't spoken. "If we had a boat like that, we'd have put it in the lake, not in the ground."

Max wasn't sure what he expected to find at the farm. He'd conjured up a vague notion of a rotted-out hulk with lanterns hung on its gunwales. He was therefore not at all prepared for what he saw when Ginny led him into the barn.

"My God," he said. "You're kidding me." The yacht was bright and sleek even under strings of bare lightbulbs. Will was right: It belonged on Lake Winnipeg, not stored in an old farm building outside Fort Moxie.

Ginny read his eyes. "We have no idea where it came from," she said. "None."

It was mounted on a trailer. The mainmast, which was hinged, had been folded over. Several piles of white canvas were shelved along the wall. "Those are the sails," Ginny said, following the direction of his gaze.

A moist, animal smell alerted him to the presence of horses in stalls at the rear. He saw a lamp forward on the hull, long and teardrop-shaped, but it was not lit. Nor was any other part of the vessel lit. The keel was broad and deep and ran the length of the hull. A wheel was installed in the stern, and there was probably another in the pilothouse just forward of the cockpit. Black spidery characters unlike anything he had seen before were stenciled across the bow, below the lamp.

"Did you turn them off?" he asked. "The lights?"

"Not exactly," said Ginny. She flipped a wall switch.

The barn went dark. It was a tangible dark, absolute, universal. The horses sounded uneasy.

"Ginny?" he asked.

"Wait."

Something began to glow. It reminded him of phosphorous, ambient and silver and amorphous, not unlike moonlight through thin clouds. As he watched, the effect brightened. It was green, the color of a lawn after a spring rain, of ocean water just below the surface when sunlight filters down. It penetrated the stalls, illuminated pitchforks and hoes, and threw shadows from the tractor and the feeding troughs across a side wall. He gaped at the light, suddenly aware why she had been spooked.

"There's one on the other side," said Ginny. "A white light."

"Running lights," he said. "But that's not right, is it? This is the port side. The light should be red."

"I don't know."

"Sure. Red to port, green to starboard." He walked around and looked at other light. "White's not even in the ballpark," he said. He touched the hull. It felt good, the way carved mahogany feels good, or a leather chair. He turned back to her. "How old is this supposed to be?"

She threw up her hands in exasperation. "I don't know."

Max folded his arms and circled the boat. First things first: Why would anyone want to bury something like this? "No one's called to claim it?"

"No."

"This thing's in showroom shape." He stared at its gleaming bow, its polished masts, its color. He walked over to the shelves where the sails had been folded. They did not feel like canvas.

"We washed it," Ginny said.

"It can't have been in the ground long."

"I can't believe anybody buried it while *I* was living here."

He looked at her. That went back a few years. "What's inside it? You find any bodies in there?"

"We thought the same thing. No, no bodies. And no drugs."

"How about an identification number? There ought to be something that would allow you to trace the previous owner."

"If there's anything like that, we haven't been able to find it." She stayed close to him. "Max," she said, "it also doesn't have an engine."

"That can't be. It has a propeller." He noticed that the shaft was broken off. "Or at least it *had* one."

"I know. The propeller tied into a little green box. We can't open the green box, but it doesn't look much like an engine."

She turned the lights back on. Max cupped his hand over the running light and watched it fade.

"Scares me silly," said Ginny. She folded her arms over her breast. "Max, what *is* this thing?"

It didn't look like any boat that Max had seen before. "Let's go back to the house," he said.

He was happy to be away from the boat. Ginny insisted her two sons bring their bedding down to the living room. Jerry was delighted by the opportunity to camp downstairs, and anyhow he was jittery, too. Will didn't really mind, although he pretended to be annoyed. "Humor your mother," Max told him, adopting the just-us-guys mode from the airport.

The kids complied, and they all bunked together. Ginny left lights on all over the house.

✠ 4 ✠

Glides through misty seas
With its cargo of time and space . . .

—Walter Asquith, "Ancient Shores"

Max did not sleep well. He had put on a show of good-natured amusement at Ginny's fears and her insistence they stay together, as if some demonic spirit had come in off the plains and invaded the barn. But it was he who suggested they leave a few lights on outside. Best that the glow leaking in through the windows be coming from GE sixty-watt bulbs rather than from the whatsis. But he felt a degree of pride that she had turned to him for support.

It was not the presence in the barn, however, that caused his restlessness. It was rather the sense of *home*, of a family drawing together. He had known this kind of atmosphere as a child but never as an adult. Lasker occasionally joked about the assorted pleasures of Max's social adventures. Never the same woman twice. And Max played along, because it was expected. But he would have traded it all to get a Ginny in his life.

In the morning they located Tom. The previous evening's

alarms now seemed overblown, and if Ginny had a difficult time explaining why she had summoned help, Max felt uncomfortable at his presence in the rambling farmhouse. "I wouldn't want you to think I was nervous," she told her husband over the phone. "But it was really spooky here. I'm in favor of getting rid of the damned thing."

Lasker was on the speaker. He couldn't believe that the lights had come on, and he kept asking whether she was sure. Finally he seemed satisfied, although Max knew he would not believe it until he'd seen it for himself. As for getting rid of it: "I don't think we want to make any quick decisions," he said. "Let's find out what we've got first. We could throw some canvas over it, if you want. That way you wouldn't be able to see the damn thing."

Ginny looked at Max. "I don't think that's going to make me feel much better, Tom."

"Max," he said, "what do you think about this? Does it make any sense to you?"

"No," said Max. "I have no idea. But I'll tell you one thing—that boat hasn't been in the ground any length of time at all."

There was a long pause on the other end. "Okay," Lasker said at last. "Look, I'm on later this morning. I'll do my stuff and leave right after. Be home this afternoon."

It was a cold, gray, dismal day, threatening rain or snow. During breakfast a few people arrived and banged on the front door. Could they see the boat? Ginny dutifully unlocked the barn, hitched the trailer to an old John Deere, and pulled it out into a gray morning. Signs posted on the trailer requested people not to touch anything.

"Why do you bother?" asked Max, deeply engrossed in a plate of pancakes and bacon. "Leave it in the barn and all this will stop."

"I'd do it in a minute," she said. "But Tom thinks it would be unneighborly. He thinks if people come all the way from Winnipeg or Fargo to see this thing, they should get to see it." She shrugged. "I don't really disagree with that, but it *is* getting to be a hassle." More cars came while Max was finishing breakfast. "We figure they'll get bored soon. Or frozen. Whichever." Ginny's cool blue eyes touched him. She was still frightened, even in the daylight. "Max, I'd like very much to be rid of it."

"Then sell it." He knew she could have her way with her husband.

"We will. But it's going to take a while. I don't even know whether we have a free claim to it."

Max finished off his pancakes and reached for more. He usually tried to be careful about overeating, but Ginny's cooking was too good to pass up. "I wonder," he said, "if there's anything else buried here."

She looked momentarily startled. "I hope not."

Max was trying to piece together a scenario that would account for the facts. He kept thinking about the Mafia. Who else would do something this weird? Maybe the boat was a critical piece of evidence in a Chicago murder case.

Someone knocked at the kitchen door.

Ginny opened it to a middle-aged woman wrapped in furs, accompanied by a stolid, gray-haired chauffeur. "Mrs. Lasker?" she asked.

Ginny nodded.

The woman came in, unbuttoned her coat, and saw Max. "Good morning, Mr. Lasker," she said.

"My name's Collingwood," he said.

Her only reaction was a slightly raised eyebrow. She turned back to Ginny. "I'm Emma McCarthy." She had sharp, inquisitorial features and the sort of expression one gets from a lifetime of making summary judgments. "May I inquire, dear, whether your boat is for sale?" She closed the door behind her, leaving the chauffeur outside on the step.

"Oh, I don't think so," said Ginny. "My husband's quite fond of it. We're planning to use it ourselves this summer."

McCarthy nodded and lowered herself into a chair. She signaled Max for coffee. "I understand perfectly. I'd feel the same way. It *is* a lovely boat."

Ginny filled a cup and handed it to her.

"You *do* want to explore your options, dear," she continued. "But I can assure you no one will offer a better price. I wonder if you'd be willing to let me look at it a little more closely. I'd like to see the cabins. And the motor."

Ginny sat down across the table from her. "I must tell you in all honesty, Ms. McCarthy—"

"*Mrs.*," she corrected. "My husband, George, God rest him, would never stand for it if I abandoned him now."

"*Mrs.* McCarthy." Ginny smiled. "I'll be happy to show you around the yacht. But I'm not ready to entertain an offer just now."

Mrs. McCarthy pushed her coat off and let it fall back over the chair. *Let's talk turkey,* she seemed to be saying.

Max excused himself and went to pack. It was time to go back to Fargo. With Tom coming in and the crowd wandering the premises, he could see no reason why he was needed. From the living room, Max watched cars continue to arrive. Rain was beginning to fall. Beyond the driveway, the fields were gray and bleak and rolled on forever.

Where had the yacht come from?

No serial number. No plates of any kind.

Sails that had to have been in the ground, Ginny insisted, for more than twenty years. Crazy. He *knew* that wasn't true.

He dropped his bag at the front door and went back out to

the barn to look at them. They were neatly stacked in plastic sheaths. He opened one and removed the fabric. It was bright white. And soft. More like the texture of a shirt than a sail.

When Ginny returned, he didn't have to ask how it had gone. She looked ecstatic.

"She's in your business, Max," she said. "Do you believe that? Except that she restores *boats*." She held out a business card. *Pequod, Inc.*, it read. *Mrs. George McCarthy, director. Boating as It Used to Be.*

"I take it she made an offer?"

Ginny's eyes grew big and round. "Yes!" she said, and her voice escalated to a squeal. "Six hundred thousand!" She grabbed Max and hugged him so hard she knocked him off balance.

A van pulled into the driveway and opened its doors. Its passengers, who appeared to be a group of retired people, hesitated about getting out into the rain.

Max shook his head. "Don't jump too quickly," he said.

"What? Why not?"

"Because it's probably worth a lot more. Look, Ginny, boats are not my specialty. But it's never prudent to rush into a deal." He screwed his face up into a frown. Damned if he could figure this out. "I don't think you stand to lose much by waiting. And, depending on what it turns out to be, you might have a lot to gain."

Ginny put on her jacket and walked outside with Max, where they stood on the porch with five or six tourists. The rain wasn't much more than a light drizzle, but it was *cold*. "Ginny," he said, "do you have any pictures? Of the yacht?"

"Sure."

"May I have a few? And one other thing: I'd like to make off with a piece of sail. Okay?"

She looked at him uncertainly. "Okay," she said. "Why?"

"I'd like to find out what it's made from."

"It feels like linen," she said.

"That's what I thought."

She smiled. "Sure," she said. "Let me know what you find out." A curtain of hard rain was approaching from the west. "I better put it away." She jumped down off the porch, climbed into the tractor, and started the engine. Most of the visitors, seeing the sky, decided to get out while they could and ran to their cars.

She had to back the boat into the barn. It was about halfway in, and she was turned around in the operator's seat, trying to ease between stalls, when she stopped and stared. "Max." She waved him forward. "Look at this."

"It's raining out there," he protested.

But she waited for him. He sighed, jammed his hands into his pockets, and walked across the squishy lawn. "What?" he said. The rain got heavier. It drove against him, drilled him, took his breath away.

She was pointing at the prow, paying no attention to the downpour. "Look."

He looked. "I don't see anything."

"I don't think," she whispered, "it's getting very wet."

A haze had risen around the boat, much the way it will on a city street during a downpour. Max shrugged. "What's your point?"

"Look at the tractor."

No mist.

Well, maybe a little. The tractor had been recently polished. It shimmered, and large waxy drops ran down its fenders.

But the boat: The rain fountained off the hull and was shot through with rainbow colors. It was almost as if the water was being *repelled.*

✠ · ✠ · ✠

An hour later the P–38J rolled down the runway at Fort Moxie International Airport and lifted into a gray, wet sky. Max watched the airstrip fall away. The wind sock atop the lone hangar was around to the southeast at about twenty knots. North of the airport, frame houses and picket fences and unpaved streets mingled with stands of trees and broad lawns. The water tower, emblazoned with the town's name and motto, *A Good Place to Live*, rose proudly above the rooftops. The Red River looked cold.

He followed Route 11 west, into the rain, flying over wide fields of wilted sunflowers waiting to be plowed under. Only a farm truck, and a flock of late geese headed south, moved in all that vast landscape. He cruised over Tom's place. The driveway was almost empty now, and the barn was shut against the elements. He turned south.

The rain beat on his canopy; the sky was gray and soupy. He looked over at his starboard tail boom, prosaic and solid. The power plant consisted of two 1,425-horsepower liquid-cooled Allison engines. *White Lightning* had been manufactured sixty years ago by the Lockheed Aircraft Corporation of Seattle. It was magic, too, like the boat. But this was *real;* it was magic held aloft by physics. There was no room in the same world for a P–38J and a buried yacht with working lights.

None at all.

He climbed to seventeen thousand feet, his assigned altitude, and set course for Fargo.

Max dropped the fragment of sail off at Colson Laboratories, asking that they determine the composition of the material and, if possible, where it might have been manufactured. They promised to get the results back to him within a week.

Stell Weatherspoon was his executive assistant. She was an overweight, bright-eyed, matronly type with three kids in high school and an ex who was constantly delinquent with his payments. Her prime responsibility at Sundown was to handle the administrative details of the operation. She wrote contracts, scheduled maintenance, hired subcontractors. She was also a born conservative who understood the difference between risks and gambles, and who thereby exercised a restraining influence on Max's occasional capricious tendencies. Had she been along, Kerr would have had his Lockheed Lightning, no questions asked. "Don't get emotionally involved with the planes," she warned him now and then. "These are business ventures, not women."

She greeted him on his arrival at the Sundown offices with a disapproving stare. "Hello, Max."

"He wasn't the right guy for the P–38," he said.

Her eyes drifted shut. "Our business is to restore and sell airplanes. Not find homes for them."

"He was a jerk," Max said. "No good comes from that kind of money."

"Yeah, right. Max, the world is full of jerks. If you're not going to sell to them, we are going to eliminate most of the population."

"The *male* population," said Max.

"*You* said it; I didn't."

Max picked up his mail. "I was up on the border last night."

"Really?" she said. "Doing what?"

"I'm not sure. Tom Lasker dug up a yacht on his farm."

"I saw it on TV," she said. "That's Lasker's place? I didn't realize that."

"It is. I spent the night up there." Max drew a chair over beside her and sat down. "I need your help, Stell." He opened his briefcase. "Ginny gave me some pictures." He handed over six nine-by-twelve glossies.

"It's in pretty good condition," she said, "for something that was buried."

"You noticed that, huh? Okay, look, what I'd like you to do is find out who made the damned thing. There's no ID on it of any kind. Fax these around. Try the manufacturers, boat dealers, importers. And the Coast Guard. Somebody'll be able to tell us something."

"Why do we care?" she asked.

"Because we're snoops. Because your boss would like to know what the hell's going on. Okay?"

"Sure. When do you want it?"

"Forthwith. Let me know what you find out." He went into his office and tried to call Morley Clark at Moorhead State.

"Professor Clark is in class," said his recorded voice. "Please feel free to leave a message at the beep."

"This is Max Collingwood. Morley, I'm going to fax you some photos. They're of a yacht, and there's a piece of writing on the hull. If you can identify the language, or better yet get a translation, I'd be grateful."

Everett Crandall came out personally to usher Lasker into his office. "I saw your boat the other day, Tom. You're a lucky man, looks like to me." Ev was more or less permanently rumpled—both he and his clothes.

"That's why I'm here," said Lasker.

"What's going on? Whose boat is it?"

"Don't know."

"Come on, Tom. You must have *some* idea."

Ev's office was packed with old law books, framed certificates, and photos, most of which had been taken during his tenure as county prosecutor. Prominently displayed on his desk was a picture of Ev and Senator Byron Glass at last year's Fourth of July celebration.

Lasker sat down. "Ev," he said, "I've got a prospective buyer."

"For the boat?"

"Yes. Is it mine to sell?"

Ev nodded, but his dark eyes said no. He took off his glasses, wiping them with a wrinkled handkerchief. "Hard to say," he said.

"It's on my property. That should make it mine, right?"

Ev's hands were in his lap. He looked down at them. "Tom, if I left my RV over at your place, would it be yours?"

"No. But this was *buried.*"

"Yeah." Ev considered that. "If I chose to hide my family silver by burying it out back of your house, would it be yours?"

"I don't know," said Tom. "I don't guess it would."

"Have you heard from anyone? I mean, has anybody put in a claim for the boat?"

"No. Nobody."

"Have you exhausted reasonable means to establish ownership?"

"Is that my responsibility?"

"Who else's? Listen, for all we know it could be stolen. The thieves hid it in your ground. For whatever reason. In that case, it would belong to the original owner." Ev was a careful man, a model of caution. He took pride in not committing to a view until all the facts were in. Which meant, of course, that he was never quite on board. Or in opposition.

"The question here, as I see it, is one of intent. Was the property abandoned? If so, then I think your claim to ownership would be valid. And I believe that claim would be substantiated in court, if need be. If someone challenged it."

"Who would challenge it?"

"Oh, hard to say. A relative might claim the owner was not competent when he, or she, abandoned the boat. Burying it might constitute a sound argument in that direction."

"So how do I establish ownership?"

"Let me research it, Tom. Meantime, it would help if we could find out how it came to be where it was."

✠ 5 ✠

Antiquities are remnants of history which have casually escaped the shipwrecks of time.

—Francis Bacon, *The Advancement of Learning*, II

Stell pursued her mission for three days. No one could identify a manufacturer. There were two more or less similar models of yachts, but nothing identical. Max asked her to keep at it.

Morley Clark had no idea whatever about the symbols on the hull. In fact, Max found it impossible to convince him he was serious. "These characters," Clark told Max, "are not part of any language of any industrialized society." There were eleven of them, presumably the name of the craft. They were cursive, rendering it difficult to be sure of the exact shape of an individual character. Max recognized an *O* but nothing else.

They were sitting in Clark's office on the campus of Moorhead State. Outside, the sun was shining, and the temperature was a balmy forty degrees. "That can't be right, Morley," he said. "You must have missed something."

Clark smiled tolerantly. He was lanky, broad-shouldered, athletic. A softball nut. "I agree, Max. But I can't see where. Maybe the data banks aren't as complete as they're supposed

41

to be. But as a practical matter, I think we have damned near everything. Your stuff won't make a match. Well, a couple of the symbols do. One's Hindustani, another's Cyrillic. Which means it's pure coincidence. You put a few lines and loops together and you have to come up with something." He looked down at the photo on his desk. "Max, it's a joke."

Max thanked Clark and drove back to Chellis Field wondering who was the joker and who the jokee. He was by turns mystified and irritated. It had to be some kind of gang thing. Had to be.

He was up on I–29 when Stell reached him on his cellular phone. "You got a call from Colson Laboratories. Can you take it?"

Already? It was only two days. "Okay," he said. "Put them through."

"Roger. And Max?"

"Yes?"

"They sound excited."

The phone clicked. "Mr. Collingwood?" A woman's voice. And Stell was right: She sounded as if she'd just run up two flights of stairs.

"Yes, this is Max Collingwood. Can I help you?"

"My name's Cannon. I'm calling for Colson Labs. About the samples you left the other day."

"Okay."

"I assume you're not at your office now?"

"I'll be there in ten minutes," said Max. "What have you got?"

"Can I meet you there?" she asked.

She was black, slender, in her mid-thirties. Her business card indicated she was a lab director for Colson. Good smile, high cheekbones, and an aura of barely-suppressed excitement. She wore a navy blue business suit and carried a leather briefcase. "Pleasure to meet you, Mr. Collingwood," she said, extending her hand. "I'm April Cannon."

Max took her coat. "I didn't expect results quite so soon."

Her smile implied there was a secret between them. She sat down, keeping the briefcase on her lap, and looked at him sharply. "I'll admit we don't usually do home delivery, Mr. Collingwood," she said. "But you and I both know you've got something very unusual here."

Max nodded as if that was all very true.

Her eyes cut into him. "Where did you get it?"

Max wondered briefly whether he should keep the source quiet. But what the hell, it'd been on TV. "It was buried up on the border."

"The *boat?* The one they found on the farm?"

Max nodded.

"The *boat.* I'll be damned." Her eyes lost their focus. "May I see it?" she asked.

"Sure," he said. "Everybody else has been up there." She seemed to be drifting away from him. "What exactly can you tell me?"

"Let me ask *you* something," she said, as if he had not spoken. "Did you drop any samples off anywhere else?"

"No," said Max.

"Good." She released the snaps on the briefcase, withdrew a folder, and handed it over. "How's your chemistry?"

"Shaky."

"That's okay. Listen, Mr. Collingwood—"

"I think this'll go quicker if you call me Max."

"Okay, Max." She smiled. Max had the feeling. that she wasn't really seeing him. "Colson's a small operation. I did the lab work myself. Nobody else knows."

"Knows what?"

She pointed at the folder.

Max opened it and glanced over a one-page form.

"I wonder if you'd translate it for me."

She looked around the office. "Can we be overheard?"

That startled him. "No," he said.

"Okay. The material's a fiber. It's very fine, and it's woven." Her voice dropped almost to a whisper. "It has an atomic number of one-sixty-one. It's a transuranic."

"What's a transuranic?"

"An artificially-created element."

"Is that a problem?"

"Max, this is a transuranic in spades. We've got one out there now so new it hasn't even been named yet. It has an atomic number of one-twelve. That's the top of the chart. Or it used to be. This stuff— " She shook her head. "It shouldn't exist."

"So what are we saying here?"

Her features were tense. "Nobody has the technology to manufacture this kind of stuff. Even if we did, the element should be inherently unstable. And hot."

"*Hot?* You mean radioactive?" Max began reviewing how much time he'd spent close to the sails.

"Yes. That's what it *should* be." She produced what remained of the sample, and held it up to a lamp. "But it's okay. Maybe at those levels, elements lose their radioactivity. I don't know. Nobody does."

"Are you sure about this?" he asked.

"Yes. Of course I'm sure."

Max got up and walked to the window. A Cessna was just touching down. "I don't think I understand what you're telling me."

She did not answer for a long time. "Somebody," she said

ANCIENT SHORES

at last, "somewhere, has made a technological leap over the rest of us. A *big* one."

"Okay," he said. "So is it important?"

"Max, I'm not talking about a moderate advance. I'm talking *light-years*. This shouldn't be possible."

Max shrugged. "Obviously it is."

She got that faraway look again. "Apparently," she said.

"So, what are the implications? Is there a commercial advantage to it?"

"Oh, I would think so. The electrons are extremely stable. *Extremely*. I've already done some tests. It does not interact with other elements."

"I'm still not following."

"It's virtually indestructible."

Max knew better. "That can't be right," he said. "The sample I sent you was cut with a pair of scissors."

She shook her head. "I don't mean that kind of indestructibility. Obviously you can cut it. Or crunch it. But it won't decay. It won't fall apart on its own." She was watching him closely, trying to decide, he thought, whether he knew more than he was saying. "Do you think if I drove up there, they'd let me see it tonight?"

"Sure," he said. "I'll make a call for you, if you like." Something that had been floating in the back of his mind suddenly took form. "You said it won't decay. How old is the sample?"

"No way to know," she said. "It's hard to say how you'd date this kind of thing. I'm not sure you could." She was on her feet.

"Would it wear out?" Max asked.

"Oh, sure. Everything wears out. Eventually. But this stuff would be pretty tough. And it'd be easy to clean because other elements won't stick to it."

45

Max thought about the haze with its rainbow effect. "Why don't I go with you?" he said. "I'll fly you up."

A light blue government car pulled into Lasker's driveway, swung around the gravel loop at the front of the house, navigated past a couple of parked cars, and stopped. A middle-aged, thick-waisted man got out. He slid a worn black briefcase out of the trunk, quickly surveyed the scene, and made for the front door.

"Jeffrey Armbruster," he announced when Lasker opened up, "Internal Revenue Service." He produced credentials so smoothly that they appeared to come out of his sleeve.

Lasker swallowed. "Is there a problem?" he asked.

"No, no," Armbruster said easily. "No problem at all."

Lasker stood away from the door, and Armbruster thanked him and came in.

"Cold day," said Lasker, although by local standards it wasn't.

"Yes. Yes, it is." Armbruster unbuttoned his coat. "I understand you've recently had a piece of good fortune, Mr. Lasker?"

Tax implications. He had never thought of that. "You mean the boat," he said.

"Yes." Armbruster nodded. Their eyes met briefly. It occurred to Lasker that this was not a man who enjoyed his work. "Yes, that's right. You've begun proceedings to establish your claim."

Lasker offered a chair by the coffee table. "That's true," he said. "I have."

"If that happens, Mr. Lasker, please be aware that the item will be taxable as ordinary income."

"How much?"

"I really can't say. The first step in the process would be to get an appraisal." He opened his briefcase. "You should complete these." He pushed some forms across the table.

Lasker looked at the documents.

"No hurry," said Armbruster. "However, if you *do* acquire title to the boat, you will be required to make an estimated payment." He produced a card. "Call me anytime, and I'll be happy to advise you."

Out in the laundry room Ginny started the washer, and the house began to vibrate. "I'm surprised," said Lasker, "that you were on top of this so quickly. I hadn't even thought about taxes."

"It's my job, Mr. Lasker." He closed his case and got up.

There was a sadness in the man's manner. Lasker wondered what it was like to have a job that probably involved continual confrontation. "How about some coffee?" he asked.

Armbruster looked pleased. "Yes," he said. "If you have it ready. I wouldn't want to put anyone to any trouble."

"It's no trouble."

The tax man followed him into the kitchen, where they were joined by Ginny. She put on a fresh pot and broke out a cherry cheesecake. Armbruster told them how much he admired the house.

"My father built it," said Lasker proudly. "I was about twelve."

It was spacious, with hardwood floors, a big wraparound porch, and thick carpets that Ginny had bought in St. Paul. The living room had a cathedral ceiling, rare in that harsh climate. They sat for almost an hour, talking about the yacht. Armbruster thought it was no coincidence that it had been found a mile south of the border. "Somebody trying to get away with something," he said. But he couldn't explain what they might be trying to get away *with*.

Eventually the conversation turned to Armbruster's job. "People usually get nervous when they find out who my employer is," he observed. "My wife doesn't tell anyone who I work for." He smiled.

Tax collectors have no friends, thought Lasker. Except other tax collectors.

"Nobody is as abused as tax collectors," Armbruster continued. "It's always been that way. But by God, we are the people who held Rome together. And every other place that was ever worth a damn."

With that he looked momentarily embarrassed. Then he thanked them both, swept up his briefcase and coat, made his good-byes, and strode out the door.

Minutes later Will pulled up out front with Max and April Cannon. Max did the introductions, but the woman had a hard time keeping her eyes off the boat.

"You wanted to take a look, Dr. Cannon?" said Ginny.

"Please. And call me April."

"What's going on?" said Lasker. "What did we find out?"

Max, who enjoyed playing with a mystery as much as anyone, suggested that Ginny give April the tour while he brought Tom up to date. The men went inside and threw another log on the fire.

The women were gone almost an hour, and they looked half frozen when they came back. Lasker poured a round of brandy.

"Well, April," said Max, "what do you think?"

April sipped her drink. "You really want to know? I don't see how anyone could have built that yacht."

Max listened to the fire and watched April struggle with her thoughts.

"I know how that sounds," she said.

"What exactly do you mean?" asked Max.

"It's beyond our technology. But I knew that before I came here."

"*Our* technology?" said Lasker.

"*Way* beyond."

"So you're saying, what?" said Max. "That the boat was built in Japan? Or on Mars?"

"Maybe Mars. Or a pre—Native American super-high-tech civilization in North Dakota."

Max glanced at Ginny to see how she was reacting. She looked skeptical but not surprised. They'd had at least part of this conversation outside.

"That's crazy," said Lasker.

"Crazy or not, nobody alive today could duplicate the materials in that boat." She finished off her drink. "I don't believe it, either."

"It looks like an ordinary yacht to me," said Ginny.

"I know. Maybe if it didn't look so ordinary—" She shook her head.

"April," said Max, "think about it. Do you really believe they'd manufacture sailboats like that on *Mars?*"

"The fire feels good." She dragged her chair closer. A log broke, and sparks flew. "Look," she said, "it wouldn't really matter whether you were building it out at Alpha Centauri. There are only a few designs for a practical sailboat. Some-body somewhere built this, and I can guarantee you it wasn't anyone we've ever heard of."

The wind sucked at the trees. A couple of automobile engines started. "I wish I could have seen it before you took it out of the ground," said April. "Before it got washed."

"Why?" asked Lasker.

"We might have been able to make some inferences from

the clay. But maybe it won't matter." She took a white envelope out of her pocket.

"From the mooring cables," Ginny explained to Max and her husband. "We found some splinters."

"What good will that do?" asked Max.

April got a refill of her brandy. "I usually go pretty light on this kind of stuff," she said. "But today I feel entitled." She turned to Max. "Each of the cables has a loop at one end and a clip at the other. The clips still work, by the way. I don't know much about yachts, but this part is simple enough. When you're tying up, you secure the loop over one of the cleats on the boat. And you tie the other end, the end with the clip, to the pier."

"So what does it tell us?" asked Max.

"We should be able to figure out what it's been tied to. And maybe that'll tell us where it's been." She put the envelope back and looked at Lasker. "Tom, was the boat upright when you found it?"

"No," he said. "It was lying on its starboard side. And angled up."

"How much?"

"Oh, I don't know. Maybe thirty degrees."

"Okay." April seemed pleased. "The slope of the ridge is close to thirty degrees."

"Which means what?" asked Max.

"Probably nothing," she said. "Or maybe that's where it came to rest."

"Came to rest?" Lasker was having trouble following the conversation.

"Yes," said April. "When it sank."

✠ 6 ✠

Where lies the final harbour, whence we unmoor no more?

—Herman Melville, *Moby Dick*

April had almost changed her mind about flying with Max when he showed her the P–38 he intended to use. Although designed as a single-seat fighter, the Lightning could accommodate a second seat behind the pilot. Many of the aircraft purchased by collectors after the war had been modified in this way. *White Lightning* was among these.

Now, on the return trip, she was too excited even to think about the plane, and she climbed in without a murmur. Max taxied out onto the runway, talking to Jake Thoraldson, who was Fort Moxie's airport manager and air traffic controller. Jake worked out of his office.

"Max?" she said.

He turned the plane into the wind. "Yes, April?"

"I'd like to take a look at something. Can we go back over the Lasker farm?"

"Sure." Max checked with Jake. No flights were in the area. "What did you want to see?"

"I'm not sure," she said.

51

When they were in the air, he leveled off at three thousand feet and headed west. The day was beginning to turn gray. He had a strong headwind, and the weather report called for more rain or possibly sleet by late afternoon. Probably rain along the border and snow in the south, if the usual patterns held.

The fields were bleak and withered. They had been given up to the winter, and their owners had retired either to vacation homes in more hospitable latitudes or to whatever other occupations entertained them during the off-season.

It was impossible to know precisely where the Lasker property began. "Everything north of the highway for several miles belongs to him," Max explained. Usually houses were set more or less in the middle of these vast tracts of land. But when Lasker's father had rebuilt, he'd opted for a site at the southwestern edge of the property, near the highway, and in the shadow of the ridge in which Tom had found the yacht. The idea had been to gain a degree of protection from the icy winds that roared across the prairie.

Beyond the ridge the land flattened again for several miles and then rose abruptly to form the Pembina Escarpment.

The escarpment consisted of a spine of hills and promontories and peaks. Unlike the surrounding plain, they were only very lightly cultivated. Their tops were dusted with snow, and they ran together to form a single, irregular wall. There were occasional houses along the crests and narrow dirt roads that tied the houses to one another and to Route 32, which paralleled the chain along its eastern foot.

"Ten thousand years ago," April said, "we'd have been flying over water. Lake Agassiz."

At her direction, Max banked and followed the chain south. She was looking alternately at the crumpled land and at the valley, which was flat all the way to the horizon.

"Where was the other side?" asked Max. "The eastern shore?"

"Out toward Lake of the Woods," she said. "A long way."

Max tried to imagine what the world had been like then. A place of liquid silence, mostly. And Canada geese.

"It only lasted about a thousand years," she continued, "scarcely an eyeblink as such things go. But it *was* here. That's all lake bottom below us. It's why Tom can raise the best wheat in the world."

"What happened to it?" asked Max.

"The glaciers that formed it were retreating. They finally reached a point where they unblocked the northern end." She shrugged. "The water drained away."

They were beginning to run into a light drizzle.

"Some of it is still here," she continued. "Lake of the Woods is a remnant. And lakes Winnipeg and Manitoba. And a lot of the Minnesota lakes."

Max's imagination filled the prairie with water, submerging Fort Moxie and Noyes in the north, Hallock over on Route 75, and Grand Forks and Thief River Falls and Fargo to the south.

"You can find all kinds of evidence in the soil if you look. Remains of shellfish, plankton, whatever." Her eyes were far away. "I suppose it might come back, for that matter. During the next ice age."

It suddenly occurred to Max where this was leading. "You think the boat is connected with the lake, don't you?"

She was silent.

April arrived at Colson Laboratories toward the end of the afternoon, in a downpour. She was met at the front doors by a swarm of employees headed out. "Let's go," Jack Smith told her, taking her arm and turning her around. "You need a ride?"

Ride where? It took her a few moments to recall: retirement party for Harvey Keck.

She liked Harvey, but she didn't want to go. Her samples were all she cared about at the moment. She could claim she had a rush assignment. Had got behind. Wasn't feeling well. But she owed a lot to Harvey.

Damn.

She locked her samples in the safe, told herself it would be just as well to tackle it in the morning when she was fresh, and went back downstairs to her car. Forty minutes later she pulled into the parking lot at the Goblet.

Celebrations were encouraged at Colson. When a big contract came in, when someone won a major award, when somebody found a better way to do things, they celebrated. The Goblet was more or less traditional for these kinds of affairs. It was a midpriced family restaurant with a good bar. They called it Colson West, and for each event they hung corporate logos and banners around its Delta Room. On this occasion, a blowup of Keck's management philosophy, which advocated taking care of the help as well as the customers, was mounted behind the lectern. Also adorning the front of the room were his potted rubber tree and a hat rack on which hung the battered Stetson he'd worn during most of the last three decades.

Most of the employees were there when April arrived, and a substantial number were already well into the mood.

She picked up a rum and Coke and sat down with several of her friends. But the routine conversations, detailing struggles with kids, complaints about one or another of the bosses, problems with reports coming back from various subcontractors, seemed extraordinarily dull on this night.

She had a major mystery on her hands, and she was anxious to get working on it.

Everyone liked Harvey. It looked as if the entire work force had turned out for his farewell. He was stepping down as associate director, a post that April had set her sights on. She wasn't in position yet. The new AD would be a temporary appointment, Bert Coda, who was himself close to retirement. As things now stood, April would have the inside track when Coda retired. The position, if she got it, would mean a salary increase of $25,000; and she would still be young enough to aspire to the top job. Not bad for a kid who had started out washing dishes.

But tonight she just didn't care. Compared to what she had in her safe, the directorship was trivial. It was all she could do not to seize the lectern and announce what she had found. *Hey, listen up. We've been visited. And I've got proof!*

When she'd first come to the Dakotas, as an undergraduate at the University of North Dakota, April had attempted a weekend automobile tour that was to include the Black Hills. But western states tend to be a lot bigger than eastern states, and she'd run out of patience with the endless highways. She'd circled back and encountered the Sioux reservation along the south shore of Devil's Lake. (The north shore was occupied by a prosperous prairie town named for the lake.)

Subsequently she became interested in the tribe, made some friends, and in time acquired what she liked to think of as a Sioux perspective: *I would live where the sky is open, where fences are not, and where the Spirit walks the earth.*

One of the friends was Andrea Hawk, a Devil's Lake talk show host, who captured for April the sense of a people bypassed by history. April was saddened by the poverty she saw on the reservation and by Andrea's frustration. "We live too much on the largesse of the whites," Andrea had told her. "We have forgotten how to make do for ourselves." Andrea pointed out that Native-American males die so young, from drugs and disease and violence, that the most prosperous establishment on many reservations is the funeral home.

April's own life was hedged in by fences. A marriage had gone sour. She wanted both family and career but had been unable to balance the needs of a husband with the long hours her job required. She was in her mid-thirties now, and she had no sense of satisfaction from all the activity. Accomplishments, yes. But if she died tonight, her life would not have counted for anything. She would leave nothing behind.

At least, that was how she had felt until running the test on Max Collingwood's piece of cloth. Curiously, she had been only vaguely aware of her dissatisfaction until the test results came in and she realized what she had in her hand.

The tributes for Harvey were moving. Several people described how much they had enjoyed working for him, how he had inspired them, why he was a good boss. Two former employees of Colson who had gone on to greater things attributed their success to his inspiration. The first principle of his credo, said one, had carried her through dark days: *Do the right thing, regardless of consequences.* That was Mary Embry, who had become an operations chief with Dow. "It's not always a path to promotion," she said. "But it made me realize that I had to be able to respect myself before others would." She smiled warmly at Harvey, who looked embarrassed.

The director added his own praise. "Forty years is a long time," he said. "Harvey always said what he thought. Sometimes I didn't want to hear it." Laughter. "Sometimes I *really* didn't want to hear it." Louder laughter. "But you never ducked, Harv. And I'm grateful for that." Applause.

"I'll add this for everyone in the room who wants to be a manager: Look for someone like Harvey on your staff, to tell you what you need to hear. Treat him well. Make him your conscience."

They cheered, Harvey stood, and April actually saw tears around her. He beamed in the rush of affection. When things subsided, he symbolically dragged the lectern to one side. (His refusal to use a lectern was part of the body of corporate myth.) He thanked his coworkers for their kindness and, as he always did, spoke to them about themselves. "In some ways," he said, "this is the finest moment of my life. I'd like to think that Colson Laboratories has a more solid foundation than it had before I came, and that its employees and customers are better off. If that's true, and if I can claim *some* credit for that, I'd feel that my years here have been successful."

April suspected she had never seen him this happy. Not during her twelve years with Colson Labs. And she thought how very sad that was.

The associate director had devoted his life to the success of the company and its employees. He had refused to settle for anything less than excellence. And now, addressing his colleagues on this final night, he was saying it again. "Never confuse perfection with production. People who don't make mistakes aren't doing anything."

His subordinates loved him.

She watched him now as he thanked the rank and file. He was walking into the dark. At the end of this celebration he would go back to his office for the rest of the week, and then it would be over.

In some ways, this is the finest moment of my life.

My God, was that all it had come to? A few dozen people at a dinner party, teary-eyed for the moment, but who would disperse soon enough to their own lives and leave Harvey Keck to find his way as best he could?

Surreptitiously she wiped her eyes.

Nothing like this was going to happen to *her*. She would make sure her life counted for something more than being a nice person down at the office. And Tom Lasker's enigmatic yacht was going to be her passport.

✠ 7 ✠

The distant roar of receding time . . .

—Walter Asquith, "Ancient Shores"

Lasker had been out working on his tractor all morning, replacing a leaky cylinder and a drive belt. He'd just come back into the house and was headed for the shower when the doorbell rang. It was Charlie Lindquist and Floyd Rickett.

Charlie was a three-hundred-pounder, about six-three, amiable, a man who thought the world could be had by figuring out what people wanted to hear and telling it to them. Actually, Charlie had done fairly well with that philosophy. He'd built half a dozen businesses in Fort Moxie, and now owned Intown Video, the Tastee-Freez (which was, of course, closed for the winter), and four duplexes over near the library. Charlie was director of the Fort Moxie Booster Association and president of the city council.

Floyd also sat on those esteemed bodies. He was tall, gray, sharp-nosed, pinched-looking. A postal clerk, he had strong opinions and a strong sense of the importance of his time. *Get to the bottom line,* he was fond of saying, jabbing the air with three fingers. Floyd did a great deal of jabbing: he jabbed his way into conversations, jabbed through political opposition on the council, jabbed through conflicting opinions of all kinds. *Life is short. No time to waste. Cut to the chase.* At the post office he specialized in sorting out problems caused by the general public. Floyd disapproved of sloppy wrapping, of clumsy handwriting, of people who failed to use zip codes properly.

Not surprisingly, Charlie and Floyd did not get along.

They shook hands with Lasker, heartily in Charlie's case, prudently in Floyd's. "Still got people coming by to see the yacht, I see," said Charlie, trying to be casual. He thought of himself as a man of considerable subtlety.

"A few. Depends a lot on the weather." He led them into the living room, where they gathered around the coffee table. "It's getting old, I think."

"Getting cold, too," said Floyd. His hand chopped through a brief arc to emphasize the point.

"We've been noticing it in town," said Charlie. "We aren't seeing as many people as we did." He shook his head. "Pity it didn't happen in the spring."

"Doesn't matter," said Lasker. "We've about had it with this donkey drill, anyway. I'm tired of hauling it in and out of the barn every day. I'm going to lock it away and that'll be the end of it."

"Wish you wouldn't, Tom," said Charlie in an easy tone that suggested the action was selfish and ill-conceived.

Floyd nodded. "Bad for business," he said. "The folks that come out here, a lot of them, eat in town. They do some shopping. Some even stay overnight." He sat back and crossed one leg over the other. "Fact is, we could use more stuff like this."

"You have to understand," Charlie said, "that a lot of the people downtown are depending on you."

"Charlie," said Lasker, "it's only a *boat*."

"That's where you're wrong," said Floyd. "It's a national news story. And it's sitting right here in Fort Moxie."

"It is *not* a national news story," said Lasker. "We've been on *one* TV show. And anyhow, most of the people who come out here think I buried the boat myself. They think the whole thing's a scam."

Floyd looked shocked. "There's no truth to that, is there, Tom?"

Lasker glared at him, and Floyd subsided.

"Listen." Charlie was a picture of magnanimity. "All of this is beside the point. There's a lot of money to be made, and it occurred to us you haven't been getting your share, Tom. Now, what we propose to do is to organize this in a more businesslike way."

"How do you mean?"

"First thing," said Floyd, "is to get the attraction off the trailer. I mean, no offense, but what we have here feels like a garage sale. I can understand why people don't take it very seriously."

"The attraction?" said Lasker. "It's an *attraction* now?"

"No offense, Tom." Charlie shifted his weight and his chair sagged. "We just thought it would be a good idea to put it on a platform."

"Ed's volunteered to make the platform," said Floyd. That would be Ed Grange, who usually took charge of parades and other ceremonials. "He'll do a good job, don't worry."

"We'll put a tent over it," continued Charlie, "and install some heaters."

Lasker made a face. "I don't want a tent on my front lawn," he said.

"We know that." Charlie's benign expression signified

that everything was under control. "We wouldn't do that to you, Tom. We thought it would look better over where you dug it up, anyhow." His eyes suddenly clouded. "You haven't filled in the hole, have you?"

"Sure I have. We filled it in the day we got the damned thing out of the ground."

"That's too bad," said Floyd. "Shouldn't have done that."

"Why not? The hole was thirty feet deep. If somebody'd fallen in there, they would have got a terrible bruise."

"Well, it's too late now," said Charlie. "Wish we'd thought of that right away." He rapped his fingers against the table. "Anyway, we'll put up the shelter. We know where we can get an old circus tent. Old, but in good shape. But don't you worry, that's only temporary."

"What do you mean, *temporary?*"

"The bottom line on this," said Floyd, "is that we might have a permanent draw here if we play our cards right. We need to think about a museum."

Lasker's head was beginning to hurt.

"Well, not right away," said Charlie. "Look, we're going to do a publicity push. We'll start charging an admission fee. You'll get a cut, of course. And we'll see how it goes."

"Wait a minute. You can't charge for *this.*"

"Why not?" Charlie was into his take-charge mode. "You want people to react seriously, you have to make them pay something. Not a lot. But something. I bet we'll double the crowds the first week. We were thinking thirty percent for you; the rest goes to the town. Okay? It'll all be pure profit for you. Cost you nothing." He nodded at Floyd, and Floyd nodded back. "The city will pay for everything. Now, we've got a T-shirt design. Let me show you—"

His eyes found Floyd, and Floyd produced a folder. He opened it and pulled out several drawings. All featured the boat, in various aspects. But there were several legends. *The Devil's Boat,* read one. And *My Folks Visited Fort Moxie, ND, and All I Got Was This Lousy T-shirt.* Another featured a map of the upper Red River, with the location of the "devil's boat" site marked with an inset.

"What's this 'devil's boat' routine?" asked Lasker.

"It was Marge's idea," said Charlie. Marge Peterson was the town clerk. "Part of the public-relations initiative."

"I think it's a little overboard."

"Listen," said Charlie, "people love that kind of stuff. And this whole business does have a kind of *Twilight Zone* flavor. Right?"

"And it lights up, doesn't it?" said Floyd. "You find the power source yet?"

Lasker shook his head.

"Good. No known power source. We need to push that, Charlie. And the markings. The markings are good."

"Yeah." Charlie reached for his coat. "Listen, enjoyed talking with you, Tom. We've already started the ball rolling on this thing. Couple of the boys'll be out tomorrow to get it going. You just relax. You won't have to do anything except sit back and watch the money roll in."

They were up and headed for the door. "Oh, one more thing." Charlie stopped, and Floyd almost collided with him. "A rest room. We'll need a rest room."

"No," said Lasker.

"It's okay. We'll set something up outside. Put it back in the trees. Out of sight."

They shook his hand, opened the door, and looked out. There were maybe twenty visitors, and two more cars were pulling up. "See what I mean?" Charlie said.

✠   ✠   ✠

April held the packet where the light from the window could shine through it. "What we have here," she said, "are a few fibers taken from the mooring lanyards. The fibers are *wood*. They're from *spruce* trees." She passed it over.

Max squinted at the samples. "What does that tell us? There aren't any spruce trees around here."

"Not anymore. But there *used* to be. At one time they were quite common, as a matter of fact."

"When?"

"When the lake was here."

They were in a steakhouse. Max listened to the murmur of conversation, the clink of silverware. "You're sure?"

"I'm sure."

Max's insides churned. A waitress arrived, and he settled for a Caesar salad rather than the club sandwich he'd been planning. "So what we're saying is that we've got a ten-thousand-year-old boat up there?"

April squirmed. "I'd rather not jump to conclusions, Max. Let's just stick with the facts for now. One, the boat will not rot, rust, or decay over extremely long periods of time. Two, the lanyards that are in the Lasker barn were once tied up to a piece of wood that was cut from a spruce tree. The tree that the wood fibers came from was alive ten thousand years ago."

"But the boat," said Max, "is *new*."

"The boat will always *look* new, Max. You could put it back in the ground and dig it up to celebrate your sixtieth birthday, and it would look exactly as it does today."

"That doesn't sound possible."

April nodded. "I know. Look, it's outside our experience. But that doesn't make it irrational." Her voice dropped. "I'm not sure what kind of alternative explanation might fit the facts. The age of the wood fibers is not in dispute. Neither is the composition of the original samples. I think somebody was here. A long time ago somebody with advanced technology went sailing on Lake Agassiz. They tied up at least once to a tree or a pier."

"So who was it?" asked Max. "Are we talking UFOs? Or what?"

"I don't know. But it's a question worth asking."

Diet Cokes came. Max took a pull at his while he tried to get his thoughts in order. "It doesn't make much sense," he said. "Assume for a minute you're right. Where does that leave us? With the notion that people came here from another world to go *sailing*? I mean, are we seriously suggesting that?"

"It's not out of the realm of possibility. Try looking at the big picture, Max. And I mean *big*. How many water lakes are there, I wonder, within a radius of, say, twenty light-years? Agassiz might have looked pretty good to a load of tourists." She smiled. "Look, let's stay away from the speculation and concentrate on what we know. What we know is that we have an artificial element that's unique in the world."

"How do we know that?" asked Max.

"I guarantee it."

"*You* guarantee it. April, I hate to say this, but a couple of days ago I wouldn't have known who you were. No offense, but maybe you're wrong."

"Maybe I am. In the meantime, Max, consider this: If I *do* know what I'm talking about, the boat is literally beyond value." She realized she was getting too loud; she leaned closer and lowered her voice. "Look. You'd like a second opinion. I know we don't need one. Get a second opinion, and we get a second chemist. I'd just as soon keep this as exclusive as we can. We are sitting on a monumental discovery, and we are all going to be on the cover of *Time*. You. Me.

The Laskers." Her dark eyes filled with excitement. "There's another reason to keep this close for the time being."

"What's that?" asked Max.

"There might be something else out there."

Lisa Yarborough had launched her professional career as a physics teacher in a private school near Alexandria, Virginia. But she had been (and still was) an inordinately striking woman who just flat-out enjoyed sex. While she discussed energy and resistance by daylight, she demonstrated after dark a great deal of the former and hardly any of the latter.

Lisa discovered early that there was profit to be made from her hobby. Not that she ever stooped to imposing tariffs, but men insisted on showing her a substantial degree of generosity. Furthermore, indirect advantages could accrue to a bright, well-endowed young woman who had never been shackled by either inhibition or an undue sense of fair play. She left the Alexandria school in the middle of her second year amid a swirl of rumors to take a lucrative position with a firm doing business with the Pentagon; her new company thought she could influence the military's purchasing officers. She proved successful in these endeavors, using one means or another, and moved rapidly up the corporate ladder. If it was true that, in her own style, she slept her way to the top, she nevertheless refrained from conducting liaisons with men in her own chain of command, and in that way maintained her self-respect.

Eventually she developed an interest in government and took a position as executive assistant to a midwestern senator who twice sought, without success, his party's presidential nomination. She moved over to lobbying and did quite well for the tobacco industry and the National Education Association. At the law firm of Barlow and Biggs, she functioned as a conduit to several dozen congressmen. She received a political appointment and served a brief tour as an assistant commissioner in the Department of Agriculture. And eventually she became a director in a conservative think tank.

It was in the latter role that Lisa discovered a facility for writing. She had kept scrupulous diaries since she was twelve, a habit that began around the time she'd first retired into the backseat of her father's Buick with Jimmy Proctor. Jimmy had been her first real connection, so to speak, and she'd found the experience so exhilarating that she'd wanted to tell someone. But her girlfriends at the Chester Arthur Middle School weren't up to it. And her parents were Baptists.

Lisa should have been a Baptist, too. She had been exposed to the full range of ecclesiastical activities. She'd gone to youth group meetings on Tuesdays and Thursdays, services on Wednesdays and Sundays. But by senior year she'd slept with half the choir.

While she was at the think tank helping demolish Dukakis's bid for the White House, she'd decided to use her diaries to write an autobiography. Her promise to go into delicious detail about an array of prominent persons throughout government and the media produced a seven-figure advance. The think tank had promptly fired her because she did not confine herself to prominent Democrats.

Old paramours and one-night stands had come to see her, pleading for selective amnesia. When persuasion and bribes didn't work, they resorted to tears and threats, but she went ahead with the project. "If I don't tell the truth," she told a TV talk show host, "what will people think of me?"

The book was *Capitol Love*. It became a best-seller and

then a TV movie, and Lisa bought a chain of auto-parts stores with the proceeds. The rest, as they say, is history.

Lisa had first met April Cannon while Lisa was working at the Department of Agriculture. She'd gone to a dinner hosted by an environmental-awareness group. Her date had been one of the speakers, a tall, enthusiastic stag burdened with the conviction that the loss of forests had already exceeded the limits from which recovery might be possible. He also believed that women in general and Lisa in particular could not resist his charms. Lisa, who had planned to cap the evening in her usual style, changed her mind. April had been unimpressed with her date as well, and the two had fled together into the Washington night.

They had been close friends since.

Lisa was therefore not surprised when April called and asked to see her. Her interest grew when her friend refused to state the reason for the meeting.

The day after the phone call, April arrived with a nondescript individual in tow. "Lisa," she said, "this is Max Collingwood."

The women knew each other too well to indulge in small talk. April quietly explained what had been happening at Tom Lasker's farm. When she had finished, Lisa was slow to respond. "You're certain?" she asked. "How about fraud?"

"There's no mistake. And fraud is not possible." April slid a manila envelope onto the table, opened it, and took out a handful of photos. They were pictures of the yacht. Interior. Exterior. Sails. Close-ups of rails and stanchions. And the markings.

"They *are* odd," Lisa agreed. "And there's no language match?"

"None that we can find," said April.

Lisa continued to study the pictures, but her mind shifted to April. The information was so outrageous that she drew back to reassess her old friend. She knew what was coming, and she had to ask herself whether this was an effort to con her. April wouldn't do it, she was sure. But what about this Collingwood?

"So what are your conclusions?" she asked. "Where did the element, the boat, come from?"

April smiled wearily. "Everything's guesswork beyond what we've told you. We have no conventional explanation."

"Do you have an *unconventional* one?"

"Yours is as good as anybody's," said April.

Lisa nodded, walked over to her desk, and took out a checkbook. "Where do you go from here?"

"We want to take a close look at the area. See if there's anything else buried up there."

"What do you need to do that?"

"A ground-search radar. We can rent one at a reasonable price."

"But what could you possibly find? Another boat?"

"Maybe," said Max.

"But you've already got *one*. I can understand that two is better than one, but in what way would a second boat advance your knowledge?"

"There might be remains," said April.

"Ah. After ten thousand years? And some of it in the water? I hardly think so. You'd do better to think about where they might have stopped for hot dogs."

The chemist leaned forward, and their eyes locked. "Lisa, they had to have a way to get here. There's a possibility they never went home."

Lisa listened to everybody breathe. "How much do you need?"

When GeoTech's ground-search radar unit showed up to begin its probe, Max was there. He and the Laskers assumed that if anything was actually still in the ground, they would find it right away. If they found nothing, that would be the end of it.

Max did not like being associated with UFOs. Didn't look good for him or for Sundown Aviation, and he resolved to keep a low profile. But on the other hand, if there *was* anything to it, intense media coverage and maybe a lot of money was not out of the question.

The GeoTech team consisted of three people working out of a large sand-colored van. The crew chief was an energetic, rather precise young woman who made the company jumpsuit look pretty good. Her name was Peggy Moore, and she opened the conversation by asking Max what they were looking for. "The work order's a little vague on that point," she added.

"Anything unusual," said Max.

That was not a satisfactory reply. Moore had intense eyes, a quick frown, and a schedule that kept her far too busy to cope with someone who wanted to mess around. "Try me again," she said in a tone that bordered on hostility.

"We're not sure what we're looking for," Max explained. "We think there may be some artifacts buried in the area. We'd like *you* to tell *us* what's in the ground. If anything."

"What, generally, are we talking about here, Mr. Collingwood? Arrowheads? Indian burial ground? Old oil cans? It makes a difference in the way we proceed."

"They dug up a boat last month."

"I saw that on TV. This is the place, huh?"

"Yeah. We'd like to know if there's anything else down there."

"All right. It saves time," she said, "when you tell us what we need to know."

"Okay," said Max.

"We already found a rake. While we were calibrating."

The van was lined with computers, printers, display

screens, and communications gear. The radar unit itself was mounted on a small tractor. "The images are relayed to the van by radio link," Moore explained. "It goes up on the main screen. We'll be watching for shadows, unusual coloring, anything that suggests a formation that isn't obviously natural."

It was by then mid-November, and the day on which the GeoTech crew started was miserably cold. Snow threatened throughout the afternoon, although only a few flakes fell.

The other two technicians were Charlie Ramirez, a somber-looking man who drove the tractor and ran the radar, and Sara Winebarger, the communications specialist. Sara was stick-thin with straight blond hair.

Because of the extreme cold, Moore and Charlie rotated assignments on the tractor. Charlie did not like cold weather, and he talked a lot about Nevada. "Only reason I'm here is because they eliminated my job on the southern border. Soon as it opens up again, I'm out of here."

Max's fascination with the project worked on him, and he asked if he could watch from inside the van. "It's against the rules," said the crew chief.

"I wouldn't create a problem."

"I'm sure you wouldn't, Mr. Collingwood. But there are insurance implications." Her demeanor was as cold as the weather. "You understand."

They laid out a search pattern, and Charlie took off, headed for the top of the hill. He plunged through the windbreak, mounted the ridge and, at a range of about a hundred yards from the site of the original find, executed a sharp right turn. Eventually he completed the first of a series of overlapping rectangles.

Max went into the farmhouse and took over the Laskers' dining room, near a window. Outside, the tractor rumbled methodically through the long afternoon.

✠ 8 ✠

This antique coast,
Washed by time . . .

—Walter Asquith, "Ancient Shores"

*During the course of the afternoon, the GeoTech team found noth-*ing. When at last they quit for the day, Max exchanged reas-surances with the Laskers, and flew home. The second day of the search, a Friday, also produced no results, and the operation shut down for the weekend.

April had encouraged Max and the Laskers to say as little as possible about the find. She had followed her own advice and revealed nothing to her colleagues at Colson. But she needed someone to talk to. Max's enthusiasm matched her own, and so, during the succeeding days, while the radar unit searched Tom Lasker's property without result, they found themselves meeting after hours for dinner and drinks and long intense conversations.

These conversations had the effect of fortifying their hopes and creating an informal alliance. However, they rarely produced specifics about what those hopes really were: hers, that a way might be found to master transuranic technology; his, that there had indeed been unearthly visitors, and that proof might lie nearby. But Max suspected that a more mundane explanation would eventually surface, that April *had* to have overlooked something. Nevertheless, she could usually, over beer and pizza, allay those doubts. For a time.

For her part, April had no one to lean on. She considered herself rock-solid, not the sort to be carried away by passion or gulled by ambition. Nevertheless, she would have liked a second opinion, some confirmation from one of the experts in the field. But the stakes were so high that she knew where premature disclosure might lead: the heavyweights would move in and Cannon would be pushed aside.

She needed someone to talk to. The Laskers, sitting on what might turn out to be the discovery of the ages, seemed to look on the entire business with a degree of complacency that irritated her. They were interested, the possibilities intrigued them, and yet they lacked fire. It was her impression that, had Tom Lasker been informed there was a crashed UFO on his land, he'd go look at it, but only after feeding the horses.

Max was different. And during this difficult period, he became her sole support.

They tended to approach the more electrifying possibilities obliquely: they joked about the effects they would have on their personal lives. April conjured up an image of Max on the cover of *Time*, stepping down from the cockpit of the Lightning, his flying jacket rakishly open. Man of the Year.

And he speculated about a Nobel for the woman who had given the world the lifetime automobile guarantee.

Meantime, the days passed without tangible result from the ground-radar unit, and Max's conviction returned that it was all just too good to be true. April pointed out that the search was a long shot, but even if they found nothing else, they already possessed an artifact of incalculable value. "Nothing is ever going to be the same," she said, adding that she had written a paper revealing her findings. "Which I will not publish until we can be reasonably sure there's nothing else out there. We don't want to start a treasure hunt."

"I agree," said Max. They were sitting in a food court in the mall at the intersection of the two interstates in Fargo, splitting a pepperoni pizza. "If there really is something out there, what would you think our chances are of finding it?"

Her eyes fluttered shut. "Almost nil. There's too much lake bottom." She stirred a packet of artificial sweetener into her coffee. "We're talking about substantial pieces of the U.S. and Canada. For that matter, there could be something *here*." She indicated the floor. "The Fargo area was underwater, too, for a while. Who knows?"

Max looked down at the tiles. "I wonder what the yacht is worth?"

"If it is what we think it is, Max, you couldn't put a price on it." She watched a mother trying to balance a squalling child and an armload of packages. "I hope we can actually get some answers to the questions. Truth is, I have a bad feeling that we're likely to be faced with a mystery no one will *ever* solve."

"It would be nice," he said, "to find something that would help pin down who owned the boat."

"*Remains*," she said. "What we need are remains." Her manner was so intent that two kids trooping past with balloons turned to stare. "Look. They left the boat. That suggests something unexpected might have happened. A storm. Maybe they were attacked by natives."

"Or," suggested Max, "maybe they just never came back for it."

"It's a nice boat," said April. "I'd sure take it with me when I left. I wouldn't just leave it somewhere. No, I think there's a good chance something went wrong." Her voice softened, became very distant. "Oh, Max, I don't know. I hate to speculate about this thing." She took a bite of pizza and chewed very deliberately before continuing. "If something *did* do wrong, there's a decent chance their means of transportation is still here."

Max should have been feeling good. The Vickers Museum in South Bend was expected to get a substantial grant, an award that opened serious possibilities for the company. In addition, there had been two good offers for a Catalina flying boat on which Max had an option, and *Popular Aviation* had notified him they wanted to do an article on Sundown. The company's condition looked strong enough that he was toying with the possibility of keeping *White Lightning*.

Nevertheless, he was restless. The ground-search radar was approaching the western limits of Tom Lasker's farm with no indication of anything untoward. April had hinted at a vehicle. But maybe they were looking in the wrong place. After all, a vehicle wouldn't have gone into the lake.

Maybe they hadn't thought this out too well. What was it Lisa Yarborough had said? *Think about where they might have stopped off for hotdogs.*

The weather stayed cold. He took to watching the *Ben at Ten* news team out of Grand Forks, which came in on cable. *Ben at Ten was* covering the Fort Moxie story as a kind of light windup feature each evening. First there was the "devil's boat" T-shirts. Then there had been footage of angry citizens warning the city council that more people would be frightened away than attracted to Fort Moxie by talk of a devil. They interviewed a man who claimed to have unearthed an intact 1937 Chevrolet in a rock garden in Drayton. They reported on the reactions of out-of-state visitors: the boat was a sign of the last days; it had fallen out of an aircraft; it was a publicity stunt by a boat manufacturer; it was an attempt by the American government to entice Canadian visitors.

Tom complained on the phone that the tent smelled of elephants and that for the first time in his life he was grateful the wind rarely blew out of the south. April was almost frantic that the boat was not locked away securely and not even kept away from the public, but Tom felt a responsibility to his lifelong neighbors to keep it on display. He also sent along a brochure and a T-shirt with a picture of the yacht and the slogan *I Had a Devil of a Time in Fort Moxie*. The artwork for the brochure wasn't bad: The boat lay atop its ridge, silhouetted by a full moon with a devilish aspect. The story of the discovery was told in a few terse lines, below a Gothic leader proclaiming that "scientists are baffled." There were also photos of the Lasker farmhouse and downtown scenes prominently displaying the Prairie Schooner, Clint's Restaurant, and the Northstar Motel.

Max kept thinking they were looking in the wrong place. On the day that the T-shirt and brochure arrived, he decided to investigate the possibility.

The main branch of the Fargo library is located downtown, at the intersection of First Avenue and Third Street. It's a square two-story structure, wedged into an area of weary stone-and-brick buildings, softened by trees and occasional shrubbery.

It was midafternoon, just before rush hour, when Max passed the police station and pulled into a parking place in front of the civic center. The temperature had risen, the snow that had been falling since lunchtime had turned to rain, and the asphalt glistened in a cold mist. The streetlights were on, creating a spectral effect, and a heavy sky sagged into the rooftops. He climbed out of the car, pulled his jacket around him, and hurried the half-block to the library.

High-school kids crowded the stacks and tables, and the air was thick with the smell of damp cotton. He went back into the reference section, pulled out all the atlases he could find, and dragged them to a table.

Lake Agassiz had been the largest of the many Pleistocene lakes of North America. It was a sea in every sense of the word, covering at its maximum expanse a surface area of 110,000 square miles. It had formed from the meltwaters of the continental ice sheet near the end of the last ice age. But within a few thousand years those same glaciers, retreating north, had uncovered access to Hudson Bay, and Agassiz had drained.

The ancient lake lived on in Lake of the Woods, the Assiniboine River, Rainy Lake, Red Lake in Minnesota, the Red River of the North, Lake Winnipeg. But in the days of its greatness, the water had filled the valley to a depth of more than three hundred feet.

He checked the dates on Native Americans. They had been here early enough to have seen Agassiz. What else had they seen?

The spruce fibers in the loops of the mooring cables indicated that the boat had been tied up rather than simply anchored. That implied a harbor. Where within a reasonable range of Tom Lasker's farm had there been a sheltered harbor?

Where, along the shores of Lake Agassiz, would you build a pier?

The size of the coastline was dismaying. It stretched from north-central Saskatchewan to St. Anthony's Falls in Minneapolis.

Probably ten thousand miles of shore. Hopeless. But there was a fair chance that the boat had been moored, that it had broken loose, and that it had been driven onto a reef or sunk by a storm shortly afterward. Not a tight chain of reasoning. But it was possible. If so, then the mooring place lay in the neighborhood. Say, along the western coastline between Fargo and Winnipeg.

He looked a long time at the maps.

What did a good harbor need? Obviously the water had to be at the right level. That made it a problem of altitude. Okay, he could check that out. It would have to provide shelter from current and wind. And enough depth to tie up without grounding during low tide. That meant no shallow slopes. There couldn't be too many places like that.

He hoped.

Max lifted off, climbed into a clear sky, and turned west, looking for the shoreline. He didn't find it. The Red River Valley rises in the south, and the escarpment, which is so pronounced near the border, sinks to invisibility. From offshore, the coast would have looked flat. That meant there could have been no deep-water approaches.

He turned north, flying over a snow-covered landscape marked by silos and occasional towns connected by long, quiet two-lane roads. The ancient coast did not appear until he crossed into Cavalier County.

Near Herzog Dam, Route 5 passes through a cut. He went down to four thousand feet for a better look. The snowfields had been abandoned to winter, and nothing moved in all that landscape save a lone pickup, approaching from the east. It was possible the cut disguised an ancient harbor, and he flew overhead several times without coming to a firm conclusion. Unfortunately, if this was it, he doubted there would be much left to look at. He photographed it and flew on.

He found another potential landfall south of Walhalla, off Route 32.

And another candidate in Canada.

Three possibilities in all.

The site at Walhalla was closest to the Lasker farm. That one first, he thought, turning east.

He called April from the plane. "No big thing," he said. "But it's a possibility."

"Sure." She didn't sound particularly enthusiastic. "Anything's better than what we're doing now. Who owns the land?"

"I can find out, if you want me to pursue it."

"Yes," she said. "Go ahead. Get us permission to look around."

Tom met him at Fort Moxie International. He was equally unimpressed, but he shrugged and took the same tack. "We can ride over now, if you want," he said.

They drove west on Route 11, past the farm, and out to the edge of the Pembina Escarpment, where they turned south on Route 32. The hills and ridges on the west side of the road formed a solid chain, with clumps of forest scattered across their summits and piles of rock at ground level. Walhalla nestled in this section, a prosperous prairie town of frame houses, lumberyards, and feed stores.

Ten minutes south of town, the trees parted, and they were looking into a horseshoe canyon.

"Johnson's Ridge," said Lasker.

The canyon walls were rocky and almost sheer on the south and west. The northern slope rose more gradually toward the summit. It was heavily wooded, as was the valley floor. Two men were stopped just off the road, cutting firewood, stacking it in the back of a pickup.

The canyon was two hundred yards wide at its mouth and maybe twice as deep. It narrowed by about a third toward the rear wall. An access road left the highway, plunged into the trees, and climbed the northern ridge in a series of hairpin turns.

Lasker pulled over and stopped. The sun was sinking toward the top of the western promontory, which was lower by fifty to a hundred feet than the summits on either side. "Where was the water level?" he asked.

"Depends on which period you're talking about. It was never high enough that the southern side could have served conveniently as a harbor. But for a long time you could have taken a boat up there"—he indicated the rear wall—"tied up at your dock or whatever, and stepped out onto dry land."

Lasker squinted through the sunlight. A squadron of birds, too far away for him to see clearly, cruised over the summit. "Could be," he said. "I think it belongs to the Indians," he added.

Arky Redfern's law offices were located in a professional building on the outskirts of Cavalier, the county seat. He was flanked by an orthodontist and a financial advisor. The building was flat gray slate with maybe twenty parking places, about half of which were filled when Lasker pulled in and found an open slot next to the handicapped space.

Inside, a brisk young woman looked up from a computer terminal. "Good afternoon, gentlemen," she said. "Can I help you?"

She took their names and picked up a phone. Fifteen

minutes later they were ushered into an interior office dominated by a mahogany desk, leather furniture, and an array of glass-door bookcases. The walls to either side were crowded with plaques and certificates; the one behind the desk was conspicuously reserved for a hunting bow and a spread of five arrows.

Arky Redfern was a lean young man in a gray tweed jacket. He was of about average height, with dark, distant eyes, copper skin, and thick brown hair. Just out of law school, Max thought. Redfern came through an inner door, greeted Lasker with easy familiarity, asking about his family, and shook Max's hand.

"Now," he said as they settled down to business, "what exactly is it you gentlemen want to do on Johnson's Ridge?"

As they'd agreed, Lasker took the lead. "We'd like to have permission to conduct a ground-radar search. To look for artifacts."

The lawyer cocked his head as if he hadn't heard correctly. "Really? Why? What would you expect to find?"

Lasker said, "It's a general survey. We want to see if there's anything up there. And we'd agree not to remove anything."

Redfern took a pair of spectacles from his jacket pocket and fitted them carefully over his eyes. "Why don't you tell me straight out what you're looking for? Is there another yacht up there, Tom?"

Lasker looked at Max. "We're looking at places all over the area, Mr. Redfern," Max said. "You can never tell where you might find something."

Lasker mouthed, "Trust him," and Max sighed. Trust a *lawyer?* It flew in the face of his most cherished principles.

Redfern was apparently not satisfied with Max's answer. He seemed to be still waiting for a response.

"We think," said Max, "there might be some objects left over from the Paleolithic."

The lawyer's eyes narrowed, and he turned toward Lasker. "This *is* connected with the boat, Tom? Right?"

"Yes," said Lasker. "There's an outside possibility, and that's all it is, that something might be buried on top of Johnson's Ridge. It's a long shot."

Redfern nodded. "Why don't you tell me exactly what you know about the yacht?" he said.

"It's been in the newspapers," said Max.

"Nothing's been in the newspapers. Old boat dug up on a farm. It's in very good condition, suggesting that it hadn't been in the ground more than a week. And it lights up at night." He stared across at the two men. "You want access to Johnson's Ridge? Tell me what's going on."

"Can we get a guarantee of confidentiality?" asked Lasker.

"I would like to be free to confer with the chairman if need be. But I can assure you that otherwise what you tell me will go no farther."

"Who's the chairman?" asked Max.

"The head of the local Sioux," said Lasker. "Name's James Walker."

"The head of the Sioux is a *chairman?*"

"*Movie* Indians have chiefs," said Redfern. "Now tell me about the boat."

Max nodded. "It might be a lot older than it looks." A tractor-trailer went by and shook the building. Max described April's findings, watching Redfern while he talked, expecting at every moment to be dismissed as a crank.

Instead he was heard without comment or visible reaction. When he'd finished, Redfern sat silently for a few moments. "You're suggesting," he said, "someone sailed a *yacht* on Lake Agassiz?"

When people put it like that, it always sounded dumb. "We're not sure," Max said. "It's possible."

"Okay." Redfern opened a drawer, and took out a piece of memo paper. "How much are you willing to pay for the privilege?"

Lasker pushed back in his chair. "Since we won't be doing any damage to the land, Arky, we'd hoped you'd just let us look around."

Redfern nodded. "Of course. And I hope you understand, Tom, that if it were up to me, I'd say yes without hesitation. But the tribal council has its rules, and I have no alternative except to abide by them." He looked at his visitors.

"I guess we'd be prepared to invest a hundred," said Max.

Redfern nodded yes, not yes to the offer, but yes to some hidden impression of his own. "How exactly do you intend to conduct the search?"

"We'll be using a ground-radar unit," said Max.

Redfern wrote on his sheet of paper. His brow wrinkled, he made additional notes. Then he looked up. "It's hard for me to see how I can accept less than a thousand."

Max got to his feet. "That's ridiculous," he said.

"It's customary," said Redfern. He let the statement hang, as if its validity were obvious. Max thought it over. There were other places to look, but Johnson's Ridge was an ideal harbor. If the boat had been housed anywhere in the area, it would have been there.

"We can't manage a thousand," he said. "But you might want to consider that if we *do* find something, everyone will benefit."

"I'm sure of that," said Redfern. He sighed. "Okay. I tell you what I'll do. Let me speak with the chairman. He might be willing to make an exception and come down for a worthy cause. What kind of figure can I offer him?" He smiled politely at Max.

"How about five hundred?"

Redfern's eyes slid momentarily shut. "I suspect he'll consider that a bit tightfisted. But I'll try." He wrote on the paper again. "I'll draw up a contract." He smiled. "Of course you understand that any Native-American artifacts you might find will remain the property of the tribe. Anything else of value, we will share according to usual conditions."

"What are those?" asked Max.

Redfern produced another piece of paper. "In this case," he said, "section four would seem to apply." He handed the document to Lasker. "These are our standard guidelines for anyone applying to do archeological work on tribal land."

"I think," said Max, "we need a lawyer."

Redfern looked amused. "I always recommend that anyone entering into a legal transaction seek counsel. I'll draw up the agreement, and you can come by later this afternoon and sign, if you like." He rose, business apparently concluded. "Now, is there anything else I can do for you?"

Max had been admiring the bow. "Have you ever used it?"

"It was my father's," he said, as if that answered the question.

Peggy Moore had grown up in Plymouth, New Hampshire, in the shadow of the White Mountains. She'd gone to school in New York, left three marriages in her wake, and had little patience with people who got in her way. She handled a wide range of duties at GeoTech, and running a ground-search radar team was what she most preferred to do. Not because it was challenging, but because it could yield the most satisfying results. There was nothing quite like sitting in front of a monitor and spotting the rock formations that promise oil. Except maybe the Nebraska find that had been the highlight of her career: a mastodon's bones.

She had assumed that the hunt on Lasker's farm had been for another boat. But now, without explanation, her team had been sent to the top of Johnson's Ridge. What in hell were they looking for?

It was a question that had begun to keep her awake nights. Moore suspected there was something illegal going on. Nothing else explained the compulsive secrecy. Yet Max (who reminded her of her first husband) seemed too tentative to be a criminal, and the Laskers were clearly up-front types. She was not sure about April Cannon, with whom she'd spent little time. Cannon possessed a streak of ruthlessness and was probably not above bending the law, given the right reason. But that still did not answer the basic question. What were they looking for? Hidden treasure? Buried drugs? A lost cache of nerve gas?

She watched Sara track the input from Charlie's radar. The weather had moderated somewhat, warmed up after the last few days, and Charlie was cutting his pattern across the top of the ridge. The scans were fed into the system and translated into images of rock and earth.

They'd had a couple of days of unseasonable warmth, and the snow cover had melted. The ground was consequently wet and dangerous, so Moore had drawn the survey course carefully, keeping Charlie safely away from the edge of the precipice. She kept a close eye on his progress and occasionally warned him back in, sacrificing coverage to safety.

The ground-search unit was giving them reasonable imagery to about a hundred feet. For archeological purposes—

assuming that was the real reason they were here—that would be more than adequate.

The western section of Johnson's Ridge, the summit of the rear wall, was grassy and flat, a long plateau about two thousand yards north to south and a hundred fifty yards across the spine. On the south, a ravine split it off from the rising hills on its flank. The north side ended in a wall of trees.

"Concentrate along the rim," Max had said.

"Slower," she told Charlie, who was still uncomfortably close to the edge.

"Roger," said Charlie. He was wearing an outsized lumberjack coat and a woolen hat with its earflaps pulled down.

Moore wanted to find *something*. Not only because she wanted to know what was going on, but because she was a professional and intended to deliver a product to the customer even when he made the project unnecessarily difficult. Still, it was irritating that Max and his associates wouldn't trust her. Nobody was going to steal their beads and arrowheads, or whatever. And that was another aspect of this that pointed toward a geological motif: These did not seem like people who would be interested in digging up old cookpots. But she had explained that if they wanted to find, say, gold, they had to tell her about it if they expected to get results.

She was seated with her feet on one of the workbenches, sipping coffee, when a very peculiar picture worked its way onto the bank of screens. "Son of a bitch," she said, freezing the image on her personal display.

✠ 9 ✠

For the moonlit places where men once laughed
Are now but bones in the earth . . .

—Walter Asquith, "Ancient Shores"

Max was in Tucson to bid on a Halifax bomber when the call came in.

"I think we got it right out of the box." April's voice, hushed. "Something's buried on the lip of the ridge."

"What? Another boat?" Max was standing near a window in the lone terminal of a small private airport. The Halifax was out on the runway, surrounded by the competition.

"No. This is a lot bigger. About a hundred fifty feet across. And it's right where you thought it might be. On the brink of the summit."

"Damn."

"Max," she said, "it's *round*."

"What?"

"You heard me."

The word brought a long, pregnant silence at both ends.

✠   ✠   ✠

On the radar printouts, it looked like a roundhouse with a bubble dome. "I'm damned if I've ever seen anything like it," Moore said. "It's not a ranger station and it's not a silo. And it sure isn't a farmhouse." She looked suspiciously at Max. "I assume you know what it is."

Max knew what he was hoping for. But the trace image didn't look aerodynamic. He contented himself with shaking his head.

"What else can you make out?" April asked.

"Nothing. *Nada*. It's just a big, round building. About five hundred feet in circumference."

"How high is it?"

"Twenty feet at the perimeter. Thirty feet or so at the top of the bubble." They were in the GeoTech van, which was parked uncomfortably close to the cliff edge, directly over the object. The wind pushed against the side of the vehicle. "Now here's something else that's strange," Moore said. "The top of the summit is mostly rock, with a few feet of dirt thrown on top. Okay? But this thing is built inside a cut in the rock. Look, see these shadows? That's all granite."

April asked her to enlarge the image.

"The cut is also round," Moore said. "Uh, I would have to say it was made specifically to accommodate the roundhouse."

Max and April exchanged glances.

"Here's something else," said Moore. She pointed at dark shadings below and in front of the object. (If, that is, one could assume that the front was at the lip of the cliff.) "This is a channel cut through the rock." It passed from a point directly under the structure out to the edge of the precipice.

"What's the roundhouse made of?" April asked.

"Don't know. I can tell you it isn't rock, though."

"How can you be sure?"

"Quality of the return. It almost reads like glass." Moore

tapped her fingers against the top of her work table. "I just can't imagine what anything like this is doing up here. If we were down on the plain, I'd say it was an abandoned storage facility. It's big enough. But why would anyone put a storage building up here? It almost looks like a place where people came to sit on the front porch and look out over the valley. Right?" She looked hard at Max. "But this thing doesn't *have* a front porch." Max squirmed under her irritation and was tempted to blurt everything out. But what was he going to tell her? That he thought she'd just found a flying saucer?

They climbed out of the van and stood looking down into the ground as if, by sheer will, they could see what lay beneath. It had snowed during the night, but the wind had been blowing hard all day and had swept the summit clear. It was just after sunset, and the temperature was dropping fast.

The radar tractor crisscrossed the ground at a distance, looking for other objects. The periodic roars of its engine knifed through the still air. Far below, a pair of headlights moved south along Route 32, and a couple of farmhouses lit up the gathering gloom. The landscape was fading, becoming intangible.

April surprised him. She put her arm through his and walked him along the brink, away from Moore. "The channel," she said. "Are you thinking what I am?"

He nodded. "It was for the boat."

She shivered with excitement. "I think we've hit the jackpot."

"I think so," said Max.

Neither spoke for a time. Max was savoring his feelings.

"Do you think," she said, "the Sioux will agree to our digging up the area?"

"Sure. They stand to profit from this, too."

They turned their backs to the wind and looked out over the void. "I don't like the idea," she said, "of putting this on a profit-and-loss footing. I wish we could just sneak in here and do this without saying anything to anybody. But we're talking about a major project now."

Max agreed. "An excavation's not going to be easy. This thing is a lot bigger than the boat." The ground crackled beneath his feet. "I wonder whether we shouldn't wait for spring."

"No." April's jaw tightened. "I am not going to sit on this for six months. We can get a small army of volunteers out here pretty quickly. When we show Lisa what we've got, I'm sure she'll fund us. There'll be no problem there." She snuggled down into her coat. "We can post ads at UND and get some student workers. There are a lot of people in Fort Moxie, Cavalier, and Walhalla with not too much to do this time of year. I don't think we'll have any trouble assembling a workforce. First thing we need is to get some heavy equipment up here." Her eyes were shining. "What do you think, Max? Have we got one?"

She was warm and vulnerable. Like Max, she was reluctant to give too much credence to the find until they knew for sure. "I don't know," he said.

Toward the east, the Red River Valley stretched away to the stars.

Lisa Yarborough had spent a pleasant evening with a half-dozen friends watching *Cats*, after which they had retired to the Thai Lounge. At about 1:30 she pulled into her garage. She let herself into the house, bolted the door, and checked her calls.

April's voice said: "When you can, call me."

She debated waiting until morning, but there had been a note in the voice that excited her curiosity.

April picked up on the second ring.

"What've you got?" said Lisa.

"Something's buried on the ridge. We don't know what it is yet, but it shouldn't be there."

"Is it connected with the boat?"

"We won't know until we dig it up. I don't want to make promises. Maybe somebody started to put a silo in up there. I just don't know. But it's *big*. And round. Lisa, I'm not objective about this anymore. But the present owners have had the property since the 1920s. They say there shouldn't be anything there."

"Okay. How much do you need?"

They fell quickly into the habit of creating prosaic explanations for the roundhouse. There were, after all, any number of things it might have been. A sanitarium for people who had needed to get away. A government test facility of one kind or another. A forgotten National Guard training installation. But there was a distinct division between what they said and what they were thinking.

Max took charge of getting a steam shovel up to the site. The night before the Northern Queen Construction Company was to start, Max, April, and the Laskers gathered under Christmas lights at the Prairie Schooner for a celebration that was ostensibly connected with the season but which somehow touched on Max's hunt for a harbor and its possibly successful conclusion. To add to the mood, which was simultaneously exuberant and tentative, Redfern delivered congratulations from the tribal chairman.

They sat at a corner table, watching couples lit by electric candles moving slowly to Buck Clayton's "Don't Kick Me When I'm Down, Baby." The music caught at Max, made him feel sentimental and lonely and happy. Too much wine, he thought.

A man he had never seen before invited April to dance. She smiled and went off with him. He was blond and good-looking. About thirty. "His name's Jack," said Lasker. "He works over at the depot."

Max was irritated to observe that she seemed to enjoy herself.

The important thing, she said a few minutes later, was that whatever happened up on the ridge, they still had the yacht. They had, in her opinion, indisputable evidence of the presence of an advanced technology. "But," she added, "I can't wait to get a close look at the roundhouse." Her eyes glowed.

When Max asked Lasker almost offhandedly what he intended to do with the boat, the big man looked surprised. "Sell it," he said. "As soon as I can get a handle on how much it's worth."

"It's priceless," said April.

"Not for long," he said. "I'm anxious to be rid of the damned thing."

This shocked April. "Why?" she asked.

"Because I'm tired of the circus tent and the T-shirts. I'm tired of being made to feel I'm not doing enough for the town. No, I'm going to cash it in at my first reasonable opportunity."

Max relished the prospect that he might really be instrumental in finding a UFO. He pictured himself showing the President onto its flight deck. *This would have been the navigational system, Mr. President. And here, on your right, is the warp drive initiator.* No, there would not be a warp drive. It would be, what, hyperlight? Quantum? *We estimate Alpha Centauri in eleven days at cruising speed.* Yes. That was a line he would like very much to deliver.

He anticipated a TV movie and speculated who would play Max Collingwood. Preferably somebody both vulnerable and tough. He pictured himself among *Esquire*'s most eligible bachelors. Interviewed by Larry King. (He wondered whether he would get nervous when the TV cameras rolled.) If things went well, he decided, he would keep the Lightning and construct a warbird museum in which it would be the centerpiece.

The Collingwood Memorial Museum.

They were trying not to draw attention to themselves, but as the liquor flowed and spirits picked up, it became more difficult. They drank to one another, to Lisa Yarborough, to the ground-radar crew, to Lake Agassiz, and to Fort Moxie ("the center of American culture west of the Mississippi").

"I think what we need here," said Max, "is an archeologist. Seems to me we could hire one to direct the dig. That way we avoid the screwups we'll make if we try to do it on our own."

"I disagree," said April.

"Beg pardon?"

"We don't want an archeologist." She studied her glass in the half-light of the electric candles. "We don't want anybody else involved if we can help it. Bring in an archeologist and he'll tell us we're amateurs and try to take over the operation. Eventually he'll wind up getting the credit." Her expression suggested she knew about these things and Max should trust her. "You have to understand about academic types. Most of them are predators. They have to be to survive. You let any of them in and they'll never let go." She took a deep breath. "Look, let's be honest. This is not a standard archeological site. Nobody knows any more about this stuff than we do."

"You mean," said Max, "you're the only scientific type associated with this, and you'd like to keep it that way."

She looks exasperated. "Max, this is *our* baby. You want to bring in some heavy hitters? Do that, and see how long we keep in control of things."

The Northern Queen Construction Company supplied a baby steam shovel and a crew. The steam shovel had trouble negotiating the switchback that ran up the escarpment, but once it arrived its operators went to work single-mindedly.

"You're sure you guys won't damage this thing, right?" asked Max.

"We'll be careful," said the crew chief, a gray-haired, thickset man bundled inside a heavy coat. He'd been told the object was an old grain storage facility in which several major works of art were thought to be hidden. (Max was becoming creative.) "Of course," he continued, "you understand we only get you close to the thing. Afterward there'll be a lot of digging to do, and that's going to be up to you."

They used stakes and string with pieces of white cloth fluttering in the wind to mark out the target area. Peggy Moore was standing just outside the radar van, her arms folded over a Boston Red Sox jacket (the weather had warmed up), while the Northern Queen crew moved into position. A few yards away, Charlie was posted on the radar tractor.

In the van, the atmosphere was electric. April had assumed a post near the main screen (the rule that noncompany people had to stay out of the van had been long since forgotten), from which she was directing the excavation. Max was losing confidence now that the moment of truth was near and had become convinced that they were going to unearth a silo or a long-forgotten Native-American habitation. April's Martians were light-years away.

The steam shovel lined itself up just outside the markers and stopped. The man in the cab looked at a clipboard, got on his walkie-talkie, and then rolled the engine forward a few yards. The jaws rose, opened, and paused. They plunged into the earth, and the ground shook.

The operator moved levers and the saws rose, trailing pebbles and loose dirt, and dumped their load off to the side. Then they swung back. The plan was to dig a broad trench around the target. Tomorrow April's volunteers, who were mostly farmers without too much to do at this time of year, would begin the actual work of uncovering the roundhouse.

A few snowflakes drifted down from an overcast sky.

Peggy Moore had a video camera and was recording the operation. The woman was no dummy. Max realized he should have thought of it himself. The videos might be worth a lot of money before this was over.

In fact, they were going to have to break down soon and call a press conference. How long would it take before the media figured out something was happening on Johnson's Ridge? But there was a problem with a press conference: What did you tell them? You couldn't talk about UFOs and then dig up an old outhouse.

By sundown a twelve-foot-wide, thirty-foot-deep trench had been driven into the promontory. Like the canyon, it was shaped like a horseshoe, enclosing the target area on three sides, within about fifteen feet of the object. They laid ladders and planking in the ditch and threw wooden bridges across. "You'll want to be careful," the crew chief explained. "There's a potential for cave-ins, and if you dig around the bridges, which you will probably have to, you'll want to make adjustments so they don't collapse. I suggest you get a professional in, somebody that knows what they're doing."

"Thanks," said April. "We'll be careful."

He held out a document for her to sign.

April looked at it.

"It explains about hazards, safety precautions, recommends you get somebody."

"It's also a release," said April.

"Yeah. That, too." He produced a clipboard.

She glanced across the document and signed it. The crew chief handed her a copy. She folded it several times and slid it into a pocket.

The steam shovel began to move away, rolling toward the access road through a light wind that blew a steady stream of snow over the summit. The crew chief surveyed his work with satisfaction. "Good night, folks," he said. "Be careful."

When he had left, they walked slowly around the trench, poking flashlight beams down into it. "That's going to be a lot of digging," said Max.

April nodded. "We've got a lot of people."

✠ 10 ✠

Shopkeepers, students, government officials, farmers,
Ordinary men and women, they came,
And were forever changed . . .

—Walter Asquith, "Ancient Shores"

In the morning, a horde of volunteer workers crowded into the auditorium at the Fort Moxie City Hall. The press was represented by Jim Stuyvesant, the town's gray eminence and the editor and publisher of the weekly *Fort Moxie News*. Stuyvesant didn't know much about why there had been a call for workers, other than that there was going to be an excavation on Johnson's Ridge, but in a town where the news was perpetually slow, this was front-page stuff.

At eight sharp April tapped her microphone, waited for the crowd to quiet, and thanked everyone for coming. "We don't know much about this structure," she said. "We don't know how durable it is, and we don't know how valuable it is. Please be careful not to damage anything. We aren't in a hurry." Stuyvesant, who was his own photographer, took some pictures. "If you find anything that's not rock and dirt, please call a supervisor over."

"Is it Indian stuff?" asked a man in a red-checked jacket up front.

"We don't know what it is." April smiled. "After you help us find out, we'll let you know. Please stay with your team. Tomorrow you can report directly to the work site. Or come here if you prefer. We'll have a bus leaving at eight and every hour after that, on the hour, until two P.M. We'll quit at four-thirty. *You* can quit when you want, but please check out with your team leader. Unless you don't care whether you get paid."

The audience laughed. They were in a good mood— unexpected Christmas money was coming, and the weather was holding.

"Any questions?"

"Yeah." One of the students. "Is there going to be something hot to drink out there?"

"We'll have a van dispensing coffee, hot chocolate, sandwiches, and hamburgers. Hot chocolate and coffee are on the house. Please be careful about refuse. There'll be containers; *use* them. Anyone caught littering will be asked to leave. Anything else?"

People began buttoning parkas, moving toward the doors.

They poured out of the old frame building and piled into buses and cars and pickups. Stuyvesant took more pictures and waited for April. "Dr. Cannon," he said, "what actually is on the ridge?"

"Jim," she said, "I honestly don't know, and I don't want to speculate. It's probably just an old storage facility from the early part of the century. Give me a few days and you can come look at it."

Stuyvesant nodded. The *Fort Moxie News* traditionally reported stories that people *wanted* to see printed: trips to Arizona, family reunions, church card parties. He was therefore not accustomed to people who dodged his questions. He had an additional problem that daily newspapers did not: a three-day lead time before the *News* hit the street. He was already past the deadline for the next edition. "I can't believe anybody would put a storage shed on top of a ridge. It's a little inconvenient, don't you think?"

"Jim, I really have to go."

"Please bear with me a minute, Dr. Cannon. You're a *chemist*, aren't you?"

"Yes, I am."

"Why is a chemist interested in an archeological site?"

April had not expected to be put under the gun. "It's my hobby," she said.

"Is there an archeologist here somewhere? A *real* one? Directing things?"

"Well, as a matter of fact, no. Not really."

"Dr. Cannon, several weeks ago somebody dug up a yacht in the area. Is this project connected with the yacht?"

"I just don't know," April said, aware that she was approaching incoherence. "Jim, I'm sorry. I have to go." She saw Max, waved, and started toward him.

But Stuyvesant kept pace. "There's a rumor it's a UFO," he said.

She stopped and knew she should think before she said anything. She didn't. "No comment," she blurted out.

It was, of course, among the worst things she could have said.

They rented three vans: one to use as a kitchen, the second to serve as a control center, and the third to be a general-purpose shelter. They also erected a tent in which to store equipment.

Max had established himself at the Northstar Motel in Fort Moxie. He called Stell to tell her he'd be staying near the site for several days and asked her to arrange to get his car delivered so he would have local transportation.

Lasker agreed to take over the administrative aspects of the dig. He wasted no time designing an overall plan, appointing supervisors, devising work teams and assigning them rotating responsibilities, and putting together a schedule that allowed the workers almost as much time in shelter as exposed to the elements.

He also thought nothing of throwing a few spadefuls of earth himself. His attitude caught on, especially when April and Max joined in. Consequently, things happened quickly. And on the same day that the *Fort Moxie News* hit the stands with its UFO story, Lem Hardin, who worked part-time at the lumberyard, broke through to a hard green surface.

UFO ATOP JOHNSON'S RIDGE? SCIENTISTS: "NO COMMENT"
by Jim Stuyvesant

Fort Moxie, Dec. 17—

Dr. April Cannon, who is directing an excavation effort on Johnson's Ridge, refused today to deny escalating rumors that she has found a flying saucer.

Cannon heads a workforce of more than two hundred people who are trying to unearth a mysterious object, which was found recently after an intensive radar search. Archeologists at the University of North Dakota commented that Johnson's Ridge is an unlikely site for Native-American artifacts, and they are at a loss to explain the reasons behind the Cannon initiative.

The story was picked up immediately by the major wire services.

Max's first intimation of the breakthrough came with a loud round of distant cheers. He got up from his desk and was reaching for his coat when the phone rang. "The roof," Lasker told him.

The word passed quickly around the site, and people scrambled up ladders and dropped wheelbarrows to hurry over to see. What they saw, those who could get close enough, was a small emerald-colored patch protruding out of the dirt at the bottom of a ditch.

April was already there when Max arrived. She was on her knees, gloves off, bent over the find. Max climbed down beside her.

"Feels like beveled glass," she said. "I think I can see into it." She took out a flashlight, switched it on, and held it close to the patch. But the sun was too bright. Dissatisfied, she removed her jacket and used it to create shade.

"What is it?" asked one of the workers.

"Can't tell yet." April looked at Max. "The light penetrates a little bit."

"You're going to freeze," he said. But he put his head under the spread jacket. He *could* see into the object.

April produced a file, took off a few grains, and put them in an envelope. Then she looked up and spotted Lasker. "Be careful," she said. "We don't want any spades near it. I don't care if it takes all year to get the dirt out. Let's not damage this thing." She put her jacket and gloves back on and climbed out of the hole. "Don't know, but that doesn't look to me like the roof of a shed. Maybe we've really got something." The envelope was the self-sticking kind. She sealed it and put it in a pocket. "Max," she said, "I need a favor."

"Name it."

"Fly me back to Colson?"

"The action's here."

She shook her head. "Later it will be. But this afternoon the action will be at the lab."

April never understood how the media found out so quickly. The *Ben at Ten* TV news team arrived before she and Max could get off the escarpment, and they were quickly joined by some print reporters.

"No," she told them, "I don't know anything about a UFO."

She told them she had no idea how the story had got started, that they weren't looking for anything specific, that there'd been reports of a buried object atop the ridge, and that they had found some thick glass in the ground. "That's it," she said. "It's all I can tell you for now."

Carole Jensen from *Ben at Ten* pressed for a statement.

"How about tomorrow morning?" said April. "Okay? Nine o'clock. That'll give us a chance to try to figure out what we've got. But please don't expect any big news."

Max flew them back to Chellis Field. April wasted no time jumping into her car, declining his invitation for lunch. "I'll call you when I have something," she promised.

Max checked in at the office, ordered pizza, and turned on his TV just as the noon news reports were coming on. And it was not good. There he was, standing beside April and looking foolish, while she transparently dodged questions. Worse, the reporter identified him as the owner of Sundown Aviation.

The anchor on *The News at Noon* referred to the delusions often associated with UFO buffs, and cited a gathering two weeks earlier on an Idaho mountaintop to await the arrival of otherworldly visitors. "Is the Fort Moxie dig another example?" he asked. "Stay tuned."

In midafternoon the clips showed up on CNN, which lumped Johnson's Ridge in with a report on the crazy season. They interviewed a visibly deranged young man who maintained there was a power source within the Pembina Escarpment that allowed people to get in touch with their true selves. In Minnesota a group of farmers claimed to have seen something with lights land in the woods near Sauk Centre. There were stories of alien abductions in Pennsylvania and Mississippi. And a man in Lovelock, Nevada, who'd crashed into a roadside boulder and tested positive for alcohol, swore he was being chased by a UFO.

"Max, you're a celebrity," Ceil told him. He hadn't seen her standing in the doorway. She was wearing an immaculately pressed Thor Air Cargo blazer, dark blue with gold trim. Her hair was shoulder-length, and it swirled as she pulled the door shut.

Max sighed. "On my way to fame and fortune," he said.

She sat down opposite him. "I hope you make it." Her expression was set in its whimsical mode. "I was down looking at the Zero today."

"And?"

"If you really have a UFO up there, the rest of this stuff is going to look like pretty small potatoes."

He grinned. "Don't bet the mortgage on it."

"I won't, Max." She smiled. Max felt warmth flood through him. "Listen, I'm going up to Winnipeg. You busy?"

He shook his head. "Just waiting for a phone call. How long are you going to be there?"

"Up and back. I'm delivering a shipment of telecommu- nications parts." Her eyes went serious. "Max, is it really there?"

"I doubt it," he said.

She looked disappointed. "Pity. Anyhow, why don't you come along? You can show me where you're digging."

Max saw himself coming out of a Washington studio after an interview with Larry King. Ceil would be waiting, but as she approached he would wave her away. "Talk to you later," he'd say. "I'm on my way over to do the *Tonight* show."

"Max?" she said.

"Yeah. Sure, I'll go." He *did* want to hear April's results as soon as they became available. "Which plane?"

"*Betsy.*"

"Okay. Let me finish up here and I'll meet you outside."

He called April, got her answering machine, and told her how to raise the C–47. Then he left a note for Stell (who was at lunch), pulled on his jacket, and wandered out onto the runway.

Ceil was already on board. He could see her up in the cockpit, going through her checklist. The C–47 still carried its original insignia. The only external concession to its real mission was the corporate mallet and the legend *Thor Air Cargo* tucked away on the tail.

Max climbed in through the cargo door and closed it. The interior was filled with packing cases. He threaded his way through to the cockpit. Ceil, talking to the tower, raised a hand to acknowledge his presence. Max took the copilot's seat.

The engines were turning slowly.

"What's the big rush on the telephones?" he asked. Usually he would have expected a shipment like this to go by land.

"Somebody screwed up. Production is waiting. So I get

the assignment. Most of my business comes from picking up the pieces when people get things wrong." She grinned. "I'll never lack for work."

She taxied out onto the north runway. A few clouds floated in a gray sky. Snow tonight, Max thought. He liked the feel of the C–47. It was a durable and exceptionally stable aircraft. If you were going to haul cargo through hostile skies, this would be the plane you'd want to have.

"On our way," she said. She gunned the engines, and the C–47 rolled down the tarmac and lifted into the early afternoon.

Max had discovered more than a year earlier that romance with Ceil wasn't going to happen. Once that had been got out of the way, he found her easy to talk to. She was a good listener, and he trusted her discretion absolutely. "What scares me," he said, "is that all this is becoming so public. The whole country now thinks that *we* think there might be a UFO up there. It makes us look like kooks."

"What *do* you think?"

"That it'll turn out to be something else."

"Then why are you going to all this expense?"

Max thought about it. "On the off chance—"

Her laughter stopped him. "See? You *are* kooks. Anyhow, I wouldn't worry about it. You'll be fine if you really *do* have a UFO." It was cold in the cabin, and she turned up the heat. "If it's there, Max, I want to ride in it." She looked at him, and he laughed and gave her a thumbs-up.

She climbed to fourteen thousand feet and turned north. Life was good in the cockpit of the C–47, where the sun was shining and everything was peaceful. "Who would own it?" she asked.

"I guess it would belong to the Sioux."

"The Sioux?"

"It's on their land." The thought of the Sioux winding up with the world's most advanced spacecraft amused him. "I wonder what the Bureau of Indian Affairs would say to that."

"You can bet your foot," she said, "that the Sioux wouldn't be allowed to keep it."

They picked up the Maple River near Hope and followed it north. When they were over Pleasant Valley, the phone rang. Ceil picked it up, listened, and handed it to Max.

It was April. She sounded out of breath. "It's one-sixty-one, Max," she said.

"Just like the boat?" He squeezed the phone and caught Ceil's eye. "You're sure?"

"Yes, Max. I'm sure." She made no effort to suppress her delight.

"Congratulations," said Max. Ceil was watching him curiously.

"You, too. Listen, we should go back up."

"Actually, I'm more or less there now. I'm on my way to Winnipeg. I'll be back this evening, and we can fly up tonight. Okay?"

"Sure. That's fine. Call me when you get here."

Max said he would. "Have you thought about the press conference tomorrow?"

"Yes," she said. "I've thought about it."

"Seems to me we have no reason to keep it quiet anymore."

"What?" asked Ceil, forming the word with her lips.

Max could almost hear the wheels go round in April's head. "I'd feel better," she said, "if we waited until we have the thing dug up."

"You probably won't have that luxury."

"I take it," Ceil said moments later, "you have a UFO."

"No, the news is not *that* good. But it *is* good." He explained.

She looked at him, and her eyes grew round and warm. "I'm happy for you, Max," she said.

Johnson's Ridge was coming up. Max looked down on the flanking hills, smooth and white in the afternoon sun, and the saddle, low and flat and emptying off abruptly into space.

"You've got a lot of people down there," said Ceil.

Too many, as a matter of fact. There were people everywhere, and the parking lot overflowed with vehicles. "I guess we've got some sightseers," he said.

Ceil banked and started a long, slow turn. "It's probably just the beginning," she said. "You might want to start thinking about crowd control and security." She extracted a pair of field glasses from a utility compartment and raised them to look at the ridge. "I don't think your people are getting much work done."

Max reached for the phone, but she touched his wrist. "Why don't we do it in person?" she said. "I'd like to see it for myself, anyhow."

She put the glasses down and pushed the wheel forward. The plane began to descend. "You aren't going to land down *there*, are you?" Max asked. "There's an airport a few miles east."

She pointed down. "Is that the road?"

The two-lane from Fort Moxie looked like stop-and-go traffic. "That's it."

"We don't have time to negotiate that. Look, Max, I'd love to see a UFO up close. You've seen the ground. Any reservations?"

The top of the escarpment was about two thousand yards long. It was flat, treeless as long as she stayed away from the perimeters, marked with occasional patches of snow. "You've got a pretty good crosswind," he said.

She looked down, and her expression indicated no sweat. "It's less than twenty knots. No problem for Betsy."

"Whatever," he said.

She laughed. "Don't worry, Max. If anyone complains, I'll tell them you protested all the way down."

Ten minutes later she set the big plane on the ground without jostling the coffee. Everyone turned to watch as they taxied close in to the site. Lasker was waiting when Max opened the door.

"I should have known it was you," he said. Before he could say anything else he saw Ceil, and he got that same goofy expression that seemed to afflict every man she got close to.

"Ceil," Max said, "this is Tom Lasker. Our straw boss."

They shook hands.

Tourists and sightseers were everywhere. They engaged workers in conversation, blocked bridges, and generally got in the way. Many were standing on the edge of the excavation, others were dangerously close to the precipice. "We need to do something," Max said.

Lasker sighed. "I had some people trying to keep them away. But they're aggressive, and there are just too many to control. Anyway, nobody up here has any real authority."

Max watched an unending stream of cars approaching across the top of the plateau. "Okay," he said, "we'll ask the police to establish some controls on the access road. Maybe limit the number of tourists they allow up here at any one time."

"They don't want to do that."

"They're going to have to. Before somebody gets killed. We'll need to make up ID cards for our people."

"What do we do in the meantime? We're almost at dead stop here."

Max took a deep breath. "Send everyone home early." He looked at the swarms of people. "Who's the chief of police?"

"Emil Doutable."

"Do you know him?"

"Yeah. We don't run in the same social circles, but I know him."

"Call him. Explain what's happening and ask for help. Tell them we've been forced out of the excavation, and ask him to send some people to clear the area."

He nodded. "Okay."

"Meantime," Max said to Ceil, "I guess you'd like to see the whatsis?"

"Yes," she said. "If you don't mind."

They crossed a wooden bridge over the main trench. In the inner area, heaps of dirt were thrown up everywhere, and several other ditches had been dug. Max peered into each as they advanced. Finally he stopped. "Here," he said.

The excavation was wider than it had been in the morning. And the green patch had also grown. "It looks like glass," Ceil said.

Several minutes later, Lasker rejoined them. "Cops are coming," he said.

"Good. By the way, Tom, April says this is more of the same stuff. Maybe we've really got ourselves a UFO."

Lasker shook his head. "I don't think so."

Max had been careful not to allow himself to get carried away by his hopes. But Lasker's comment, and something in his tone, disappointed Max. "Why not?" he asked.

Lasker looked pained. "Follow me," he said.

He led the way back to the main ditch and descended

one of the ladders. Max and Ceil followed. It was cold and gloomy in the trench. Boards had been laid along the ground. People were digging everywhere. Others hauled dirt away and loaded it into barrels. The barrels were lifted by pulley to the surface, where they would be dumped.

"Here," said Lasker. He pointed at a curved strut that emerged from the earthen wall about five feet over his head and plunged into the ground. "There are several of these," he said. "The upper end is connected to the outside of the object. This end," he added, pointing to the lower section, "is anchored in rock. Whatever else this thing might be, it sure as hell wasn't meant to go anywhere."

✠ 11 ✠

The entire macroindustrial system is predicated on a persistent and sta-
tistically predictable level of both dissolution and waste. That is, on
major components of what is normally defined as use. A significant
reduction in either of these two components could be relied on to pro-
duce immediate and quite volatile economic disruptions.

—Edouard Deneuve, *Industrial Base and Global Village,*
third edition

"I'd like to start by putting an end to the flying-saucer rumor."
April spoke directly into the cameras. She was flanked by
Max, who would just as soon have been somewhere else but
was trying not to look that way. A state flag had been draped
across the wall behind them. "I don't know where that story
came from, but it didn't originate with us. The first I heard
about it was in the *Fort Moxie News.*" She smiled at Jim
Stuyvesant, who stood a few feet away, looking smug.

They were in the Fort Moxie city hall. Max had been
shocked at both the number and the identities of the journalists who had turned up. There were representatives from
CNN and ABC, from the wire services, from several major

midwestern dailies, and even one from the *Japan Times*. Mike Tower, the *Chicago Tribune*'s celebrated gadfly, was in the front row. For at least a few hours, the little prairie town had acquired national prominence.

April and Max had made a decision the previous evening to hold nothing back but speculation. If they were going to show up on CNN, they might as well do it with a splash. April had rehearsed her statement, and Max had asked every question they could think of. But doing it with the live audience was different. April was not an accomplished speaker, and there were few things in this life that scared Max more than addressing any kind of crowd.

April pulled a sheaf of papers out of her briefcase. "But we do have some news. These are lab reports on a sample of sail found with the Lasker boat and on a sample of the exterior of the object on the ridge. The element from which these objects are made has an atomic number of one hundred sixty-one."

Photojournalists moved in close and got their pictures.

"This element is very high on the periodic chart. In fact, it would be safe to say it is *off* the chart."

Several hands went up. "What exactly does that mean?" asked a tall young woman in the middle of the room.

"It means it is not an element we have seen before. In fact, not too long ago I would have told you this kind of element would be inherently unstable and could not exist."

More hands. "Who's capable of manufacturing this stuff?"

"Nobody I know of."

Cellular phones were appearing. Her audience pressed forward, holding up microphones, shouting questions, some just listening. April asked them to hold their questions until she completed her statement. She then outlined the sequence of events, beginning with the discovery of the yacht. She named Max and Tom Lasker, giving them full credit (or responsibility) for the find on the ridge. She described in detail the test results on the materials from the boat and from the excavation site. "They will be made available as you leave," she said. She confessed an inability to arrive at a satisfactory explanation. "But," she added, "we know that the object on the ridge is a *structure* and not a vehicle of any kind. So we can put everyone's imagination to rest on that score." She delivered an engaging smile. "It looks like an old railroad roundhouse."

Hands went up again.

The *Winnipeg Free Press:* "Dr. Cannon, are you saying this thing could *not* have been built by human technology?"

CNN: "Have you been able to establish the age of the object?"

The *Grand Forks Herald:* "There's a rumor that more excavations are planned. Are you going to be digging somewhere else?"

She held up her hands. "One at a time, please." She looked at the reporter from the *Free Press.* "Nobody I know can do it."

"How about the government?"

"I wouldn't have thought so. But you'll have to ask them." She turned toward CNN. "The element doesn't decay. I don't think we'll be able to date it directly. But it appears that the builders did some rock cutting to make room for the roundhouse. We might be able to come up with a date when the rock cutting took place. But we haven't done that yet."

A woman to her left was waving a clipboard. "Do you have some pictures?"

April signaled to Ginny Lasker, who was standing beside

a flip chart. She lifted the front page and threw it over the top, revealing a sketch of the roundhouse. "As far as we can tell," April said, "the entire outer surface is made of the same material. It feels like beveled glass, by the way."

"Glass?" said ABC.

"Well, it *looks* like glass."

More hands:

"What's inside?"

"Are you sure you haven't made a mistake here somewhere?"

"Now that we have this material, will we be able to reproduce it?"

And so on. April responded as best she could. She had no idea what lay within. She had arranged to have the samples tested by a second lab, and the results were identical. And she had no idea whether anyone could learn to manufacture the material. "If we could," she added, "we could make sails that will last a long time."

"How long?" asked the *Fargo Forum*.

"Well." She grinned. *"Long."*

They had the security problem under control. ID badges were passed out to workers, and police kept tourists from wandering onto the excavation site.

The press conference, if nothing else, had alerted Max to the nature of the beast he was riding. He gave several interviews but was careful not to go beyond the limits they'd set. *What is really happening here? Who built the roundhouse?* Max refused to be drawn in. *We don't know any more than you do.* He was, he said, content to leave the speculation to the media.

Journalists at the excavation outnumbered the workforce.

They took pictures and asked questions and stood in several lines to look at the translucent green surface, which had now been reached in several locations.

Just before noon Tom Lasker caught up with Max in the control van. The phones were ringing off the hook, but they'd brought a few people in from the dig to help out. "They've broken in on the networks with this story, Max," he said. "Bulletins on all the stations. By the way, Charlie Lindquist called. He loves us."

"Who's Charlie Lindquist?"

"President of the Fort Moxie city council. You know what he said?"

"No. What did he say?"

"He said this is better than Nessie. So help me." Tom's grin was a foot wide. "And the wild part of it is that it's true, Max. This is the biggest thing in these parts since Prohibition. Cavalier, Walhalla, all these towns are going to boom." There were raised voices outside. Max looked out the window and saw April trading one-liners with a contingent of reporters. "I think they like her," he said.

"Yeah, I think they do. She gave them one hell of a story."

The door opened, and April backed in. "Give me an hour," she shouted to someone, "and I'll be glad to sit down with you."

"We're into my childhood now," she said, safely inside. "Some of them want to turn this into another story about how a downtrodden African-American makes good." She sighed, fell into a chair, and noticed Lasker. "Hi, Tom. Welcome to the funny farm."

"It's like this at home, too," he said. "Huge crowds, unlike anything we've seen before, and an army of reporters. They were interviewing the kids when I left this morning."

April shrugged. "Maybe this is what life will be like from now on."

"I can deal with it." Max was enjoying himself.

"Hey," she said, "I'm hungry. Have we got a sandwich here anywhere?"

Max passed over a roast beef and a Pepsi from the refrigerator. April unwrapped the sandwich and took a substantial bite.

"You were good out there," Max said.

"Thanks." Her lips curved into a smile. "I was a little nervous."

"It didn't show." That was a lie, but it needed to be said.

Someone knocked. Lasker leaned back and looked out. He opened the door, revealing a thin, gray-haired man of extraordinary height.

The visitor looked directly at April, not without hostility. "Dr. Cannon?"

"Yes." She returned his stare. "What can I do for you?"

The man wore an air of quiet outrage. His hair was thin but cropped aggressively over his scalp. The eyes were watery behind bifocals that, Max suspected, needed to be adjusted. His glance slid past Lasker and Max as if they were furnishings. "My name's Eichner," he said. "I'm chairman of the archeology department at Northwestern." He looked down at April from his considerable height, which his tone suggested was moral as well as physical. "I assume you're in charge of this—" He paused. "—operation?" He coated the term with condescension.

April never took her eyes from him. "What's your business, Dr. Eichner?" she said.

"My business is preserving the past, Dr. Cannon. You'll forgive me for saying so, but this artifact, this whatever-it-is that your people are digging at, may be of great value."

"We know."

He flicked a cool glance at Max, as if challenging him to disagree. "Then you ought to know that the possibility of damage, and consequently of irreparable loss, is substantial. There are no controls. There is no professional on site."

"You mean a professional *archeologist*."

"What else might I mean?"

"I assume," said Max, "you're interested in the position."

"Frankly," Eichner said, still talking to April, "I'm far too busy to take over a field effort just now. But you have an obligation to get *somebody* up here who knows what he, or she, is doing."

"I can assure you, Dr. Eichner," said April, "that we are exercising all due caution."

"All due caution by amateurs is hardly reassuring." He produced a booklet and held it out for her. The legend *National Archeological Association* was printed on the cover. "I suggest you call any university with a reputable department. Or the Board of Antiquities. Their number is on page two. They'll be happy to help you find someone."

When she did not move, he dropped the booklet on the table. "I can't prevent what you're doing," he said. "I wish I could. If it were possible, I would stop you in your tracks this moment. Since I cannot, I appeal to reason."

April picked up the booklet. She slipped it into her purse without glancing at it. "Thank you," she said.

He looked at her, looked at the purse. "I'm quite serious," he said. "You have professional responsibilities here." He opened the door, wished them all good day, and was gone.

Nobody spoke for a minute. "He's probably right," said Lasker.

Max shook his head. "No," he said. "Not a chance. The

archeology department at Northwestern doesn't know any more about digging up this kind of thing than we do."

"I agree," said April. "Anyhow, Schliemann was an amateur."

"Didn't I read somewhere," said Lasker, "that he made a mess of Troy?"

Everything April had hoped for was on track. She was living the ultimate scientific experience, and she was going to become immortal. April Cannon would one day be right up there with the giants. And she could see no outcome now that would deny her those results. She was not yet sure precisely what she had discovered, but she knew it was monumental.

They made all the networks that evening and were played straight, without the crazy-season motifs. The *NewsHour with Jim Lehrer* produced a panel of chemists who generally agreed that there had to be an error or misunderstanding somewhere. "But," said Alan Narimoto of the University of Minnesota, "if Dr. Cannon has it right, this is a discovery of unparalleled significance."

"How is that?" asked Lehrer.

"Setting aside for the moment where it came from, if we are able to re-create the manufacturing process and produce this element—" Narimoto shook his head and turned to a colleague, Mary Esposito, from Duke, who picked up the thread.

"We would be able," she said, "to make you a suit of clothes, Jim, that would probably not wear out before you did."

ABC ran a segment in which April stood beside the roundhouse with a two-inch wide roll of cellophane tape. "Ordinary wrapping tape," she said. She tore off a one-foot strip, used it to seal a cardboard box, and then removed the tape. Much of the box came with it. "Unlike cardboard, our element interacts very poorly with other elements," she continued. She tore a second strip and placed it against the side of the building, pressed it down firmly, loosened the top, and stood clear. The tape slowly peeled off and fell to the ground. "It resists snow, water, dirt, whatever. Even sticky tape." The camera zeroed in on the green surface. "Think of it as having a kind of ultimate car wax protection."

The coverage was, if cautious, at least not hostile. And April thought she looked good, a model of reserve and authority. Just the facts, ma'am.

Atomic number way up there. Over the edge and around the corner and out of sight. *This element is very high on the periodic chart. In fact, it would be safe to say it is off the chart.* The science writer from *Time* had positively blanched. What a glorious day it had been. And tonight researchers across the country would be seeing the story for the first time. She hadn't published yet. But that was all right, because she had proof. And she was, as of now, legend. It was a good feeling.

There was no bar at the Northstar Motel. April was too excited to sleep, and, unable to read, she was about to call Max and suggest they go out and celebrate some more (although they both had probably already had too much to drink at a rousing dinner in Cavalier with the Laskers) when her phone rang.

It was Bert Coda, the associate director at Colson. Coda had been around since World War II. He was a tired, angry, frustrated man who had substituted Colson Labs for wife, family, God, and country a long time ago.

His greeting was abrupt. "April," he said, "have you lost your mind?"

That caught her attention. "What do you mean?"

"You talked to all those cameras today."

"And?"

"You never mentioned the lab. Not *once*."

"Bert, this had nothing to do with the lab."

"What are you talking about? Last time I noticed, you were working for us. When did you quit? Did you pack it in when I wasn't looking?"

"Listen, I was trying to keep the lab out of it."

"Why? Why on earth would you want to do *that?*"

"Because we're talking UFOs here, Bert. Maybe little green men. You want to be associated with little green men? I mean, Colson is supposed to be a hard-nosed scientific institution."

"Please stop changing the subject."

"I'm *not* changing the subject."

"Sure you are. This is about publicity. Tons of it. And all free. I didn't hear much talk out there today about UFOs."

"You will."

"I don't care." It was a dangerous rumble. "April, you are on every channel. I assume that tomorrow you will be in every newspaper. *You*, April. Not Colson but Cannon." He took a long breath. "You hear what I'm telling you?"

"But it's *bad* publicity."

"There is no such thing as bad publicity. When they line up again in the morning, as they assuredly will, please be good enough to mention your employer, who has been overpaying you for years. Do you think you can bring yourself to do that?"

She let the seconds run. She would have liked to defy the son of a bitch. But the truth was that he intimidated her. "Okay," she said. "If that's what you want."

"Oh, yes. That's what I want." She could see him leaning back with his eyes closed and that resigned expression that flowed over his features when he confronted the world's foolishness. "Yes, I would like that very much. By the way, you might mention that we're especially good in environmental services. And listen, one other thing. I'll be interested in hearing where you were and whose time you were on when this business first came to your attention."

✠ 12 ✠

A little gleam of time between two eternities; no second chance to us forever more!

—Thomas Carlyle, *Heroes and Hero Worship, V*

Temperatures fell to minus twenty on the Fahrenheit scale the day after the press conference. The ground froze, people came down with frostbite, and Mac Eberly, a middle-aged farmer who'd brought half his family with him to the ridge, suffered chest pains. During the holidays the weather deteriorated further, and April reluctantly gave up and closed the operation for the season. She paid a generous bonus and announced they would restart the project when they could. In the spring, she added.

The following day a blizzard struck the area. And the wind-chill factor on New Year's Eve touched a hundred below. The story quickly dropped out of the newspapers, shouldered aside by the run-up to the Super Bowl, a major banking scandal involving lurid tales of sex and drugs, and a celebrity murder trial.

April published her findings, and, in accordance with tradition, the new element was named cannonium in her honor. The NAACP awarded her its Spingarm Medal, and the National Academy of Sciences hosted a banquet in her honor. She was, of course, ecstatic. But nevertheless the long delay weighed on her spirits.

Max returned to Fargo, resumed his life, and proceeded to cash in on his newfound fame. People who were interested in buying, selling, or restoring antique warplanes were making Sundown their preferred dealer. Furthermore, Max found he was now in demand as a speaker. He'd never been comfortable speaking to groups of people, but offers were in the range of a thousand dollars for a half-hour. He took lessons in public speaking and learned that, with experience, he was able to relax and even became good enough to command interest and get a few laughs. He talked at Rotary Club affairs, business luncheons, university award presentations, and Knights of Columbus gatherings. When he found out April was getting an average of *six* thousand per appearance, he raised his price and was surprised that most groups were willing to meet it.

He spent a weekend with his father. The colonel was delighted. For the first time in Max's memory, his father seemed proud of him and was anxious to introduce him to friends.

April, meantime, became a regular dinner companion. Somewhere during this period Max recognized a growing affection for her and made a conscious decision to maintain a strictly professional relationship. He told himself that the Johnson's Ridge project was potentially too important to risk the complications that might come out of a romantic entanglement with the woman who had emerged as his partner in the venture. Or it might have been more complicated, a mix of race and Max's reluctance to get involved and a fear that she might keep him at arm's length. She had, after all, done nothing to encourage him. But when she introduced him to a police lieutenant she was dating and confided to Max that she really liked the guy, he was crushed.

Occasionally they took out the Lightning and flew over the escarpment. The blowing snow had filled in most of the excavation; only heaps of earth remained as evidence of the frenetic activity on the ridge. It was almost as if they had never been there. On one occasion, a cold, frozen day in late January, she asked him to land.

"Can't," he said.

"Why not? Ceil landed here."

"I don't know how deep the snow is. Ceil had an inch. We might have a foot. And there's probably ice underneath."

"Pity," she said.

Unseasonably warm weather arrived in February. After several successive days in the fifties, April drove to Fort Moxie, picked up Tom Lasker, and toured the excavation with him. It was too early in the year to start again, and they both knew it. But she could not bear the prospect of waiting several more weeks. "Maybe we'll get lucky," she said. "When it gets cold, we can work around it."

Lasker said he didn't think it was a good idea. But April cleared it with Lisa Yarborough, and the spring drive got underway.

The weather held for eight days. The excavation teams returned and took full advantage of their opportunity. They dug the snow out of the trenches and dumped it into the canyon. They attacked the hard ground with a will and methodically uncovered a wide area of roof. They worked their way down the front of the structure, exposing a curved

wall of the same emerald-green color and beveled-glass texture. To everyone's disappointment, no doorway or entry
was visible.

They had assumed that the front, the portion that looked
out over the edge of the precipice, would provide an
entrance. But its blank aspect was disappointing. There was
considerably more work to be done, and because it was on
the lip of the summit, the effort would be both slow and
unsafe.

The roundhouse curved to within three feet of the void,
from which it was separated by a shelf of earth and loose
rock. This shelf covered the channel they'd seen on the
radar printouts. The channel might provide a quick entrance
but its proximity to the edge of the cliff rendered it dangerous. Before April would consent to excavating the channel,
she wanted to dig out the rest of the structure. Surely somewhere else they would find a door.

They also erected several modular buildings to serve as
storage and communications facilities.

The workers had got into the habit of bringing flashlights
with them, which they periodically used to try to peer into
the cannonium shell. Several swore they could see through,
and a couple even claimed that something looked back. The
result was that the ridge began to acquire a reputation that
at first lent itself to jokes and later to an inclination by many
to be gone by sunset.

On Washington's birthday, the weather went back to
normal. The Red River Valley froze over, and Max celebrated
his own birthday on the twenty-third with April and the
Laskers during a driving snowstorm. But the winds died
during the night, and the morning dawned bright, clear, and
cold. So cold, in fact, that they were forced by midafternoon
to send everyone home.

By then they had almost freeed the roundhouse from of its tomb. Earth and rock still clung to it, but the structure was attractive in its simplicity. The wall was perfectly round and, like the bubble roof, it glistened after it had been washed.

Max was watching the first cars start down the access road when he heard shouting and laughter out of sight around the curve of the roundhouse.

A small group was gathered near the rear of the building. Two men were wiping the wall. Others were shielding their eyes against the sun to get a better look. Several saw Max and waved excitedly.

They had found an image buried within the wall.

A stag's head.

It was clear and simple: a curved line to represent a shoulder, another to suggest an antler. Here was an eye, and there a muzzle.

The image was white, contrasting sharply with the dark cannonium shell. Like the structure itself, its most compelling characteristic was its clean fluidity. There was no flourish. No pretense.

April unslung a camera from her shoulder and studied the roundhouse in the failing light. "Perfect," she said. Snow drifted down through the somber afternoon.

She snapped the shutter, changed her angle slightly, and took a second picture.

The snow whispered against the wall. "It's lovely in the storm," she said. They walked slowly around the perimeter while she took more pictures. "In our whole history," she continued, "this is only going to happen once." She shot the roundhouse, the stag's head, the surrounding hills, the parking lot. And Max. "Stand over here, Max," she told him, and when he demurred, she laughed and dragged him where she wanted him, told him to stay put, and took more pictures. "All your life, you're going to remember this," she said. "And there'll be times when you would kill to be able to come back to this moment."

Max knew it was true.

And he took her picture with the great building crouching behind her like a prehistoric creature. "Good," she said. "That's good."

And when he least expected it, she fell into his arms and kissed him.

The TV crews returned in force the next day. They interviewed everybody and showed particular interest in the stag's head. Max stayed late on the summit that evening, working. There was still some light on the escarpment when Tom Brokaw led into the final feature of the evening news broadcast, which was traditionally chosen to leave a positive impact. "In North Dakota, a team of researchers has begun digging again at the site of a very mysterious object," he said. Aerial and ground pictures of the excavation site and the roundhouse appeared. "The object you are looking at was discovered several months ago a few miles from the Canadian border. The people who are directing the excavation aren't talking much, but persons close to the effort think it may have been left by extraterrestrial visitors. Was it?" Brokaw smiled. "Carole Jensen, of our affiliate KLMR-TV in Grand Forks, has the story."

Close-up. Jensen stood in front of the curving wall, wrapped in a stylish overcoat. She was wearing no hat, and the wind played havoc with her hair. She looked cold. (It was hard to believe that elsewhere in the country pitchers and catchers were reporting to spring training.) "Tom, we've heard a lot of speculation about this site since we first found out about it last November. Experts across the country are saying that the test samples that were taken from the object they call the roundhouse should not be possible. They are also saying that they have no idea how such an element could be manufactured. But it's here. And a small group of amateur archeologists has begun digging again. Before it's over, we may have the first convincing evidence of a visit by extraterrestrials."

Yeah, thought Max. That's good. As long as we're not the ones saying it.

The other networks took the same approach. They were all cautious. But it was a great story, and the media, once they were reasonably assured that nothing was amiss, would be trumpeting it.

Max pulled on his coat and went outside. Moonlight fell on the excavation, illuminating the roundhouse, throwing shadows across the circular cut in which it stood. Peggy Moore's theory that the cut was artificial, that someone had sliced a piece out of the rock to accommodate the structure, now seemed beyond question. The rocky shore had been too high above water level, Max thought, visualizing the ancient lake. So they'd removed a piece, installed their boathouse, and cut a channel through the last few feet.

Eventually the inland sea had gone away, leaving the thing high and dry. And over ten thousand years the wind had filled everything back in.

Might it be possible to find the piece they had taken out? He walked close to the edge and peered down.

Harry Ernest was Fort Moxie's lone delinquency problem. He'd acquired a passion for spray-can art in Chicago and had come to North Dakota to live with relatives when his mother died. (Harry never knew his father.)

Harry's major problem was that in a place like Fort Moxie, no free spirit can hide. He was the only known vandal north of Grand Forks; and consequently when an obscene exhortation showed up on the water tower or on one of the churches or at the Elks hall, the deputy knew exactly where to go to lay hands on the culprit.

To his credit, and to his family's dismay, Harry was dedicated to his art. But since he knew he would inevitably have to pay the price, he learned to choose his targets for maximum impact. When the roundhouse showed up on TV, Harry experienced a siren call.

Tom Brokaw had hardly signed off before Harry was collecting the spray paint he'd hidden in the attic. Gold and white, he thought, would contrast nicely with the object's basic color.

He gave a great deal of consideration to the appropriate message and finally decided that simple was best. He would express the same sentiments he'd left on countless brick walls in and around Chicago. Harry's response to the world.

At around eleven o'clock, when the house had settled down, he took the car keys from the top of his uncle's bureau, climbed out his bedroom window, and eased the family Ford out of the garage. A half-hour later he discovered that a police presence had been established at the access road. He therefore drove past and parked a half-mile beyond. From there he cut through the woods, intercepted the access road, and *walked* up.

The roundhouse was a dark cylindrical shadow cast against subdued starlight. It overlooked the valley, and whatever he wrote would be spectacularly visible from Route 32 when the sun hit it.

Several temporary buildings had been erected around the thing. He noted lights in one and somebody moving inside. Otherwise the area was deserted.

He strolled across the summit, whistling softly, enjoying himself. In the shadow of the roundhouse he paused to check his spray cans. It was getting cold again, but they worked okay. Satisfied, he stood for a minute letting the wind blow on him. Yeah. This was what life was about. Wind in your hair. Snow coming. And sticking it to the world.

He smiled and walked out onto the narrow strip of rock across the front of the roundhouse. The void beside him did not touch his sensibilities. He reached the center, turned to survey his canvas, and backed up until his heels ran out of shelf. Fortunately, the wind was coming from the west, so the structure protected him. That was important if you were trying to work with a spray can.

He was relieved to note that the wall was made of beveled glass. There had been some disagreement on the TV about that. But people had been talking about glass, so he'd brought enamel.

He pointed his flashlight at the wall, and the beam seemed to penetrate. He moved in close, tried to see inside. It occurred to him that there might *be* no inside, that the object might be solid.

He shrugged and took out his spray can.

He would do the first word in gold. He looked up and measured his target with his eye. The angle wasn't so good because he was too close. But there was no help for that.

The only sounds were the wind and a far-off plane.

He aimed and pressed the nozzle. Paint sprayed out of the can in a fine mist, and the satisfying sense of changing pressures flowed down his arm.

But unlike water towers and churches, the roundhouse tended to resist interaction with the world. The mist did not cling. Some of it liquefied and dribbled down the face of the wall. Some very little of it lodged in chinks and seams. But the bulk of it skimmed off into the air and formed a golden cloud.

The cloud held its shape only briefly and then began to dissolve and descend.

Harry could not have understood what was happening. He knew only that his face was suddenly wet. And his eyes stung.

He dropped the can, cried out, and fell to his knees. His fists were in his eyes, and he scraped his arm against something in the dark, and he knew where he was, could not forget where he was. Then the ground was gone and he was falling. In his office a hundred yards away, Max heard the scream, poked his head out the door, and assigned it to an animal.

✠ 13 ✠

In all that vast midnight sea,
The light only drew us on. . . .

—Walter Asquith, "Ancient Shores"

Searchers found Harry by noon. His family reported him missing at eight o'clock, his car was discovered at nine-thirty, and workmen found an enamel spray can and a flashlight on the shelf in front of the roundhouse at a little after ten. The rest was easy.

Max was outraged to think that anyone would want to damage the artifact. He found it hard to sympathize until he stood at the brink in the middle of the afternoon and looked down.

Arky Redfern appeared near the end of the day. He examined the shelf with Max and shook his head. "Hard to believe," he said.

Max agreed.

"There is the possibility of a lawsuit," he added.

The remark startled Max. "He came up here to vandalize the place," he said.

"Doesn't matter. He was a child, and this is a dangerous

132

area. A good lawyer would argue that we failed to provide security. And he would be right."

Max's breath hung in the sunlight. It was a cold, crisp day, the temperature in the teens. "When do we reach a point where people become responsible for their own actions?"

Redfern shrugged. He was wearing a heavy wool jacket with the hood pulled up over his head. "There's not much we can do now for this kid, but we'll act to ensure there's no repetition. That way, at least, we can show good faith if we have to." He directed Max's attention toward the parking area. A green van was just emerging from the trees at the access road. "I want you to meet someone," he said.

The van parked and the driver's door opened. A Native American wearing a blue down jacket got out, looked toward them, and waved. He was maybe thirty years old, average height, dark eyes, black hair. Something about the way he looked warned Max to be polite. "This is my brother-in-law," said Redfern. "Max, meet Adam Kicks-a-Hole-in-the-Sky."

The brother-in-law put out his hand. "Just *Sky* is good," he said.

"Adam will direct the security force," Redfern continued.

"What security force?" asked Max.

"It came into existence this morning," said the lawyer.

Sky nodded. "My people will be here within the hour." He surveyed the escarpment. "We're going to need a command post."

"How about one of the huts?" suggested Redfern.

"Yes," he said. "That would do."

Max started to protest that they didn't have space to give away, but the lawyer cut him off. "If you want to continue operations here, Max, you'll have to provide security. I recommend Adam."

Sky shifted his weight. He looked at Max without expression. "Yeah," Max said. "Sure. It's no problem."

"Good." Sky took a business card from his wallet and gave it to Max. "My personal number," he said. "We'll be set up here and in business by the end of the day."

Max was beginning to feel surrounded by con artists. What were Sky's qualifications? The last thing they needed was a bunch of gun-toting locals. Redfern must have read his thoughts. "Adam is a security consultant," he said. "For airlines, railroads, and trucking firms, primarily."

Sky looked at Max and then turned to gaze at the round-house. "This is a unique assignment," he said. "But I think I can assure you there'll be no more incidents."

Within an hour a pair of trucks and a work crew had arrived to begin putting up a chain-link fence. The fence would be erected about thirty feet outside the cut and would extend completely around the structure. Anyone who wanted to fall off the shelf now would have to climb eight feet to do it. "There'll be no private vehicles inside the fence," Sky explained.

That was okay by Max. He was still wondering how the young vandal had managed to spray paint in his own eyes. He was aware that a rumor was circulating that the kid had used his flashlight to look through the wall. And had seen something.

The fence went up in twenty-four hours. Sky's next act was to set up a string of security lights around the perimeter of the cut. He mounted cameras at five locations.

Uniformed Sioux guards appeared. The first that Max met fit quite closely his notion of how a Native American should look. He was big, dark-eyed, and taciturn. His name was

John Little Ghost, and he was all business. Max's views of Native Americans were proscribed by the Hollywood vision of a people sometimes noble, sometimes violent, and almost always inarticulate. He had been startled by his discovery of a Native-American lawyer and a security consultant. The fact that he was more at ease with John Little Ghost than with either Sky or Redfern left him paradoxically uneasy.

The police investigation of Harry Ernest's death came and went. Forms got filled out, and Max answered a few questions. (He had been on the escarpment until midnight, he said, and he didn't think there had been anyone else here when he left. He had completely forgotten the "animal" cry he'd heard.) It was an obvious case of accidental death resulting from intended mischief, the police said. No evidence of negligence. That's what they would report, and that would be the finding.

Max went to the funeral. There were few attendees, and those seemed to be friends of the boy's guardians. No young people were present. The guardians themselves were, Max thought, remarkably composed.

The next day Redfern informed him that no legal action appeared likely.

Tourists continued to arrive in substantial numbers. They were allowed onto the escarpment, but they were required to remain outside the fence. Police opened a second access road on the west side of the escarpment and established one-way traffic.

No one had yet found a door.

The security fence ran unbroken across the front of the roundhouse. Now that the area had been rendered safe, workers began to excavate the channel.

With TV cameras present, they brought in a girl in a wheelchair from one of the local high schools to remove the first spadeful of dirt. She was a superlative science student, and she posed for the cameras, smiling prettily, and did her duty. Then the work teams got started.

They knew it would be a drawn-out process because of the confined space. Only two people could dig at a time. Meanwhile, the sky turned gray and the temperature rose, a sign of snow. Around the circumference of the building, an army of people wielding brooms was clearing off the walls and the half-dozen braces that anchored the structure to its rocky base. April and Max watched through a security camera in the control module.

This was to be the last week for all except a few designated workers. The rest would be paid and thanked and released. Charlie Lindquist was planning an appreciation dinner at the Fort Moxie city hall, and he'd arranged certificates for the workers which read *I Helped Excavate the Roundhouse.* (At about this time, the structure acquired a capital *R.*) Media coverage was picking up, as was the number of visitors. Cars filled Route 32 in both directions for miles.

Periodically April went out, climbed down into the excavation, and strolled along the wall. She liked being near it, liked its feel against her palms, liked knowing that something perhaps quite different from her had stood where she now stood and had looked out across the blue waters of the long-vanished glacial lake.

But today there was a change in the wall. She stood at the rear, near the stag's head, looking past the long, slow curve at the wooded slope that mounted to the northern ridge, trying to pin down what her instincts were telling her. Everything *appeared* the same.

She touched the beveled surface. Pressed her fingers to it.

It was *warm*.

Well, not warm, exactly. But it wasn't as cold as it should have been. She let her palm linger against it.

The west grew dark, and the wind picked up. Max watched the storm teams assemble and begin distributing tarpaulins. The digging stopped, and workers rigged the tarps around the excavation to prevent it from being filled with snow. When that was completed, they sent everyone home.

No one wanted to be caught on the road when the storm hit. Including Max. "You ready?" he asked April.

"Yes," she said. "Go ahead. I'm right behind you."

Max put on his coat. The wind was beginning to fill with snow. Visibility would soon go to near zero.

"Hey," he said, "how about if I stop and get a pizza?"

"Sure. I'll see you back at the motel."

Max nodded and hurried out the door. The wind almost took it out of his hands.

He walked to the gate and was greeted by Andrea Hawk, one of the security guards. She was also a radio entertainer of some sort in Devil's Lake, Max recalled, and she was extremely attractive. "Good night, Mr. Collingwood," Andrea said. "Be careful. The road is treacherous."

"How about you?" he asked. "When are *you* leaving?"

"We'll stay here tonight, or until our relief comes. Whichever."

Max frowned. "You sure?"

"Sure," she said. "We're safer than you."

Whiteouts are windstorms, gales roaring across the plains at fifty miles an hour, loaded with dry snow. The snow may accompany the storm, or it might just be lying around on the ground. It doesn't much matter. Anyone trying to drive will see little more than windshield wipers.

April resented the delay caused by the storm. She seldom thought about anything now other than the Roundhouse. She was desperate to know what was inside and who the builders were, and she spent much of her time watching the laborious effort to clear the channel.

The day she'd seen Tom Lasker's boat, she had begun a journal. Chiding herself for an attack of arrogance, she had nevertheless concluded that she was embarked on events of historic significance and that a detailed record would be of interest. During the first few days she'd satisfied herself with accounts of procedures and results. After Max had found Johnson's Ridge, she'd begun to speculate. And after she had closed the operation down for the winter, she had realized that she would eventually write a memoir. Consequently, she'd begun describing her emotional reactions.

The stag's head intrigued her. It seemed so much a human creation that it caused her to doubt her results. Somehow, everything she had come to believe seemed mad in the face of that single, simple design. She had spent much of the afternoon trying to formulate precisely how she felt and then trying to get the journal entry right. Important not to sound like a nut.

She put it in a desk drawer and listened to the wind. Time to go. She signed off the computer, and headed out into the storm. She was about ten minutes behind Max.

At the entrance, John Little Ghost forced the gate open against the wind and suggested that maybe she should stay the night. "Going to be dangerous on the road!" he said, throwing each word toward her to get over the storm.

"I'll be careful," April said.

She was grateful to get to her car, where she caught her breath and turned the ignition. The engine started. There was an accumulation of snow on the rear window. She got her brush out of the trunk and cleared that off, and then waited until she had enough heat to keep the snow off the glass. Then she inched out of the lot and turned toward the opening in the trees that concealed the access road. She drove through a landscape in motion. The storm roared around her.

Maybe Little Ghost had been right.

She turned left, toward the western exit. It was a long run across the top of the escarpment, several hundred yards during which she was exposed to the full bite of the storm. But she kept the wheel straight and opened the driver's door so she could see the ruts other cars had made. The wind died when she arrived finally among a screen of elms and box elders.

She passed an abandoned Toyota and started down.

Snow piles up quickly in a sheltered section, and one has to maintain speed to avoid getting stuck. It obliterates markers and roadsides and hides ditches. To make matters worse, this was the second road, just opened by police, and April wasn't used to it.

She struggled to keep moving. She slid down sharp descents and fought her way around curves. She gunned the engine through deep snow, but finally lost control and slid sidewise into a snowbank. She tried to back out, but the car only rocked and sank deeper.

Damn.

She buttoned her coat, opened the door cautiously against the wind, and put one foot out. She sank to her knee. Some of the snow slid down inside her boot.

An hour and a quarter later, scared and half frozen, she

showed up at the security station. "Thank God for the fence," she told her startled hosts, "or I'd never have found you."

Andrea Hawk was a talk show host on KPLI-FM in Devil's Lake. She'd worked her way through a series of reservation jobs, usually exploiting her considerable Indian-maiden charm to sell baskets, moccasins, and canoe paddles to well-heeled tourists. She'd done a year with the reservation police before discovering her on-air talents, which had begun with a series of public-service pleas to kids about drugs and crime. She was still selling automobiles, deodorants, CDs, and a host of other products to her dewy-eyed audience. Along the shores of Devil's Lake, everybody loved the Snowhawk.

She was twenty-six years old and hoping for a chance to move up. Two years ago a Minneapolis producer had been in the area, heard her show, and made overtures. She'd gone to the Twin Cities thinking she had a job, but the producer drove his car into a tractor-trailer, and his replacement, a vindictive middle-aged woman with the eyes of a cobra, did not honor the agreement.

Andrea was planning to do several of her shows on the scene from Johnson's Ridge. It was clear to her that she was sitting on a big story, and she planned to make the most of it. She'd got Adam's permission, worked out her schedule so that it would not conflict with her air time, and stocked the security module with equipment.

It was cold inside, despite the electric heater. The modular buildings were well insulated, but they weren't designed to withstand winter conditions atop a North Dakota escarpment. The wind blew right through the building. Andrea sank down inside her heavy woolen sweater, wishing for a fireplace.

She wondered whether she'd be able to keep her teeth from rattling when she went on at nine o'clock via her remote hookup. As was her habit, she had begun making notes on subjects she wanted to talk about during the broadcast, and she was reviewing these when April stumbled in.

Little Ghost caught her and lowered her into a chair. "Hello," she said with an embarrassed smile. And then she recognized her old friend. "Andrea," she said, "is that really *you?*"

"Hi," said the Snowhawk.

When April woke, the windows were dark, and the air was filled with the sweet aroma of potatoes and roast beef. A bank of monitors flickered in a corner of the room. "How are you feeling?" asked Andrea.

"Okay." April pushed the toes of one foot against the other ankle. Someone had put heavy socks on her feet. "What are you doing here?" She vaguely remembered having asked the question before but couldn't recall the answer.

Andrea pulled her chair forward so April could see her without having to sit up. "Security," she said. "It pays well."

"Why didn't you come see me?"

"I would have, eventually. I wasn't sure it was appropriate." She felt April's forehead. "I think you're okay," she said. "What were you doing out there?"

"Waited too long to leave."

Andrea nodded. "How about something to eat? We only have TV dinners, but they're decent."

April decided on meatloaf, and Andrea put one in the microwave. "Max called," she said. "We told him you were here."

There was a coziness in the hut that warmed April. Little Ghost didn't talk much, but he was a good listener, which is a faculty guaranteed to make people popular. He stayed close to the monitors, although they showed little more than dancing blobs of light and curving shadows. They talked, and April saw that Andrea was fascinated by the Roundhouse.

"I'm going to do the show on it," she explained.

April smiled. "The Snowhawk at the cutting edge."

"That's right, babe. I was wondering whether you'd be interested in going on tonight. Want to be a guest?"

April considered it. She owed the woman, but she didn't want to face phone calls. "I think I'd better pass," she said.

But she was interested enough to stay and watch.

The Snowhawk's show ran from nine until midnight. If the subject for the evening was the excavation, it didn't stop people from calling in to comment on the new property tax initiative, the schools, the tendency of the county to run up postage costs unnecessarily, or other nongermane topics. The Snowhawk (funny how Andrea seemed to change personalities and become more dominant, even confrontational, in front of her microphone) dealt with these callers summarily, slicing them in midsentence. "Eddie," she might say, "I'm on Johnson's Ridge, freezing my little butt off, and *you* are out of here. Please try to stay on the rails, folks. We're talking about the Roundhouse tonight."

On the whole, however, April was impressed by the level of dialogue. She wasn't sure what she had expected. The Snowhawk's callers were reasonably rational. They were excited by the mystery surrounding the find, but by a ratio of about four to one resisted far-out resolutions in favor of the more mundane. It'll turn out to be a mistake, they said, one after another. April was reminded of Max.

Toward the end of the show the storm began to weaken. April could make out the dome of the Roundhouse rising over the blowing snow.

It seemed to be *glowing*.

She turned away and looked back.

It was a trick of the security lights. Had to be. But they were dull and indistinct in the general turmoil of the storm.

Furthermore, the snow looked *green*.

It was hard to see clearly from the illuminated interior of the security station. She pulled on her boots and took down her jacket. Little Ghost glanced at her. "I'll be back," she whispered, and walked out the front door.

April caught her breath. A soft emerald halo had settled over the Roundhouse.

The Snowhawk saw that something was happening, but she was talking with Joe Greenberg in Fort Moxie and did not have a portable mike. She frowned at John Little Ghost and nodded at the door by which April had just left.

"It's lit up," Little Ghost said.

"What is?"

"The Roundhouse." This exchange, of course, went out live. No damage yet. That came a moment later: "Son of a bitch, I hope it's not radioactive."

✠ 14 ✠

Fear has many eyes.

—Cervantes, *Don Quixote*

Walhalla, Cavalier, and Fort Moxie, like prairie towns across the Dakotas, are social units of a type probably limited to climatically harsh regions. They are composed of people who have united in the face of extreme isolation, who understand that going abroad in winter without checking the weather report can be fatal, who have acquired a common pride in their ability to hold crime and drugs at arm's length. From Fort Moxie, the nearest mall is eighty miles away, and the nearest pharmacy is in Canada. The closest movie theater is within a half-hour, but it's open only on weekends, and not even then during the hunting season. Consequently these communities have developed many of the characteristics of extended families.

Mel Hotchkiss was sitting in the kitchen of his home on the outskirts of Walhalla half-listening to the Snowhawk and enjoying his customary bedtime snack, which on this occasion was cherry pie. He was just pouring a second cup of coffee when she conducted her exchange with the unfamiliar voice. Something untoward was obviously happening. He put the pot down, intending to walk over to the window and look out toward Johnson's Ridge, when Little Ghost delivered the remark that galvanized the area: *Son of a bitch, I hope it's not radioactive.*

An eerie green glow *did* hang over the top of the promontory.

Ten minutes later, having paused only to call his brother and a friend, Mel, his wife, his three daughters, and their dog were in their pickup with a couple of suitcases, headed west out of town.

Within an hour the population was in full flight. Beneath the baleful light atop the escarpment, they loaded kids, pets, jewelry, and computers and took off. Those few who, out of principle, refused to believe in anything having to do with astrology, numerology, crop circles, or UFOs were nevertheless bullied into leaving their warm homes by frightened spouses and well-meaning teenagers. They headed southwest toward Langdon, east to Fort Moxie, and north to the border, where the closed port was defended only by warning signs and highway cones. But nobody planned on stopping for international niceties, and the flood rolled into Canada.

State police flew in a Geiger counter and by about one-thirty in the morning pronounced the area safe. Radio and TV stations broadcast the news, but by then it was too late. The town lay effectively deserted, and its roads were littered with wrecked and abandoned vehicles.

April, John Little Ghost, and the Snowhawk listened to the reports and watched the long lines of headlights moving away on the two-lane roads with a growing sense of horror.

Fortunately, nobody died.

There had been three fires and a half-dozen heart

attacks. Several men had intercepted Jimmy Pachman as he was trying to get out of his driveway and forced him to open his gas station. The men paid for the gas, but Pachman claimed he'd been kidnapped. Police, fire, and medical facilities had been strained to the limit and would announce before the end of the week sweeping reviews of their procedures. The City of Walhalla spent nine thousand dollars to rent equipment and pay for overtime out of its perennially hard-pressed treasury. And there was talk of lynching some of the people on Johnson's Ridge.

Max found out over breakfast. It was, he decided, the same effect that had lit up the boat in Tom Lasker's barn and scared the bejesus out of Ginny. Except this time it was on a wider scale. This time there would be lawsuits.

He left his bacon and eggs, called the security station to talk to Adam, and got April. "It has not been a good night," she said.

"I don't guess." Max took a deep breath. "I'm on my way."

He passed several wrecks along the highway.

Police helicopters roared overhead.

At the turnoff to the access road, a man in a Toyota was arguing with the cop on duty. The cop spotted Max, rolled his eyes, and waved him around. This action infuriated the driver of the Toyota.

Max took his time going up, noting the large piles of snow on either side where the plow had gone through. At the crest he passed one of the Sioux security people. This was the topside traffic coordinator, looking cold, carrying a radio in one hand, waving Max on.

The 8:00 A.M. shift had arrived and begun removing the tarps. Max took a long look at the Roundhouse. In direct sunlight it was hard to see whether it was putting out any illumination of its own. He stopped the car in his accustomed place and sat holding one hand over his eyes, trying to get a good look.

"It faded with the dawn," April told him a few minutes later.

"Just like the boat."

"Yes. Except that this time it wasn't just a set of running lights that came on. The entire building lit up." They'd taped the early-morning news shows. April ran one of them for him. The segment included views from an aircraft. The top of the ridge glowed softly.

"More like phosphorous than electricity," he said.

"That's what we thought." She sipped coffee. Outside, they heard a few cheers.

Max looked through the window but saw nothing out of the ordinary. "Any reaction yet from the city fathers in Walhalla?" he asked.

"Reaction? What do you mean?"

He sighed. "I think we threw a scare into the town last night. They are probably not happy with us."

She smiled. "Max, nobody's dead. Although I'm going to see that Adam grounds the Snowhawk. We don't need any more live broadcasts up here. At least not by our own people."

"The *who?*"

"Andrea Hawk. One of the Sioux security people." She explained how the incident had begun.

"Well," said Max, "maybe we can ride it out. Chances are that before this is over, Walhalla will have an NBA franchise."

The phone rang. April picked it up, listened, frowned. "You're kidding." She listened again. "*Who?*" She gave Max a thumbs up. "We're on our way."

"What?" asked Max.

"We're inside," she said.

While the main effort was being made in front, one of the security people had got through a door near the rear. At the stag's head.

A crowd had already formed. At its center stood the man of the hour. "Well done, George," said Adam Sky, who arrived simultaneously with Max.

The man of the hour was George Freewater, a young Sioux with an easy smile. But Max saw no entrance. Tom Lasker came around the curve of the building from the other direction.

Freewater, standing beside the stag's head, beamed at them. Then, almost casually, he extended his right hand, tugged his glove tight the way a ballplayer might, and touched the wall. Directly over the muzzle.

The stag's head rode up and uncovered a passageway. The crowd applauded. They also backed away slightly.

The passageway had neither windows nor doors, and it was short: After about twenty feet it dead-ended. There were no features of any kind, save for a half-dozen rectangular plates about the size of light-switch covers. These were mounted on the walls waist high, three on a side.

April made for the opening, but Freewater grabbed her sleeve. "Let me show you something first."

"Okay. What?"

"Watch."

Voices in back demanded to know what was happening. Someone was trying to identify herself as UPI.

Without warning, the door came back down. No seam or evidence remained that it had ever been there.

"What happened?" asked April.

Freewater was looking at his watch. "It stays up for twenty-six seconds," he said.

"Thanks, George," April said. She pressed the stag's muzzle. The door didn't move.

She looked at Max. "What's wrong?"

Freewater ostentatiously removed one of his gloves. It was black and quite ordinary. "Try it with this," he said.

April frowned, pulled off the mitten she was wearing, and put on the black glove. "Does it really make a difference?" she asked.

The smile was all the answer she needed. She touched the wall, and the passageway reappeared.

"I'll be damned," said Lasker.

Max noticed a wave of warm air at the opening. *The interior was heated.*

April compared the glove with her mitten. "What's going on?" she asked.

Freewater didn't know. "It only works," he said, "if someone is wearing *my* glove."

"How could that be?" asked Max.

"Don't know," continued the guard. "Bare hands won't do it, either."

"Odd." April looked down the passageway and then again at the glove. "George, if you don't mind, I'm going to hang onto it for a few minutes." She stuffed it into a pocket and looked at Max. "You ready?"

"To do what?"

"Go inside."

Max's jaw dropped. "Are you kidding?" he said. "We could get sealed in there."

"I'd like to go," said Freewater.

"No. No one else. I'll feel better if you're out here to open the door if we can't do it from the inside. I assume both gloves work?"

They tested the other one, and it did. "Give us five minutes," April said. "If we're not out, open up."

"April," said Max, "you know how the Venus flytrap works?"

She smiled at Max as if he were kidding and stepped into the passageway. Max hesitated, felt everyone's eyes on him. And followed.

The space was barely six feet high, maybe four across. It was too small, almost claustrophobic. The walls were off-white and so thick with dust it was hard to make out their composition. Dirt covered the floor.

"We're getting heat from somewhere," said April. She held out her hands to detect air currents.

Max was looking for a door opener. The only thing he saw that offered itself as a candidate was the series of six plates. Two pairs were directly across from each other. The fifth and sixth seemed positioned near either end of the passageway. He fixed the one closest to the entrance in his mind so he could find it when the door closed and they lost their light.

April ran her palms across the wall and then wiped the dust from them. "Heat seems to be coming from everywhere," she said.

The door started down. Max resisted an urge to duck under it while he could, and watched it shut.

The lights did not go out. A gray band running horizontally across the back of the door gave them enough illumination to see by. When Max wiped his sleeve on the band, it brightened, and in a moment he was looking through it at the people on the other side. "It's transparent," he said.

April grinned. "Okay," she said. She also had been studying the wall plates. She approached the one at the far end of the corridor and put on Freewater's glove. "You ready, Max?"

"Do it."

She inhaled. "It's one small step for a woman. . . ." She touched the plate. Pushed it.

Something clicked in the wall. A door opened up directly in front of her. They were looking into a rotunda. "Yes," breathed April. She stepped inside.

The light was gray and bleak. Just enough to see by.

"This is it," she said. "Main stage."

It was empty. A few columns reached up to connect with a network of overhead beams. And that was all. A trench ran from the middle of the floor toward the other side of the dome, which would have been the front.

The door slid down.

He felt a momentary twinge until he saw a plate identical to the ones outside.

"That's our channel," said April, indicating the trench. "Boat came in through the front, tied up right here." There were even a few posts that would have served the purpose.

It was getting hard to breathe. "Heads up," Max said. "The air's bad." How could it have been otherwise?

They propped the doors open and used a couple of blowers to circulate fresh air inside. When they felt it was safe, they opened it up for their people and for the journalists.

The trench was about fifteen feet deep. The dimensions were sufficient to accommodate the boat. They'd have had to fold the mainmast over to get it inside. But it would have worked.

Four rooms opened off the passageway. Two might once have been apartments or storage areas but were now simply bare spaces. The others contained cabinets and plumbing. The cabinets were empty. A sunken tub and a drainage unit not unlike the device on the ketch suggested one had been a washroom. The other appeared to be a kitchen.

Max noticed almost immediately a sense of anticlimax and disappointment. April especially seemed down. "What did we expect?" he asked.

It was just *empty*.

No interstellar cruiser. No ancient records. No prehistoric computers. No gadgets.

Nothing.

✠ 15 ✠

The true power centers are not in the earth. But in ourselves.

—Walter Asquith, "Ancient Shores"

Tom Brokaw displays just the right amount of skepticism. "There is," he says, "more evidence tonight that extraterrestrials may have visited North America near the end of the last ice age. Scientists today entered a mysterious structure that may have been buried for thousands of years on a ridge near the Canadian border." A computer graphic of the Walhalla–Fort Moxie area appears beside him, and the camera cuts quickly to overhead shots and silhouettes of the Roundhouse. "This building is constructed of materials that, we are being told, cannot be reproduced by human technology. Robert Bazell is on the scene."

Bazell is standing in front of the Roundhouse, and he looks cold. The wind tries to take the microphone out of his hand. "Hello, Tom," he says, half turning so the camera can get a better look at the structure. "This is the artifact that scientists think may have been left by someone ten thousand years ago. No one knows where it came from or who put it here. It is constructed of a material that experts say we've

153

never seen before. A team led by Dr. April Cannon got inside today for the first time, and this is what they saw."

The interior of the dome rises above the viewer. Accompanied by strains from Bach's Third Concerto for Organ, the camera glides along the green curves and over the gaping trench.

To Max, watching with April and the Laskers at the Prairie Schooner, it only stirred his sense of disappointment and bad luck. Even the cabinets had been empty! At the very least, Max thought, it would have been nice to find, say, a discarded shoe.

Something.

"If the Roundhouse is really as old as some of the experts are saying, Tom," Bazell continues, "we are looking at a technological marvel. The temperature inside is almost sixty degrees. As you can see, it's cold up here. So we have to conclude that there's a heating system and that it still works." They cut back to the top of the ridge, where snow is blowing and people are standing around with their collars tugged up. "I should add that the structure glows in the dark. Or at least it did last night. So much so that it frightened people in nearby Walhalla and emptied the town."

Split screen. Brokaw looks intrigued. "Are we sure it's not a hoax?"

"It depends on what you're asking about, Tom. The experts don't all agree on the age of the Roundhouse. But they seem to be unanimous that the material it's made from could not be produced by any human agency."

They cut to a bearded, older man seated at a desk before a book-lined wall. The screen identifies him as Eliot Rearden, chairman of the Department of Chemistry, University of Minnesota.

"Professor Rearden," says Brokaw, "can you hear me?"

"Yes, Tom."

"Professor, what do you make of all this?"

"The claim appears to be valid." Rearden's gray eyes blaze with excitement.

"Why do you say 'appears,' Professor?"

He thinks it over. "I wouldn't want to imply there's any problem with the evidence itself," he says. "But the implications are of a nature that causes one to hesitate."

Brokaw asks quietly, "What are the implications?"

Rearden gazes directly into the camera. "I think if we accept the results of the analyses, we are forced to one of two conclusions. Either there were people living here at the end of the last ice age who were technologically more advanced than we are and who somehow managed to get lost, or—" He looks directly out of the screen. "Or we have had visitors."

"You mean UFOs, Professor. Aliens."

Rearden shifts uncomfortably. "If there is a third possibility, I don't know what it might be." He purses his lips. "We are faced here with an imponderable. I think it would be a good idea to keep our minds open and not jump to any conclusions."

The illuminated image of the Roundhouse under a bright moon appears onscreen. It is a live aerial shot. "Now that scientists are inside," says Brokaw, "hard answers should come quickly. NBC will be doing a special on the Johnson's Ridge enigma tonight on *Special Edition* at nine."

Tom Lasker speared a piece of steak and pointed it at the screen. "I'm glad to hear we're on the verge of hard answers," he said.

In the morning, April and Max arrived on Johnson's Ridge at dawn, just in time to watch the green aura fade. A helicopter circled overhead. Press vehicles pulled onto the access road behind them.

Their fax machine had run out of paper during the night, and several thousand e-mail messages had piled up. Everyone on the planet was asking to tour the Roundhouse. "We'll have to work something out," April said. "But I don't know how we're going to do this. We aren't going to be able to accommodate all these people."

Journalists and VIPs were already arriving in substantial numbers. April talked to the media for a while. She described her fears that the results of her investigations would cause her to be written off by her scientific colleagues. "That hasn't happened," she added. "Everyone's being very open-minded about this." She explained the need to protect the premises from hordes of visitors until they could glean whatever information the Roundhouse might contain. "Therefore," she said, "we'll allow six pool reporters inside. Three TV, three print. You folks decide. Give me thirty minutes to set it up. Those who do go in will be asked to stay with the guide. Anybody who wanders off gets the boot. Agreed?"

Some grumbled, most laughed. While they tried to sort out their representatives, she and Max walked around to the stag door. It had been braced open all night with a spade while exchangers ventilated the interior. April took the spade away, and the door closed. She removed her own glove and pressed her fingers against the stag's head. As Max expected, nothing happened.

"So we have established," she said, "that it is George's glove, yes?"

"Apparently," said Max.

"But why should that be?" She produced a scarf and held it up with a flourish for Max's inspection. "Bought it at

156

Kmart," she said. "Six bucks, on sale." She draped it across her fingers and again touched the image.

The door opened.

"*Voilà!*" She wedged the spade back into the doorway.

"Why does it respond to the scarf?"

"Not sure. What does the scarf have in common with George's glove that it does *not* have in common with my mitten or my bare hand?"

"Damned if I know," said Max.

"George's glove—" She removed it from her pocket. "—is made from polypropylene. The scarf is polyester. They're both products of a reasonably technological society."

Max frowned. "Explain, please."

"It's only a guess. But when the Roundhouse was in use, there may have been natives in the area. Who knows what else might have been here? Bears, maybe. Anyway, how would you set up the door to make sure your people could use it, but not the natives, or anything else?"

"I don't know."

"I'd use a sensor that reacts to, say, plastics. Anything else, bare skin, fur, whatever, the door stays shut."

The hordes descended. They poured through U.S. border stations and overwhelmed I–29 and the two-lane highways north from Fargo and Dickinson. They arrived in charter flights at Fort Moxie International Airport, where they discovered that the car rental service had only one car and there was only one taxi. A five-car pileup near the Drayton exit of I–29 stopped northbound traffic for two hours. On State Highway 18, near Park River, frustrated motorists found themselves in stop-and-go traffic for miles. By sundown on the first day after blanket coverage began, two were dead, more than twenty injured, and almost a hundred were being treated for frostbite. Property damage was estimated at a quarter of a million dollars. It was believed to be the single worst day of traffic carnage in North Dakota history.

Police broadcast appeals throughout the afternoon. At 2:00 P.M. the governor went on radio and TV to appeal for calm. (It was an odd approach, since unbridled emotions were by no means the reason for the problem.) "The traffic in and around Walhalla," he said, "is extremely heavy. If you want to see what is happening on Johnson's Ridge, the best view, and the safest view, is from your living room."

We are fond of charging that most people have no sense of history. That claim is usually based on a lack of knowledge of who did what or when such-and-such an event occurred. Yet who among us, given the chance to visit Gettysburg on the great day or to share a hamburger with Caesar, would not leap at the opportunity? We all want to *touch* history, to be part of its irresistible tide. Here was an opportunity, an *event* of supreme significance, and no one who could reach Johnson's Ridge was going to stay home and watch it on TV.

The chief of police was a thick-waisted, gravel-voiced man whose dull features and expressionless eyes belied a quick intelligence. His name was Emil Doutable, which his force had changed to *Doubtful*.

He arrived on the escarpment during the late morning. By then Max and his team of assistants had spent hours on the phone with metallurgists and archeologists and industrialists and politicians and curiosity-seekers from around the world.

Doutable was not happy. The presence of this abomination was complicating his work. He understood that events of major significance were unfolding in his jurisdiction, but he wished they would unfold somewhere else. "We might need a Guard detachment," he told Max. "We're hearing that most of North America is headed this way."

"Tell me something I don't know," Max said. "Maybe we ought to close off the access road. Keep people off the ridge altogether."

Doutable glanced around as if someone might overhear. "Are you serious? Business is booming in the county. If I shut it down, my job goes south." He looked out the window. The parking area was filled with hundreds of cars. "Listen, this is an ideal situation for the towns. It's still pretty cold. Nobody can stay up here very long. They come up, take a look, and go down. Then a lot of them go into one of the towns for a hot meal and wind up doing some shopping. Everything keeps moving. Or at least it used to. Now, though, we've got just too much traffic."

Max nodded, happy that it wasn't his problem.

Doutable was quiet for a minute. "Max," he said, "you're not planning on letting them walk around inside that place, are you?"

"Inside the Roundhouse? No. We're restricting it to the press and to researchers."

"Good. Because that would slow things down even more. We need to keep them out in the cold. As long as we can do that, we should be okay." He nodded vigorously. "Don't change your mind." He got up and started for the door. "If we get lucky, maybe it'll go below zero. That's what we really need."

Helicopters were arriving every few minutes, bringing in fresh loads of journalists and VIPs. Lasker needed help keeping things organized, and Max found himself appointed head greeter. They deluged April with questions and requests for photos, and she tried to respond. But it was an exhausting day, and they were all glad to see the sun go down.

"It's ridiculous," April complained. "I've got the world's most interesting artifact waiting, and I can't get away from the reporters. I want to get a good look at the *inside*." The reality was that the journalists were getting more time than she to look around the interior of the Roundhouse.

There were other distractions. Although she didn't realize it yet, April had become overnight the best-known scientific name in the country. She had already, during the first twenty-four hours of what they had begun to think of as their appearance on the world stage, received offers from three major cosmetics companies who wanted her to endorse their products, from Taco Bell ("Our burritos are out of this world"), from a car rental agency, and from MCI.

She conducted crowds of visitors through the Roundhouse. She granted interviews and conducted press briefings. The photographers had by now discovered they had a photogenic subject, and flashbulbs went off continuously. She was obviously enjoying herself, and Max was happy for her. She was brighter, quicker on her feet than he was. In addition, her smile won everybody's heart, and she had a penchant for delivering sound bites.

On the third day after penetrating the Roundhouse, they started the slow process of screening and removing the accumulated dirt. Selected sections of the walls were cleaned, admitting diffused sunlight into the dome.

The light was of the texture that might fall through a forest canopy in late afternoon. But there were no trees here, of course. Green walls, presumably more cannonium, and apparently identical in design to the exterior, rose around them. A wraparound window, chest high, curved for two hundred seventy degrees, centered on the front.

Lasker asked Max to oversee the restoration. April described the precautions they needed to take and then turned him loose. Also during this period, they hired ex-mayor Frank Moll to act as their public-relations director.

Max thought the real information would come out of the walls. He wanted to know how systems could be built that would still work after ten thousand years. Still, he regretted that first contact might bring little more than a better heating system.

He left a note for April and started back to the motel. But he got caught up in traffic and arrived two hours later, exhausted and annoyed, in Fort Moxie. The town was under siege. Cars were parked everywhere, and the streets were filled. Max negotiated his way through and pulled into the motel lot, where there was no room. He eventually had to park over on Leghorn Street, six blocks away.

Walking back, he saw a teenager wearing a shirt depicting the Roundhouse. The legend read FORT MOXIE, ND–OUT OF THIS WORLD. The Lock 'n' Bolt had put together a display of Roundhouse glasses, dishes, models, towels, notebook binders, and salt and pepper shakers. Across Bannister Street, Mike's Supermarket featured more of the same.

Two school buses were moving leisurely toward him. Bright banners fluttered from both, displaying a picture of the Roundhouse. Across the nose of the leading vehicle, someone had stenciled *Misty Spirit*. They were filled with young people, mostly college age or a little older, and they waved at him as they went by.

Max waved back, hurried along the street (for he was by now cold), and let himself into his motel room. The sudden rush of warm air drained his energy, and he dropped his coat over a chair and sank onto the bed.

The buses stopped at Clint's. The restaurant was already too full to accommodate an additional sixty hungry people, but Clint was not one to miss an opportunity. He offered to make up sandwiches and coffee to go, and he accepted reservations for the evening meal. When they had left, Clint noted that his stores of lunch meats, pickles, and potato salad were moving more quickly than he'd anticipated. He dispatched his son to Grand Forks with an order for replenishments.

At the Lock 'n' Bolt, Arnold Whitaker was watching automotive supplies jump off his shelves. Also moving very quickly were games for kids to play while traveling and, ominously, firearms. And binoculars. Sales of Roundhouse merchandise were going through the roof. He'd picked the stuff up on consignment, what he thought was a generous supply, but it would be gone by tomorrow afternoon.

When he called for more, his Winnipeg supplier put him on back order.

The Northstar Motel was completely full for the second consecutive week. During its entire history, that had never happened before. At about the same time that Max was falling asleep in his room, management was contemplating doubling the rates.

The price of a drink at the Prairie Schooner had, for some, already risen measurably. The proprietor, Mark Hanford, was careful to install separate rates for regulars and visitors. Ordinarily Mark would have considered such a practice unethical. But these were extraordinary times. A businessman had to adjust to changing conditions. He didn't expect that anyone would notice, and nobody did.

Mark had also decided to propose that the town council award Tom Lasker a certificate of appreciation. He knew that the motion would ride right through.

Charlotte Anderson, seated in the front of the lead bus, could *feel* the lines of force. They filled her, washed through the emptiness, and carried her to a level of awareness higher than she had ever known. The grinding of gears in the stop-and-go traffic subsided, and she knew only the triumph of drawing close to a primal destination.

The power source was to the southwest, achingly near. Years ago she had approached such a point in Alaska, near Barrow. It too had put her at one with the cosmos, had established a link between her inner being and the greater universe outside, had tied her to the great web of existence. That too had been a time of exhilaration. But that source, whatever it was, had been buried in a mountain pass beneath glaciers.

Charlotte was trim, honey-blond, clean-cut. There was a kind of forced cheeriness in her manner, an exuberance that seemed reflexive rather than spontaneous. She was from Long Island, had graduated *magna cum laude* from Princeton, and now possessed a master's with a specialization in modern European history. She'd been reared Catholic, but during high school Charlotte had become uncomfortable with a faith that seemed to lay everything out so neatly. God the scorekeeper. At graduation she'd announced that she had become a Unitarian. Creation is beyond logic or explanation, she'd told her dismayed father; one can only sit back and await the wind that blows between the stars. Her father had assured her mother that everything would be all right, that it was all nonsense and Charlotte would get over it.

Some of the boys with the group, she knew, were more interested in her than in centers of power, but that wasn't necessarily a bad thing. Given time, they would come around, and that was enough.

The buses had come from Minneapolis, where Charlotte was a manager at a McDonald's, having left home to find her true self. When the boat had turned up on the North Dakota farm, she'd known it was pointing toward something more. And so had Curie Miller in Madison. They'd talked about it online, the Manhattan group, and Curie and her people, and Sammy Rothstein in Boise, and the Bennetts in Jacksonville, and their other friends around the country, in Philly and Seattle and Sacramento. When the situation had ripened, more than sixty members of the network, wanting to be on hand, had flown into Grand Forks, where Charlotte and a few people from the Twin Cities area had met them with the buses. They'd rented the Fort Moxie city hall and had spent two nights there waiting for stragglers. Now they were ready. And their timing had been perfect: The latest news accounts out of Johnson's Ridge had fired their enthusiasm (if indeed it had needed firing), and she knew, as they all did, that pure magic lay ahead.

April wasn't sure which member of Max's restoration crew had first noticed the series of images in the wall at the rear of the dome. Several claimed credit for finding the icons; but she was struck by the fact that battalions of journalists and physicists, mathematicians and congressmen had marched innocently past the figures. She herself had never noticed them.

There were six, embedded within the glassy surface. They were unobtrusive, black rather than white, and consequently easy to miss in the dark green wall.

The workers had retreated from the area, leaving wheel-barrows and shovels. April stood on a couple of inches of dirt, studying the icons. They were arranged in two columns, each about the size of her palm. Several were pictographic: a tree, a curling line that looked like smoke, an egg, and an arrow. There was also a pair of interlocking rings, and a figure that vaguely resembled a *G* clef.

They appeared to be three-dimensional, and they were all executed in the representational style of the stag. April peered closely at the tree, the top left-hand figure. Like the others, it was located just beneath the surface. She took out a handkerchief and wiped the wall, trying to see more clearly.

And the tree lit up.

She jumped.

Like neon, it burned with a soft amber glow.

She held her hand against the wall but felt no localized heat.

Nothing seemed to be happening anywhere. No doors opened. There were no changes in the texture of the light. She touched the icon again to see if the light would go out.

It continued to burn.

And a bright golden aura ignited a few feet in front of her. It expanded and stars glowed within its radiance. She tried to call out, but her voice stuck in her throat.

Then, as quickly as it had come, it faded. And snapped off.

There had not been a sound.

April stood, not moving, for a full minute. Where the light had been, a clean circle of floor glittered in the filtered sunshine.

✠   ✠   ✠

165

Charlotte inspected the cartons at the back of the bus. One had worked loose and was threatening to fall into the aisle. She reached for it, but Jim Fredrik, from Mobile, got there first and secured it. She thanked him and went back to her seat.

They were behind schedule. The buses had been stalled in heavy traffic about nine miles northeast of the excavation for almost two hours. Signs posted along the route warned them that the site would be closed at six. They were not going to make it.

The members of the network tended to be students or young professionals. They were predominantly white, they were joggers and aerobics enthusiasts, and they had money. During the sixties they would have ridden the freedom buses. They were believers, convinced that the world could be made better for everyone and that the means to act lay at hand.

The bus was drafty and the windows were freezing over. Nevertheless, Charlotte's fellow passengers retained their good spirits. They opened thermos bottles and passed around coffee and hot chocolate. They sang traveling songs from Tolkien and Gaian chants from last year's general council at Eugene. They wandered up and down the aisle, trying to keep their feet warm. And they watched the Pembina Escarpment grow.

The buses turned onto Route 32 just before sunset. Traffic was moving faster now. But it was after six when they reached Walhalla. Charlotte was tempted to call it off for the night and stop here for coffee and hamburgers. But when a couple of her lieutenants approached her with the same notion, she resisted. "Let's at least make the effort," she said. "And if they won't let us in tonight, there's something else we can do."

Back out on the two-lane, they moved at a good clip. Her driver, a rock-band guitarist from New Mexico whose name was Frankie Atami, jabbed his finger ahead. "That's it," he said.

There were lanterns off the side of the road, and barricades were up. Cars were being turned away. "Pull over," she told Frankie.

Two police officers stood beside a barricade at the entrance. They wore heavy jackets. Frankie stopped and opened the door. She leaned out, but the cops just waved them back. "We've come a long way, officer," Charlotte said, shivering.

"Sorry, ma'am," said the taller of the two. "We're closed for the night. Come back tomorrow."

"What time do you open up?"

But the cop was finished talking and jabbed a finger at the road. Frankie checked his mirrors and pulled cautiously out onto the highway.

"Pull off when you can," Charlotte told him. "Let's try to get a look at it."

He glanced doubtfully at the drainage ditches on both sides, which had already claimed several cars. "I don't think so," he said.

Frustrated, they continued south while their angle of vision to the ridge narrowed and vanished. Charlotte fished out a map. "Okay," she said. "Left just ahead."

She brought them around so that, as it grew dark, they were moving along a county road several miles distant from the escarpment but with an excellent view of it. "Find a place to stop, Frankie," she said.

They pulled off onto a shoulder. The second bus swung in behind them and parked. People drifted between the vehicles, drinking coffee and hot chocolate. At the back of the bus, Jim Fredrik was opening cartons. May Thompson and Kim Martin dug into them and brought out lanterns. Along the roadside they filled them with kerosene, and everybody took one.

A few started to sing, and the last of the light fled down the horizon. The stars blazed overhead.

And suddenly, as if someone had thrown a switch, the emerald glow appeared atop the escarpment.

They went dead silent.

After a minute someone moved up close to Charlotte. Manny Christopher, a software designer from Providence. "That's it," Manny said.

Silently they embraced each other and murmured congratulations. Charlotte lit her lantern. It was a signal for the others, and they lined up in the communal glow, forming a human chain, facing Johnson's Ridge.

Charlotte felt the pull of the object on the summit. The Roundhouse, the media called it. But in another time it had borne a different name, given by a different entity. The faces of her friends, despite the cold, were warm and alive in the flickering lights. Beacons, she thought. The lanterns and the faces. Beacons for the universal power.

She raised her lamp, and the others followed her lead.

In that moment she loved them all. And she loved the magnificent world into which she'd been born.

For a few brief moments she saw her friends, the whole complexity of life on earth, and the wheeling stars through the eyes of God.

"Our guest on *CNN Matchup*," said the host, "is Alfred Mac-Donough, from the University of Toronto, winner of the Nobel prize for physics. Dr. MacDonough, what is really happening at Johnson's Ridge?"

MacDonough, thin, white-haired, fragile, looked over the top of his glasses. "I would have to say, Ted, that we're seeing the first real evidence that we've had visitors from somewhere else."

The host nodded. "The Roundhouse is reported to have power."

"Yes. There seems to be no question that this—" He paused, weighing his words. "—*place* is putting out light and heat."

"Do we know how that's being done?"

"To my knowledge, no one has yet looked at the mechanism."

"Why not?"

"Because it's not in an obvious place. It appears that we'll have to break through some walls in order to determine how things work. Naturally everyone is reluctant to do that."

"Dr. MacDonough." The host's voice changed slightly. "We have been hearing that there's reason to believe the artifact is more than ten thousand years old. How do you react to that?"

"It's not impossible."

"Why not? How could the lights work after all that time?" The host smiled. "We have to buy maintenance contracts to protect us against toasters that fail within a couple of years."

MacDonough smiled and inadvertently dropped the bomb. "I can assure you, Ted, that if the reality on Johnson's Ridge turns out to be what it now appears to be, it won't take us long to adapt that technology to our own needs. I think we could give you a pretty durable toaster." He sat back in his chair, looking quite pleased. "In fact, I think we could give you the first multigenerational toaster."

✠ 16 ✠

I can't help wondering how it would have come out had it not been for Wesley Fue's garage door opener.

—Mike Tower, *Chicago Tribune*

"What happened to the dirt? That's what I really don't understand."

Several inches of dirt had been removed, revealing a stone disk. The disk was about five feet in diameter and rose an inch or two off the surrounding gray floor. It was lime-colored and ribbed with a gridwork of black spokes.

"It looks as if we've discovered a high-tech vacuum cleaner," Max said. He put the minicam down and inspected the grid from a respectful distance. There were too many unknowns here, and Max had no interest in getting rearranged the way the dirt had.

"This one," April said, pointing toward the tree emblem. "All you have to do is touch the wall."

"How about if we try it again?" he said.

"But something more distinguishable than dirt this time," said April.

A few wooden chairs had been set inside the dome for the convenience of the workers. Max retrieved one and put it on the grid. Then he set up to record everything on video. He signaled when he was ready.

April pressed the flat of her hand against the wall in front of the tree.

It lit up.

"Okay," she said.

But nothing happened. With a bleep, the light went out.

And there were no special effects.

Max looked at the six icons. They were tastefully done, but they did have the appearance of being functional rather than decorative. He noticed a recessed plate near the base of the wall. Another sensor?

"Go ahead," she said. "Try it."

He pushed it and felt something click. A panel door popped open. It was round, several inches across. Inside, he could see cables.

"Well," he said, "we've got something. Our wall switches *do* tie in to a power source."

"How about," said April, "we try one of the other icons?"

He pointed the minicam at the chair and started it.

"Maybe," she said, "we should make sure we're not standing on another one of these grids."

Max brushed away some of the earth with his heel. No sign of a gridwork. "I think we're okay," he said.

The smoke symbol was next. She pushed on the wall.

The icon stayed dark.

"I don't think it's working," said Max.

"Apparently not."

Almost casually, she tried the egg icon.

It blinked on. "We got a light," she said.

Max backed up a few steps and started the minicam again.

April glanced at her watch.

The red lamp glowed in the viewfinder. The minicam got heavy, and Max shifted it higher on his shoulder.

He was beginning to suspect the phenomenon would not repeat when a tiny star began to glow in the middle of the viewing field.

"Twenty-three seconds," she said.

The star expanded and grew brighter.

"My God," said Max. "What *is* that?"

It enveloped the chair.

He watched it glitter and swirl until it hurt his eyes. Then it was gone.

So was the chair. They had a clean grid.

Edward (Uncle Ed) Crowley was in his third year as CEO of the Treadline Corporation, which had been a subsidiary of Chrysler but had gone independent three years before and was scoring a major success with its line of quality cars at reasonable prices (the company motto) and its emphasis on customer service.

Treadline was doing everything right. It had gone for a legitimate team concept, had got rid of its autocrats and replaced them with managers who understood how to motivate, had encouraged employees to make decisions, and had seen to it that everyone had a stake in success. Now, at last, things were coming together. The previous quarter had given Treadline its first net profit, and the curve was now decidedly up. He could see nothing ahead but prosperity.

His calendar lay open on his teak desk. German trade reps were due in fifteen minutes. That would spill over into lunch. Staff meeting at one, reflection at one-forty-five, wander down to the Planning Effectiveness Division at two-fifteen. Uncle Ed subscribed to the theory of management by walking around. He understood the importance of being seen. Conference with the legal director at three, and with Bradley and his technicians at four. Open door in effect from four-thirty. Anyone could pop by and say hello to the boss.

In fact, he got relatively few visitors. The line of command immediately below him, because they normally had easy access, were prohibited from taking advantage of his time. People further down the food chain were somewhat reluctant to drop in on the head man. But they did come by on occasion. And anyhow the open door was a valuable symbol, both to the rank and file and to his chiefs.

He had been going over the plans for restructuring Treadline's long-term debt, in the hope of finding a way to finance needed R and D. But he was tired of looking at numbers, and his back was starting to hurt. He glanced at his watch and realized he'd been at it for an hour and a quarter. Too long.

Time to take a break and clear his mind. He got up, walked over to the window, and looked out at the Indianapolis skyline. The intercom beeped.

"Yes, Louise?"

"Mr. Hoskin on line one."

Walt Hoskin was his vice president for financial operations, a fussy little man who had never learned to think outside the parameters. Which was why he would never rise higher than he was now. It was Hoskin's plan that lay on his desk. And it was perfectly satisfactory within the general rules and principles of company policy and past practice. But the man did not know how to kill sacred cows. If Treadline was to take full advantage of recent market trends, they had to get out of the old buggy Hoskin was driving. He picked up the phone. "Yes, Walt?"

"Ed, have you seen the news this morning?" Hoskin's voice was reedy and thin.

As a matter of fact, he hadn't. Uncle Ed was a bachelor.

On days when he worked late, as he had last evening, he often stayed overnight at the office. He hadn't been near the TV either last evening or this morning. "No," he said quietly. "Why? What's going on?"

"We opened seventeen points down." Hoskin delivered the news like a sinner announcing the Second Coming.

Uncle Ed prided himself on his ability to react coolly to crises and shocks. But this blindsided him. *"Seventeen points?"* he bellowed. "What the hell's going on?" He knew of nothing, no bad news, no market speculations, that could produce this kind of effect.

"It's that *thing* in North Dakota."

"What *thing* in North Dakota?"

"The UFO."

Uncle Ed had discounted the reports from Johnson's Ridge as a mass delusion. "Walt," he said, struggling to regain his composure. "Walt, what are we talking about?"

"There are reports that it's about to become possible to make automobiles that will run damn near forever!"

Uncle Ed stared at his phone. "Nobody's going to believe that, Walt."

"Maybe not. But people might think other shareholders will. So they're dumping their stock. There was a woman on ABC this morning saying that a car made of this stuff would last the lifetime of the owner. Provided he changed the oil and didn't have any accidents."

Hoskin was on the verge of hysteria. Uncle Ed eased into his chair.

"Are you there, Ed?" asked Hoskin. "Ed, you okay?"

The markets had opened mixed, unable to make up their minds for an hour or so. Then a wave of selling had set in.

By late morning they were in free fall. The Nikkei Index lost 19 percent of its value in a single day, while the Dow Jones Industrial Average closed down 380 points.

They ran the sequence through the VCR.

The chair.

The light.

The empty grid.

They ran it a frame at a time, watching the incandescence build, watching it acquire a sparkle effect, watching it reach out almost protoplasmically for the chair. "Go slow," said April.

The chair looked as if it was fading.

There were a couple of frames during which Max thought he could see through the legs and back. It looked like a double exposure.

They were in the control module. Around them, phones continued to ring. Helicopters came and left every few minutes. April had hired a bevy of graduate students to conduct the tours and coordinate visits by VIPs. Two of these students, wearing dark blue uniforms with a Roundhouse shoulder patch, were busy at their desks while simultaneously trying to follow April's progress.

"We need to try this again," said Max. "And use a filter."

But they would apparently have to try a different icon: Like the tree, the egg seemed to have only one charge to fire and was no longer working.

She seemed not to be listening, but was instead staring into her coffee cup. At last she looked up. "What do you think it is, Max?"

"Maybe a garbage disposal." The thought amused him. He looked back at the image on the monitor. Something caught his eye.

"What?" she said, following his gaze.

Behind the nearly transparent chair, against the wall, Max could make out two vertical lines.

"Those are *not* in the Roundhouse," he said. He tried to visualize the space between the grid and the rear wall. There was nothing that might produce such lines. Nor anything on the wall itself.

"What are you thinking?" she asked.

Max's imagination was running wild. "I wonder," he said, "whether we haven't sent an old chair into somebody's vestibule."

Randy Key was rendered even more desperate by the conviction that he was probably the only person on the planet who understood the truth about the ominous structure on Johnson's Ridge. He had tried to warn his brother. Had tried to talk to his ex so she could at least hide their son. Had even tried to explain it to Father Kaczmarek. No one believed him. He knew it was a wild story, and he could think of no way to convince his family and friends of their danger. To convince anyone. So he had no choice but to take the situation into his own hands.

The thing they called the Roundhouse was in fact a signaling device left to sound the alarm that the human race was ready for harvest. Randy suspected it had been atop the ridge far longer, many times longer, than the ten thousand years the TV stations were talking about. He could not be sure, of course, but it didn't matter anyhow. The only thing that *did* matter was that he understood the danger. And knew how to deal with it.

Randy worked for Monogram Construction. He was currently assigned to a road crew that was out restoring Route

23, in the Ogilvie area, north of Minneapolis. It pained him to think what it would all look like, these pleasant little white-fenced homes, and the lighted malls, and the vast road network, after the enemy had come.

It was, of course, too late now to stop the signal from being sent. It was on its way. All that remained to do, all that *could* be done, was to punctuate that signal in such a way that the creatures at the other end would understand there would be no free lunch on Earth. He would show them we knew about them and that they should be prepared for a long, hard fight if they came.

He would ride to the top of the ridge and gun the engine and crash into the son of a bitch. There were five hundred pounds of C4 in back of his Isuzu Rodeo, connected to a remote-control device that he'd purchased with a model car outfit. If everything went well, he would get out of the Isuzu quickly, warn any bystanders to take cover, and turn the Roundhouse into rubble. He hoped nobody inside would be killed, but he couldn't help that. In the end, people would understand. It might take a while, but once they realized what he had done, he would be on television. And his ex would be sorry she hadn't listened to him. But it would be too late then for her because he'd be damned if he was going to take the bitch back. Not even to get his boy.

He cruised along the expressway, staring placidly out at the barren, snow-covered fields. A sense of repose had been creeping over him since he'd left Minnesota. He'd be at Fort Moxie by midafternoon. He had read there was no space in the Walhalla motels, but Fort Moxie was close enough. He hadn't figured out how he would return to his motel after he'd destroyed his means of transportation. But that was okay. Once they saw the inner workings of the Roundhouse, they would be grateful, and someone would understand and give him a ride.

He'd used the workings of the model car to make the switch that would blow his bomb. He'd armed it but had put a wooden wedge between the electrical contacts to make sure they could not accidentally close.

Randy ran into two pieces of bad luck that afternoon. The first occurred as he passed Drayton on I–29. A red station wagon with Manitoba plates cut in front of him; Randy slammed on his brakes, slid sidewise, and bounced out onto the median. A tractor-trailer roared past, almost taking his front end off. But it missed him, and Randy, who ended up facing south, felt very fortunate. He shouldn't have. His wedge had shifted, and it shifted again when he had to gun his engine to climb the narrow snow-covered embankment below which the pickup had come to rest. By the time he got back onto the freeway, it no longer served its purpose, and the contacts, although not actually touching, were close enough to permit a spark to cross. The bomb was, in effect, armed.

At the northernmost exit, just before entering Canada, he turned east onto Route 11 and followed it into Fort Moxie. Randy's second piece of bad luck came when he approached the intersection at 20th Street. He was on the edge of town, and there wasn't much out there, other than a lumberyard and the forlorn white building that housed the Tastee-Freez and Wesley Fue's house. It happened that Wesley, who'd been fighting a cold for six weeks, had come home from his job at the bank, planning to make himself a good stiff drink and go to bed. It also happened that Wesley's garage door opener was tuned to precisely the same frequency as the radio-controlled toy that Randy had converted into a firing switch.

ANCIENT SHORES

The garage stood with its back to 20th Street. Wesley pulled into his driveway as Randy approached from the west. The driveway was partially blocked by his daughter's sled. Wesley angled carefully around it, promising himself to speak with her when she got home from school, and reached up to activate his door opener, which was clamped to the top of the dash. He squeezed the remote just as its directional angle swept across Bannister Street. The radio beam caught Randy entering the intersection and closed the circuit on his bomb.

The intersection erupted in a sheet of flame. The explosion blew out the western end of the lumberyard, leveled the Tastee-Freez, knocked out all of Wesley's windows, and demolished his garage. Wesley suffered two broken arms and a mass of cuts and burns, but he survived.

One of the few pieces of Randy's vehicle that came through more or less intact was a vanity plate that read *UFO*.

Traffic was so heavy that Max decided to do something about it. In the morning he contacted Bill Davis at Blue Jay Air Transport outside Grand Forks and scheduled a helicopter pickup service. They established an operating schedule among Fort Moxie, Cavalier, Devil's Lake, and Johnson's Ridge.

Matthew R. Taylor had come to the White House by a circuitous route. His father had run a candy store in Baltimore, which had provided a meager existence for Matt and his six siblings. But the old man had provided his kids with one priceless gift: He'd encouraged them to read, and he didn't bother too much about the content, subscribing to the theory that good books ultimately speak for themselves.

By the time he was nineteen, Taylor had devoured the Greek and Roman classics, Shakespeare, Dickens, Mark Twain, and a wide array of modern historians. He was also a decent outfielder in high school and at Western Maryland University. In 1965 he went to Vietnam. During his second patrol he took a bullet in the hip. Doctors told him he would not walk again, but he had stayed with a six-year-long program of therapy and now needed only a cane to get around the White House. Eventually, of course, the cane would become a symbol of the man and his courage.

He married his nurse and invested his money in a car wash, which failed, and in a fast-food outlet, which also failed.

Taylor was never very good at business, but he was scrupulously honest, and he was always willing to help people in the community who got in trouble. During the mid-seventies, when he was working as a clothing clerk at Sears Roebuck, he allowed himself to be persuaded to run for the county highway commission by people who thought they could control him.

He proved to be a surprisingly shrewd steward of the public money. Before he was done, several county officials and a couple of contractors were in jail, costs were down, and the road system had improved dramatically.

Taylor was elected to the House in 1986 and to the Senate eight years later. He chaired the ethics committee and introduced a series of reforms that brought him national prominence and the vice presidency. But within sixty days after his accession to office, a stroke incapacitated the chief executive, and Taylor became acting President under the Twenty-fifth Amendment. He was subsequently elected in his own right.

The country loved Matt Taylor as they had no other president since FDR. He was perceived by many as a new Harry Truman. He possessed several of Truman's finest characteristics: an unbending will when he believed he was right, uncompromising integrity, and a willingness to say what he meant in plain English. This latter tendency sometimes got him in trouble, as when he offhandedly remarked within the hearing of journalists that it might be prudent, during the visit of a certain Middle Eastern potentate, to hide the White House silver.

Taylor explained his solid ratings by saying that the American people understood that he did what he thought was right, and to hell with the polls. "They like that," he would say. "And when they reach a point where they don't trust my judgment anymore, why, they'll turn me out. And good riddance to the old son of a bitch."

The President's political alarms over the North Dakota business had been sounding all winter. His advisors had told him not to worry. It was just a crop circle flap, the sort of thing to stay away from, to deflect at press conferences. A chief executive who starts talking about flying saucers is dead. No matter what happens, he is dead. That was what they said. So he had kept away from it, and now it was blowing up. The stock market today had dropped 380 points.

"They're already calling it Black Wednesday," said Jim Samson, his treasury secretary. Samson was now trying to pretend he'd been warning the President all along to take action.

It was a turbulent time. There were six wars of strategic interest to the United States being fought with varying degrees of energy, and another fifteen or so hotspots. Famine was gaining, population growth everywhere was shifting into overdrive, and the UN had all but given up the dream of a new world order. The American transition from an industrialized economy to an information economy was still creating major dislocations. Corruption in high places remained a constant problem, and the splintering of the body politic into fringe groups that would not talk to each other continued. On the credit side, however, the balance of trade looked good; the long battle to reduce runaway deficits was finally showing positive results; racism, sexism, and their attendant evils seemed to be losing ground; drug use was way down; and medical advances were providing people with longer and healthier lives. Perhaps most important for a politician, the media were friendly.

The truth was that Matt Taylor could not take credit for the latter trends any more than he could be blamed for the former. But he knew that whatever else happened, he had to have a strong economy. If he lost that, the dislocations accompanying the evolution through which the western world was now passing were going to get a lot worse. He could not allow that. He was not going to stand by and watch hordes of homeless and unemployed reappear on the American scene. No matter what it took.

"A blip," Tony Peters said. "These things happen."

Peters was chairman of the President's Fiscal Policy Council. He was also an old ally, with good political instincts. Of the people who had come up with him from Baltimore to the White House, no one enjoyed a greater degree of Taylor's confidence.

"Tony," the President said, "it's only a blip if there's nothing to it. What happens if they really have a metal up there that won't break down or wear out?"

"I agree," said Samson. "We need to find out what the facts are here."

Peters frowned. "As I understand it, Mr. President, it's not a metal."

"Whatever." Taylor pushed back in his chair and folded his arms. "They can make sails out of it. And they can make buildings. The issue is, what happens to the manufacturing industries if they suddenly get materials to work with that don't break down periodically?" He shook his head. "Suppose people buy only one or two cars over a lifetime. What does that mean to GM?" He took off his glasses and flung them on the desk. "My God," he said, "I don't believe I'm saying this. All these years we've been looking for a way to beat the Japanese at this game. Now we have it, and it would be a catastrophe."

Taylor was short and stocky. He wore nondescript ties and well-pressed suits that were inevitably last year's fashion.

"Mr. President," said Peters, "it's all tabloid stuff. No one is going to be able to mass-produce supermaterials."

"How do you know? Have we looked into it?"

"Yes. Everybody I've talked to says it can't happen."

"But we have samples."

"We saw a lot of lightning before we learned how to put it into a wall switch. What we need to do is get everybody's mind off this thing. Pick one of the wars, or the Pakistani revolution, and start sounding alarms."

There was this about Tony Peters: He was the only person Taylor had ever known who seemed to understand what drove economies, and who could make that insight clear to others. He also knew the Congress, the power brokers, and the deal makers. He was an invaluable aide to an activist President. But Taylor knew his chairman's limits. To Peters, experience was everything. One learned from it and applied its lessons succinctly, and one could never go far wrong. But what happened when you ran into a problem that transcended anything you'd seen before? What good was experience then?

"I want you," said Taylor, "to talk to some of the people who've been out there. *Top* people, right? Find out what's really going on. What the risks are. Not what your experts say *can't* happen."

Peters stared back. "You're not serious," he said. "We shouldn't get anywhere close to this thing, Mr. President. We start asking questions, and it'll get around."

"Try to be discreet, Tony. But goddammit, the markets are in the toilet. Find somebody who understands these things and get me some answers. Definitive ones. I want to know if that thing is for real. And if it is, what's it going to do to the economy." He felt tired. "I don't want any more guesswork."

✠ 17 ✠

We walk by faith, not by sight.

—II Corinthians 5:7

Al Easter was the most aggressive shop steward the Dayton, Ohio, subsidiary of Cougar Industries had ever known. The rank and file joked that managers did not go out alone at night, fearing Al might be roaming the streets. Management cautiously sought union advice on any decision that could be construed as a change in work conditions. And they tended to be very lenient with the workers. Even Liz Mullen, who'd been caught taking staplers, computer disks, and assorted other office supplies home, where she'd been running an independent retail operation, had survived. She'd gotten a reprimand when she should have been fired and gone to jail.

Al's most effective tactic was the threat of the instant response. He was quite willing (or at least management believed he was, which amounted to the same thing) to call a work stoppage or slowdown to protest the most trivial issue. No attempt to warn a recalcitrant employee or to revise a work schedule was immune to reprisal, should Al consider principle at stake.

The steward made no secret of his view that everyone in management was on a power trip and that only he stood between the vultures in the executive suite and the well-being of the workers.

He was not empowered by the national union to act in so arbitrary a manner, but their occasional formal rebuffs were halfhearted and hypocritical. They knew who held the cards in Dayton. When Al announced a slowdown or called the workers out, everyone in the plant responded as one person. The National Affiliated Union of Helpers, Stewards, and Mechanics might get around several days later to chiding him, but in the meantime he would have made his point.

Management tried on several occasions to promote him. Double his money. But he wouldn't take it. "They need me," he'd told plant manager Adrian Cox, "to keep you and the rest of your crowd from eating them alive." Yeah. Adrian knew the real reason: Al liked power too much to give it up. And no mere supervisor at Cougar possessed the kind of power Al had.

The shop steward disliked Cougar's managers both personally and on principle. He made it a point not to be seen in their company, save when he was bullying them. It came, therefore, as an uncomfortable surprise when Cox's secretary notified him that Al had arrived downstairs and was on his way up.

Cox's first reaction was to take a deep breath. "Did he say what he wanted?"

"No, sir. Janet asked him, but he just walked past her."

Moments later Al strolled through Adrian's outer defenses and walked into the inner office while the intercom buzzed a late warning.

It was a spacious office, with framed awards and certificates of appreciation and a couple of expensive oils that his wife had picked out. Cox sat behind his mahogany desk in sunlight softened by an array of potted palms. It annoyed him that the shop steward pretended not to notice all this. Al advanced into the center of Cox's Persian carpet, insolently neglecting to remove his cap, and leveled his gaze at the plant manager. "Mr. Cox," he said, "I assume you've seen what's been happening in North Dakota."

Al was a little man, round, long out of shape, with uncombed thinning hair. His belly pressed against his greasy shirt, and a stained handkerchief was stuffed into his breast pocket. It was all part of the act.

"The UFO?" Cox felt instant relief that there was not a problem on the floor.

"Yeah." Al dropped into one of the wing chairs. "What are we doing about it?"

Cox leaned forward. "About *what?*" He knew what was coming, of course. There had already been talk in the boardroom and with corporate about the materials that might emerge from the Johnson's Ridge discovery.

"About a tougher tire." Al rocked back and forth. "What happens to Cougar if the industry begins to produce tires that will run two hundred thousand miles?"

"That won't happen," said Cox.

"I'm glad to hear it." The man's eyes never blinked.

"What do you want me to say?" asked Cox. "All I know is what I see on the TV."

"Yeah. Me, too." Al's face had no range. The only emotion it ever revealed was sarcasm. "You know I've always said that we should work together more. After all, we have the same objectives. A healthy company means good jobs."

Cox couldn't resist smiling. "I couldn't agree more, Al."

The steward scowled. "If this stuff can do what they're saying it can, there won't be any tire and rubber business in this country in another three years. If I were sitting in your chair, I'd have somebody up there making an offer."

Cox frowned. "Offer? To do what?"

"To buy them out."

Cox stared at Al. "There's no need to panic," he said finally. It felt like a weak response, but he couldn't think what else to say.

Al shook his head. "If the worst happens, you'll wind up getting a government bailout. There'll be hard times, and the company will go Chapter Eleven. But *you'll* do fine. You'll vote yourself a bonus and complain about the business cycle. Along with everybody else up here. The rank and file will get walked on, like they always do. In the end, they won't get nothin'."

Cox's skin crawled. "Al." He tried to sound forceful but knew his voice was shaking. "Al, you're overreacting. None of this is going to happen."

"Yeah. Well, if I were you, I wouldn't just sit around up here hoping it'll all blow over."

April cleaned the icons with a couple of damp cloths. Each lit up when she touched it, with the exception of the smoke, which stayed dark no matter what. But there were no special effects at the grid. She interpreted it to mean that there had to be something *on* the grid to produce the lights.

Near the pit she found a seventh icon. Bigger than the others, it resembled a kanji character. Like the smoke, it stayed dark when she touched it.

Marie McCloskey had always been able to feel the imminence of the divine presence. There had never been a time, not even during her most difficult days—when the news had come of Jodie's death in the wreck on I–29, when her husband had first assaulted her, when they'd told her she had diabetes—there had never been an *instant* when she had not been aware that Jesus walked beside her. That sure and certain knowledge had carried her through all these years and had brought her, in spite of everything, an inner peace that she would not trade for any of life's more tangible assets. Marie McCloskey was a fortunate woman.

She came to Fort Moxie to visit her sister, and she would not ordinarily have shown any interest in the events atop Johnson's Ridge. But the town, which had been so quiet and orderly in past years, was overrun with tourists and salesmen and journalists and college students and busloads of people from all over North America. So it was natural that her curiosity would be aroused, and anyhow her sister's husband, Corky Cable, wanted to go see the Roundhouse. They drove out and got in the line of cars over on Route 32. They rode up one side of the escarpment, cruised past the odd green building that looked like a fancy salt cellar, and rode down the other side, talking about Martians the whole time. It didn't mean anything special to Marie or to her sister, but Corky raved about it.

They had dinner in Walhalla at the Cat's Eye, and afterward drove back toward Johnson's Ridge. It was dark now, a cold, crystal night with silent stars and no moon and a few wisps of cloud. They were riding three across the front seat in Corky's Mazda when they rounded a curve and saw the soft green glow at the top of the ridge.

"Look at that," said Marie's sister.

Corky would have pulled off somewhere so they could watch, but the road was lined with cars. Instead he slowed down and crept along at about twenty.

To Marie, there was something supernatural in that quiet radiance. As though God himself had provided a lighthouse for His lost children. A reassurance that He was still here.

Oddly, she had felt nothing when she'd been alongside the structure two hours earlier, in broad daylight. But now the full weight of its significance caught her.

"We can see it all the way out to the border," said Corky. He was a customs inspector at the Fort Moxie border crossing, and that statement was exaggerated. The border was too far away. But tonight it seemed possible. Tonight everything seemed possible.

"Slow down, Corky," Marie said.

Corky was already creeping along, and some headlights had come up behind them.

Marie's sister said, "I wonder what causes it. Maybe it's made of phosphorous."

Marie began to see an image. If you backed away a little bit mentally, stayed away from the details, and looked just so, you could make out a woman's face. And she knew the woman.

"It's the Virgin," she said.

Arky Redfern ushered his guest to a seat, sat down behind his desk, and smiled politely. "Dr. Wells," he said, "what can I do for you?"

Paxton Wells was a tall, lean man with a gray mustache and a manner that would have been aristocratic had he not been burdened with oversized ears. "Mr. Redfern," he said, "I understand you represent tribal interests on Johnson's Ridge."

The lawyer nodded.

"I have an offer to make on behalf of the National Energy Institute." He released the catches on his briefcase, searched inside, and withdrew a contract. "We would like to have permission to investigate the power source in the Roundhouse." His eyebrows rose and fell, signaling, Arky thought, a fair degree of stress, which otherwise did not evince itself in Wells's manner. "There's a possibility we might be able to develop some of the technologies in the building. If indeed there *are* any technologies that can be adapted. We don't know that, of course."

"Of course," said Redfern.

"Nevertheless, we would be willing to offer a substantial sum of money for the property and assume all the risk and expense of developing it."

"I see." Redfern picked up the document.

"We can offer a million dollars," Wells said. He underscored the amount and left himself slightly breathless.

The lawyer flipped methodically through the pages, stopping occasionally to examine an item that had caught his attention. "I see," he said, "you would get all rights for development and use."

"Mr. Redfern." Wells leaned forward and assumed an attitude that he obviously thought was one of friendly no-nonsense sincerity. "Let's be honest here. This is a crapshoot. NEI is willing to gamble a lot of money on the off chance that there's something usable on the ridge. We don't know that to be the case. Nevertheless, in everyone's interest, we'll assume the risk. And the tribe can just sit back and collect. One million dollars. To do nothing."

Redfern folded the contract and handed it back. "I don't think so," he said.

"May I ask why? What can you lose?"

The lawyer got out of his chair. "Dr. Wells, I'm quite busy today. If NEI wants to make a serious offer, you know where to find me."

"Aren't you overstepping your authority, Mr. Redfern? I would think your responsibility is to consult your employer."

Redfern let Wells see that he was not impressed. "I believe I understand my responsibility, Dr. Wells. Now, I hate to rush you—"

"All right." Wells leaned back in his chair. "You drive a hard bargain, Redfern. To save us both time, I'll go right to the bottom line. I'm authorized to offer *two* million."

Redfern glanced up at his father's bow. There were times, he thought, when he regretted that they'd given up the old ways.

✠ 18 ✠

A man without money is a bow without an arrow.

—Thomas Fuller, *Gnomologia*

During the two years he'd served on the city council, Marv Wick-
ham had never seen more than a dozen people attend the
monthly meeting. But tonight was different. Fort Moxie's
total population of nine hundred twenty-seven must have
been at city hall, where they overflowed the spacious
second-floor meeting room and spilled out into the corri-
dors. (The presence of the New Agers to whom the mayor had
rented the lower-level auditorium did nothing to alleviate
matters.) They were still coming in when the council president, Charlie Lindquist, launched the evening's proceedings.

There were several routine items on the agenda: a zoning
ordinance request, a proposal to issue highway improvement bonds, and a suggestion that Fort Moxie participate in
a consolidated school scheme. But the issue that had drawn
the crowd, and which Lindquist consequently scheduled
last, would be a request that the city approve a demand that
the Johnson's Ridge excavation site be shut down.

Lindquist, who considered himself the town's Solomon,

guided the deliberations methodically through the prelimi-
naries. At twelve minutes past nine he gave the floor to Joe
Torres, a retired farmer now living in town.

Torres, reading nervously from a sheet of paper,
described the chaotic conditions existing in Fort Moxie. Traffic had become impossible. There were drunks and fights
and crowds of hoodlums. Visitors were parking their cars
everywhere. They were overflowing the restaurants and
stripping the supermarket so that ordinary citizens had to
drive eighty miles to Grand Forks. They were even drawing
lunatics with bombs, like the one who had taken out the
Tastee-Freez the day before. "I know it's good business for
Mike and some of you other boys, but it's pretty tough on
the rest of us."

Agnes Hanford stood up. "We need to take advantage of
this while we can. In the end, the whole town'll be better
off." Agnes's husband owned the Prairie Schooner.

Joe shook his head. "That's easy for *you* to say, Agnes.
But it's getting worse. And I think we need to do something." As if to underline his argument, they heard an automobile roar past, horn blaring, radio shaking the building.
"If we allow this to go on, we're going to have to hire some
police officers." Historically, Fort Moxie had received what
little law enforcement support it needed from Cavalier. "I
therefore propose," he continued, reading again, "that the
council demand that the persons digging on Johnson's Ridge
cease and desist. And that the structure known as the
Roundhouse be demolished." He looked around. "Torn up
and hauled away," he added.

Lindquist recognized Laurie Cavaracca, who owned the
Northstar Motel. Laurie had lived in Fort Moxie all her life.
The motel had been built by her father in 1945, after he
came back from the Pacific. Laurie was now sole owner and

manager. "We have eight units at the Northstar," she said. "Until two weeks ago, we never had consecutive days in which I could turn on the No Vacancy sign. Now there is never an empty room. We are booming. Do I like the problems that we are currently having in Fort Moxie? No, of course not. None of us does. But the solution isn't to close down and crawl back in our holes." Her voice sounded a little fluttery at first, but she gained confidence quickly. "Listen, people," she said. "Most of us have stayed in Fort Moxie because we were born here. We love this town. But the economy has always been touch and go. Now, for the first time in anyone's memory, we have a chance to make some real money. And not just the store owners. Everyone will profit. Healthy businesses are good for everybody. For God's sake, don't kill the golden calf."

"Goose," someone said. "It's a golden *goose*."

"Whatever," said Laurie. "This won't last forever. We should milk it while we can."

"Meantime," said Josh Averill, rising with his usual dignity, "they're going to kill somebody, the way they race around the streets. What happens then?"

"This town has never had two dimes to rub together," said Jake Thoraldson, whose airport had suddenly become a hub. "What's the matter with you people? Can't you stand a little prosperity?"

"Prosperity?" howled Mamie Burke, a transplanted Canadian who worked for the railroad. "What kind of prosperity is it to have all these people running wild? Joe's right. Close it down."

Arnold Whitaker, the self-effacing owner of the Lock 'n' Bolt Hardware, argued against the proposal. "I can't see," he said, "where anyone is being hurt by current conditions."

That remark infuriated Morris Jones, a ninety-year-old

postal retiree known around town primarily for his interest in electric trains. Two inebriated Canadians had driven a pickup into Jones's den, demolishing a forty-year-old HO layout. Jones sputtered and shook his finger accusingly at Whitaker. "Attaboy, Arnie," he said, "take care of yourself. Don't worry about anybody else."

The vote to demand a shutdown passed by a majority of eighty-seven. Floyd Rickett volunteered to head up the committee that would write the draft.

Lindquist took him aside when opportunity offered. "Keep it reasonable, Floyd," he said. "Okay? We don't want to offend anybody."

The rain beat incessantly against the windows of the Oval Office. It was a sound that tended to heighten whatever emotion the President was feeling. Today he didn't feel good.

A copy of the *Washington Post* lay on his desk. The headlines reported civil war in India and famine in the Transvaal. They also revealed the results of a new poll: "60% Think Roundhouse Is Related to UFOs." An additional twenty percent thought it was a government project. Eight percent believed it was of divine origin. The rest didn't know or hadn't heard of Johnson's Ridge.

Tony Peters sat disconsolately in his chair, one leg crossed over the other. "Almost everybody thinks there's a government cover-up," he said. "But that's inevitable. We might as well get used to it."

"Did you see the signs outside?" There were roughly six hundred pickets on the circle. *Come Clean on Johnson's Ridge*, the posters read. And *Tell the Truth About the Roundhouse*. "So what *is* the truth? What do we know?"

Peters uncrossed his legs and got up. "We've talked to a dozen people in as many fields who have either been there or had access to the test results. They're all having a hard time accepting the notion that it's extraterrestrial, but there's nobody who can provide a satisfactory alternative explanation."

"I don't think we care about where it came from or how it got there." Taylor took a deep breath. "My concern is, where do we go from here? What kind of power does the place use?"

"No one's had a chance to look. All they're letting people do now is walk around inside. Guided tours."

"Okay." Taylor pushed back in his chair and folded his arms across his chest. Crunch time. "Prospects, Tony. What are we facing?"

"Hard to say, Mr. President." Peters scrunched his face up, and pockets of lines showed at the corners of his mouth and eyes. "The experts do not agree about our ability to reproduce the new element. But they do agree that if we *can*, any products made from it will not decay."

"Will they wear out?"

"Yes. Although most of these people think they'll be a lot tougher than anything we have now."

Taylor sighed. He would talk to his economists, but he knew what that would mean to the manufacturing interests.

"Something else, sir. Did you know someone saw the Virgin Mary out there last night?"

The President's eyes rolled toward the ceiling. "What next?" he asked.

"Seriously." Peters grinned, a welcome shift in the tension. "It was on CNN ten minutes ago. Woman saw a face in the lights."

The President shook his head. "Goddamn, Tony," he said. "What about the market? What's going to happen today?"

"The Nikkei got blasted again. And I'm sure the slide will continue on Wall Street."

Taylor pushed himself wearily to his feet and looked out the window. The grass was green and cool. Days like this, he wished he were a kid again. "We have to get a handle on this, Tony."

"Yes, sir."

"Before it gets out of control. I want to take it over. There should be a national security provision or something. Find it."

"That might be tricky," he said.

"Why?"

"My God, Mr. President, it's Indian land. If it were just some farmer, yeah, we could declare a health hazard or something. But this is Sioux property. We try to move in, there'll be a heavy political price. Your own people won't like it, and the media will beat you to death with it."

Taylor could feel the walls closing in. "I don't mean we should simply *seize* it. We can recompense them. Buy them off."

"Sir, I think our best strategy is to wait it out. Not get stampeded into doing something that'll come back to haunt us."

Taylor was by nature inclined to act at the first sign of trouble. But he'd been around politics long enough to know the value of patience. And anyway, he wasn't sure of the right course. He didn't like the idea of maneuvering Native Americans off their land. That had a bad taste. And it was bad politics. But so were collapsing markets.

"It'll blow over," Peters assured him soothingly. "Give it time. We may not really have a problem. Let's not *create one*. What we need to do is concentrate on Pakistan."

"Pakistan?"

"No voters in Pakistan. But a lot of people are getting

killed. Make another statement. Deplore the violence. Maybe offer to act as an arbitrator. It looks as if it's going to play out soon anyway. Both sides are exhausted. We might even be able to get credit for arranging a settlement."

The President sighed. Peters was a hopeless cynic, and it would have been easy to dislike him. It was a pity that American politics degenerated so easily to such blatant opportunism. Even where good people were concerned.

Arky Redfern grew up near Fort Totten on the Devil's Lake reservation. He was the youngest of five, the first to collect a degree. That his siblings had pursued early marriages and dead-end jobs had broken the heart of his father, who'd promised to do what he could to support any of his children seeking a higher education. Redfern was given his father's bow to mark the occasion of his graduation from the law school at George Mason University.

He had also received encouragement from James Walker, one of the tribal councilmen, who had remarked proudly that the government no longer had all the lawyers. Redfern was fired with the idea of becoming the defender of the Mini Wakan Oyaté, as the Devil's Lake Sioux called themselves in their own language. (The term meant *People of the Spirit Lake*.) He'd passed the bar exam on the first try, and he returned to North Dakota to establish a practice writing wills and overseeing divorces, which paid reasonably well. He also became the tribal legal representative, which didn't pay so well. But it had its rewards.

At about the time Matt Taylor was looking for a course of action, Redfern was taking Paxton Wells into the reservation to make a new offer in person. Wells, wrapped in a somber mood, had apparently decided that the lawyer was hopelessly against him and had given up all efforts to placate the younger man. He sat staring moodily out the window at the flat countryside.

It had finally turned warm. Piles of melting snow were heaped along the side of the road, and there was some flooding.

The tribal chambers were located in a blue brick single-story structure known as the Blue Building. Old Glory and the flag of the Mini Wakan Oyaté fluttered in a crisp wind. Redfern pulled into the parking lot.

"This it?" said Wells, gazing at the open countryside stretching away in all directions.

Redfern knew Wells's type: Unless he was dealing with those he knew to be his superiors or those in a position to injure him, he wore an air of restrained self-importance. That attitude was in place now because he perceived the lawyer as no more than a means to an end, a guide to the Sioux equivalent of a CEO. That was, of course, a mistake.

They climbed out of the car, and Redfern led the way inside.

The Blue Building was home to the post office, the Bureau of Indian Affairs, the Indian Health Service, and the tribal offices. Redfern let the tribal secretary know they were there and headed for the chairman's office.

James Walker would not have been easy to pick out of a crowd. He was less than average height, and might have struck Wells as a man more likely to be at home in a grocery store than in a council hall. There was no hint of authority in his mien or his voice, nor was there a suggestion of the steel that could manifest itself when the need arose. His eyes were dark and friendly, his bearing congenial. Redfern believed Walker's primary strength lay in his ability to get people to tell him what they really believed, a talent as rare among Native Americans as among the rest of the population.

Walker rose from his desk as they entered and offered his hand to his visitor.

Wells took it, pumped it summarily, commented on how happy he was to have a chance to visit the reservation, and sat down.

The office was decorated with tribal motifs: war bonnets, totems, medicine wheels, and ceremonial pipes. A bookcase and a table supporting a burbling coffee pot flanked the desk. Sunlight flooded the room.

Wells cleared his throat. "Chairman," he said, "I represent an organization that would like to help the tribe achieve prosperity. Great possibilities are opening before us."

"Arky tells me," Walker said, as if Wells had not spoken, "you have an interest in buying some of our land."

"Yes, sir." Wells looked like a man trying to appear thoughtful. "Chairman, let me not mince words. The National Energy Institute is a consortium of industrial and banking interests that would like to offer you a great deal of money for the property known as Johnson's Ridge. A great deal, sir."

Walker showed no expression. "You wish to buy the property outright?"

"That's correct. And we are prepared to pay handsomely." He smiled. It was a thin smile, and conveyed no warmth. Defensive. Redfern decided that Wells had been one of those kids whom everybody beat up. "Let's put our cards on the table," he said.

"By all means."

"Chairman, it's doubtful that there is anything of real value on that ridge. You know that. I know that. The government's been there and they've already decided there's no need for them to be concerned." Redfern doubted that was true. "So it's a shot in the dark. But on the off chance there might be something that could be turned to a profit, we are willing to pay for the chance to look. And pay quite well, I might add."

He produced a blue folder and a leather-covered checkbook and took a gold pen from his pocket. "Why don't we just settle it now? Say, five million?" He removed the cap from the pen. "You could do quite a bit with that kind of money. Truth is, Chairman, I'd like to come back in a few years to see how the reservation will have changed."

Walker was able to conceal his surprise at the amount. He glanced at Redfern, who gave him no encouragement. Whatever they offer now, Arky thought, is too little. "A number of corporations," the chairman said, "have already shown interest. They would like to build hotels up there. And restaurants. Disney wants to build a theme park. I would not wish to sound greedy, Dr. Wells, but five million is small potatoes at this stage."

Redfern was proud of the chairman.

Wells's eyebrows went up. "I see," he said. "And you have firm offers?"

"Oh, yes. They are very generous. And these people only want to *lease* property. *You* want to get at the heart of the property's value. If we were to sell to you, we would have nothing save the cash in hand. Dr. Wells, under the circumstances, that would have to be a lot of cash in hand."

Wells looked down at his checkbook. "You drive a hard bargain, sir. But I understand your point. And I am authorized to compete. May I ask what you would consider a serious offer?"

Walker closed his eyes briefly. "Why don't you simply go to your final offer and save us both some time?"

Wells looked uncomfortable. Arky could see the wheels going around.

"Fifty million." He spoke in a voice the lawyer could barely hear.

"That's very good," said Walker. "And the money would be payable . . . ?"

Redfern caught his eye. *Don't do it.*

"Ten percent on signing the contract. The balance on the actual deed transfer." He offered his pen to the chairman. "Do we have an agreement?"

This time Walker was unsuccessful in masking his shock. "You must understand," he said, "that I cannot make the decision. It will be up to the council."

"Of course. But Mr. Redfern assures me you have considerable influence. I'm sure that if *you* are in favor of this action, the council will go along with it."

Walker tried to look doubtful. But it wasn't working. Wells smiled, confident the council would take the money and run. "Arky is inclined to overstate my influence, I think." Walker glanced over at his lawyer. "I wonder, Dr. Wells, if you would excuse us for a minute."

"Of course." Wells threw a quick grin at Redfern. *You son of a bitch,* it said, *you cost me, but let's see you change his mind.* "I'll be in the other room," he said. He opened the blue folder, which contained a contract, pushed it toward Walker, and left the office.

The chairman smiled broadly. He could barely contain his pleasure.

"I advise against it," said Redfern.

"Why not?" Walker beamed. "*Why* in God's name should we not take this kind of money?"

"The value isn't going to go away. Why would they offer so much?"

"It might be worth *nothing*. We could wind up selling T-shirts over there. Listen, Arky, we don't *need* more than fifty

203

million. Do you realize what that could do for us? He's right, you know. That kind of money could put a lot of logs on front porches. I think we should not get greedy. And I will so advise the council."

"This is not a man," said Arky, "who is going to *give* us anything. He's offering fifty million because he thinks it's worth more. Considerably more. Advise the council to seek a second offer. You might be surprised at the result."

Walker's delight began to drain away. "You seriously expect me to go before them and recommend against this kind of money? When we could conceivably end up with nothing? Even if I did take a stand against the proposal, they'd sweep me aside." He took a deep breath. "Give me a real reason. If you have one."

Arky did not like the position he was in. If things went wrong, he knew who would be hanging out there. "If Wells and his people get hold of it, they'll treat it exclusively as a source of wealth. Who knows what might get lost?"

"That's not exactly a war cry," said Walker.

"No, it isn't. But we may be looking at another Manhattan island."

"Maybe you weren't listening, Arky. He isn't talking twenty-six bucks."

"Maybe not. But if you want a war cry, keep in mind that we now possess a discovery that may release whole new technologies. The road to the future, Chairman, might run directly across the top of Johnson's Ridge. And you're ready to give it away."

"I'd see it the same way," said Max. "Take the money and run."

Arky looked disgusted. "That is precisely what they will do."

He was working his way through a plate of fish and chips. April, Arky, and Max were in a back booth at Mel's Restaurant in Langdon. It was no longer possible to get near the Prairie Schooner, which was overwhelmed with customers. "The council will feel that it would be criminal to turn down an offer of that magnitude. And, to be honest, I'm not comfortable advising against accepting it." He looked extremely unhappy. "Do you have any idea what would happen to me if they took my advice and the ridge turned out to be worthless?"

"You'd get scalped?" Max asked innocently.

Arky didn't seem to have heard. "Not that it matters. They'll take the money and run. Just as you say."

"Damn," said April. "If the project gets sold off, we'll be out the following day."

"I don't think there's much question about that," said Max. He listened to the low murmur of conversation around him, to the clink of silverware and occasional bursts of laughter.

"Arky," April said, "I can't deal with the prospect of not being here when the discoveries get made."

The lawyer looked sympathetic. "I know. But I think the matter is past my being able to control events."

"How long do we have?" asked April.

"Wells's people probably have teams ready to go as soon as the paper gets signed. There'll be a special council meeting late tomorrow afternoon to consider the offer. If they approve it, which they will, Wells will make a phone call, and you'll be history."

Devil's Lake, ND, Mar. 15 (AP)—
    A consortium of business interests is reported to be ready to offer one hundred million dollars to the Devil's

Lake Sioux for the Johnson's Ridge property on which the Roundhouse, an archeological find rumored to be of extraterrestrial origin, is located. According to informed sources, the tribal council will meet in extraordinary session tomorrow evening to consider the offer, which has been increased several times over the last few days. Officials on both sides declined to comment.

When they got back to the Northstar, there was a package waiting for Max. "Filters," he explained. "For the minicam. Maybe we can get a better look at what happens when the lights come on."

They retreated gloomily to their rooms. But minutes later April appeared at Max's door.

"Come in," he said. "I was going to call you."

She looked frantic. "What do we do?"

There was only one chair in the room. Max left it for her and sat down on the bed. "I don't think there's much we *can* do. Not with all that money out there."

"Max," she said, "fifty million's peanuts. Listen, we may have found a link to *somewhere else*." She forced it out, as she might an appeal to the supernatural. "The chair did not just get annihilated. It *went* somewhere."

"You think."

"I think." She rubbed her forehead wearily. "Did you know there's a *seventh* icon?"

"No," said Max, surprised. "Where?"

"Beside the ditch. Where they used to tie up the boat."

Max pictured the area. "On one of the posts?"

"Yes. It's got a design that looks like a kanji character. It doesn't light up when you touch it. I even tried putting a chair in the ditch, and it still didn't work. But Max, I

206

think that's the way they brought the boat in. Directly from *wherever*."

Max shook his head. "I'm sorry. But I just can't buy any of this. You're talking *Star Trek* stuff. Beam me up, Scotty."

They sat and listened to the wind blow.

"I think it's really true, Max."

"Well, good luck proving it. Whatever they are, the icons seem to work only once. What good is a long-range transport system that only works once?"

She pulled her legs up onto the chair and hugged her knees. "I think they work only once because the stuff we've been sending blocks the reception area. Somebody has to move it and clear the grid on the other end. If they don't, the system shuts down."

"That's the wildest guesswork I've ever heard."

"Max, we watched the chair fade out. It *faded*. It didn't blow up. It didn't disintegrate. It went somewhere. The question is, where?"

Max shook his head. "I think the whole idea is goofy."

"Maybe." April took a deep breath and let it out slowly. "I think we better tell Arky what we know."

"You mean, tell him we think we have a portal to another dimension? Or to Mars? He'll think what I think: It's goofy."

Her eyes were pools of despair. "He wouldn't think that if we did a demonstration for him."

"What kind of demonstration? All we can do is make things disappear. That doesn't prove anything."

Neither of them wanted to state the obvious.

✠ 19 ✠

Joyous we too launch out on trackless seas,
Fearless for unknown shores.

—Walt Whitman, "Passage to India"

April squeezed her eyes shut. The eternal prairie winds shook the windows. She was unnerved, but the conviction that she was right was going to help her get through it.

She heard a car pull up outside. The doors banged, and voices drifted in.

If there were time, she might have devised a test that would remove some of the risk. But there was no time. She sighed. Use it or lose it.

Through the wall, she could hear the mindless burble of Max's TV.

What were the dangers?

She might be annihilated. But no piece of the chair had remained, and there was no indication of a violent event. It had simply lost its corporeality. *It had gone somewhere.*

She might find herself in a hostile environment. For example, in a methane atmosphere. But the visitors had presumably thrived in North Dakota. Surely whatever

208

lay on the other side, through the port, was essentially terrestrial.

She might be stranded. But who ever heard of a port you could enter from only one side?

At midnight she filled her thermos and put two sandwiches and some fruit into a plastic bag. She loaded her camera and pulled on her Minneapolis Twins jacket, feeling pleased with herself. Forty minutes later she passed the police blockade at the access road and drove up the winding incline and out onto the ridge. The glow from the Roundhouse, out of sight in its excavation ditch, seemed brighter tonight. She wondered if it was still charging its batteries and made a mental note to start logging the luminosity.

It was cold, down in the teens. She parked just outside the security gate, opened her glove compartment, and took out a notebook. She sat thinking for several minutes before she knew what she wanted to say. When she'd finished, she laid the notebook open on the passenger seat, picked up a flashlight, and got out.

One of the guards, a middle-aged man whom she knew only as Henry, appeared in the door of the security station. "Good evening, Dr. Cannon," he said. "Forget something?"

"No, Henry." Her breath misted in the yellow light of the newly installed high-pressure sodium lamps. "I couldn't sleep. Thought I'd come out and see if I could get some work done."

He looked at his watch, not without a sense of disapproval. "Okay," he said. "Nobody else here. From the staff."

She nodded. "Thanks."

He disappeared back inside. April walked through the gate and went directly into the Roundhouse, shutting the door against the cold.

At night the dome was a patchwork of light and dark, a

scattering of illuminated alcoves. The lights shifted and moved as she did, following her, illuminating the ground in front, fading behind. As she approached the grid, it also lit up, spotlighted for her as if the place *knew* what she intended.

She hesitated. It was just as well Max wasn't here, because then it would be impossible to back away. And until now she had believed she *would* back away. But the fear had almost dissipated. Something was out there, waiting for her. The illuminated grid looked both safe and inviting. Time to move out.

She switched on the flashlight and approached the icons. The triggers.

Touch the icon and you get twenty-three seconds to walk over and take your place on the grid.

She looked at the arrow, the rings, and the *G* clef.

The arrow.

It gleamed in the half-light. She touched the wall, just her fingertips. And pressed.

The light came on.

She took a deep breath, crossed the floor, and stepped onto the grid. The trench that had once been a channel extended out into the shadows. Across the dome, the wall was lost in the dark and the lights faded out and the night went on forever. She hitched the camera strap higher on her shoulder, taking comfort from the mundaneness of the act. She zipped her jacket almost to her neck and fought down a sudden urge to jump off the grid.

It was still dark when the telephone brought Max out of a deep sleep. He rolled over, fumbled for the instrument, picked it up. "Hello?"

"Mr. Collingwood? This is Henry Short. Out at the security gate."

He immediately came awake. "Yes, Henry? What is it?"

"We can't find Dr. Cannon," he said.

He relaxed. "She's sleeping next door."

"No, sir. She came out here at about twelve-thirty. Went inside the Roundhouse. But she's not in there now."

Max looked at his watch. A quarter after three.

"We've checked the other buildings. She's not anywhere. We can't figure it out."

"Is her car still there?"

"Yes, sir. She hasn't come back through the gate."

Max was genuinely puzzled. To him the conversation earlier that evening, with its implications and pointed omissions, had been purely hypothetical. "Henry, did you check the rear apartments in the Roundhouse?"

"We looked everywhere."

"Okay. Call the police. I'm on my way."

He hung up and rang her motel number. No one answered. He stared at the phone and finally recognized the possibility that she might have used the grid. Thoroughly alarmed, he dressed hastily, climbed into his car and started for Johnson's Ridge. He should have told Henry to look in the channel. Maybe she'd fallen in there. It would have been easy enough for the security people to miss her.

He picked up his cellular phone, dialed the gate, and got a new voice. George Freewater. "How are we doing?" he asked.

"Still no news. The police are on their way." Long pause. "Max, if she's outside, she won't last very long. It's cold."

"I know. Did you look in the channel?"

He heard a brief conversation on the other end, and then George came back. "Yes, we looked in the channel.

Listen, Mr. Collingwood, we found something else. There's a message addressed to you. It was on the front seat of her car."

"Me?" Max's stomach lurched. "What's it say?"

"You want me to read it?"

"Yes, George. Please."

"Okay. It says— Wait a minute; the light's not so good here. It says, 'Dear Max, I'm following the arrow. Since you're reading this, something may have gone wrong. Sorry. I enjoyed working with you.'" George grunted. "What's she talking about?"

Max's headlights lost themselves in the dark. "I'm not sure," he said. But he knew.

The Man in the White Suit is alive and well. Those who remember the classic British film starring Alec Guinness as a man who invented a cloth that resisted wrinkling and dirt may understand what's happening these days to the clothing industry. Capitalization has been shrinking for clothing manufacturers since the first rumors surfaced of the possibility of developing a cloth very much like the one in the film. Numerous experts are on record that it is only a matter of time before the Roundhouse technology, which created superresistant materials on Johnson's Ridge, becomes generally available. What will happen when that occurs is uncertain. But for now, tens of thousands of jobs have disappeared, and an entire industry is in chaos. This newspaper is a reluctant advocate of government intervention. But in this case, the time has come.

(Lead editorial, *Wall Street Journal*)

When Max walked into the Roundhouse, he was angry with April Cannon. She had put him in a terrible position. He berated himself for not guessing what might happen and heading it off.

What the hell was he supposed to do now?

The dome was oppressive.

Henry Short was inside with two police officers. One was looking down into the pit. He was young, barely twenty-one. Sandy-haired, long, angular jaw, prominent nose.

The partner, who was bald and irritable, broke off his conversation with George Freewater as Max entered. "Sir, you're Mr. Collingwood?"

"Yes," said Max.

"I'm Deputy Remirov," he said, producing a notebook that Max recognized as belonging to April. "What does this mean?"

I'm following the arrow.

"What's the arrow?" the younger one asked.

Max hesitated briefly. "I don't know," he said.

Remirov looked unhappy. "You have no idea what she was trying to tell you?"

"No," said Max. "Not a clue."

The policeman didn't believe a word of it. "Why would she write you a note you can't understand?" he asked angrily.

Max squirmed. He wasn't good at lying. And he didn't like being evasive with police officers. He'd had little contact with them during his life, and they made him nervous. "I just don't know," he said.

Exasperated, Remirov turned back to George. "You're sure she didn't go out through the gate without being seen?"

"We've got a camera on the gate," George said.

"That doesn't answer my question."

"I guess it *is* possible. But we always have somebody on the monitors."

"So you really don't know," said Remirov.

"Not without checking the tapes."

"Why don't we check the tapes?" he asked with exaggerated politeness.

Max wandered away to look at the grid. He saw no way to confirm whether she had actually used it. There were no footprints, no marks that told him anything.

Redfern, wearing a buckskin jacket and heavy boots, came into the dome. He spoke briefly with George and the two policemen before he saw Max. "They're going to organize a search party," he said.

"Good," said Max.

A long, uncomfortable silence followed. "George told me she left a note for you. Max, where is she?"

"My guess is she's dead," said Max. Saying what he had been thinking ever since he'd heard about the note somehow made it less real.

Redfern's jaw tightened. "How?" he asked.

Max thought about doing a demonstration, but since each of the icons seemed to work only once, he hesitated. Instead he simply pointed out the grid and the set of triggers, and explained what had happened. "This," he said, directing the lawyer's attention to the symbol at the top of the second column, "is the arrow."

"You're telling me there's a device here that *annihilates* things, and you think she used it on herself?"

"That's what I think," said Max.

"Son of a bitch," he said. "Don't you people have any sense at all?"

"Hey, I didn't know anything like this was going to happen."

"Yeah. Well, maybe you should've been watching a little closer."

Max started to protest, but Arky waved it aside. "We can figure out who to blame later. She thought she was going somewhere. How did she expect to get back?"

"I don't know. She didn't exactly talk this over with me. But I assume she hoped there'd be a similar device at the other end. If there *is* an other end."

Arky turned to George, who had joined them. "How long ago, did you say?"

"She came through the gate at twelve-thirty."

Arky looked at his watch. Ten after four. "I guess we can assume she isn't coming back on her own." He folded his arms. "So where," he asked accusingly, "do we go from here?"

Max felt like an idiot. *Damn you, Cannon.*

Arky's face was dark. The shadows of an internal struggle played at the corners of his mouth and in his eyes. "Maybe it would be best," he said, "if the tribe did sell. People die a little too easily here." He got up and headed toward the door. "We'll let the police go ahead with their search. There *is* a chance she wandered off and got lost on the mountain." He hesitated. "Max—"

"Yes?"

"I would like your word that you will not try to follow her."

The demand embarrassed him. Max Collingwood would *never* try that kind of stunt. It was flat-out stupid. But in some dark corner of his mind it pleased him that Arky believed he might be capable of it. "No," he said, meaning it. "I won't."

Emotion flickered across the lawyer's features. "Good," he said. "Let's let the search run its course. Meantime, you should find out about her next of kin."

Next of kin? Max knew very little about April Cannon. He would have to check with Colson Laboratories.

Arky paused at the door. "Max, is there anything else about this place I should know?"

"No," said Max. "At least, not anything that *I* know about."

Max listened to the negative reports coming in from the search parties while the first vague streaks of dawn crept into the sky. The little girl with the brown curls was looking at him again from the cabin window. It was a memory he had thought he'd shut away. Buried.

He liked April Cannon, and he couldn't bring himself to believe she was gone, vanished into a dark never-never land. The image of the fading chair, the vertical lines just visible through its legs and seat, was paused on each of the monitor bank's four screens.

The lines might have been anything—a defect in the film, a momentary reflection. Or they might have been a glimpse of another place. They looked vaguely like a column. He pictured the wooden chair set in the portico of a Greek temple.

If in fact it was a transportation system, it *had* to work in both directions. Why, then, had she not come back?

Because the system was old. After all, the smoke had not worked. Maybe she was simply stranded.

There was a test he could run.

Max installed a filter in his minicam, got a spade and collected a pile of snow, and went back to the Roundhouse. It was empty; the search was concentrated on the surrounding hillsides. His boots crunched on the dirt floor, and it occurred to him that it was the first time he'd been alone in here.

He made a little mound of snow in the center of the grid.

Then he propped the camera on a chair, aimed it, and started it.

He pressed the wall over the arrow.

It lit up.

Max backed away, watching the pile of snow, counting down without meaning to.

Above the grid, the air ignited. It burned and expanded and threw off a golden cloud that shimmered and grew so bright he had to look away. Then it winked out.

The snow was gone. Not so much as a trickle of water remained.

Okay. He gathered up the camera, hurried back to the van, and loaded the videocassette into the VCR.

He played it through at normal speed first to be sure he had the entire sequence. And there was no doubt that the snow went transparent before vanishing altogether.

He rewound it and began again. When the effect started, he froze the frame and walked it through. The light brightened, grew misty, and expanded. Within the mist, stars ignited. The luminosity seemed almost to *seek* the pile of snow. Bright tendrils embraced the snow, and then it began to fade. Frame by frame it grew less distinct, without losing its definition. When it was almost gone, no more than a suggestion, another image appeared.

It paralyzed him.

He was looking at her headless torso. She was crumpled, arms dangling.

A sense of loss engulfed him. And as tears of blind rage began to flow, he realized that it *might* be only her jacket.

Was only her jacket.

Minnesota Twins. He could read the logo. There was no question. But the front didn't look right. An object, a cylinder, a tube, something, hung from it.

A flashlight. It was the barrel of a *flashlight*. Minus its cap. The barrel looked crushed.

It was one of the standard-issue cheap plastic models they had used at the site. But what had happened to it?

He puzzled over it for several minutes. What would he have done if he were stranded over there, wherever *there* was? He would try to send a message.

I am here.

And . . . what?

The flashlight's broken?

He took a deep breath.

Something's broken.

The transportation system is broken.

He called Arky. "She made it," he said. "The thing's a *doorway*. A passage."

"How do you know?"

"Her coat's on the other side. I've got pictures."

The lawyer seemed to have trouble speaking. Max could picture him shaking his head, trying to make sense of all this. "You're sure?"

"Yes. I'm sure."

"So what do we do now?"

It was painfully obvious. "We need a hardware store."

They got the proprietor out of bed and bought a generator, two gallons of gas, a voltage meter, a one-and-a-half-horse-power industrial-strength drill, and a few additional pieces of equipment and took it back to the Roundhouse. Max used the drill to cut through the rear wall.

The space behind the wall was occupied by a flat rectangular crystal mounted in a frame. It was roughly the dimensions of a sheet of standard-sized stationery and about a quarter-inch thick. It was translucent, and there were several small burn marks. The device was connected to the icons by color-coded cables. "It's probably a circuit board," said Max.

Arky looked horrified. "We can't repair this kind of stuff," he said.

"Depends what the problem is. If it's something integral to the crystal, then probably not. But April might just be looking at a loose wire. Or a dead power source." He shrugged. "I wouldn't want to *build* one of these, but it doesn't look all that complicated."

"I don't think it could be the power supply," Arky said. "If there were no power over there, she wouldn't have arrived in the first place."

"That's probably true, Arky. But who knows? Let's see what else is here." He dug into the wall behind the crystal.

There were other cables in back, one running down into the floor, others curving into the overhead. One group was banded together. "One of these has to be the power source," said Max. "And I'll bet the cluster activates the transport mechanism itself. Whatever and wherever that is."

"It's going to take a while to figure out where these go," said Arky.

"Maybe we can cut a few corners." Max knelt on a rubber mat and took hold of the cable they thought might lead to the power source. He tugged on it, gently, and to his delight, it slipped off as easily as if the connection had been cleaned and oiled the day before, revealing a prong. "Okay," he said. "Hand me the voltage meter."

It was difficult getting at the cable, and eventually he was forced to make a bigger hole. But he got his reading. "Direct current," he said. "Eighty-two volts."

"That's an odd number," said Arky.

"They don't play by our rules, I guess."

Arky poured gas into the generator tank. He used the regulator to adjust its flux and took a True Hardware cable connector apart and reconfigured it to clip to the back of the crystal. Max pressed the arrow, and the icon lit up.

"Okay," he said. "I guess it's time to bite the bullet."

Max had almost hoped it wouldn't work. Then he'd have been able to justify in his own mind that there was no point trying to follow. But he was cornered, and he wondered whether he could really bring himself to stand on the grid.

He disconnected the generator and replaced the original cable. Then he put the generator on the grid, plunked a toolbox down beside it, and picked up a legal pad.

"I'm not so sure about this," said Arky. "If something goes wrong, I could lose my license." He grinned at Max, and Max suddenly realized he had the lawyer's respect. It was almost worth it. "What's the paper for?"

"Communication." Max held up a black marker. "If we get stuck over there, if this stuff doesn't work, I'll post a message."

He climbed stiffly onto the grid and closed his eyes. Then, deliberately, he opened them again. "Okay, Arky," he said. "Hit the button."

✠ 20 ✠

Unpathed waters, undreamed shores . . .

—William Shakespeare, *The Winter's Tale*

The world filled with light. The arching walls grew transparent and leaked blue-white sunlight. Violet hills swam in and out of focus. The floor fell away, and he was afloat, not falling, but drifting. A sudden vertigo washed through him. Then he sprawled forward on solid ground.

He was looking at the *Minnesota Twins* logo. The jacket was draped over a broken tree branch, which was propped against a glass wall.

He was inside a cupola, near the top of a low hill. Around him lay the forest he had glimpsed when the transition started. Except that it was solid now. And it did not look like any forest he had ever seen.

There were no greens. The vegetation favored a deep violet hue. Enormous white and yellow blossoms hung from trees that looked half human, like people who had defied the gods and taken root. Plump red and yellow fruit hung from thick, gnarled branches. The ground was thick with leaves.

The sun hovered on the horizon, but whether it was early evening or morning was impossible to say.

The cupola appeared to be made of clear glass. It had a door, which was ajar. The ground beyond was higher than the floor of the cupola by more than a foot. Which meant what? That the cupola, like the Roundhouse, was long abandoned?

The forest was silent, save for the hum of insects and the occasional flutter of wings. Where was April?

Surely she would not have left the area voluntarily. Unless she was taken. It was a thought he tried to put aside as he smelled the warm, sweet air.

He pushed on the door. It crashed into the grass. Max jumped, and then smiled at his own nervousness.

When April had arrived, the door (which apparently hadn't been used in a long time) was jammed shut by the higher ground outside. So she had removed the bolts from the hinges.

Max stepped through the opening. A large bird flapped across the sky and disappeared into the trees. In the distance, he could hear the roar of surf.

He called April's name. Something screeched back.

Where the hell was she?

He looked at the tangled grass and brush and surveyed the sweep of woodland. There was a glade at the bottom of the hill, and the shrubbery was not so dense as to preclude walking. She could have gone in any direction.

He turned back to the cupola and went inside. The structure was shaped like a bell jar, approximately twelve feet in diameter, its top almost at tree level. He had arrived on a circular dish, the same size as the grid in the Roundhouse. A post, in which was mounted another array of icons, rose behind the dish. The icons were three-dimensional and took the form of glyphs. They were earth-colored, and the symbols were different from the other group (save one), although the styling was the same.

The exception was the stag's head. His ticket home. He touched it, very gently, and then pressed it.

Nothing happened.

He visualized April standing here, with a jammed door at her back, trying to get it to work.

He looked doubtfully at the icons. It was possible she had gone on to another terminal in another reality. Possibly in the hope she would find a link home.

That was a dark possibility.

But going through another port would have been an act of desperation. No: She'd left her jacket. It said, in effect, *I am here. Come find me.*

There were eight icons this time. Five were geometrical figures, a sixth might have been a flower, another had wings.

Seven new destinations, presumably. What in God's name had they stumbled into?

He took another look at the forest, to be sure nothing was sneaking up on him. His first priority was to make a way out.

He opened his tool kit.

The disk seemed to be hard rubber. Its center was rounded and raised.

He used his drill to cut into the post. Again, it was tough going, and he worked for almost forty minutes before he broke through. By then it had become clear that the sun was setting.

Inside the post, he found a mounted crystal similar to the one he'd seen at the Roundhouse. Good so far. The power cable looked okay. He checked the wiring behind the icons.

The pattern was the same: strands from each of the icons formed a color-coded cluster, as before, which disappeared up into the post. Three, however, were missing, not connected at all. Unfortunately, the stag's head was not among them.

He looked at the crystal and started to worry. If the problem was buried in the technology, he was dead.

The post was about ten feet high. It tapered as it rose and curved out over the disk, widening finally into an amber lens. A ladder was connected to the rear. He picked up his drill, climbed the ladder, and cut into the post just below the lens. The cable cluster had broken apart and the individual lines were tied into connectors. The line from the stag's head, which was white, had pulled loose.

He tried to tighten it, then went back down and returned with a piece of electrical tape. It seemed to work.

He took his pad of paper and a marker and wrote:

Arky,

I'm okay. April has gone off somewhere, and I am going to find her. Wait.

He removed the broken flashlight and took the jacket off the tree branch that supported it. He tore off the sheet of paper and stuffed it in a pocket, leaving a corner jutting out, and laid the jacket on the grid. When he'd finished, he took a deep breath and pressed the stag's head. The icon lit up and, twenty-three seconds later, he was gratified to watch the light burst appear. When it had faded, the jacket was gone.

Bingo.

On a second sheet, he wrote another message and taped it to the door:

ANCIENT SHORES

April,

I'm here. Please stay put. I'm looking for you and will be back in a few minutes.

Max

The hill on which the cupola stood might not have been entirely natural. Worn stone steps, all but buried, descended to the forest floor. He went down cautiously, regretting that he had not thought to bring a weapon. The colonel would have been dismayed.

He called her again. The cry echoed back.

He was both fearful and annoyed. She'd have wanted to explore, and he could understand she would not have waited by the cupola for a rescue party that might never come. (How much confidence *did* she have in him, anyway?) But it would have been nice to find her there.

Which way?

He listened to the distant rumble of the sea.

That was the direction she would have gone. Anybody would.

Now that he was down among the trees, the sky was concealed by the overhang. But the light was failing rapidly.

He wanted to find her and get back before it got dark. The hill on which the cupola stood was higher than any other ground he could see. But things could get dicey at night.

He set off. It was easy walking; the vegetation was luxuriant but not thick or high enough to impede him. The soil was rocky, and he periodically piled several stones together to mark a trail. He saw no animals, although he heard them, and occasionally saw shrubbery move.

225

He noticed also that he felt more energetic, and maybe even stronger, than normal. Probably it had to do with the weather. He was outside, and the air was fresh and clean.

He traveled at his best speed for about a half-hour. Dusk came on, and the vegetation grew sparser. Finally he left the trees behind altogether and walked out onto a wide beach. Gray-red cliffs rose on his left, backlit by the last light from a sun that was below the horizon. Blue water opened before him, and a cool salt wind stung his nostrils. Wherever he was, he had come a long way from North Dakota.

He saw her almost immediately. She was out near the tide line, seated beside a flickering fire. The surf boomed and roared, so she did not hear him when he called her name. She was gazing at the sea, and he was almost beside her before she realized he was there.

She jumped to her feet. "Max," she cried. "Welcome to the other side." A long wave broke and rolled up the strand. She extended a hand, then shrugged and fell into his arms. "I'm glad to see you," she said.

"Me, too. I was worried about you."

She hung onto him. Squeezed him. "I've got bad news," she said. "We can't get home."

He pushed her away so he could see her face. "Yes, we can," he said. "It works."

Tears welled up in her eyes, and she pulled him close again and kissed him. Her cheeks were wet.

It was cool, and after a minute they sat down by the fire. A few birds flapped across the incoming tide. They had long beaks and webbed feet. As he watched, one landed behind a retreating wave and poked at the sand. "I thought I was stuck here, Max."

"I know."

"This place is nice, but I wouldn't want to stay forever." And, after a second thought: "You're sure? You tried it?"

"Yeah. I'm sure."

That seemed to satisfy her.

"We wouldn't have left you," Max said.

She held a bag out to him. "Peanut butter," she said, offering him a sandwich.

He was hungry.

"This is all I had left."

Max took a bite. "It's good," he said. And, after a moment: "Do you know where we are?"

"Not on Earth."

He moved in closer to the flames. "I should have brought your jacket," he said.

"I'll be fine."

The sea had grown dark. Stars were starting to appear. "I wonder who lives here," Max said.

"I haven't seen anyone. And I don't think anybody's used the transportation system for a long time."

Max watched a breaker unroll. "Are you sure? That this isn't Earth? I mean, that's a lot to swallow."

"Take a look around you, Max."

The Alice-in-Wonderland forest had grown dark.

"And the gravity's not right. It seems to be less here." She studied him. "How do you feel?"

"Good," he said. "Lighter."

"Did you see the sun?"

"Yes."

"It's not ours."

She didn't elaborate, and Max let it go. "We should be getting back," he said. He looked at his watch. "Arky will be worried."

She nodded. "In a way, I hate to leave. Why don't we stay out here tonight? We can go back tomorrow."

It wouldn't occur to Max until several hours later that there might have been a proposition in the offer. He was too unsettled by events and not thinking clearly. "We need to let them know we're okay."

"Okay," she said.

The sky was becoming a vast panorama. It was almost as if the stars switched on with a roar, a million blazing campfires, enough to illuminate the sea and prevent the onset of any real night. Great black storm clouds had appeared, and Max blinked at them because they too seemed swollen with stars. "Odd," he said. "The sky was clear a few minutes ago."

"I don't think," she whispered, "the clouds are in the atmosphere."

Max frowned. The breakers gleamed.

"Look." She pointed out over the sea. A thunderhead floated above the horizon, flecked with liquid lightning and countless blue-and-white lights. "I've seen that before," she said.

So had Max. It looked like an oncoming storm, but it had the distinct shape of a chess piece. A knight.

"I think it's the Horsehead Nebula," he said.

She stood up and walked down to the shoreline. "I think you're right, Max." Her voice shook.

Max watched her; he listened to the fire crackle and to the melodic roar of the surf. Perhaps for the first time since the child had died in the burning plane, he felt at peace with himself.

✠ 21 ✠

Thou dread ambassador from Earth to Heaven . . .

—Samuel Taylor Coleridge, "Hymn Before Sunrise"

London, Mar. 14 (BBC News Service)—

The recent rise in workplace murders in the United Kingdom can possibly be ascribed to events on Johnson's Ridge, according to Timothy Clayton, an industrial psychologist writing in the *Economist*. "People are more fearful for their jobs than they've been since the Great Depression," Clayton says. "They're not sure who's responsible, but to a remarkably increasing degree, they're gunning down bosses, secretaries, newspaper vendors, and anyone else who happens to get in the way."

The five members of the tribal council, four men and a woman, were arrayed across the front of the chamber behind a long wooden table. Behind them hung the banner of the Mini Wakan Oyaté, the shield of the Devil's Lake Sioux, with its buffalo skull and half-sun devices. Chairman Walker occupied the center of the group.

Jack McDevitt

The chamber was packed so tightly with journalists and photographers there wasn't much room for the tribe's members. Some nevertheless managed to squeeze in, while others waited in the hallways and outside the Blue Building. The mood was jubilant, and when Wells stepped forward, there was a smattering of applause.

"Chairman," he said, "esteemed council members, as you are aware, I represent the men and women of the National Energy Institute, which hopes to be allowed to examine the archeological find on Johnson's Ridge and to preserve the find for future generations. In order to accomplish this, we are offering to pay the Mini Wakan Oyaté two hundred million dollars in exchange for the property."

The crowd caught its collective breath. Applause began, but Walker quickly gaveled it down. Wells smiled, enjoying himself. He took out a letter and gazed at it. "I have, however, been directed by my superiors to inform you that some of our investors doubt that this is a wise use of their money, and they are threatening to pull out. The offer could be withdrawn at any time." He crumpled the letter and pushed it back into his pocket. "Ladies and gentlemen," he said, looking concerned, "take the money while you can. Unfortunately, once I walk out that door, anything might happen."

The chairman nodded. "Thank you, Dr. Wells. The council appreciates your coming here this evening to speak with us."

Wells bowed slightly and sat down.

"We have one other person on the agenda for this matter." He looked to his right, where April and Max were seated with Arky. "Dr. Cannon?"

April looked like a world-beater. She wore a dark blue business suit and heels and the expression of someone who'd just found a cure for cancer. "Chairman," she said, "and members of the council. Two hundred million dollars sounds like a lot of money—"

"It *is* a lot of money," said a middle-aged woman up front.

"—but something happened today that changed the value of your property." April paused. "The Roundhouse has a doorway. It's a port to another world."

The audience did not react, and Max realized that people did not understand what she was saying. Even the media representatives were waiting for more.

"This morning two of us walked into that building and walked out onto *another world*. This means that the Roundhouse contains the secret of instantaneous travel. There is a technology that would allow any of us to travel to Fargo, to Los Angeles, to China, *in the blink of an eye.*"

An electric charge rippled through the crowd. Flashbulbs went off, and cellular phones appeared.

Walker pounded his gavel.

In accordance with Arky's advice, April described the land through the port as a place where the world felt young, a wilderness of virgin forests and starlit seas. "Moreover," she said, "we think there are several ports. Perhaps to other forests. We don't know yet. What we do know is that the Mini Wakan Oyaté have a bridge to the stars.

"Do not sell it for a few million dollars. Don't sell it for a few *billion*. It's worth far more."

She sat down, and near pandemonium erupted. It was almost a full minute before the chairman could restore order. "We will now," he said sternly, "hear comments from the floor."

Andrea Hawk stood up to be recognized.

"I would like to remind the council that we are talking here about *two hundred million dollars*.

"I know April Cannon, and I am happy for her. This port she talks about, if it really exists, is of supreme importance. But that is in the future. The reality is that we have people suffering *now*. We can do a great deal for ourselves, and for our kids, with this kind of money. I implore the members of the council not to let it slip away."

A tall man in a worn buckskin jacket told a story about a coyote who, by trying to grab too much, got nothing.

One by one they rose and related stories of children gone bad, of men and women ruined by drugs, of what it meant to be powerless in a rich society. Wells sat looking piously at the ceiling.

"The outside world," said a man who looked ninety, "only knows we are here when they want something from us. However much they offer, they are trying to cheat us. Be careful."

It was the most encouraging comment Max heard until Arky got up. "Tonight," he said, "I am saddened at what I hear, and I worry for my people. Once again, the white man offers money, and we are quick to snatch it from him. We pay no heed to the nature of the bargain.

"The problems that you have described do not happen because we have no *money*. Rather, they happen because we have lost our *heritage*. We have forgotten who we are and what we might have been. I tell you, brothers and sisters, if we allow ourselves to be seduced again, it would be better for us if we never saw another sunrise."

A murmur ran through the crowd. The journalists were holding up cassette recorders, aiming TV cameras, getting it all. Arky turned back to the council.

"We have been shown a new world. Maybe it's time we stopped trying to live on pieces of land that the whites dole out. Maybe it's time to do what our fathers would have done. Let us hold on to this forest world that April Cannon has found. Let us see if we cannot make it ours. That is the choice before you tonight: take this man's money, or live again as we were meant to live."

After the council had filed out to deliberate, the media jumped April. While she answered questions, Max took Arky aside. "I don't think you convinced the crowd," he said.

The lawyer smiled. "I wasn't trying to," he said. "I was pointed in their direction, but I was talking to the old warriors."

Devil's Lake, ND, Mar. 15 (AP)—

The tribal council of the Devil's Lake Sioux today turned down a two-hundred-million-dollar offer from a consortium of business interests to purchase the Johnson's Ridge property on which a controversial excavation site is located. Their action is related to the alleged discovery of a "star bridge." (See lead story, above.) Unrest among tribe members has been reported. Several mounted a demonstration here today, and police are bracing for more. . . .

They made a second trip through the port and took some reluctant reporters along. That night the nation developed what Jay Leno dubbed "Roundhouse fever." Pictures of the beach and the Horsehead Nebula and of people vanishing in a splash of golden light were on the front page of every newspaper and on every channel. As daylight moved around the globe, the Roundhouse and the wilderness world made headlines everywhere.

Security was beefed up. VIPs arrived, mostly by helicopter, from major universities, research facilities, state and federal agencies. Foreign dignitaries dropped in, and at one point a flustered Max was introduced to the French president. April put together a slide presentation, which highlighted Tom Lasker's boat, results of the various tests of the material used to construct the boat and the Roundhouse, early stages of the excavation, and aerial views of Johnson's Ridge at night.

By now, April had been granted leave by Colson Labs. She was the only person with the excavation group who was even remotely qualified to address the various researchers. (The waiting list to visit the Roundhouse, and with it the new world, had already grown into the thousands.) On the sixteenth she announced that a committee of prominent scholars would meet in ten days to formulate an investigative and developmental strategy. The immediate questions posed to the committee would be, "What should we do about the world across the bridge?" and "How do we prepare for first contact?"

Columbus, Ohio, Mar. 16
President Matthew R. Taylor
The White House
Washington, DC 20003

Dear President Taylor,

I know that you are very busy, but I hope you can find time to help my dad. He lost his job last week at the paper mill. It happened to some other kids, too.
I am in the fifth grade at the Theodore Roosevelt School, and I told some of my friends I was going to write to you. We know you will help. Thank you.

Richie Wickersham

April Cannon had planned to treat everyone, Max and the Laskers and Arky Redfern, to dinner the evening after the tribal council voted down Wells's offer. But she hadn't counted on the effects of rising from the status of minor celebrity to international fame.

Once the pictures of the wilderness world, taken by a pool camera crew, flashed around the globe, any chance of anonymity for her and Max was shattered forever. Reporters appeared at the Blue Light in Grafton while patrons crowded around her table and asked for autographs.

There were more reporters at the Prairie Schooner. In the end they went to the Laskers' home and held a good-natured impromptu press conference from the front porch. When April, hoping for some privacy, suggested they cut the celebration short, Max demurred. "This is part of the story," he said. "Let them have it. It costs us nothing and gains their good will. We may need it before we're done."

In talking to the press, Max had planned to deliver a bromide, a general comment about someone having left behind an inestimable gift for the human race. But when he got up in front of the cameras and the recorders, his emotions took hold. (He had perhaps drunk a little too much by then, not enough to induce a wobble, but enough to loosen his inhibitions.) "You've seen pictures of the new world," he said. "But the pictures don't really carry the effect. The sea is warm and the beach is wide, and I suspect we're going to discover the fruit is edible. I was fortunate to find a beautiful woman on the beach, and I was not anxious to come back to North Dakota." The reporters laughed. April caught his eye and smiled and must have known where he was going because her lips formed a *no*. But it was too late. Max was rolling. "The place is like nowhere you've ever been before. It's pure magic." He glanced out through the window at the plain and watched the wind blowing snow around the corner of the barn. "It's *Eden*," he said.

Within a few minutes, every major television network on the planet was breaking into its regular programming.

The Reverend William (Old-Time Bill) Addison, former beer truck driver, former real-estate salesman, former systems analyst, was the founder and driving force of the television ministry he called Project Forty, a reference to the years in the desert and the flagship TV channel which carried his show. He was also pastor of the Church of the Volunteer, in Whitburg, Alabama. Bill was a believer. He believed the end was near, he believed people were intrinsically no damned good and needed divine help every step of the way, and he believed Bill Addison was an exception to the general rule.

He was a recovered sinner. He had been a womanizer. He had known the evils of drink, and he had hot-wired more than one Chevrolet during his adolescent years in Chattanooga. He had defied authority in all its manifestations. Even the divine.

And it happened to him, as it had happened to Paul, that a highway had led him directly to the Lord. In Bill's case, the highway was I–95. Bill was headed to Jacksonville on a rainswept evening, planning a night in the company of sinful women, when his car spun out of control and rolled into a ditch. He should have died. The car exploded and Addison was thrown at the foot of a tree a hundred feet away. But between the moment of the explosion, and the arrival of the police some ten minutes later, the Lord spoke to him, and gave him his mission. Now that mission went forward from a small country church on the south side of Whitburg to 111 affiliated stations across the nation and in Canada.

ANCIENT SHORES

The morning after Max's injudicious remark, Bill broached the subject to his electronic flock. He was standing in the book-lined study set that he habitually used to lend a scholarly glow to his perorations. "Last night," he explained, "I could not sleep very well. I don't know why that should have been. I usually have no trouble sleeping, brothers and sisters, because I never go to bed with a heavy conscience. But last night something kept me awake. And I wondered whether someone was trying to speak to me.

"Now I don't say it was God." He pronounced the name as if it had two syllables. "Hear me well, friends, I don't say it was God. But, as St. Paul tells us in the book of Romans, it was time to awaken out of sleep.

"I went downstairs and read for a while. The house was quiet. And I put on the television, CNN, that I might have the company of a human voice.

"If you read your newspapers this morning or looked at the news broadcasts, you know what I saw. Scientists claim to have found a door into a new world. I watched, fascinated. They showed pictures of this new world, of its broad purple forest and its blue sea. And its brooding sky.

"Now I don't know what it is that we, in our insatiable curiosity, have blundered into. But it is disquieting to any good Christian. At first I thought it was a joke, but that cannot be, because it would be too easily found out. To those of you who have asked, therefore, I say yes, I believe the reports coming out of North Dakota are true.

"Some of you have also asked, 'Reverend Bill, what do you think about this news? What is this place they call the Roundhouse?' I have no answers. But I will tell you what I suspect and why I think we should close that door forever.

"These scientists are, by and large, godless men and women. But one of them seems to have had an inkling of what I believe is the truth about the land across the Dakota bridge. He was attracted by it, and said he would have liked to stay among its quiet forests. And he called it Eden.

"Brothers and sisters, I propose to you that that is exactly what it is. That some part of this man, atheist as he may be, as he probably is, some living part deep in his soul recognized its long-lost home and yearned, no, *cried out*, to return.

"We know that God did not destroy Eden. Perhaps He wanted it to remain to remind us of what we had lost. What our arrogance had cost. I do not know. No one knows."

The faithful caught their cue. "Amen," they cried.

"You may say, 'But Reverend Bill, the Bible makes no mention of purple forests. Nor of strange cloud formations.' But neither does it exclude them. It says that the Lord God made two great lights, one to rule the day and the other to rule the night. Do we really know that the second light was our present-day moon, and not the great cloud that we saw on our televisions earlier today?

"Brothers and sisters, I tell you, we take a terrible risk if we go back through that door. If it is indeed Eden, we are defying the will of the Almighty."

Akron, OH, Mar. 17 (UPI)—

Goodyear Tire and Rubber Company today denied reports that massive layoffs announced last week were tied to revelations coming out of Johnson's Ridge. "Laughable," said a company spokesman. "We are reengineering and reorganizing. But we are confident there will always be a strong market in this country for tires."

ANCIENT SHORES

The stock market is down 650 points as of this hour. The biggest losses have been in the auto and airline industries. Analysts attribute the sell-off to fears that a revolutionary new transportation system is on the horizon, based on Roundhouse technology.

In Boston, United Technologies denied today that massive layoffs are planned.
(*CNN Noon Report*)

Jeremy Carlucci was so excited he was having trouble breathing. He had been an astronomer, he liked to tell people, since he was four years old, when he sat out back on the open porch of his grandfather's farm north of Kenosha to look for Venus and Mars. Carlucci was near the end of a long and distinguished career.

Now he stood on a beach five thousand light-years from Kenosha, in a night filled with diamonds and stellar whirlpools. The great roiling clouds beneath the Horsehead were lit by inner fires, summer lightning frozen in place by distance.

"Magnificent," someone said behind him.

A cloud-wrapped globe was rising in the east.

The young Class A blue giants were particularly striking. The nebula was a cradle for new stars. Jeremy's joy was so great that he wanted to cry out. "We need to put an observatory here," he whispered to Max.

"A Hubble," said Edward Bannerman, who was from the Institute for Advanced Study. "It should be our first priority. We have to figure out how to enlarge the port so we can get equipment over here."

The wind worked in the trees, and the sea broke and rolled up the beach.

Bannerman, who was a diminutive, sharp-featured man with thinning white hair, watched it come, and then glanced out at the Horsehead. "We are less than two miles from Johnson's Ridge," he said.

The wave played itself out and sank into the sand.

"It's absurd," he continued. "What happened to the laws of physics?"

MIRACLE IN NORTH DAKOTA

The port works.

A team of eleven people stood today on the surface of a world that astronomers say is thousands of light-years from Earth. . . .

(*Wall Street Journal*, lead editorial, Mar. 18)

Are there people in Eden? If so, we may be hearing from them shortly. Whoever built the bridge between North Dakota and the Horsehead Nebula will probably be less understanding than the Native Americans were when their neighborhood went to hell.

(Mike Tower, *Chicago Tribune*)

Tony Peters left his office in the Executive Office Building just after the markets closed. His face was ashen, and he felt very old. His cellular telephone sounded as he strode out onto West Executive Avenue. "The Man wants you," his secretary said. The President was at Camp David for the weekend. "Chopper will be on the lawn in ten minutes."

Peters had known the call would come. He dragged his briefcase wearily through the crowds and the protesters along Pennsylvania Avenue ("Bomb the Roundhouse") and entered through the main gate just as a Marine helicopter started its descent toward the pad. The wildest of wild cards had been introduced into the global economy. And he could think of only one recommendation to make to the President.

"The world needs to be reassured," Peters was telling him a half-hour later in the presence of a dozen advisors. "The wheels came off the markets last fall because people thought that automobiles might not wear out every five years. Now they think automobiles might become obsolete altogether. And aircraft and elevators along with them. And tires and radars and carburetors and God knows what else. You name it, and we can tie it to transportation."

The people seated around the conference table stirred uneasily. The Vice President, tall, gray, somber, stared at his notebook. The secretary of state, an attack-dog trial lawyer who was rumored to be on the verge of quitting because Matt Taylor liked to be his own secretary of state, sat with his head braced on his fists, eyes closed.

The President looked toward James Samson, his treasury secretary. "I agree," Samson said.

When the secretary showed no inclination to continue, the President noted something in the leather folio that was always at his side and tapped the pen on the table. "If we assume this device really works, and it can be adapted to ordinary travel, what are the implications for the economy?"

"Theoretically," said Peters, "technological advance is always advantageous. In the long run we will profit enormously from developing a capability for cheap and virtually instantaneous travel. The equipment requires, as I understand it, no more power than would be needed to turn on your TV. The benefits are obvious."

"But over the short term?"

"There will be some dislocation," he said.

"*Some* dislocation?" Samson smiled cynically. He was small, washed-out, possibly dying. He'd been wrong during the winter in the reassurances given the President concerning the Roundhouse, but he was nevertheless generally credited with having the best brain in the administration. "Chaos might be a little closer to the truth." His voice shook. "Collapse. Disintegration. Take your pick." He coughed into a handkerchief. "Keep in mind, Mr. President, we are not concerned here with the next decade. Allow this to continue, and there may be no United States to benefit in the long term. And there certainly will be no President Taylor." He subsided into a spasm of coughs.

Taylor nodded. "Who else has a comment? Admiral?"

Admiral Charles (Bomber) Bonner was the chairman of the Joint Chiefs. He was right out of central casting for senior military officers: tall, well-pressed, no-nonsense. He appeared to be still in good shape, although he was in his sixties. He walked with a limp, compliments of a plane crash in Vietnam. "Mr. President," he said, "this device, if it exists, has defense implications of the most serious nature. Should this kind of equipment become generally available, it would become possible to introduce strike forces, maybe whole armies, into the heart of any nation on earth. With no warning. And probably no conceivable defense. All that would be necessary, apparently, would be to assemble a receiver station." He looked around to gauge whether his words were having the desired effect. "No place on earth that could be reached by a pickup truck would be safe from assault forces."

Taylor took a long, deep breath. "You are suggesting we appropriate the device, Admiral? And do what?"

"I am suggesting we *destroy it*. Mr. President, there is no such thing as a long-term military secret. When this device becomes part of anyone else's arsenal, as it will, it negates the carriers, the missile force, SAC and TAC, and everything else we have. It is the ultimate equalizer. Go in there, buy the damned place from the Indians if you can, seize it if you must, but go in there, get the thing, and turn it to slag."

Harry Eaton shook his head. Harry was the White House chief of staff. "The Sioux just turned down two hundred million for the property. I don't think they're interested in selling."

"Offer them a billion," said Rollie Graves, the CIA director.

"I don't believe they'll sell," Eaton said again. "Even if they did, this is high-profile. Give them a billion, and the media will be asking questions right up to election day about what the taxpayers got for their money. What do we tell them? That we did it to protect General Motors and Boeing?"

"I don't much care what you tell them," said Bonner. "That kind of capability converts the carrier force into so much scrap metal. Think about it, Mr. President."

Mark Anniok, secretary of the interior, leaned forward. Anniok was of Inuit heritage. "You can't just take it away from them," he said. "It would be political suicide. My God, we'd be pictured as stealing from the Native-Americans *again*. I can see the editorials now."

"We damned well *can* take it away from them," said Eaton. "And we should immediately thereafter arrange an accident that blows the whole goddamn thing off the top of the ridge."

"I agree," said Bonner. "Put a lid on it now while we can."

Elizabeth Schumacher, the science advisor, sat at the far end of the table. She was a gray-eyed, introspective woman who was rarely invited to strategy meetings. The Taylor administration, committed as it was to reducing the deficit, was not generally perceived as a friend of the scientific community. The President knew this, and he was sorry for it, but he was willing to take the heat to achieve his goal. "Mr. President," she said, "finding the Roundhouse is an event of incalculable importance. If you destroy it, or allow it to be destroyed, be assured that future generations will never forgive you."

That was all she said, and Peters saw that it had an effect.

They talked inconclusively for two more hours. Eaton was on the fence. Only Anniok and Schumacher argued to save the Roundhouse. Tony Peters was torn, and he gradually came around to the view that they should try to exploit the ridge and take their chances with the economy and whatever other effects the artifact might have. But he was cautious by nature, and far too loyal to the welfare of his chief executive to recommend that course of action. Everyone else in the room argued strenuously to find a way to get rid of the artifact.

When the meeting ended, the President took Peters aside. "Tony," he said, "I wanted to thank you for your contribution tonight."

He nodded. "What are we going to do?"

Taylor had never been indecisive. But tonight, for the first time that Peters could recall, the President hesitated. "You want the truth? I don't know how to proceed. I think this thing will disrupt the economy, and nobody knows how it will look when we come out the other side. But I also think Elizabeth is right. If I allow the Roundhouse to be destroyed, history is going to eviscerate me."

His eyes were deeply troubled.

"So what do we do?"

"I don't know, Tony," he said. "I really do not know."

✠   ✠   ✠

"Go ahead, Charlie from the reservation."

"Hi, Snowhawk. I wanted to comment on the meeting."

"Go ahead."

"When I went down there last night, I thought the way you do. I thought we should take the money."

"What do you think now, Charlie?"

"Have you seen the pictures?"

"From the other side? Yes."

"I think Arky was right. I think we should pack up and move over there and then pull the plug on the system."

"I don't think that's what Arky said."

"Sure he did. And I'm with him. Listen, Snowhawk, all the money in the world isn't going to get us off the reservation. They can keep their two hundred million. Give *me* the beach and the woods."

"Okay, Charlie. Thank you for your opinion. You're on, Madge from Devil's Lake."

"Hello, Snowhawk. Listen, I think that last caller is absolutely right. I'm ready to go."

"To the wilderness?"

"You got it. Let's move out."

"Okay. Jack, from the reservation. You're on."

"Hey, Snowhawk. I was there, too."

"At the meeting?"

"Yeah. And you're dead wrong. This is a chance for a fresh start. We'd be damned fools not to take it. I say we pack up and go. And this time we keep out the Europeans. After we're over there, do what what's-his-name said. Bar the door."

✠ 22 ✠

Our knowledge is a torch of smoky pine
That lights the pathway but one step ahead
Across a void of mystery and dread. . . .

—George Santayana, "Sonnet III"

Arky was adamant: "Nobody else goes across into this wilderness
world until we're sure it's safe."

April was ready to explode. "Damn it, Arky. We'll never
be sure it's *safe*. Not absolutely."

"Then maybe we ought to write everything off. Take the
best price we can get for the Roundhouse and let somebody
else worry about the lawsuits."

"*What* lawsuits?"

"The lawsuits that will be filed as soon as one of your
pie-in-the-sky academics gets eaten."

"Nobody's going to get eaten."

"How do you know that? Can you guarantee it?"

"Of course I can't."

"Then maybe we better think about it." He took a deep
breath. "We need to ask ourselves whether we really want
all these people blundering around over there."

"They aren't blundering." April took a moment to steady her voice. "These are trained people. Anyhow, we can't keep all this to ourselves. We have to let as many people get a look at it as we can."

"Then let me ask you again: What happens if one of them gets killed?"

"There are no large predators," she said.

"You haven't seen any large predators, April. There's a world of difference. How about diseases? Any exotic bugs?"

"If there are, it's too late. Max and I have been there and back."

"I know." Arky looked sternly at her. "I didn't care much for that, either. Look, until now this has been a shoot-from-the-hip operation. It's time we got a handle on things. Before we get burned. First off, I want you and Max to get full physicals. Complete workups. Meantime, we're going to stop the tours until Adam certifies it's safe. Okay? I don't want *anyone* going over there until that happens. Not even *you.*"

"Arky," she protested, "we can't just lock the door and tell people it's unsafe."

"We just did," he said.

Adam put together his team. They included Jack Swiftfoot, Andrea Hawk, John Little Ghost, and two more April did not know. He parceled out M–15's, grenades, and pistols. "You look as if you expect to run into dinosaurs," she said.

He shrugged. "Better safe than sorry." He signaled his people onto the grid, pressed the arrow icon, and joined them. "See you tonight," he told April. He was slipping an ammunition clip onto his belt when they began to fade.

Max walked in carrying a couple of yellow balloons and

his minicam. "I wouldn't mind," April told him, "but this sets a bad precedent. What do we have to do now? Send a SWAT team in before we can look at any of these other places?"

"Assuming there *are* other places," said Max. "I don't know. But I'm not sure it's a bad idea."

She grumbled but said nothing.

"Do you think," Max asked, "whoever built the system is still out there somewhere?"

Her eyes lost their focus. "It's been ten thousand years," she said. "That's a long time."

"Maybe not for these people."

"Maybe not. But the Roundhouse was abandoned a long time ago. And there's no evidence of recent usage in Eden, either. What does that tell you?"

Through the wraparound window, Max could see tourists taking pictures. "I wonder where the network ends," he said.

Her eyes brightened. "I'm looking forward to finding out."

The outside door opened. They heard footsteps in the passageway, and Arky Redfern appeared. He waved, peeled off his jacket, and laid it on the back of a chair. "There's some talk," he said, "of making you two honorary tribal members."

"I'd like that," said April.

The only other person Max could think of who had been so honored by a tribe was Sam Houston. Not bad company. "Me too," he said.

"So what's next?" asked Arky, gazing pointedly at the balloons.

"We want to see what else we have."

The balloons sported the legend *Fort Moxie* and a picture

of the Roundhouse. Two long strings dangled from each. Max, enjoying center stage, pulled over two chairs and set them on either side of the grid, outside the perimeter. He tied one of the balloons to the chairs so that the balloon itself floated directly over the grid.

"What are you trying to do?" Arky asked.

"We don't want to clog the system," said April. "If we send a chair and nobody moves it off the receiving grid, that's the ball game. We lose that channel. We need to send something that won't stay put."

Arky nodded. "Good," he said.

"Ready?" asked April, who was now standing beside the icons.

Max focused on the balloon and started the videotape. "Running," he said.

April pressed the rings icon.

Max counted twenty-three seconds and watched the balloon disappear. Two severed pieces of string, one on either side of the grid, dropped to the floor.

"I've got a question," said Arky. "What happens if somebody isn't all the way on when the thing activates? Does half of you get left here?"

April looked like a kid caught with her hand in the cookie jar. "That's a good question, counselor," she said.

They repeated the process with the final icon, the G clef, and returned to the control module to see the results.

The rings had implied, to Max, an artificial environment. Here, at last, they might come face to face with someone.

And perhaps they would. There *was* a secondary exposure, a ghost in the photo. The ghost was a wall with a window. The wall was plain, and suggested perhaps a vessel or military installation. The window was long, longer than the image. And it seemed to be night on the other side.

"Indoors, I think," said April.

Arky was sitting on the work table. He leaned forward, trying to see more clearly. "How do we respond if someone's there?" he asked.

"Say hello and smile," said Max.

The lawyer frowned. "I think we need to be serious about this. Listen, this station, terminal, whatever, has been out of business for a long time. But it doesn't mean the entire system is down. We need to decide how we're going to respond if someone shows up." He looked reluctant to continue. "For example, should we be armed?"

April shook her head slowly. "Seems to me," she said, "the last thing we'd want to do is start a fight with whoever put this thing together."

"He's right, though," said Max. "We should be careful."

Arky slipped into a chair. "Why don't we take a look at the other one?"

The G clef. Max let the videotape run ahead to the second sequence.

Again they watched the balloon fade. This time the background image appeared to be a carpeted room. The walls might have been paneled, but they were bare. No furniture was visible. "Light coming from somewhere," said April.

"What do you think?" asked Max.

"It might be just another Roundhouse."

April was ready to go. "Only one way to find out."

Max hesitated. "I think we should leave it alone," he said. "If someone really is over there, we are going to screw it up. Let's use that committee of yours to figure out how to do this stuff."

"That's six days away," said April. "The more information

we can get for them, the better able they'll be to do their work. Anyway, what kind of experts would you want for a project like this? I mean, it's not as if anyone has any experience."

"I can see where this is leading," said Max.

"Nevertheless, I agree," said Arky. "No one is equipped for this kind of meeting. If anyone goes, it might as well be us." Max noticed the pronoun.

April did, too. "Arky," she said, "no offense, but we don't need a lawyer along. Let us try it first."

He got visibly taller. "I don't think so," he said. "The tribe should have representation."

"You're kidding," said Max.

Arky smiled. "I never kid."

Max assembled a travel kit, which included a generator, a tool box, two flashlights, two quarts of water, and the now-standard writing pad with black markers.

Dale Tree (who was acting security chief while Adam was leading the survey of Eden) handed a .38 to Arky.

"How about me?" said Max.

"You qualified?" asked Dale.

"Not really." Max had never fired a weapon in his life.

"Then forget it," said Arky. "You'll be more dangerous than anything we might meet." He glanced at April.

"Me, neither," she said.

Dale looked concerned. "I think you should let me go along," he said.

"We'll be fine," said Arky.

April looked disgusted. "This is probably somebody's living room. I don't think we're likely to need a lot of fire-power."

Max set his travel kit in the middle of the grid and laid a

spade beside it. "When we get there," he told Dale, "I'll try to send the spade back. Give me a half-hour or so, in case we have to repair something. If nothing happens by then, send sandwiches."

"We'll put up a message if we get stuck," said April. "Nobody comes after us unless we ask them to." She glanced at her companions. "Right?"

Arky nodded. Max did, too, but less decisively.

They walked onto the grid. Dale stood by the icons. "Are we ready?" he asked.

April said yes.

The room smelled of musk. The walls were covered with a light green fabric, decorated with representations of flowers and vines. A pallid illumination radiated from no particular place, much in the style of the Roundhouse.

They did not move for a few moments, other than to glance around the large, bare chamber in which they found themselves. Max could hear no sound anywhere. The grid on which they stood was of different design but of the same dimensions as the other two. He stepped down onto a red carpet and pulled his foot back in surprise when it sank beneath him.

"What the hell kind of floor is this?" said April.

He tried again. It supported him, but the walking was going to be difficult. Who, he wondered, would be comfortable here?

In front of him, the light brightened.

The room was L-shaped, half as long on one side as on the other. There were two exits, located at either end of the stem, both opening into shadowy passageways. On the wall behind the grid, Max saw the by now familiar set of icons.

They were located in an angled panel. There were nine this time, motifs set inside disks that were inserted smoothly in the wood. One of them was the stag's head. None of the others duplicated anything Max had seen before, either in the Roundhouse or on Eden.

April stood a long time, examining them. "World without end," she said.

Max nodded. He put the spade on the grid and tried the stag's head. The icon glowed warmly.

The spade vanished in a swirl of light that was green rather than gold. "Matches the decor," April said, impressed.

"Well," said Arky, "it's good to know we can get out of here in a hurry if we have to."

The ceiling was high, and sections of it were lost in shadow behind a network of beams. "The balloon's not here," Arky said. But a look of surprise had appeared on his features, and Max followed his gaze. There was a rectangular hole in the ceiling, through which they could see into another room.

Lights were on, but they were no brighter than in this chamber.

"I don't think anyone's up there," said April.

The opening in the ceiling was rectangular, maybe six by eight feet. There was no staircase. "The balloon," Max said, "probably floated into the upper room."

It was a few degrees cooler here than in the Roundhouse. Max zipped his jacket and turned back to remove his equipment from the grid. "I feel light," he said.

"I think you're right," said April. "Gravity again."

"Not on Earth?" asked Arky.

She shook her head.

The lawyer kept switching his gaze from one doorway to the other. He was not showing a weapon, but his right hand was inside the pocket of his jacket.

No window opened into the room. April unslung her camera and took some pictures. Max and Arky looked into the passageways. The light brightened before them as they moved, and darkened again behind. The carpet remained spongy.

One corridor dead-ended in a large chamber shaped like a rhombus. The other passed additional empty rooms before it turned a corner. There were still no windows. And no furniture.

They went into a huddle. "I don't like a place where we can't see very far," said Arky. "I suggest we go back."

"Without knowing where we are?" April sighed loudly and looked at Max. "What do *you* say, Max?"

Max agreed with Arky. But he wasn't going to say so in April's presence. "Why don't we go a little farther?" he said.

April smiled. "Two out of three."

"I wasn't aware," said the lawyer, "we were running a democracy here." Ahead, the passageway made a ninety-degree right turn. "Okay," he said reluctantly. "Let's try it."

They turned the corner. More rooms. And another opening in the ceiling.

Still no windows. And no indication of recent occupancy.

"This place doesn't look abandoned," said April. "There's no dust. It just looks *empty.*"

They made a left turn, and Max started a map.

"Where," asked Arky, "are the windows?"

Max's ankles were starting to hurt. Walking on a floor that sank with every step was not easy.

They passed into a long, narrow room. Max, who was busy with his map, put a foot down. The floor wasn't there, and he fell forward; suddenly he was looking down two stories! April grabbed his jacket and held on for the instant required for Arky to get an arm around Max's shoulder.

They dragged him back, and Max knelt on the soft floor waiting for his stomach to settle.

The hole was several feet wide and extended the length of the room. On the other side, the floor continued and a doorway opened onto another passageway.

After satisfying herself that Max was not hurt, April knelt down by the edge. "This isn't damage," she said. "This is designed this way. It's a *shaft*."

"In the middle of the floor?" said Arky. "Who the hell is the architect?"

There was no way around it, so they reversed course and took another turn. They found other areas where their passage was blocked by missing floor, and to a degree their route was determined by these curious phenomena.

They looked in all the chambers along their passage. Gradually it struck them that these weren't rooms at all in the standard sense. They were rather spaces in an endless variety of shapes. Some were too narrow to have been comfortable for human occupancy. Others, like the room they had arrived in, were neither square nor rectangular, but had walls that came in at odd angles or that destroyed the symmetry of the space.

There was no furniture. And no sign of a staircase or any other rational means of getting from one floor to another. The color and texture of carpets and walls changed from place to place. And, perhaps strangest of all, they never found a window, leading to the inevitable suggestion that they were underground.

Max was ready to clear out the moment his companions dragged him out of the shaft, and he only waited for someone else to make the suggestion. Meantime, he busied himself with his map, although he was very cautious where he walked.

Lights continued to brighten before them and to fade behind. This effect created the mildly unnerving impression that there was always something moving just outside their field of vision. Max began to pretend he was working on the map while he watched out of the corner of his eye for some untoward movement. Eventually he saw it.

"Where?" asked Arky. "I don't see anything."

"Right there." Max pointed at a turn in the corridor, which they had just rounded only a minute earlier.

"I saw it, too," said April.

"Saw what?" The .38 appeared in Arky's hand.

"The light changed," said Max. "Look—there's a bright patch back there."

Air currents stirred.

The pool of light matched their own. Then, as they watched, it shifted toward them. The effect was that of being stalked.

"There's nothing there," said Arky, trying for a steady voice. "It's just the lights."

But they backed away, and the light flowed forward. April's eyes widened. "Max," she said, "can you get us back to the grid?"

Max was already consulting his map. "I don't think so. The only way I know of is back the way we came." He looked toward the approaching light.

"That's not going to work," said Arky. They set off again in the direction they'd been traveling. The lawyer took a position in the rear. "Try to find a way around," he said.

They went left at the first cross-passageway, hoping to find another place to turn again and get behind the thing in the corridor. (For Max had now begun to think of it as a *thing*. Every horror movie and vampire book he'd ever digested bubbled up in his psyche.)

"You know," said April, "I keep thinking that everything connected with the ports seems to be laid out for visitors. Tourists. People riding a boat around a lake. The Horsehead. They're vacation stops. Maybe this place is, too."

"Is *what?*" asked Max. "A maze?"

"Maybe. I don't know. Maybe it's a funhouse." They were moving at a quick walking gait. The change in illumination behind them was keeping pace. Finally April slowed and turned around, letting Arky draw abreast. "Hello," she said with nervous cheerfulness. "Is anyone there?"

Max was behind April, watching the thing advance, backpedaling, fighting down an urge to run, when his vision blurred. Suddenly he was looking at her from the *front*. She blinked on and off, like an electronic image, and his head swam. His stomach turned over and he went down on one knee, fighting faintness. He closed his eyes, tried to shake it off, and saw her face, saw her lips moving, hands outstretched, eyes riveted. He was looking *down* from near the ceiling.

"Come on, Max," said Arky. "Get in the game." He pulled Max to his feet, then caught April by the shoulder and drew her back. Now they were in full retreat.

They ran through a wedge-shaped room into another passageway and turned left and then right. Max's head cleared quickly, probably from the adrenaline he was pumping.

"I think we lost it," said Arky.

They were retreating across a wide chamber and around a shaft. They paused at the exit on the far side. When the lights didn't change, Max tried to put his thoughts in order.

The way he did that was to assign the distorted perspective

he'd experienced to his momentary weakness and to concentrate instead on getting them back to the grid. He'd always been proud of his directional sense. Even in this labyrinth, he was confident he knew which way they had to go. He showed them on the map. "We're here," he said. "And we've got to get *here*." Roughly a mile away.

He took them out through the exit and into the passageway. A moment later they turned left and walked into the room with the grid.

A chill ran through Max's stomach. "This can't be right," he said.

But Arky looked immensely relieved. "Max," he said, "you're a genius."

Max was shaking his head. "Not possible. It *can't* be the same room."

They crossed the chamber, anxiously eyeing the other entrance, which was the one by which they'd left. Max looked at the triggers. They looked like the same set he'd seen earlier. The room *looked* identical.

April waved it away. "We'll figure it out later. What bothers me is that this isn't the way to handle first contact." But she kept her voice down. "Running home is not going to look good when they write the history books."

"To hell with the history books," said Max. "The history books will only know what *we* tell them. Let's go."

"You really want to stay?" Arky asked her in a tone that challenged her to do it if she meant it. *Otherwise, don't waste our time.*

"We're going to have to come back," she said. But she stepped onto the grid.

"Next time we'll write." Max punched the stag's head and joined them.

The countdown was interminable. Max remembered

having visited an empty house once as a boy and being frightened out by noises in the attic. It was like that, and when the light folded over them and the Roundhouse formed, he recalled how it had felt to escape back into the sunshine.

✠ 23 ✠

The business of America is business.

—Calvin Coolidge

JOHNSON'S RIDGE EXPLORERS OPEN
SECOND WORLD

Walhalla, ND, Mar. 22 (AP)—

A team of explorers passed through a second port today and entered a world that was described as being "pure indoors." No evidence of recent occupancy was discovered, according to press spokesman Frank Moll, who added that visitors will not be permitted until the exact nature of the terminus can be established.

There was no indication of danger, so they reopened Eden to the press and to researchers on the twenty-third. Groups crossing over were accompanied by a guide and a member of the security force. The tours went every two hours. People were fairly nervous about the method of transit, and some in fact backed out. But those who went invariably came back elated.

Everyone signed a release, although Arky warned darkly that such documents rarely influenced liability judgments.

Blood tests for April, Max, and all the security people who had been across came back negative.

April was pleased that Eden was finally a going concern, and she loved showing it off to the world's academics. (As to the second terminus, which they had begun to refer to as the Maze, they decided to postpone further investigation until they had a chance to think things out. Max could not believe he'd got so completely lost and began to suspect that the second terminus was a sphere.)

She held informal conferences, and arranged special field trips when the requests seemed justified. She was beginning to think of herself as the Steward of the wilderness world, and she confessed to Max that she enjoyed being famous. They were all showing up on the covers of the news weeklies. A movie was being rushed into production, and early reports had it that she would be played by Whitney Houston.

Andrea Hawk was tending the port when two geologists came back through the system from the Eden terminus. They were bearded and gray-eyed, and both were talking. They seemed so deeply involved with each other that they did not even notice her. But one word caught her attention: "Oil."

An hour later, it was the number one story on the wire services.

The main item during the plenary session of the General Assembly was to have been a motion by Tanzania suggesting a further weakening of global trade barriers. But the newspapers, which had been full of speculation about the star bridge in North Dakota, now carried stories that oil had been found in Eden.

If the delegates in attendance at the United Nations had found all the talk about other worlds and dimensional intersections confusing and largely irrelevant to real-world politics (they perceived themselves as, if nothing else, hard-headed realists), they *did* understand oil.

Brazil was scheduled for opening remarks on the trade policy initiative. But everyone in the building knew where the conversation was going that morning.

The Brazilian minister was a portly woman with black hair and a thick neck and quick eyes. "The question before us today," she said, "goes far beyond the issue of tariffs. We are looking at a new world, located in some curious way beyond, but not *in*, the United States. We do not have any details about this world. We don't know how extensive it is or how hospitable it may be. So far, it appears to be *very* hospitable." She looked directly across the chamber at the U.S. delegation. "Brazil wishes to submit to the members the proposition that this discovery is of such supreme importance to everyone that no single nation should claim sovereignty over it. The port should be open to all mankind." The minister paused here to listen to a comment from an aide, nodded, and sipped her glass of water.

"Brazil is confident that the United States, which has always been at the forefront in arguing for human rights, will recognize the essential human right to explore and ultimately occupy this strange new place. We urge the United States to declare itself accordingly."

✠　　✠　　✠

Margaret Yakata could never have been a serious presidential candidate. While the country *might* be willing to accept a woman in the highest office, it was not yet ready for one of Japanese ancestry. And so Yakata had put away her own ambitions, which had taken her to the governor's mansion in Sacramento, and used her considerable political influence to get the vice presidency for Matt Taylor.

Taylor had shown his appreciation by sending her to the United Nations, where she was respected as a champion of global cooperation on environmental matters. She had also shown herself to be a staunch advocate of collective security by supporting fledgling democracies wherever they arose. "Democracies," she was fond of telling representatives of police states, "are the supreme hope for peace on this planet, because they do not make war on one another."

Now she sat in her office at the UN, watching the Brazilian delegate on one screen and the President's reaction on another. Someone handed the President a note. He read it without noticeable change of expression and then looked directly at her. "Iran," he said, "is going to demand that Johnson's Ridge be inspected by the UN and placed under international mandate."

"They'll get a lot of support," said Yakata.

"I know. It's a new stick to beat us with." An expression of pain crept into his face.

"Mr. President," she said, "a lot of people are scared about Johnson's Ridge. Even the Brits are jumpy. They're telling me they'll vote with us if we can guarantee it'll go away. Otherwise they're reserving their options."

"You heard about the oil?"

"Yes, I heard."

"What do you think?"

"Considering what else may be coming out of there, I think it's trivial. But it's got everyone here thinking about natural resources. Is there gold over there, too? Uranium? Where does it end? Incidentally, I understand the Palestinians are going to demand land in Eden." She grinned. "They'll be supported by the Israelis."

"This is a *nightmare*," said Taylor.

"The Japanese want the Roundhouse handed over to the UN and destroyed. They say the port technology will destroy the global economy."

"They won't be alone," said Taylor. "The whole world is terrified of discovering that it could get a whole lot smaller. Overnight."

Yakata sighed. "Exactly how difficult would it be to reproduce the port technology, Mr. President?"

"We haven't been able to get a good look at it yet, Margaret. But my people tell me that anything we can get a working model of, we can duplicate."

"That's what I thought. Mr. President, you'd know more about this than I do, but in my opinion the people who have been raising security concerns have a point." She considered what she was about to say and did not like it. She was not among those who had lost faith in technology or in the human race itself. And yet . . . "Matt," she said, "do you want a suggestion?"

He nodded.

"Kill the damned thing. Kill it dead. Arrange an accident. Discover that it has stopped working. Do *something* to put it out of business. Then, when it's done, invite the UN to come have a look, so there won't be any question about the identity of the body."

✠　　✠　　✠

Arky's fax was pumping out paper on a full-time basis. Sonny's Barbecue, Hooters, International House of Pancakes, Wendy's, McDonald's, Steak 'n' Ale, and a dozen other chains wanted to put restaurants on Johnson's Ridge. Sheraton, Hyatt, Holiday Inn, and Best Western had all submitted bids to build hotels. Albright REIT wanted to construct a shopping mall, and five oil companies were asking to install gas stations on the approach.

Some corporations were thinking about operations on the other side of the port. Lumber companies wanted to survey Eden's forests. Real-estate developers thought that the beach beneath the Horsehead needed a boardwalk and hot-dog stands. Requests for oil surveys were coming in already.

A group calling itself Kurds for a Better World had sent an application for land, informing Max that they hoped to send sixty thousand people to establish an independent colony in Eden. Representatives of displaced peoples from around the globe were making statements to journalists that implied there'd be more requests of the same nature. A Poor People's Crusade was forming in Washington and issuing demands.

"Maybe they're right," said April. "Maybe we should open it up and let everybody use it. What's the harm?"

Arky frowned. "What happens if we try to settle and the owners show up?"

"I don't think there *are* any owners," said Max. "I wouldn't want to put anybody in the Maze, but I think Eden is empty."

Arky's eyes flashed. "Maybe the owners like it empty. I would."

"And that's the real reason," said Max, "isn't it?"

"What is?"

"You don't want anybody using the land except your own people."

Arky started to deny the charge but only shrugged. "No one else will treat it appropriately," he said. "Turn it over to any of these other groups, and within a few years you'll have something that looks like downtown Fargo. At best." He was looking past Max, focusing on some distant place. "This is a new wilderness. We allowed strangers to settle our lands once before. I don't think we are going to make *that* mistake again."

"We're concerned about the port." Jason Fleury peered at Walker through horn-rimmed trifocals. There was something vaguely unkempt about the man, a quality which contributed to an overall sense of self-effacing honesty. Not at all what the chairman had expected in a presidential representative. "Chairman," he said, "I'm sure you understand that what you have here is of such significance that it has become, in effect, a national resource. Are you familiar with what has been happening at the UN?"

"I am. People there are arguing that the Roundhouse belongs to the world."

"And what is your reaction?"

"It is the property of the Mini Wakan Oyaté."

Fleury nodded sympathetically. "I know," he said. "I think I understand. But there are political realities involved. Tomorrow the United Nations will debate a motion that the U.S. be requested to declare Johnson's Ridge an international facility. Under ordinary circumstances, the idea would be laughable. But the Roundhouse is a unique global problem. People are terrified of what will happen if its technologies become generally available. Some regional economies are already in a shambles. For example, the auto parts industry in Morocco has collapsed. The price of oil has fallen through the floor, and clothing industries in every major western country are dying. *Dying,* Chairman." He dropped wearily back in his chair. "I don't have to tell you what's been happening to the stock market. Gold is way up, several major western banks have collapsed, capital investment everywhere is paralyzed. North Korea is threatening to nuke South Korea unless it gets access to the Roundhouse. We're in a pressure cooker, sir. And something is going to have to give."

An icy rain was rattling the windows. Outside, a school bus had pulled up, and children were hurrying into the building. It would be a tour group, kids trying to learn about their heritage. "We're not unaware of these problems," the chairman said. "It seems to me they result from widespread fear rather than from any tangible effect from Johnson's Ridge. However, we are prepared to help." He liked Fleury, who seemed a decent enough man. "We think what might be needed is a review board that would pass on any proposals to exploit Roundhouse technology or information. And we would be willing to enter discussions to set up such a board."

Fleury seemed pleased. "That kind of arrangement was our first thought, Chairman. But the truth is that we don't think it would work."

"May I ask why not?" The council had expected pressure to be brought to bear, but they had all thought their proposal was eminently reasonable.

"People don't trust their governments anymore," Fleury said. "They don't trust them to be honest or to be competent. I won't debate with you whether that's a fair assessment." A smile played at the corners of his lips. "The truth is, as long as the Roundhouse exists, people are going to be terrified. They will not believe that a board of review will be a sufficient safeguard. And, frankly, neither do we. Not over the long term. In any case, if people don't believe it will work, it won't work."

Walker felt a chill creeping into the room. "What, precisely, are you saying?"

"I'd like to speak off the record."

"Go ahead."

Fleury got up and closed the office door. "The artifact has to disappear. It has to be destroyed. What we propose to do is to buy it from you. We will offer a generous amount, more than you could have got from Wells's group. And then there will be an accident."

The chairman nodded. "There will be nothing left."

"Nothing."

"How do you propose to arrange *that?*"

Fleury didn't know. "Not my department," he said. "Probably blow it to hell and claim it was an intrinsic instability or an alien self-destruct device. They're imaginative." He looked unhappy. "You'll get a fair price. More than fair."

For a long time the chairman did not move. When at last he responded, his voice was heavy. "Some of our people," he said, "are preparing to move over there."

"Beg pardon?"

"We have been given a second chance, Mr. Fleury. A chance to remember who we used to be. That has nothing to do with government payments. Or reservations. Or a world so crowded that a man cannot breathe. No, we will keep Eden. And we will maintain control over the access point."

"You can't do that."

"Mr. Fleury, we cannot do otherwise."

✠   ✠   ✠

ANCIENT SHORES

The most lucrative segment of Old-Time Bill's broadcasting empire was the morning talk show officially designated *Project Forty* but referred to off camera as *Brunch with Jesus*. At about the time Chairman Walker was speaking with the President's representative, Bill was seated on the set of *Project Forty,* taping his show. He was surrounded by Volunteers, which was the official designation bestowed on all who joined him in working for the Lord.

The format was conversational, but there was nothing particularly noteworthy about the conversation, which ranged from wringing hands over the ejection of God from the schools to pointing out disturbing similarities between violence on TV and the Roman games. Midway through the show, Bill's special guest, an author who had written a book detailing how she had recovered from a life of alcohol abuse and free-wheeling sexual misbehavior, described an incident in which her twenty-year-old son had taken advantage of her insobriety to persuade her to cosign a loan for a new car. A few weeks later, the son had announced he could not keep up the payments.

Bill was always visibly overwhelmed by such tales. His viewers loved to watch his reactions to accounts of human weakness and gullibility. He had been known to pound his fist on the table, to splutter his indignation, sometimes to squeeze his eyes shut and simply sit with tears running down his cheeks. When the crisis of the narrative arrived, the producer dutifully switched to a full frontal close-up.

On this occasion, Bill merely sat, a man in pain. The viewers could see his large chest rising and falling. And then he waved his hand in front of his face as if to clear the air. "There are times," he said, "when I truly wonder why the Lord stays His hand. I would not second-guess the Almighty, but I can tell you that if I were running the world, things would be different. I would actively protect the innocent. And I would rain fire on the heads of sinners." He heaved a great sigh. "But our God is a merciful God. And a patient God."

If anyone in his vast listening audience thought there might have been a touch of blasphemy in the remark, it didn't show up in the mail.

Mike Swenson, who owned Mike's Supermarket in Fort Moxie, was a fan of the show. He heard the comment, and something about it unnerved him. He had to think about it a long time to realize why, and the reason didn't come to him until late that afternoon, when he was preparing the week's order.

Look out what you wish for.

They loved Governor Ed Pauling in North Dakota. He'd found ways to finance the schools and simultaneously reduce the sales tax a full point. He had reorganized the state government, reducing costs while he made it more effective. He had created jobs, had found federal funds to restore crumbling bridges and roads. And Ed had even helped the farmers. Under his direction, North Dakota had moved into the sunny uplands.

From Bismarck, however, he'd watched the storm building in Johnson's Ridge. The collapse of the financial markets had, within a matter of days, ruined the state's economy and undone everything he had accomplished over the last three years. Every major bank in North Dakota had been pushed to the edge. Several corporations were in trouble. And a lot of people to whom Ed owed favors were cashing them in. *Do something.*

He knew that a phone call from the President was inevitable. When it came, they got him out of a meeting with his economic advisors. He went back to his office, closed the doors, and turned off the tape machine. "Hello, Mr. President," he said. And, with no attempt to conceal the irony: "How are we doing?"

"Hello, Ed." If things were spiraling out of control, Matt Taylor would never let you know. In fact, the impression was that with Taylor, things could *never* spin out of control. It was the essence of the man's magic. "We're doing fine," the President said.

"Good." He let it hang there.

"Ed, I don't want a record made of this call."

"The machine's off."

"You and I haven't talked yet about the Roundhouse."

Ed laughed. "I saw a poll yesterday indicating that seventy percent of adult Americans can't find North Dakota on the map."

"That's about to change," said the President.

"I know."

"Ed, is there anything you can do to shut that monstrosity down?"

Had he been able to do so, it would have been done by now. "I'd love to," he said. "But it's on Sioux land. That's the closest thing there is to sacred territory out here. What we need is for you to declare a national emergency. Do that and I'll send in the Guard."

"That's a little ham-handed, Ed. The Sioux don't present any kind of military threat. They've committed no crime. I can't just send the troops in. They'd beat me to death with it next fall." He managed a deep-throated laugh that was half growl. "I can see the editorial cartoons now, with me as Custer."

Ed sympathized. "Have you tried to buy them out? They must have a price."

"I would have thought so. I'm beginning to wonder if our Native-American brothers haven't decided to get even with the United States." He fell momentarily silent. "Ed, do you have a suggestion?"

"If the public safety were at stake, we could seize the place. Of course, even then I'm not sure what we'd do with it. It's the goddamnedest hot potato I've ever heard of."

"I can't just trump something up," the President said. "The media won't let you get away with anything anymore."

"Maybe we'll get lucky," said Ed. "Maybe something will go wrong and you can move in."

Cass Deekin returned from Eden in a state of mind that could only be described as euphoric. He was a botanist and his pockets were filled with samples of flora from a non-terrestrial evolutionary system. He wasn't supposed to bring anything back, had in fact signed an agreement stipulating he would not, but the security guards couldn't be everywhere, and it was too good an opportunity to pass up.

He had just stepped off the grid with Juan Barcera, who was an astronomer from Caltech, and Janice Reshevsky, an Ivy League mathematician. An impassive Native American stood by the icons with a clipboard. He checked off their names. There had been twelve altogether on the other side of the port, of which Cass's group was the first to return.

He and his companions were talking excitedly about the

experience of actually *walking* on another world, barely able to contain their emotions, when the grid lit up.

The guard glanced at the icons, which Cass (like everyone else on the planet) knew controlled the transportation device.

He peered into the blossoming light, expecting to see more of his party appear. The guard said, under his breath, almost to himself, "Wrong icon."

Cass had no idea what he meant, but it was obvious something had happened. The guard's hand came to rest on, but did not raise, his weapon.

The golden light, which had been intensifying for several seconds, stabilized and began to fade.

No one was there.

But Cass felt something move deep inside his head, and his senses swam. The curved walls of the dome spoke to him; its unbroken space brought a tightness to his throat. He *flowed* into the air and rode the warm currents. They mingled with his blood, and he drifted past the long window, gasping great tears of joy, finding and filling the open passageway, pouring through it and racing toward a patch of daylight that opened out into an emptiness that swept on forever.

Cass was looking at the insides of his eyelids, feeling the world spin, feeling hands lifting his head. His face was cold and wet.

"Wait," said someone. "Don't try to move."

Another voice: "You'll be okay, Cass."

And someone shouting, "Over here."

Cass opened his eyes. The person speaking to him was the Native-American guard. "Take it easy," he said. "Help's coming."

"Thanks," he said. "I'm okay."

But the dark came again, crept over him like fog. He heard people talking somewhere. And he heard again the guard's startled reaction: *Wrong icon.*

✠ 24 ✠

*Cass Deekin's phantom may not have become more famous than Ham-
let's ghostly father. But it sure as hell scared the pants off a lot more people.*

—Mike Tower, *Chicago Tribune*

Cass Deekin knew his colleagues would be waiting to hear him talk
about Eden. But he was still shaken. He'd flown back to
Chicago, unable to sleep either on the plane or in his bed.
He'd left lights on in the house all night. And he had suffered a series of bad dreams.

In the morning he called in sick, and then, feeling the
need for company, he went down to Minny's Cafe for breakfast, and then to the Lisle Public Library.

At a little after eleven he showed up at the Collandar Bar
and Grill. Cass didn't particularly like to drink because he
put on weight too easily. But this was a special occasion.

He collected a beer and soon struck up a conversation
with a salesman from the Chevrolet dealership across the
street. The salesman was middle-aged, personable, not quite
able to pull back from his marketing persona. But that was
okay; Cass didn't mind listening to chatter today.

The salesman was talking about the current uncertainty

in the industry and simultaneously extolling the pleasures of cruising America's back roads. "Let me tell ya," he said with a grin, "even if they could do that *Star Trek* thing and walk into a booth here and come out in Bismarck, it'll never replace a Blazer. I don't care what anybody says."

After a while Cass became aware that the salesman was watching him closely. "You all right, buddy?" he asked. His name was Harvey, and the smile had been replaced by a frown.

"Yes," said Cass. "I'm fine."

"You sure? You look a little out of it."

That was all it took. Cass told his story, described his flight through the dome in exquisite detail, his sense of having been *absorbed* by something, his conviction (now that he had had time to think about it) that he had been invaded. "Whatever it was," he whispered, his eyes wide, "it was invisible."

The salesman nodded. "Well," he said, looking at his watch, "got to go."

"It was *there*," Cass went on. "God help me, it came through the port. The guard knew it, but he wouldn't say anything." He knocked over his glass. "Listen, I know how this sounds. But it's true. They've turned something loose up there."

Ten minutes later a reporter was trying to interview him. By then Cass had decided to say nothing further. It was, of course, too late.

Sioux Falls, SD, Mar. 27 (Reuters)—
     Police captured accused hit man Carmine (The Creep) Malacci outside a motel near here today. Malacci, who has been the subject of a nationwide hunt

after the assassination of a federal judge in Milwaukee, was taken after his whereabouts were tipped to police by local residents who recognized his picture from the television series *Inside Edition*. Malacci was said to have been on his way to Johnson's Ridge, North Dakota, where he hoped to escape through the port into Eden.

Police indicated he offered no resistance. He was arrested as he returned from having breakfast at a pancake house. . . .

Curt Hollis was walking past a flatcar loaded with lumber. He was headed toward the depot, about two miles away, when the wind spoke.

He had been working with J. J. Bender, the train dispatcher, opening boxcars for customs inspection. They'd finished the train, which was 186 cars long, and had just started back. Bender and the customs inspector were ahead of him, maybe forty yards or so, hands shoved into their pockets, clipboards trapped against their sides.

Bender and the inspector kept close together, their heads bent into the wind, which was out of the northwest. They were all walking on the east side of the train, using the cars for shelter. Curt didn't mind the weather as much as the others. Bender and the customs inspector had spent most of their lives indoors. Curt, on the other hand, had done track work and construction jobs, had loaded tractor-trailers and laid roads. His face had turned to leather when he was still in his early thirties.

He was almost seventy now, and his body was starting to break down. Shoulders, knees, and hips ached all the time. He had diabetes and occasional chest pains. But he was afraid to see a doctor.

He slogged steadily through the snow. There would be more work for him when they got back to the depot. He was therefore content to dawdle while the others moved quickly ahead. Curt liked the long walks back after they'd cleared the train. It was late afternoon, and the sun was sinking. A couple of diesels waited on a parallel track to be exported. Between cars, he caught glimpses of Route 75. A pickup was headed north toward the border.

Curt was alone now. His kids had long since gone to live in California and Arizona. Jeannie, who had been his wife for thirty-seven years, had died in the spring.

The wind blew through the twilight. It lifted the tags on the lumber loads and peppered the boxes with dust. And it sighed his name.

Curt.

He stopped and looked at the gray sky.

His companions trudged resolutely ahead. A blue jay perched atop a tanker, watching him.

Curt.

Clearer that time. A cold breeze touched his face.

Out on Route 75, a tractor-trailer roared past, headed south, changing gears. Other than the customs inspector and the dispatcher, there was no one in sight. The cars were squat and heavy and rusting in the dying light.

"Is someone there?" he asked.

The blue jay leaped away at the sound and tracked through the sky, headed southeast. He watched until it disappeared.

Curt.

It was a whisper, a distant sigh.

Puzzled, almost frightened, he stopped. Ahead, the customs inspector had also stopped and was looking back at him.

There was no one hiding on the other side of the train. No one in the empty boxcar beside him. No one anywhere other than the two people steadily drawing farther away.

His heart pumped.

His vision shifted, blurred, cleared. He looked down on the boxcar from *above*.

And on himself.

If he had been afraid, the fear subsided, drained away. He felt the calmness and indifference of the sky. He saw without emotion his own image, lying on the ground.

And he felt Jeannie's presence. Young and laughing and fearless, as she had been before the long winters and the money problems had beaten much of it out of her. Her eyes were bright and she leaned toward him.

Then the light changed, dimmed, and he saw it was Bender kneeling beside him. The old sense of loss returned.

"Curt? What happened?"

He didn't know. "Got sick," he said. And then: "I heard my name."

"What? Listen, just lie quiet. I'll call the depot. Get a car out here."

"There's something here," Curt said, struggling with Bender.

"He's right," said the customs inspector, her eyes wide. "I heard it, too."

The deer had begun to bleed.

Jack McGuigan eased his snomobile past a screen of heavy shrubbery and looked down the trail. Bright red drops glistened on the light snow.

He could, of course, have killed the animal hours ago, but Jack enjoyed tracking. Run it down by inches. Give the beast a fair chance. But it wasn't running anymore. The prints were no longer clean and precise. The front edges were scuffed, and there were marks in the snow indicating uncertainty and, occasionally, that it had stumbled.

He caught glimpses of the animal frequently now. It was getting weaker, approaching exhaustion. He stopped and took off his ski mask and pulled a sandwich out of his utility pouch. Give it time. It didn't really matter at this stage. No need to hurry.

He poured coffee from his thermos.

The woods were full of birds today. Jack *loved* the creatures of the forest. He loved the smell of the woods and the sky wrapped over the trees and the wind moving through the branches and the clean oiled clack of a rifle bolt being slid home to remind you how alone you were. It was easy to lose yourself out here, to forget the concrete and the kids.

At home in God's woods. That was how a man was supposed to live.

Sometimes, toward the end of a hunt, he almost came to feel guilty. The prints looked pitiful. He wondered, as he had many times before, about the almost mystical connection between hunter and prey. No anger. No animosity. The buck is resigned, will accept the final round while trying to scramble from its knees, but it will know who he is, and it also will feel the bond, the ineffable connection tracking back to the other side of the ice age.

Jack did not pretend to understand it. Like the buck, he simply accepted it. In his compassion, he drank slowly. When he was done, he folded the cellophane bag in which his sandwich had been wrapped and pushed it carefully into his pouch. (He had seen people drop trash in the woods from time to time, and nothing enraged Jack like litterers. Last year, about this time, he had come upon one, a guy leaving a trail of beer cans, and he'd left him bleeding by his campfire.)

Time to end it.

The moment had come, and Jack would finish it, as he always did, with a single shot.

"I'm coming," he said, his ritualistic response to the final phase. He climbed onto the snowmobile, turned the ignition key, and felt the surge of power through his loins. Startled birds launched themselves into the wind.

He rolled back onto the trail, running behind the prints. Here the animal had paused and slipped into the under-brush. There it had scrambled down a steep slope. He had to go almost a mile out of his way to get to the bottom. Minutes later he followed it across a frozen stream.

It was an eight-point buck, and when he finally came upon it, the creature was trying to hide in thick snow-covered vegetation. But of course it could not conceal its tracks. He unsnapped his rifle and inserted a cartridge. Their eyes locked, a final moment of mutual recognition, and it tried weakly to back away.

Jack raised his weapon, put the animal's heart in his sight, and squeezed the trigger. The shot ricocheted through the woods. Surprise flickered in the buck's eyes. The trees came alive, and a storm of birds fled into the sky. Blood appeared on the buck's breast.

The animal's front legs sagged. It went down, spasmed and relaxed.

He stood enjoying the primal beauty of the scene, waiting for the quivering to stop. When it did, and the deer lay still, he turned back to the snowmobile for the sheet of plastic in which he would wrap the carcass. In that moment something dark passed across the sun.

He looked up, expecting to see a cloud. But the sky

between the tangle of branches was hard and white. He retrieved his plastic, and the snow crunched under his boots while he spread it out beside the carcass and smoothed it down. The animal had got tangled up in a bush, and he had to break off a few branches to get hold of the front legs.

The temperature began to drop.

He glanced nervously back along the trail to the point at which it curved out of sight, roughly thirty yards away. And ahead almost as far, where it topped a low hill.

A gust of wind shook the trees. Deep in his psyche, far back in the emotional tangles among which the real Jack McGuigan lived, something stirred. Some *thing* that was not part of him.

And he felt waves of anger.

Crazy.

Birds and small game were everywhere. A warm air current touched him. The distant rumble of traffic, out on the highway, merged with the pristine silence. He grew disconnected, detached. And he was watching with sudden rage the deer and the snowmobile and a standing figure that could only have been himself.

He felt the treetops, warm and alive, under his hand. They shook. Snow and broken twigs rained down.

Something moved among the branches. The sunlight changed, shifted, coruscated. Someone was here with him. He lifted his weapon and turned to look behind him. The air was getting warmer, and the deer's blood was bright on the snow.

"It's a nightmare," Taylor said. He muted the sound and pushed back in his chair.

Tony Peters massaged the place over his left eye where his migraines always started.

The television images were from the UN, where a demand for international access to the Roundhouse was about to be presented to the Security Council. "Where," the President said gloomily, "we will have to veto the damned thing."

Peters thought they could ride out the storm, and he knew his role now was to reassure the President, to prevent precipitate action. "They all know," he said, "that you can't just give away sovereign territory. We couldn't do it if we wanted to. It's private property."

Taylor laughed. "Don't know," he said. "There's plenty of precedent for giving away private property. But it really doesn't matter. It would be *wrong*."

"It would also be political suicide."

"So you think all that's happening here is that we're being sent a message?"

"No. Of course not. Everybody's scared. But there are still a lot of people who wouldn't want to miss a chance to embarrass us."

"They're doing a hell of a good job of it." The President refilled his sherry glass and offered the bottle.

Peters shook his head.

"Tony, who would have believed there's oil in paradise?" Matt Taylor sighed. "We just don't get a break."

"It shouldn't matter," the aide said. "How much oil can you throw into the world market bringing it through that whatsis one barrel at a time?"

That was a point, and the President seemed happy for that small bit of good news. "But it will matter," he said. "Eventually. If there's a lot of the stuff out there, we'll find a way to get it back. And everybody knows it. But that isn't really the problem, is it?"

"No."

Taylor understood there was more at stake here than economics and elections. Incredibly, a stairway into the sky had opened. He hardly dared consider the implications. He did not want to close it down. The man who did that would not look good a century or two from now. And Matt Taylor, like any President, was determined that history think well of him. He had believed attaining the White House would be enough. But once in the door, he began to envy Washington, Lincoln, the Roosevelts, and Truman. Theirs was a rank he had thought would be denied him because greatness is possible only in crisis. Every administration had its problems, but until the Roundhouse surfaced, his had been relatively mundane: no government to establish, no Union to save, no Hitler to oppose.

Now the crisis was here. In spades. And he had only to choose the right course.

What in hell *was* the right course?

"Tony," he said, "I think we've had enough. The Sioux won't cooperate, so we're going to have to find another way to close the operation down. I don't care what it takes, but I am not going to let this country come apart on my watch."

Walhalla, ND, Mar. 27 (AP)—

A North Dakota man died this morning when he ran out of the woods off Route 32 south of here, directly into the path of a moving van. The victim was John L. McGuigan of Fort Moxie, who was apparently hunting out of season. His snowmobile was found abandoned about a mile away. It was reported to be in good working order. Police have not explained why he left the snowmobile or why he was running. An investigation is continuing.

McGuigan is survived by his wife, Jane, and two children.

"Dr. Deekin, are you absolutely certain about what you saw?"

Cass looked into the TV cameras. "Yes," he said. "Absolutely."

"Why haven't the people at Johnson's Ridge said anything about this? Is there a cover-up?"

Deekin thought it over. "I don't think so," he said. "I mean, this thing, whatever it was, was *invisible*. They may not know it exists."

"So what you're saying is that something that cannot be seen came through the port."

"I believe so."

"And is now loose in North Dakota."

"Yes. I would think that is true."

The interviewer turned toward the camera. "So we may have an invisible visitor. We'll be back in a minute to try to determine whether there's a connection between Dr. Deekin's experience, the reports today of a disembodied voice at a remote railroad terminal, and the mysterious death of a hunter near Johnson's Ridge."

✠ 25 ✠

It is I who travel in the winds,
It is I who whisper in the breeze.

—Ojibwa poem

Excerpt from the *Newshour with Jim Lehrer*, March 28. Conversation with Doctor Edward Bannerman, of the Institute for Advanced Study, on the subject of the "Dakota port," with Jim Lehrer. Dr. Bannerman is a two-time Nobel prize-winning physicist.

Bannerman: It might actually be what physicists call a bridge, which is to say a connection between separate universes. The Horsehead Nebula in the skies of Eden, for example, need not be *our* Horsehead at all. We don't really know. And, to be quite honest, we may never know the truth of any of this. Incidentally, I should observe that were this to be the case, those people who are hoping to use this technology to travel from San Francisco to New York are going to be disappointed.
Lehrer: They will not arrive in New York?

Bannerman: Oh, I suspect they would. But it wouldn't be *our* New York.

Jeri Tully was eight years old. Mentally, she was about three, and the experts cautioned her parents against hoping for much improvement. No one knew what had gone wrong with Jeri. There was no history of mental defects on either side of her family and no apparent cause. She had two younger brothers, both of whom were quite normal.

Her father was a border patrolman, her mother a former legal secretary who had given up all hope of a career when she followed her husband to Fort Moxie.

Jeri went to school in Walhalla, which had the only local special-education class. She enjoyed school, where she made numerous friends, and where everyone seemed to make a fuss over her. Mornings in the Tully household were underscored by Jeri's enthusiasm to get moving.

Walhalla was thirty-five miles away. The family had an arrangement with the school district, which was spread out over too vast an area to operate buses for the special-ed kids: The Tullys provided their own transportation, and the district absorbed the expenses.

Jeri's mother, June, had actually grown to enjoy the twice-daily round trip. The child loved to ride, and she was never happier than when in the car. The other half of the drive, when June was alone, served as quiet time, when she could just watch the long fields roll by or plug an audio book into the sound system.

Curt Hollis's adventure had taken place on a Thursday. Jeri's father worked the midnight shift the following night, and his wife was waiting for him with French toast, bacon, and coffee when he got home in the morning. While they were eating breakfast, an odd thing happened. For the only time in her life, Jeri wandered away from home. It seemed, later, that she had decided to go to school and, having no concept of distance, or of the day (it was Saturday), had decided to walk.

Unseen by anyone except her two-year-old brother, she put on her overshoes and her coat, let herself out through the porch door, walked up to Route 11, and turned right. Her house was on the extreme western edge of town, so she was past the demolished Tastee–Freez and across the interstate overpass within minutes. The temperature was still in the teens.

Three-quarters of a mile outside Fort Moxie, Route 11 curves sharply south and then almost immediately veers west again. Had the road been free of snow, Jeri would probably have stayed with it and been picked up within a few minutes. But a light snowfall had dusted the two-lane. Jeri wasn't used to paying attention to details, and at the first bend she walked straight off the highway. When, a few minutes later, the snow got deeper, she angled right and got still farther from the road.

Jeri's parents had by then discovered she was missing. A frightened search was just getting under way, but it was limited to within a block or so of her home.

Jim Stuyvesant, the editor and publisher of the *Fort Moxie News*, was on his way to the Roundhouse. The story that an apparition had come through from the other side was going to be denied that morning in a press conference, and Jim planned to be there. He was just west of town when he saw movement out on Josh McKenzie's land to his right. A snow devil was gliding back and forth in a curiously regular fashion. The snow devil was a perfect whirlpool, narrow at the base, wide at the top. Usually these things were blurred around the edges; they possessed an indefiniteness, and they floated erratically across the plain. But *this* one looked almost solid, and it moved patiently back and forth along the same course.

Stuyvesant stopped to watch.

It was almost hypnotic. A stiff wind rocked the car, enough to blow the snow devil to pieces. But it remained intact.

Stuyvesant never traveled without his video camera, which he had used on several occasions to get footage he'd subsequently sold to *Ben at Ten* or to one of the other local TV news shows. (He had, for example, got superb footage of the Thanksgiving Day pileup on I–29 and the blockade of imported beef at the border by angry ranchers last summer.) The snow devil continued to glide back and forth in its slow, unwavering pattern. He turned on the camera, walked a few steps into the field, and started to tape.

He used the zoom lens and got a couple of minutes' worth of pictures before the whirlwind seemed to pause.

It started toward him.

He kept filming.

It approached at a constant pace. There was something odd in its manner, something almost deliberate.

The crosswind ripped at his jacket but didn't seem to have any effect on the snow devil. Stuyvesant's instincts began to sound warnings, and he took a step back toward the car.

It stopped.

Amazing. As if it had responded to him.

He stood, uncertain how to proceed. The whirlwind began to move again, laterally, then retreated a short distance and came forward to its previous position.

He was watching it through the camera lens. The red indicator lamp glowed at the bottom of the picture.

You're waiting for me.

It approached again, and the wind tugged at his collar and his hair.

He took a step forward. And it retreated.

Like everyone else in the Fort Moxie area, Stuyvesant had been deluged with fantastic tales and theories since the Roundhouse had been uncovered. Now, without prompting, he wondered whether a completely unknown type of life form existed on the prairie and was revealing itself to him. The notion forced him to laugh. It also forced him to decide what he really believed.

He started forward.

It withdrew again.

He kept going. The snow got deeper, filled his shoes and froze his ankles.

The snow devil continued to back away. He hoped he was getting the effect on camera.

It whirled and glittered in the sun, maintaining the distance between them. He slowed, and it slowed.

Another car was pulling off the highway. He wondered how he would explain this, and immediately visualized next week's headline in the *News:* "Mad Editor Put Under Guard."

But it was a hunt without a point. The fields went on, all the way to Winnipeg. Far enough, he decided. "Sorry," he said aloud. "This is as far as I go."

And the thing withdrew another sixty or so yards. And collapsed.

When it did, it left something dark lying in the snow.

Jeri Tully.

That was the day Stuyvesant got religion. The story that actually appeared in the *Fort Moxie News* would be a truncated version of the truth.

✠   ✠   ✠

Unfortunately, there was no ready-made church at hand in Fort Moxie. But the Lord provides, and in this case He provided Kor Yensen. Kor was going to Arizona to move in with his son and daughter-in-law on a trial basis. But he was reluctant to dispose of his oversized house until he saw how things went. The opportunity to rent it to the TV preacher on a short-term basis arrived at precisely the right moment. It never occurred to him that the action would cause a permanent rift with his neighbors, who were mostly Methodists and Lutherans, and who preferred a more sedate form of worship than the hosannahs and oratorical thunder provided by Old-Time Bill.

In order to fulfill its function, Kor's house needed some renovation. The Volunteers tore out three walls to get adequate meeting space. (They posted bond with Kor, promising to restore everything.) They installed a backdrop of dark-stained paneled walls and crowded bookshelves to maintain Bill's signature atmosphere. They put in an organ and a sound stage and installed state-of-the-art communication equipment. Two days after their arrival, and just in time for the regular Saturday night service, the Backcountry Church was ready to go.

At precisely 7:00 P.M. local time, Bill's exuberant theme music, "'Tis the Old-Time Religion," rocked the house, and Bill himself, about thirty bars in, walked out in front of the cameras and welcomed the vast television audience to Fort Moxie. He explained that the Volunteers had come to do battle with the devil, and he led a packed house of eighteen (which, through the wonders of electronic enhancement, sounded like several hundred) in a thundering rendition of "A Mighty Fortress Is Our God." The choir, whose location in an upstairs bedroom was disguised by drapes and handrails, joined in, and everybody got into the mood very quickly.

"Brothers and sisters," Bill said, raising his hands, "you may wonder why the Volunteers have come to the Dakota border. Why many of us felt the Lord wanted us here.

"Tonight we are in the shadow of Johnson's Ridge." He looked beyond the camera lenses, out into living rooms around the country, where the believers were gathered. People at home always said that they thought he was talking directly *to* them. "Only a few miles from here, scientists have opened their port to another—" He paused, drawing out the moment. "—place.

"Another place.

"And what kind of place have they found? They speak of trees and pools, of white blossoms and harmless creatures, of beautiful skies and warm sunlight. They speak in terms that are very familiar to anyone who has looked at Genesis." He smiled. "The scientists, of course, don't realize this. They don't recognize the place because they are too much of *this* world.

"But *we* know where they are, brothers and sisters."

"Amen," chanted his audience.

A reporter from the *Winnipeg Free Press*, Alma Kinyata, cornered him after the service. "Reverend Addison," she asked, "do you really believe that we've discovered Paradise?"

They were in his office, upstairs at the back of the converted church. It was spartan by any measure and particularly humble when contrasted against the power and influence of its occupant. He'd brought in a desk and a couple of chairs. Copies of the Bible, Metcalf's *The Divine Will*, and the *Oxford Theological Studies* stood between marble bookends. A picture of Addison's mother hung on the wall.

"Yes," he said, "I honestly believe we have. There is no way to know for certain, although I think that if I were to go there, I could give you a definitive answer."

Alma felt good about this one. He was responsive, and it was going to be a solid story. "Are you planning to go up there? To Eden?"

"No," he said. "I will not set foot in the Garden. It is forbidden to mortal man."

"You say you would know Paradise if you saw it?"

"Oh, yes. Anyone would."

"But the people who have been there haven't drawn that conclusion."

"I mean, any *Christian*. I'm sorry, I tend to think in terms of believers."

"*How* would you know?"

Addison's eyelids fluttered. "Paradise partakes of the divine essence. Adam and Eve were sent packing early. That was a smart move, if I may say." He grinned, rather like a large, friendly dog. "It kept the Garden unsullied. Pure. Oh, yes, that place is sacred, and I think anyone who pays attention to the welfare of his soul would recognize that fact immediately. You will recall the angel."

"The angel?"

"Yes. 'And he set an angel with a flaming sword.' I can tell you *I* wouldn't want to be among those who have trespassed into the things of God."

Alma left convinced that Addison didn't believe a word of it. But she got her story and scared the devil out of a substantial portion of the countryside.

And she was, by the way, wrong about Bill. He believed every word.

Andrea Hawk gave Max a hand with the travel kit and then stood aside.

The video record of the rings icon had revealed a wall

with a long window. The window was dark. The wall was plain. They knew nothing else about the last of the possible destinations tied into the Roundhouse.

Somehow the place had looked chilly, so they were all warmly dressed. "You know," said Arky, "it's just a matter of time before we get stuck out there somewhere."

"That's right," said Andrea. "We should devise a test. A way to make sure we can get home."

"If you can think of a way to do it," said April, "set something up." Max knew she had no intention of waiting around. She wanted to look at the last of the places that could be reached from the Roundhouse; and he knew she would go on from there to Eden and begin exploring *its* connections. Eventually, he believed, they would lose her.

Andrea stood by the icons while April, Max, and Arky took their places on the grid. "Ready to move out," said April.

She pressed the rings. "Usual routine," said Max, waving a spade. "We'll check the return capability before we do anything." And to Andrea: "We'll send the spade back. If it doesn't work, we'll post a message."

Andrea nodded.

Max tried to relax. He closed his eyes against the coming light and took a deep breath. That was probably what saved his life.

He'd discovered there was less vertigo if he closed his eyes. He watched the familiar glow against the inside of his lids, felt the unsettling lack of physical reality, as if he himself no longer quite existed. Then the light died, weight came back, his body came back.

And he couldn't breathe.

A wall of cold hit him and he went down onto a grid. His ears roared and his heart pounded.

Vacuum. They'd materialized in a vacuum.

April's fingers clawed at him. She staggered away, off the grid. He went after her.

They were in a long, cylindrical chamber filled with machines. The black panel they'd seen in the video *was* a window, the night beyond it unbroken by any star.

Several windows along the opposite wall admitted the only illumination: light from an enormous elliptical galaxy. Even in his terror, Max was awestruck by the majesty of the scene.

Arky stumbled through the silver glow to the rear of the transportation device, which was supported by a post like the one in Eden. From his angle, Max could see two columns of icons.

Arky looked at the icons and caught Max's eye. Max saw reproach in the distorted features. And something else.

Now.

Max read the tortured stare.

Go.

The dark eyes flicked to the grid. Max seized April while Arky pressed the icon display. One of the symbols lit up, but his fingers stuck and would not come loose.

The terrible cold pushed what air Max had left out of his lungs. The world was slipping away, fading, and he just wanted it to be over.

But April's hand held onto him. Drew him back. He staggered onto the grid, and she collapsed behind him.

Arky was on his knees, watching them.

The chamber began to fade, and Max would have screamed against the coming light if he could.

The tape, played on NBC's *Counterpoint*, had caught everything. A nationwide audience watched the eerie column of snow move with purpose across its screens. If any program in the history of television had been designed to terrify its audience, this was it.

"And the child," asked the moderator gently, "was found in the field when you drove this thing away?"

"I don't think that's exactly what happened," said Stuyvesant.

"What exactly *did* happen, Jim?"

"It was more like it was trying to show me where the child was."

The moderator nodded. "Can we run that last portion again, Phil?"

They watched the whirling snow systematically retreat and pause and advance and retreat again. Unfortunately, the audience could not see the connection with the movements of the man holding the camera, but they saw enough.

"Is it true," asked the moderator, "that Jeri never before did anything like this?"

"That's what her folks say. If they say it, I'm sure it's so."

"Why do you think she wandered off this time?"

"Don't know. I guess it just happened."

"Jim, is there any truth to the rumor that she was *lured?* That this thing was trying to get her away from the town?"

"I don't think so," Stuyvesant said.

The cameras moved in for a close-up of the moderator, who turned a quizzical expression to the audience.

✠ 26 ✠

O my son, farewell!
You have gone beyond the great river—

—Blackfoot poem

If, *during that period, a true injustice was committed against any of* the persons living in and around Fort Moxie, the victim was Jeri Tully. Jeri also received a gift of inestimable value, and the gift and the injustice were one and the same.

For reasons unknown to the corps of specialists who had examined her, Jeri had never grown properly, and her skull had never become large enough to house her brain. Consequently, the child had suffered not only a diminution in height but retardation as well. Her world was a confused jumble, a place that was arbitrary and unpredictable, in which the principle of causality seemed scarcely to operate at all.

Jeri's pleasures were limited largely to tactile experiences: her mother's smile, an astronaut doll to which she had become particularly attached, her younger brothers, and (on Friday nights) pizza. She had little interest in television, nor was she able to participate in the games normal children might play. She was delighted when a visitor paid attention to her. And she enjoyed *Star Wars* films, although only in theaters.

June Tully sensed a change in her child after Jim Stuyvesant brought her home on that cold April day. But she could not pin it down. The feeling was so ephemeral that she never mentioned it to her husband.

Jeri, by the nature of her misfortune, would never really grasp her deficiencies, and therefore they could give her no pain. This simple view provided unlimited consolation to her family. But something unique had happened to her when she sank half frozen into the snow off Route 11. She was frightened, but not for her life, because she did not understand danger. She was frightened because she did not know where she was, where her home was. And she could not stop the cold.

Suddenly something had invaded her world. Her mind opened, not unlike a blossom directed toward the sun. She had risen into the sky and ridden the wind, had known a flood of joy unlike anything she'd experienced before. She had reached far beyond her own pale limitations.

During those few moments, Jeri understood the interplay between wind and heat and the tension between open sky and swollen clouds. She soared and dipped above the land, as if she were herself a storm, a thing made equally of sunlight and snow and high winds.

For the rest of her life, her crippled brain would cling to the memory of the sky, of the time when the darkness and the chaos and the weakness had receded. When Jeri had known what it was to be godlike.

Adam and Max went back in pressure suits to retrieve Arky's body. They said good-bye to him two days later in a quiet Catholic ceremony at the reservation chapel. The priest, who was from Devil's Lake, said the ancient words of farewell in the Sioux tongue.

The mourners were equally divided between Native Americans and their friends. There were a substantial number of attractive young women, and nine members of a teenage basketball team for which Arky had been an assistant coach.

Max was informed that, as one of the beneficiaries of Arky's sacrifice, he would be expected to say a few words recounting the event. So he used a notebook to record his thoughts. But when the time actually came to speak, the notebook, which was in his pocket, seemed a long way off. It embarrassed him to have anyone think he could not, without help, describe his feeling for the man who had saved his life. "Arky did not know April or me very well," he said, speaking from the front of the chapel. "A few months ago we were strangers.

"Today she and I are here not only because of his courage but also because under extreme conditions he kept his head. He must have known he could not save himself. So he devoted himself to saving us."

Max took a deep breath. His audience leaned forward attentively. "When I first visited his office, I noticed that he kept a bow in a prominent place on the wall. It was his father's, he explained. I could see his pride. The bow is a warrior's weapon. *My* father was also a warrior. And he would have been proud to claim such a son." Max's voice shook. He saw again the little girl in the aircraft window.

He had thought that memory had been laid to rest when he'd gone through the port after April. But he understood in the cold clarity of that moment that it would always be with him.

It is the custom among the tribes of the Dakotas and the Northwest at such times to deemphasize their sense of loss. Rather than mourn, they celebrate the life and accomplishments of the spirit that had taken flesh and lived temporarily among them. Part of that celebration is a ritualized gift-giving by members of the family.

At the end of the ceremony, Max was surprised to be called forward by a teenager who identified himself as Arky's brother. "We have something for you," the boy said.

While an expectant stir ran through the party, he produced a long, narrow box wrapped in hand-woven fabric. Max thanked him and opened the package. It was the bow.

"I can't take this," Max protested.

James Walker stood and turned so the crowd could hear him. "In your own words," he said, "the bow is a warrior's weapon."

Everyone cheered.

"I'm no warrior," Max said. "I'm a businessman."

The tribal chairman smiled. "You have a warrior's spirit, Collingwood. Arky gave his life for you, and it is the family's decision you should have the bow." When Max still hesitated, he added, "He would wish that it find its home with you."

One of the students showed the visitor in, looked inquisitively at April, and withdrew.

She rose and extended her hand. "Mr. Asquith?"

"Pleased to meet you, Dr. Cannon." Asquith's grip was uncertain. He seized her by her fingers. "I don't know whether you've heard of me."

The tone carried just enough self-deprecation to imply that Asquith understood he was in fact a person of no small significance. He was, of course, Walter Asquith, two-time Pulitzer prize–winning critic, essayist, poet, and novelist, best known for a series of scathing social commentaries, the most recent of which, *Late News from Babylon,* had topped the *New York Times* best-seller list for six months. April remembered from her college years a guest instructor who was at the end of a long career as an editor and writer. They'd been assigned Asquith's *Marooned in Barbary,* a collection of blistering attacks on various literary personages and efforts, in one of which the instructor surfaced briefly to take an arrow between the eyes from the great man. He had proudly pointed out the page and line to his students, and April understood that the assault had been the apex of his career. Rather like being Dante's barber.

"I know of your work, Mr. Asquith," she said. "What can I do for you?"

He was big, round-shouldered, meaty. His hair was white and combed over a bald spot. He spoke in short, authoritative bursts and would, April thought, have made a good judge.

"I want to spend some time in Eden," he said.

April wrote down the scheduler's phone number and passed it over to him. "They'll be happy to put you on the list."

"No, I don't think you understand. I've already been there. I want to go back. To be honest, I'd like to pitch a tent and move in. For a while."

April glanced quite deliberately at her watch. She was no longer impressed by credentials. An outrageous request was outrageous, whatever its source. "I'm sorry, Mr. Asquith. I don't think we can permit—"

"Dr. Cannon, I'm aware of the scientific significance of the Roundhouse. I wonder whether *you* grasp the psychological and philosophical implications. The slow, generally upward course of the human race has forked. We have plunged into a broad forest. The world as we know it is waiting for something to happen. But it is uncertain what that something will be. That is why the world's financial markets are in chaos; why demonstrators are in front of the White House; why the United Nations is locked in its most acrimonious debate in a decade. When you stepped across the gulf a couple of weeks ago into whatever place that was, you began a new era.

"Someone needs to record all this. To tie the daily events to their historical and literary significance. We used to think that if the twentieth century would be remembered for any single moment, it would be the moon landing. But—" He looked steadily at her. "The moon landing is small potatoes, Dr. Cannon. The decisive moment, not of the century but of recorded history, is *now*. I know you have begun to bring in experts, mathematicians, geologists, astronomers, and whatnot. And that is all to the good. We need to do that. But we also need someone whose sole function will be to consider the *meaning* of what is happening here. To stand back while others measure and weigh and speculate, to apply these events against the progress of the human spirit." He placed his hands together and laid his chin against them. "I think that I am uniquely qualified for such a role. I have, in fact, already compiled extensive notes. And I would be honored to be allowed to participate."

Asquith had a point, April thought. "What did you have in mind? A series of news reports?"

"Oh, no," he said. "Nothing like that. I would want to do a major work. My magnum opus."

"Let me think about it," she said. "I'll get back to you."

"The working title would be 'Ancient Shores.'" He gave her a card. "We should start without delay."

He let himself out. April decided she would do it. That kind of publicity couldn't hurt them. But she'd run it past Max first.

She picked up her messages. Peg Moll, their scheduler and event coordinator, had received a call from a man identifying himself as the agent for Shaggy Dog. The rap group wanted to do a concert on Johnson's Ridge. "They're promising to sell two hundred thousand tickets," Peg said.

When the phone rang, Max and April were discussing plans to send a repair crew into the chamber that had taken Arky's life. (Already it had outdistanced Eden as the place that researchers most wanted to visit.)

April picked it up, listened for a minute, and said, "Thanks." She replaced the receiver and turned to Max. "There are some investors," she said, "forming a corporation to control travel to all the worlds connected to the Roundhouse. They've offered three-quarters of a billion dollars for exclusive rights."

"The price is going up," said Max.

"They call themselves Celestial Tours." She smiled sadly.

Detroit, Apr. 1 (Reuters)—

The *Detroit Free Press* today reported that the Detroit Lions may move to Fargo, North Dakota. According to unnamed sources, the club has agreed to a deal with Manuel Corazon, CEO of Prairie Industries, and the sale will be announced tomorrow. Pending approval by the rest of the league, the team would move next year and become known as the Fargo Visitors.

Jack McDevitt

Prairie Industries is a conglomerate specializing primarily in the manufacture of agricultural equipment.

Larry King special on TNT, April 1. Guest: Dmitri Polkaevich, winner of the Pulitzer prize for *Iron Dreams*, a definitive history of the USSR. Topic: the new Russian revolution. (Suggested by then-current fears that a right-wing Russian coup was imminent.)

King: You don't feel, then, that a resurgence of nationalism is likely?

Polkaevich: The world is changing very rapidly, Larry. No, it is true there are those in Russia who would give us their own peculiar brand of fascism, if they could. Just as there are those who would return to Lenin. But the tide of history is running against them all.

King: Well, I'm happy to hear it. If I may ask before we go to the phones, where is the tide of history taking us?

Polkaevich: Predicting the future is a dangerous enterprise.

King: Yes. But you just implied—

Polkaevich: That some tendencies are evident. Larry, you have of course been following the events along the Canadian border?

King: The Roundhouse? *(Smiles)* I wouldn't know how to get away from them. In fact, we'll be doing a show from there next week.

Polkaevich: The bridge to the stars is a Rubicon.

King: For Russian politicians?

Polkaevich: Oh, yes. And for the Armenians. And the Chinese. Larry, I no longer think of myself as a Muscovite. Or even as a Russian. No. You and I are citizens of Earth. The era of national borders, of governments that divide us with their petty squabbles, is passing into history.

King: Governments are becoming obsolete?

Polkaevich: Individual governments, yes. I think we will soon see a world body. Unfortunately, the transition period will be a dangerous time. People tend to disparage their governments, but they will fight to the death to keep them. And there is good reason for their fears. If a world government becomes oppressive, where does one flee? Although now perhaps we have an answer to that problem. *(Chuckles)*

King: Dmitri, your comment that you no longer think of yourself as a Russian intrigues me. I wonder if you can elaborate a little more on that.

Polkaevich: Larry, we know now we are not alone. There are others out there somewhere, and they are quite near. This knowledge will cause us to draw together.

FBI/CONFIDENTIAL
TO: Intel IV
FROM: SAC, Morton, ID
SUBJECT: Initial Report/SIR27

New right-wing hate group is forming in this area in an effort to seize the entrance to the off-world site at Johnson's Ridge, ND. They are designing a charter calling for occupation of the new world, followed by a quick drive for statehood.

Attachment A lists active insiders. Almost everyone associated with the governing board of this organization 'is on file. Attachment B contains press releases and public pronouncements by John Fielder, spokesman for the group, and Abner Wright, its founder. You will note their concern with getting the Roundhouse out of the hands of foreigners (they seem to be referring to the Sioux) and their stated willingness to use force. Will advise as situation develops.

TO: Director, Customs Management Center, Chicago, IL
FROM: Area Port Director, Fort Moxie, ND
SUBJECT: Roundhouse, Status of

As you are aware, people are entering and exiting the country through a "transdimensional door" on Johnson's Ridge. Please advise whether Johnson's Ridge should be considered a port, for customs purposes. Of course, no one is bringing back commercial merchandise, at least to our knowledge. But there are fish and game requirements and other laws that would come into play.

If instructed to establish an entry area, please note that the action will require additional personnel.

Project Forty's ratings had gone through the roof. As a consequence, criticism of Old-Time Bill also soared.

Bill's enemies were the mainstream press, liberal politicians, and left-leaning churches, which is to say all the various forces that were conniving in the moral collapse of the American people. They accused him of every conceivable crime but concentrated particularly on fraud and hypocrisy. They charged that he used religion to solicit donations, that he was a theological con artist, that he probably didn't even believe in God.

None of this, strictly speaking, was true. To deal with the last first, Bill didn't think seriously enough about theology to worry about details, but he sincerely believed that, as he often preached, everyone had a direct line into God's study. Don't hesitate to use the phone, he said; say what you really mean, and God will never put you on hold.

He sincerely believed in his own uprightness, because he gave hope to the despairing, meaning to those who had lost direction, and a sense of belonging to the unloved. To all who came to him, who wandered the various Sinais of their lives in keeping with the spirit of the Volunteers, he offered redemption, an easing of pain, and a celestial compass.

Oh, yes, Bill was a believer. God stood by Bill's side when the choir was singing and the pipes were playing and people sobbed out their sins and promised to amend their lives.

And he most certainly did *not* do it for money.

The money was nice; he never denied that. But he thought of it as a corollary benefit for doing what was right, for walking the path of the Lord, for living by the Book. His real motivation would have been found in the exhilaration of standing before audiences in English-speaking countries around the world and feeling their response to God's truth. He loved to draw them into the power of the Word, to hold their emotions in his hands, and, with his soaring rhetoric, to loosen the chains that bound them, not to an earthly existence, but to prosaic lives.

Bill understood the romance implicit in the tales of a desert God who had loved his people and who had eventually faced the Roman cross for all who had ever drawn breath. Yes! That was what people understood and what they loved. And they loved *him* because he had made himself part of the message.

His second Fort Moxie broadcast took place during the last snow storm of the season. Ordinarily, Bill didn't get to see much snow, and it inspired him. While the flakes drifted against the windows, he understood God's love for Adam in spite of his disobedience. And he felt his people's hearts beat with his.

"But Adam has gone back into the Garden."

"Amen," cried the Volunteers.

"O Lord, we need your strong arm."

"Alleluia!"

"Give us a sign. Show the faithless You stand by our side!"

He urged his listeners to write to their representatives. "Demand that we withdraw. For we are deaf to His word." Tears appeared in his eyes. The wind began to build. Bill felt the Presence. "Show them your strength, God of Abraham," he said. "I ask it in your Son's name."

The chorus, on cue, burst into "Rock of Ages." The room shook and people sobbed and the wind wrapped itself around the building. Amanda Dexter, who could always be counted on to go to pieces at the climax of a good service, shrieked her undying gratitude to her Creator and collapsed in a quivering heap.

They rolled through several choruses while the wind played with the windows. Bill felt something open in his soul, and the power of the Angel of the Almighty entered into him. He knew once again the sheer exuberance of bringing people to the Lord. He flowed into the Angel and became one with it, directing the storm, watching the snow submerge the harsh angles of roof and shutter and drainpipe, enshrouding the building, burying it, removing its harsh lines.

Abruptly, he was back inside and the organ had stopped, and the Volunteers were in the aisles, exhausted, helping one another to their feet, delivering alleluias, collapsing into chairs.

"Praise the Lord," said Mark Meyer, whose face was ashen. "Did you *feel* it?" He was looking directly at Bill.

"Yes," said Bill, shakily. "I felt it." Tonight, more than at any other time in his career, he knew he walked with the Blessed. "I think we got the sign," he added. "I think we actually got the *sign*."

He remembered the TV cameras. And at that moment, while he wondered if the network had picked up his remark, the lights went out.

"Check the circuit breakers," someone shouted.

His people didn't mind a little power failure, and they laughed their way through "Victory in Jesus."

Bill put on his headset so he could talk to Harry Staples, his maintenance chief. "I'll have the lights back in a second," Harry said.

The room was absolutely dark. Bill could not even see any illumination coming in through the windows. That suggested the streetlights had also gone out.

"Everybody stay put until we get the power working again," Bill said.

His producer reported that they were off the air. "But we went with a bang," he added. The Whitburg studio had picked up and was covering with gospel music.

The Volunteers finished with "Joshua." They cheered, conquering failed lights the same way they conquered everything else.

Harry's voice again: "Power failure's *outside*, Reverend.

We've lost the heater, too." Flashlights had appeared on the stairs.

"Okay," said Bill. "Let's close up and clear out." They were staying in motels in Morris, Manitoba, about a half-hour north of the border. He turned to his audience. "You folks have done great," he said. "Let's go home."

They were already filing toward the door, struggling into coats and boots. Bill waited, talking with his people. He heard the front door open.

And a rough masculine voice, breaking tone with the evening, said, "Hey, what the hell is this?"

Bill heard a whimper.

The door had opened on a wall of snow.

Frank Moll was at home listening to a Mozart concerto when the lights went out and the music died. Through his picture window, he could see that the streetlight located immediately in front of the house had also gone dark.

Peg came out of the den with a flashlight, headed for the circuit breakers.

"They're off all over," Frank said, reaching for the phone book.

"We are sorry," came the recorded response at the electric company, "but all our service representatives are busy. Please stay on the line."

He hung up, sat down, and propped his feet on the hassock. "Must be lines down somewhere," he said. It was cold outside, but the house was well insulated.

They talked in the dark, enjoying the interruption in their routine. Across the street, Hodge Eliot's front door opened. Hodge carried a lamp out onto his porch and peered down the street.

The phone rang.

"Frank?" He recognized Edie Thoraldson's voice. "Something's happened at Kor's place. We're sending the unit."

That was the Quick Response Team, which Frank had once directed. "What?" he asked. "What happened?"

"I'm not exactly sure," she said. "Apparently somebody got *buried*. I've got the police coming in from Cavalier. I thought maybe it wouldn't be a bad idea if you took a look."

"Okay," he said, puzzled.

Peg looked at him, worried. "What is it?" she asked.

"Don't know. Edie says somebody got *buried*. What the hell does *that* mean?" He had his coat on already. "Keep the door locked," he said.

Kor's house was only six blocks away. He paused in his driveway for a stream of cars carrying volunteer firemen. Then he backed out into the street and turned left. Two minutes later he parked behind a gathering crowd a half-block away from Kor's house. He was just behind the Quick Response Team. The neighborhood was thick with box elders, and it was hard to see what was happening. But he could hear a lot of crowd noise.

The fire engine rolled in. The crowd split and flowed away from the emergency vehicles. And Frank finally got clear of the trees.

Where Kor's house, lately the Backcountry Church, had been, there was now a two-story-high snow cylinder. The snow was swirled at the top like soft ice cream.

✠ 27 ✠

He asked for a sign.

—Mike Tower, *Chicago Tribune* (commenting on Old-Time Bill and
the freak storm at the Backcountry Church)

Harry Mills liked to say he was pure corn country, bred true. He
had spent thirty years in the Congress of the United States,
eight as chairman of the Senate Armed Services Committee,
before becoming Matt Taylor's Vice President. Harry told
people he had no political ambitions other than to serve his
nation well. He would be seventy-seven before he could
hope for a run at the top job.

He had therefore decided to retire at the end of Taylor's
first term, while he was still young enough to enjoy the
leisure. He would write his memoirs; travel the country to
spend time with his grandchildren, who were scattered from
Spokane to Key West; and get back to playing serious bridge,
a pursuit he'd abandoned a quarter-century ago.

The reality was that Harry probably *had* become too old.
He had lost his passion for politics, his taste for power. He no
longer enjoyed influencing policy, or rubbing shoulders with
the decision makers, or even making the Sunday round of

talk shows. Tonight he was at a reception for the Jordanian king, and he devoutly would have preferred to be home with Marian, shoes kicked off, watching a good movie.

As was usually the case at these outings, he was being stalked by half a dozen predators who wanted to use him to push their agendas. One was the NASA director, Rick Keough, who caught up with him near the hors d'oeuvres.

Harry didn't like Keough very much. The director was a former astronaut, so he was popular with the general public. But he was given to grandstanding, and he was less interested in the organization than he was in his own career.

Keough was nursing a rum and Coke and trying to look like a man bearing up under misfortune and bureaucratic stupidity. They exchanged pleasantries, and he came to the point. "Mr. Vice President, we have a problem. This thing on Johnson's Ridge. My people are starting to wonder whether they have a future."

Keough had headed the effort to return to an aggressive manned program when that idea was popular, and during recent years had argued just as effectively for economy, science, and safety. He was short, barely five-six, narrow of both shoulder and intellect. There was an elusiveness in his character, a tendency to become distracted or change the subject without warning. Talking to Keough, one of the capital's pundits had once remarked in print, was like trying to carry on a conversation with a man hiding behind a tree.

"How do you mean?" asked Harry.

"Are you serious? What's the point of boosters and shuttles when you can *walk?*" He finished off his drink. "What is the President going to *do* about that thing?"

Harry was tired of hearing about the Roundhouse. He

was not a man easily rattled, and he was convinced that, given time, it would all blow over. When it did, life would go on. "Relax, Rick," he said. "There will always be a mission for NASA."

"Well, maybe somebody better tell that to my people, because they are looking around. Mr. Vice President, they are going to start bailing out. These are *dedicated* people. And they can't be replaced. Once they get the feeling that what they do doesn't matter anymore, they're gone. The organization will *die*."

And your job with it. "I'll talk to the President," Harry said. "I'm sure he'll be willing to issue a statement of purpose."

"I think he'll have to do better than that. You want *my* suggestion?"

Harry fingered his glass, waiting.

"Condemn the area. Send in a flight of F–111's and take the top off the escarpment. You can apologize later, and nobody will complain. *Nobody*."

DRIVER IN FATAL CRASH CLAIMS ATTACK BY "VISITOR"

Grand Forks, ND, Apr. 2 (UPI)—

A driver charged with vehicular homicide in Saturday's seven-car crash on I–29 has claimed that "something" took the wheel out of his hand and drove the car across the median into oncoming traffic. John Culver, twenty-nine, of Fargo, insisted yesterday that he had no way to bring his 1997 Honda under control. Police have said Culver was legally drunk when he crashed head-on into a station wagon, beginning a chain of collisions that killed three.

The press conferences on Johnson's Ridge were held daily at one o'clock. Pool reporters, wearing pressure suits, had visited the galaxy terminus, which seemed to be located on an off-world platform. No one knew for certain, because no exit from the chamber could be found. But if it was indeed off-world, then it followed that artificial gravity was now within reach. An expedition was being planned.

Today, however, no one was interested in anything other than the Visitor.

Flanked by Adam Sky, April began by issuing a short statement that admitted a remote possibility that something *might* have come through the port. "We don't think so," she said. "We are reasonably sure that the only thing that happened was a brief malfunction. The malfunction opened a channel between Johnson's Ridge and one of the terminus worlds."

"The Maze?" asked Peter Arnett of CNN.

"Yes," she said.

"April," he pursued, "when are you going to open it up for us? The Maze?"

"As soon as we can be sure it's not inhabited, Peter." (Wrong word: She should have said "not occupied." Sounded less ominous.) "But I'd like to reiterate that we spent more than two hours over there. We saw no sign of life. And we were in no way molested, attacked, or threatened by anyone. After we returned, the system reactivated on its own. No one appeared, and there was no evidence to suggest it was anything but a malfunction. And I hope this puts the rumors to rest."

"You saw nothing at all?" asked *Le Parisien*.

"That's correct."

"But that's what you'd expect to see, isn't it," asked the *London Times*, "if the creature was invisible?"

"How can I respond to that?" asked April. "We didn't see anything. More than that I can't say. If the *Times* wants to speculate, go ahead."

"How do you account for Deekin's statements?" asked a reporter from *Pravda*. "Deekin swears *something* came across."

April allowed herself to look distressed. "You'll have to ask Dr. Deekin about that."

Reporters, like everyone else, love a good story. And April knew they were torn between their natural skepticism and an unexpressed hope that there was something to the rumor. Everyone understood that this was the sort of thing that sold newspapers. A *lot* of newspapers.

She had, of course, been less than candid. The guard who had seen the wrong icon light up had been George Freewater. George also believed something had come across. But they had learned the danger of going public with everything they knew.

"Tell a press conference what we really think," Max had said, "and we'll have a panic."

Adam had disagreed. "Nobody's going to panic. That's government-speak. I think we'd do best to tell the truth."

"Truth is overrated," Max had said, looking wearily at him. "Have you been out to any of these towns lately? They're barring the doors at night. And you won't find many kids outside."

The News at Noon, KLMR-TV, Fargo

Anchor: More strange goings-on in and around Fort Moxie today, Julie. First we have an exclusive interview with the man who claims to have spoken to the invisible creature that is haunting the border area.

ANCIENT SHORES

(Cut to aerial shot of the railhead, where we see the depot and a line of tankers and empty flatcars; back off gradually for perspective)

There's another report on the town's so-called Visitor. Carole Jensen is in Noyes, Minnesota.

(We see Jensen standing by a railroad track; a white tank car is behind her)

Jensen: This is where it happened, Claude. We are at the tiny depot in Noyes, Minnesota, about a mile south of the Canadian border. A railroad employee may have had an encounter here a couple of days ago with the unearthly *thing* that is reported to have escaped from the Roundhouse on Johnson's Ridge. The employee, Curt Hollis, was taken to a local hospital after the incident, although he's with us today and seems to be okay.

(Camera moves away; Hollis is standing beside the reporter)

How do you feel, Mr. Hollis?
Hollis: I'm okay, thank you.
Jensen: What actually happened here?
Hollis: (*Nervously*) There was something calling my name. The wind, it sounded like. (*Tries to imitate sound*)
Jensen: Did anyone else hear it?
Hollis: Yes. The inspector heard it. Ask her. It was here.
Jensen: Did it say anything else?
Hollis: Not words.

Jensen: Not words. What, then?

Hollis: I don't know exactly. It made me *feel* funny.

Jensen: In what way, Mr. Hollis?

Hollis: Like I was flying. Listen, you want the truth, it scared the—*(Hesitates)* It scared me pretty bad.

Jensen: And what happened next?

Hollis: I passed out.

Jensen: So there you have it, Claude.

(Camera withdraws to long overhead shot of freight yard)

At least one other person heard a voice out here. Was this depot the scene earlier this week for an unearthly encounter? Or is it just one man's imagination running wild in a place where a lot of people are reporting eerie events?

Anchor: Thanks, Carole. Now to Fort Moxie itself, for another report from Michael Wideman at the Backcountry Church, where the *Project Forty* religious television show was interrupted last night.

Participant
Holyoke Industries Pension Plan

Dear Retiree,

As you are aware, the economy has been going through an extremely difficult period. Pension funds are connected to the economic welfare of the nation, and ours is no exception. We have, over the years, made every effort to safeguard our resources by investing conservatively and prudently. But no amount of foresight could have predicted the downturn of the last several weeks, nor would any measures have guarded against it.

Your company's pension plan, like that of many other corporations, has seen the value of its securities drop substantially over a matter of days. Fortunately we have a reserve fund set aside specifically to carry us through this kind of emergency. But the sheer scale of the problems now besetting the nation requires us to manage our reserves carefully. In order to ensure that you may continue to rely on your pension, your May payment will be reduced by $421.00 to $1,166.35. We hope that this reduction will be a one-time event only. Be assured that the trustees of the pension plan are doing everything in their power to safeguard our collective future.

We appreciate your support and understanding during this difficult period.

J. B. Haldway, Acting Director

On the same day that Holyoke Industries mailed the bad news to its pensioners, a statement by Heinz Erhardt of the University of Berlin, last year's Nobel prize winner for economics, appeared in *Der Tagesspiegel*. Erhardt acknowledged that the world economy had been rocked by the news from North Dakota. "A short-term downturn," he said, "is inevitable. But if technological applications in manufacturing and transportation become possible, as there is no reason to doubt they will, the world is headed into a period of prosperity unlike anything that has gone before."

Nobody seemed to be listening. By day's end, the Dow Jones was down another 240 points and still looking for a floor.

Larry King Live. Guest: Dr. Edward Bannerman of the Institute for Advanced Study.

King: Dr. Bannerman, you've been quoted as saying that the *big* news is the so-called galaxy world. Why is that?

Bannerman: *(Laughs)* Larry, this is all pretty big news. But the possibility that the chamber in which Arky Redfern died is actually located off-world is a monumental development in a series of incredible events.

King: Why?

Bannerman: I'm talking in practical terms now.

King: Okay.

Bannerman: The people fell *down* in that room. The reports indicate that the galaxy has not changed its position in the window. Therefore the facility, whatever it is, is not rotating. Or if it is, it is doing so very slowly. Now, that's important because it implies that if the site is not located on a planetary surface, it incorporates artificial gravity.

King: I can see why that might have some importance. But—

Bannerman: Larry, if we can create artificial gravity, we can probably reduce, or even eliminate, gravity's effects. I'm talking about antigravity. Think what it would mean to the average householder, for example.

Want to move that sofa? Slap an antigravity disk on it and float it into the next room.

Horace Gibson had started life as an insurance salesman. Bored, he'd joined the Marines, risen to command a battalion, and won a Silver Star in the Gulf and the Medal of Honor in Johannesburg. His units had collected enough citations to paper his den. In 1996 he'd retired, tried another civilian occupation, real estate this time, and lasted almost a year. On the anniversary of his retirement from the Corps, he joined the U.S. Marshals Service.

Within two years he had become commander of the Special Operations Group (SOG). SOG was the marshals' SWAT team, based in Pineville, Louisiana.

Horace was liked by his people. He was willing to take on upper management when occasion required, and he did not spare himself in ensuring that operations were carried out for maximum success with least risk.

He was twice divorced. His life had been too mobile and too erratic for either of his ex-wives. He had two sons, both of whom (with some justification) blamed Horace for the domestic failures, and whose relationships with their father were cool. Horace had found nothing to replace the wreckage of his personal life, and consequently he worked too many hours. His boss, Carl Rossini, liked to joke that Horace needed a woman in his life. He did, and he knew it.

Meantime, Horace took his entertainments where he could find them. These were growing fewer with the passing years, a result of his own aging and the narrowing of his taste. But there were occasional delights, one of which took the form of Emily Passenger, a gorgeous young woman he'd met at a fund-raiser for the Pineville library. They'd gone to dinner several times, seen a couple of shows, and had taken to jogging together. He had noted some reluctance on her part, however, toward pursuing a relationship, and he ascribed it to his track record. She did not want to become a third casualty.

Consequently Horace had embarked on a campaign to demonstrate that he was now both mature and thoroughly domesticated. The first step was to invite her for dinner at his place, and when she agreed, he had enthusiastically set about preparing the evening. He got in a couple of T-bones and an expensive bottle of champagne, invested in a kerosene lamp, which would help provide an offbeat atmosphere, and spent the day cleaning up. That evening, twenty minutes after he'd opened the champagne, his phone rang.

✠ 28 ✠

Oh, for a lodge in some vast wilderness . . .

—William Cowper, "The Task"

A thin, bearded man gazed out over the Pacific from his home at Laguna Beach. A freighter moved beneath a cloud-streaked sky. The sea was flat and calm.

There was an air of uncertainty in his bearing, and an observer would have had a difficult time deciding where his attention was directed. He held a glass of Mondavi chardonnay in his right hand.

The town, like the harbor, lay spread out before him. Traffic moved steadily along the coastal highway. He glanced at his watch, as he had been doing every few minutes for the past hour.

The phone rang.

He turned away from the window and sat down at his desk. "Hello?"

"Greg. It's all set."

It was almost two in Fargo. "Okay. Do they know we're coming?"

"Not yet. Listen. How much influence do *you* have with the feds?"

"Not much."

"Ditto."

The man in Laguna Beach was looking at his plane tickets. "Have faith, Walter. See you in a few hours."

SIX DEAD, HUNDREDS INJURED, IN AEROSPACE LOCKOUT

Seattle, Apr. 4 (AP)—

Labor tensions erupted into full-scale rioting today at three major aerospace firms when management locked out workers seeking to return to their jobs after a wildcat strike. The violence was a continuation of unrest since simultaneous announcements of "corporate reengineering" last week led to widespread fear of massive job eliminations.

DOES FORT MOXIE HAVE A VISITOR?

There have been reports from several sources that something from another world came through the port atop Johnson's Ridge and is now loose in the Fort Moxie area. There are stories of voices in the wind, of child abductions, of storms that seem to target individuals. And there has been a death under mysterious, and one might even say ominous, circumstances.

Last week Jack McGuigan abandoned his snowmobile in the woods off Route 32, in Cavalier County, and ran out onto the highway, where he was struck by a moving van. The driver of the van said that McGuigan appeared to be fleeing from someone. Or something.

Cavalier County police have been inundated with sightings, and recent visitors to the area report that for the first time in memory, people are locking their doors.

Meantime, still wilder stories are getting started. Old-Time Bill Addison, who has ridden a number of celestial horses during his career, is warning that we have broken into the Garden of Eden and released an avenging angel. Or maybe a devil. The Reverend Addison is unclear on the details.

It seems that, with the unearthing of the Roundhouse, we are doomed to relive another of those popular delusions that revisit us periodically. We don't yet know the facts in the death of Mr. McGuigan. But a probable scenario is not hard to reconstruct: he was hunting out of season; he thought he might be discovered; he became disoriented; and he stumbled onto a highway. Incidents like that happen every day. The voices around Fort Moxie can undoubtedly be ascribed to the active imaginations of the tourists, encouraged, perhaps, by some of the locals, who know a good thing when they see it. It all makes interesting reading, but we recommend keeping our feet on the ground. In the end, the facts will turn out to be suitably prosaic.
(Editorial, *Fargo Forum*, April 4)

Pete Pappadopolou had worked in the shipping room of ABC Pistons, Inc., for four years, and had recently risen to his first supervisory position. His marriage had collapsed six months earlier, when his wife ran off with the operator of a beer distributorship, leaving him to care for their asthmatic son.

Pete had worked a second job, delivering Chinese food, to pay for the nurse and associated medical care. He hadn't been sleeping well. He was depressed, and his life seemed to be going nowhere. He missed his wife, and his doctor put him on tranquilizers. But the promotion came, bringing a sizable salary increase and the promise of more as ABC expanded into allied fields. Moreover, the child's attacks had begun to lessen in both frequency and intensity. They had turned a corner.

Unfortunately, ABC was going through changes as well. Their expansion was to have been financed by a secondary stock offering. But the value of the company's stock had plummeted in recent weeks, and the banks, after a long period of watchful waiting, backed off.

ABC found itself with an unexpected surplus of people. The executive suite responded by eliminating eighteen hundred middle-management and first-line supervisory jobs. Pete, who had recently separated from the union in order to move up, discovered to his horror that he had no protection whatever.

On the day before the official notification would have been delivered (the rumor mill at ABC was quite efficient), Pete bought a .38 and used it on his plant manager and a colleague who had been making it clear that he should have got the promotion that went to Pete.

The plant manager, despite being hit six times, survived. The colleague took a bullet in the heart. The company responded by hiring additional security personnel.

James Walker loved solitude. He remembered staring out the windows of the schoolhouse years ago, gazing across snow-blown prairies, imagining himself alone in the world beyond the horizon. He had pictured a place of sun-dappled forest and green rivers and gentle winds heavy with the fragrance of flowers. Where the paths were grass rather than blacktop, and the land was free of county lines and posted limits and tumbledown barns.

Walker listened to his wife, Maria, working in the kitchen, her radio playing softly. A book lay open on his lap, but he couldn't have told anyone what the title was. Events on the ridge had filled his waking hours since Arky had first called him to report the discovery. Now Arky was dead, and people on the reservation and throughout the area were afraid of the night. George Freewater had told him flat out that something had got loose. "There's no doubt in my mind," he'd said.

A jigsaw puzzle lay half done on a table near the window. It was titled "Mountain Glory," and it portrayed a gray snow-capped peak rising out of lush woodland. A rock-filled stream rushed through the foreground. He had done a thousand such puzzles during his lifetime.

It saddened him there was no wilderness for the Mini Wakan Oyaté like the landscapes on the boxes. He had dreamed all his life that the Sioux would recover their lost world. How this might occur he'd had no idea. But it seemed right that it should happen, and he therefore fervently believed that in time it would.

But the shadows were advancing now. One day soon, he knew, the long night would begin for him. The Sioux had outlived their way of life, had turned it over to the white technicians, who would map everything. That was what he most disliked about them: that they sought to know all things, and did not realize that a forest without dark places has value only to the woodcutter.

Now a road to the stars had opened. From Sioux land. Arky had understood all along, had cautioned him that the Roundhouse might prove far more valuable than any commodity that could be offered in exchange for it. Possibly, the new wilderness was at hand.

The government car drew up outside. He sighed and watched Jason Fleury get out. There were two others with him, but they did not move. Fleury seemed ill at ease.

Walker met him at the door and escorted him back to his office. "I assume," he said, "you are not bringing good news."

"No." Fleury shook his head. "There's no good news for *anyone* these days."

The tribal chairman produced two cups of coffee. "What do they propose to do?" he asked.

"I must ask you first, Mr. Chairman, whether you are taping this meeting."

"Would it make a difference?"

"Only in what I would feel free to tell you."

Walker sat down on the couch beside his visitor. "There is no device," he said.

"Good. I didn't think there would be." Fleury took a deep breath. "I hardly know how to begin."

"Let me help," said Walker. "You are about to seize our land. Again."

For a long time Fleury didn't speak. Finally he cleared his throat. "They don't feel they have a choice in the matter, sir."

"No," said Walker. "I'm sure they don't."

"Officially our position is that we are reacting in order to allay panic in the local towns and in southern Canada from the rumors that *something* has got loose from the Roundhouse."

"What panic?" asked Walker.

Fleury smiled, an attempt to break the tension. It didn't work. "It is true that people are frightened, Chairman. Surely you know that?"

"Give it a few days and it will go away of its own accord."

"No doubt. Nevertheless, there's been a death, and there's political pressure. The government has no choice but to act. It will take over Johnson's Ridge and temporarily administer the property until we can be assured the situation is stabilized."

"And when will the situation be considered 'stabilized'?"

Their eyes locked. Walker could see that Fleury was making a decision. "What I have to say may not be repeated outside this room."

"It will not be, if you wish."

"That moment will come when the port and the Roundhouse have been destroyed."

"I see."

"There will be an accident. I don't know how they'll arrange it, but it's the only way out."

Walker nodded slowly. "Thank you for your honesty," he said. "I must repeat, Johnson's Ridge belongs to the Mini Wakan Oyaté. We will resist any effort to take it."

"Try to understand," said Fleury. "There are forces at work now over which no one has any real control."

The chairman felt as if he were caught in the gears of a giant clock. "Jason," he said, "I understand quite well. But I am being asked to choose a reservation for my grandsons when they might have a wilderness. Rather, your people need to put aside their fear. There is nothing destructive in the Roundhouse. The difficulties now besetting the larger world stem from ignorance. And fear."

Fleury's eyes were bleak. "Many of us sympathize with your position. You have more friends than you know."

"But none who are prepared to come forward."

Fleury struggled with his words. "Chairman, the President counts himself among your friends. But he feels compelled, by his duty to the nation, to take action."

"I am sorry," said Walker, standing up to signal an end to the conversation. "I truly am."

"Chairman, listen." A note of desperation crept into Fleury's voice. "It's out of your hands. The court order has already been issued. It will be served on your people within the hour."

"On the tribal council?"

"On your representatives at Johnson's Ridge."

"Adam will not accept it."

"That's why I'm here. To explain what's happening. And to ask for your assistance. We will pay ample compensation."

"And what would you offer me in exchange for the future of my people? Keep off the ridge, Mr. Fleury. It belongs to the Sioux. We will not surrender it."

Max picked up his phone. It was Lasker. "Listen, Max," he said, "there's something you ought to know."

"You sold the boat," Max said.

"Yeah. Listen, they offered a *lot* of money, Max. More than I'll ever need."

"It's okay, Tom."

"I don't know if it's going to have any kind of impact up there. I was afraid—"

"Where's the boat now?"

"They're outside loading it onto a trailer."

"Wells?"

"No. It's government money. These guys are from the Treasury."

Deputy U.S. Marshal Elizabeth Silvera served the court order on Adam Sky. She was in her late forties, tall, rangy,

ANCIENT SHORES

impersonal. Her black hair was just beginning to show streaks of gray.

She was accompanied by Chief Doutable.

Adam's office in the security station was small and cramped. Its walls, which until yesterday had been bare save for a tribal drum and a framed picture of his wife, were now covered with weapons. Bows, antique rifles, Adam's old service revolver, whatever he'd been able to find had been put on display.

Silvera extracted a document from her jacket. "Mr. Sky," she said, "A federal court order requiring that this premises, the Roundhouse, and everything in it, save personal property, be remanded into the custody of the federal government.

"The action is necessitated," she continued, "because the area has been determined to be a public hazard."

When the security chief made no move to accept the court order, she laid it on his desk. "You have until midnight tonight to comply." Her tone changed, as if she were offering friendly advice: "The sooner you clear the site, Mr. Sky, the better it will be for all concerned."

"We won't be leaving," Adam said coolly.

She met his eyes. "You don't have that option. You can't defy the court."

"This is our property. If you come back to take it from us, come armed."

Silvera's eyes hardened. "I *am* sorry," she said. "You have until midnight." She turned, walked to the door, and paused. "Under the circumstances I should remind you that resisting a federal court order is a felony. I have no discretion here, Mr. Sky. I have no choice but to enforce the order. By whatever means necessary."

✠ ✠ ✠

331

Jack McDevitt

Walker had been waiting for the call from Adam. When it came, he listened intently to the security chief's narrative. When he asked for instructions, the chairman hesitated. "Adam," he said, "how far are you prepared to go?"

"I do not wish to accept this."

"Are you prepared to defend the ridge?"

"Yes. I'd prefer not to. But I don't think we have a choice."

"But," said Walker, "armed resistance will not produce a victory."

"Then what do you suggest? That we give in again?"

"The real question is whether we can find a way to keep our hold on the wilderness world."

"If the federals are prepared to come against us in force, I think not."

"So," said Walker, "we can take our money and end it here. Or we can fight with no hope of victory."

"Yes," said Adam. "Those seem to be our choices."

The chairman glanced around his office. The walls, the battered windows, even the fireplace seemed somehow mementos of captivity. "I agree. We must fight."

"Will you send us help?"

"I will come," he said. "But the police will not be so stupid as to allow your brothers and sisters to join you. Talk with those who are with you. Find out who will stay."

"I will talk to them now," said Adam.

"Good. I'm on my way." He hung up and stared at the phone.

It rang again.

He picked it up. "Hello?"

An unfamiliar voice asked to speak with James Walker.

"That's my name."

"James, I'm Walter Asquith. I've heard what's been happening."

"I don't think I know you."

"No matter. I know *you*. Listen, not everybody in this country's getting stampeded. I thought maybe you could use some help."

As Asquith talked, Walker recalled one of Jason Fleury's remarks. *You have more friends than you know.*

"And you are all going to stay?" demanded April.

"Yes," Adam said. "We will defend the ridge."

Max was shocked. "Does the chairman know about this?"

"The chairman ordered it."

"My God, Adam," he said, "you're talking about shooting it out with *United States marshals?*"

"That's crazy," said April. "You'll all wind up dead. What we need to do is talk to a lawyer."

"I don't believe," said Adam, "that talking to a lawyer would accomplish anything. Anyway, it's not my decision."

Her eyes got very wide. "Adam," she said, "the chairman would not ask you to do any such thing. There's a misunderstanding here somewhere."

Adam showed no emotion. "You can ask him when he comes," he said.

Max could not believe he was listening to this conversation. "What do you think this is," he demanded, "some sort of kids' game? You can't tell the federal government to take a hike."

"We've had some experience doing just that," said Adam.

"Like hell. Your grandfather, maybe. Not you." He looked through the window at Dale Tree, who was talking with a group of visitors. "Or anybody else here, for that matter."

Adam looked directly at Max. "We are now at a point

where we have to ask ourselves what we really stand for. Everything is about to happen again, Max. We're not going to allow that. If we have to stand our ground and make them kill us, then that is what we will do."

✠ 29 ✠

Where can I go
That I might live forever?

"Testing, one, two," said Andrea.

"That's good." Keith sounded excited. "Listen, we aren't going to lose you up there tonight, are we?"

"I hope not." Andrea thought she sounded confident. Completely in charge.

"Okay," said Keith. "We're doing a special lead-in, and we'll be cutting away to the network before we actually go over to you. So you'll be on right from the top."

"Good."

"As far as we can tell, you'll be the entire media show. No one's being allowed up the road."

"Well, I guess this is my night to become famous."

"I hope so. And listen, Hawk, take care of—" Static erupted.

Andrea switched to her alternative frequency. Same problem. The sons of bitches were jamming her. Unbelievable.

She picked up a telephone. And waited for a dial tone that never came.

✠　　✠　　✠

Joe Rescouli had been driving for almost twelve hours when he and Amy and his sister-in-law Teresa turned north onto Route 32 to travel the last few miles to the Roundhouse. They had come from Sacramento and had covered the ground in three days. Teresa was a particle physicist. Although Joe wasn't sure precisely what that meant, he knew she had a good job and did not have to work hard. He admired that. "She gets paid for what she *knows*," he'd told his friends down at the bottling plant. Joe, on the other hand, had never seen a day when he did not have to slave for every nickel.

Teresa had talked for months about nothing but the Roundhouse, and her enthusiasm had so overwhelmed Joe and Amy that when she started thinking about flying up here to visit the site, they'd all wanted to come, and it was a lot cheaper to drive.

So they were here, and Teresa was saying how she thought they should stay on the ridge until it got dark so they could see the structure glow. Amy was all for it. Amy was always in favor of anything her sister wanted to do. Joe understood that his wife entertained more than a few regrets about her marriage. She never said anything, but he could see it in her eyes. Had she not married Joe, she might also have been working at a place like Triangle Labs, with her own office and a doctorate and a sense of really going somewhere in the world.

It was already getting dark in the shadow of the ridge, and a fierce wind beat against the ancient Buick. He knew about the hairpin access road and didn't much like having to navigate at dusk with this kind of wind blowing. But the sisters were excited, so there would be no peace until they'd seen what they'd come to see.

"There," said Amy.

A board had been erected by the side of the highway. It had a big yellow arrow on it, and it said *The Roundhouse*. But someone had drawn a line through the middle of the sign and printed *Closed* on it.

"That can't be," said Teresa. "It's supposed to be open until sundown."

Just around the bend they came across the access road, but it was blocked by a barrier. A police cruiser was parked to one side, and a line of cars was being waved on. Joe eased in and rolled down the window. A policeman gestured impatiently at them.

"What's wrong, Officer?" Joe asked.

"Please keep moving, folks. It's shut down."

"Okay," said Joe, trying to hide his gratification. "What time does it open in the morning?"

"It won't. It's closed permanently."

"Closed permanently?" said Teresa. Joe could hear the disbelief in her voice. "Why? Officer, we've come a long way." Her voice was getting shrill.

"They don't tell us much, ma'am. The courts have ordered it shut down. Safety hazard."

"You can't be serious."

"I'm sorry. I'll have to ask you to move on." He stepped away, waiting for them to pull out. Another car drifted in behind them. The policeman sighed.

At that moment a black 1988 Ford, coming from the north, pulled up to the barrier. The driver was alone. An elderly Indian, Joe thought. Then he watched indignantly as they opened up. The Ford went in, and the roadblock was replaced.

"Hey," said Teresa. "What's going on? How come *he* got in?"

"Official vehicle," said the cop.

Joe glared, but the cop didn't seem to care. He looked at Joe and pointed to the highway. "Somebody's going to get a letter," Joe said, then rolled up the window and hit the gas.

Walker had anticipated trouble at the blockade. All the way over from the reservation, he had been certain they would deny him entrance. Maybe even arrest him. But they had let him through. And as he started up the access road he understood. He was old, and they were hoping he could rein in the more aggressive spirits at the Roundhouse. In any case, wherever he was, they did not see him as a threat.

Cautiously he negotiated the curves, noting a liberal supply of police scattered along the road. The trees thinned out after a while, and he emerged finally on top of the ridge. There were only a half-dozen cars parked in the lot.

The Roundhouse glistened in the fading light. It spoke somehow to the spirit. Its lines were curved and uncluttered, and he knew that its designers had loved the world as it was then, as it still was on the other side of the port. He would have liked to speak with those who had traveled so far to sail virgin seas. It seemed almost as if they had known what the condition of the Sioux would be and had left the woodland as a gift.

Adam stepped from the security hut and waved.

Walker parked the car and got out. "Good to see you, Adam," he said.

"And you, Chairman." Adam started to say something but hesitated.

"What is it?" asked Walker.

"The site is not easily defensible. Not with a handful of people."

"Would you prefer to withdraw?"

"No," he said. "I am not suggesting that."

A helicopter drifted in low and kicked up dust from the excavation ditches. "Photo recon," said Adam.

Walker nodded. "They've sealed off the access road. What *are* you suggesting?"

"That we take the initiative. That we not wait for them to hit *us*."

"And how would you do that?"

They'd reached the security station and hesitated by the door. "We could start by dropping a few trees on the access road. That'll at least slow them down."

"There are police stationed along the road."

"I know," said Adam.

And Walker understood. The police did not look as if they believed any serious deployment by the defenders would take place. This was, after all, an area where people traditionally did not shoot each other. A simultaneous series of ambushes could clear the road. And a couple of well-positioned snipers might hold it if some trees were dropped. It might work. "No," he said.

"Chairman, we cannot sit here and simply wait for the attack to come."

"And if you kill a few policemen, do you think the end will be any different?"

Anger rose in Adam's dark eyes. "If we are to travel beyond the great river, we should not go unescorted."

"No," Walker said again. "Spill blood once, and there will be no end to it until we are all dead. I prefer a better outcome."

"And how do you hope to arrange a better outcome?"

"I've been in touch with well-placed friends. Help is on the way."

"Well-placed friends?" Adam smiled. "When have the Sioux known such friends?"

"Possibly longer than you think, Adam. It may be that you have simply not recognized them."

They went into the security station. Little Ghost and Sandra Whitewing got to their feet. Both looked calm. Little Ghost was in his late twenties. The chairman knew him, had always worried about his future, because Little Ghost had a wife and two sons but no job. Today it looked as if that would no longer be a matter for concern.

And Sandra, who had once come to him for help when her father drove his car into a gas pump. Her dark eyes shone, and it struck him that she was extraordinarily lovely. Somehow, over the years, he had failed to notice. Too busy negotiating his own narrow track through the world. Pity.

She worked in a restaurant that catered to reservation visitors. He had heard that she was engaged to a white man, a carpenter or an electrician or something, who lived in Devil's Lake. She was not yet twenty-one. He considered ordering her off the ridge but knew that would be unfair, both to her and to her brothers. She had chosen to make her stand, and he could not deprive her of that privilege.

Weapons were stacked around the room. M–16s. At least they had some firepower.

"We also have a hand-held rocket launcher," said Adam. "They will not take us without paying a price."

"Who else is here?" asked Walker.

"Will Pipe, George Freewater, and Andrea are in the Roundhouse. Max and Dr. Cannon haven't left yet, but I'm sure they will do so shortly. They're with visitors."

"There are *still* visitors?" asked Walker, surprised.

"Three from the last tour."

340

He lowered himself into a chair. "We need to talk about the defense."

The door opened, and Max came in. "I wouldn't have believed this was possible," he said apologetically. "I've been trying to call Senator Wykowski, but it looks as if the lines are down."

Walker smiled. "They don't want us talking to anyone," he said. "But I don't think it matters. We are way beyond senatorial intervention." The chairman felt sorry for Max, who seemed to be a man uncertain of purpose. Courage is not easy to summon when one is at war with oneself.

He looked through the window at the sunset. It saddened him to realize he might not see another.

April was talking with the departing researchers, wondering whether they would be the last to have crossed to Eden. They were Cecil Morin, an overweight, soft-looking middle-aged bacteriologist from the University of Colorado; Agatha Greene, a Harvard astrophysicist who had been overcome by the wonders of the Horsehead; and Dmitri Rushenko, a biologist from SmithKline Beecham Pharmaceuticals.

"I'd like to move over there," said Greene.

"Is it true," asked Morin, "that the government is about to take this place?"

April nodded. "Apparently so."

Morin shook his head sadly. "God help us all."

Rushenko opened the door to his car. "You're in the right, you know." His accent was New York. Long Island, she thought.

"We know."

"I hate to think of the port in the hands of the government," he continued. "Damned shame. I wish I could help." He got into his car and started the engine.

"Well, I'll tell you something," said Greene. "If the decision were mine, they'd have to take it from me."

April held the door while she got in. "We intend to stay," she said, using the pronoun figuratively, for *she* had no intention of staying. But it felt good to say so. "And you're welcome to stay with us, Agatha, if you wish." She intended it as a joke or bravado or something and immediately felt embarrassed by the woman's confusion.

"I would like to, April," the astrophysicist said. "I really would. But I have a husband and a little girl." She blushed.

The others said nothing.

April watched for her chance to talk privately with the chairman. He was out with Adam and the others, bent into a severe wind, touring the mounds of earth that rose around the rim of the excavation pit. Those mounds, she gathered, would constitute the first line of defense.

"Max," she said, "why are they doing this? What's the point?"

Max was coming to hate the Roundhouse and everything associated with it. "I don't know," he said. "Maybe it's a cultural thing."

She knew Max was waiting anxiously for her to agree to leave. He'd warned her that going down the access road in the dark past nervous police entailed risks.

It was dark now.

"I hate to leave them here," she said, initiating another cycle of the conversation they'd been having over and over for the last hour.

"So do I."

"I wish there were something we could do."

"Why do they insist on doing this? There's nothing to gain."

At eight o'clock they killed the security lights, but the churned-up ground was still visible in the glow from the Roundhouse. "Too bad they can't throw a tarp over that thing," said Max.

When the chairman left Adam and retreated to the security station, she judged the time was right. "Max," she said, "let's go talk to him."

Max had lost all hope of making anybody see reason. To him, Adam Sky and his people, who had once seemed so rational, had been transformed into a band of fanatics who were ruled by ghosts of lost battles and ancient hatreds. The prospect of telling a federal court and a police force to kiss off was utterly foreign to Max's nature.

Walker seemed cheerful enough when they caught up with him.

"Chairman," April said with her voice fluttering, "don't do this. You can stop it."

Walker smiled warmly at her. "Are you still here?" he asked.

The wind ripped across the escarpment and hammered against the building. "We don't want to leave you here."

"I'm pleased to hear that," he said. "But you can't stay." The exchange caused Max's pulse to miss a beat. He had no intention of getting caught in the crossfire.

"There's no reason to do this," April said. "It won't change the result."

Walker stared at her. "Don't be too sure." He looked away, up at the moon, which was in its third quarter, and then out over the river valley, dark except for the distant pools of light at Fort Moxie and its border station.

"You can fight this in the courts," said Max. "I would think you'd have a good chance of getting it back. But if you put up an armed resistance—"

Something in the old man's eyes brought Max to a stop.

"What?" said April. "What aren't you telling us?"

"I have no idea what you mean, young lady." But he couldn't quite get the coyness out of his voice.

"What?" she said. "You've got the place mined? What is it?"

The helicopter was back. It rolled across the center of the escarpment.

Walker looked at his watch.

"The rational way is through the courts," she said. "Why aren't you going through the courts?"

The question hit home, and Walker simply waved it away. He didn't want to talk anymore. Wanted her to leave.

"Why?" she asked. "Why won't the courts work? You think the fix is in? Something else?"

"Please go, April," he said. "I wish there were a better way."

April's eyes widened. "You think they're going to destroy it, don't you? You don't think the courts would be *able* to hand it back."

The chairman stared past her, his eyes fixed on the sky. Then he turned on his heel and walked out the door.

"My God," she said. "That can't be right. They wouldn't do that."

But they would have to. As long as people believed the advanced technologies existed, that they could eventually surface, they would continue to work their baleful effects on the world at large. There was only one way to neutralize the Roundhouse.

"I think," said Max, "he's right. It's time for us to clear out."

April stood hesitating, dismayed. Terrified. "No," she said. "I don't think it is."

Max's heart sank.

"I'm not going," she said. "I'm not going to let it happen."

Brian Kautter was the commissioner of the Environmental Protection Agency. At eight-thirty, tracked by TV cameras, he walked into the agency's press room. There was more tension in the air and more reporters present than he had ever seen. That meant there had been a leak.

Kautter was a tall, congenial African-American. He hated what was happening right now, and he resented being part of it. He saw the necessity of the President's action. But he knew this was one of those events that would dog him through the years. He suspected a time would come, and very soon, when he would wish with all his heart for the capability to come back and relive these next few minutes.

"Ladies and gentlemen," he said, "I have an announcement to make, after which I will be happy to take questions. We have become increasingly concerned with the dangers inherent in the Roundhouse. Your government, as you know, has taken no official position on whether there actually *is* a bridge to the stars. But enough evidence is in to allow us to conclude that the land on the other side is most certainly not terrestrial.

"That brings up a number of disquieting possibilities. There are already stories that something has passed into our world. We do not know what this something might be, nor do we believe there is any truth to the account. But we cannot rule it out. Nor can we be certain that such an event might not happen in the future. There are other potential hazards. Viruses, for example. Or contaminants.

"In order to ensure the general public's safety, EPA has requested and received a court order requiring the owners of the artifact to submit it to government inspection and control. I repeat, this is only a temporary measure and is designed purely to avert local hazards." Kautter looked like a man in pain. "I'll take questions now."

Maris Quimby from the *Post:* "Mr. Commissioner, have the Sioux agreed to this arrangement?"

Kautter shook his head. "Maris, a federal court order does not require anyone's consent. But to answer your question, I'm sure they'll see the wisdom of the action." He pointed at Hank Miller, from Fox.

"Isn't it a little late to worry about bugs? I mean, if there's anything dangerous over there, we can be reasonably sure that by now it's over here."

"We don't think there's any real reason to worry, Hank. Our action in this regard is purely precautionary."

When he was finished, he went back upstairs to his office and opened the bottle of rum he kept stashed in his supply cabinet.

✠ 30 ✠

Courage is worth nothing if the gods do not help.

—Euripides, *The Suppliant Women*

This is an NBC News flash.

U.S. Marshals have sealed off Johnson's Ridge tonight, apparently preparing to seize the property. A group of Native Americans has announced they will not obey a federal court order to leave. We take you first to Michael Pateman at the White House, and then to Carole Jensen at the Sioux reservation near Devil's Lake, North Dakota.

Jensen was set up inside the tribal chambers in the Blue Building, where she had cornered William Hawk. National coverage. When you worked for the ten o'clock news in Fargo, this was the moment you lived for. She smiled at Hawk and got no reaction.

"One minute," said her cameraman, adjusting his focus.

"Just be natural, Councilman," she said. "We'll start when the red light goes on."

347

"Okay." He wore a cowhide vest, a flannel shirt, and a pair of faded jeans. She guessed he was about sixty, although his face was deeply lined.

The producer again, from Fargo: "Same routine as usual, Carole. Just like you'd do it for us. Except adjust the tag line."

"Okay," she said.

They were seconds away. The cameraman gave her five fingers, counted down, and the red lamp blinked on.

"This is Carole Jensen," she said, "in the tribal chambers at the Devil's Lake Sioux Reservation. With me tonight is Councilman William Hawk, one of the Sioux leaders. Councilman Hawk, I understand you saw the EPA press conference earlier this evening?"

"Yes, I did, Carole." His jaw was set, but she could see pain in his eyes. She hoped it translated to the screen. Tragic nobility here.

"How do you respond to Commissioner Kautter's remarks?"

"The commissioner should be aware there is no danger to anyone. No one has seen anything come through the port. And I'm sure nobody out there takes seriously the story of an invisible man. Or whatever."

"Councilman, what will you do?"

His expression hardened. "We will not let them steal our land. It belongs to us, and we will defend it."

"Does that mean by force?"

"If necessary. I hope it will not come to that."

"You told me earlier that your daughter is on the ridge."

"That is correct."

"Will you bring her home?"

"She will stay with her brothers to defend her heritage." His leathery face was defiant.

"We don't need you," said Adam. "You and Max should get out now, while you can."

"He's right," said Max. "We have no business here."

April looked at him sadly. "I think everybody has business here. We're too goddamn stupid or lazy or whatever to tackle the job of educating people, so instead we'll destroy the Roundhouse. It just makes me furious. I'm not going anywhere. My place is here—"

"Can you shoot?" interrupted Adam. "*Will* you shoot?"

"No," she said. "I won't kill anybody. But I'll be here anyhow." She knew how disjointed and weak that sounded, and tears came.

"You'll only be in the way."

"If you want me out of here," she told Adam, "you'll have to throw me over the side."

Max threw up his hands.

He was trying to begin the complex action of disengaging and heading for his car. Sometimes, he thought, it takes more guts to run than to stay. But he had no intention of throwing his life away for a lost cause. He was still thinking how best to manage it when Andrea joined them.

"There might be another way," she told Adam. "We could threaten to destroy the port. Take it from them."

"That's no good," he said. "That's precisely what they want."

"Maybe not," said Max. "There'll be a lot of media attention here tonight. It would be a public-relations nightmare for the administration."

"It's a public-relations nightmare," said Adam, "only if we can broadcast the threat. We have no capability to do that."

"You mean the Snowhawk is off the air?"

"Yes, she is," said Andrea. "But I think it would put a lot of pressure on them to stay clear if we could find a way to get to the media."

"No." April's voice took on steel. "You can't threaten the port. The whole point of staying here is to protect the place."

"We don't actually have to destroy anything. It's a bluff," Andrea said.

"And that's exactly how they'll read it," said Adam. "They would have to call us on it." Lights were moving on the access road. "They'd *have* to."

A phone rang. They looked at one another. It was coming from the control module. "I thought," said Max, "the phones were dead."

They had been standing at the rim of the cut in which the Roundhouse rested. "That'll be an official call," said April.

It was Max's phone. April picked it up, listened, nodded. "Yes," she said, "he's here." She handed it to Max.

"Hello," he growled.

A female voice asked if he was Mr. Collingwood.

"Yes," he said.

"Please hold for the President."

Max froze. He stared at the others, and they stared back. "Who?" April asked, forming the word silently.

Then the familiar clipped voice with its Baltimore accent came on the phone. "Max?"

"Yes, Mr. President." Eyes went wide all around.

"Max, are you in a place where the others can hear us?"

"Yes, I am."

"Okay. I know you can put this on a speaker if you want. But it would be better if you didn't. What I have to say is for *you*."

His throat had gone dry. "Mr. President," he said, "I am *very* glad to hear from you."

"And *I'm* glad to have a chance to talk to *you,* son. Now listen, things are going to hell in the country. They're a lot worse than you probably know about. People are losing their jobs, their savings, and God knows where it's all going to end."

"Because of the Roundhouse?"

"*Because of the Roundhouse.* Look, we don't want to take anything away from the Indians. You know that. The country knows it. But people are scared right now, and we have to get that thing up there under control. We will see that the Indians are taken care of. You have my word. But this *thing,* it's like nothing we've ever had to deal with before. It's a national treasure, right? I mean, the Indians didn't put it there or anything like that. They just happen to own the land." He paused, possibly to catch his breath, maybe to get his emotions under control. His voice sounded close to breaking.

"I know about the problems, sir."

"Good. Then you know I have to act. *Have to.* God help me, Max, the last thing we want to do is to spill blood over this."

"I think everybody here feels the same way."

"Of course. Of course." His voice changed, acquired a tone that suggested they were now in accord. "I know about your father, Max. He served this country damned well."

"Yes, sir. He did."

"Now *you* have a chance." He paused a beat. "I need your help, son."

Max knew what was coming. "I don't have much influence up here, Mr. President."

"They don't trust us, do they?"

"No, sir. They don't."

"I don't blame them. Not a damned bit. But I am willing to give my personal assurance that they will be amply compensated for giving up their rights to Johnson's Ridge."

"You want me to tell them that?"

"Please. But I also need you to try to persuade them to see our side of this problem. I need you to convince them to give this up, Max. The only thing that can come out of this if they persist is to get themselves killed. Now please, I need your help."

"Why *me*, Mr. President? Why didn't you call Chairman Walker? Or Dr. Cannon?"

"Walker's mind is made up. Dr. Cannon may be too young to have much influence over a group of Indians. You understand what I mean. I'll be honest with you, Max. We've looked at the profiles of the people up there with you, and you seemed to us to be most open to reason."

Max took a deep breath. He was the weak link. "I'll tell them," he said. "May I ask *you* something?"

"Go ahead, Max. Ask anything. Anything at all."

"There's a rumor here that the government intends to destroy the Roundhouse. Will you give me your word there's no truth to it?"

Max could hear breathing on the other end. Then: "Max, we wouldn't do that."

"Your word, Mr. President?"

"Max. I can promise generous compensation."

"What's he saying?" whispered April.

Max shook his head.

"I don't think that's enough, Mr. President."

"Max, you can help. Talk to them."

"They won't listen to *me*. Anyhow, I think they're right."

The long silence at the other end drew out until Max

wondered if the President was still there. "You know, Max," he said at last, "if there's bloodshed, you'll have to live the rest of your life knowing you could have prevented it." Max could visualize him, a little man who looked somehow as if he should be running the neighborhood print shop. "I feel sorry for you, son. Well, you do what you have to, and I respect that. But stay on the line, okay? They'll give you a number so you can get through if you change your mind. If we can get out of this peacefully, I'd be pleased to have you up to the White House."

Then he was gone, and Max copied down the number and handed it to Adam. Without looking at it, Adam tore it into small pieces. He opened the door and gave it to the wind. And it occurred to Max that the only person who thought that Max Collingwood was going to stay with the Sioux was the President of the United States.

The white *Ben at Ten* news van rolled east across the prairie, bound for Johnson's Ridge. Carole could barely contain her excitement. She kept replaying the interview in her mind, relishing the drama. *She will stay with her brothers to defend her land.* And, at the end, her own closing line, *From the Sioux reservation at Devil's Lake, this is Carole Jensen for NBC News.*

And it wasn't over. Robert Bazell was coming, but in the meantime she would be the network's voice on the front line. She hoped that Bazell's plane would get socked in somewhere.

Carole fell back against her seat and let the sheer joy of the moment surge through her.

They passed through the Pembina Mountains, and turned north again on Route 32. After a while they saw the emerald glow in the sky.

Jack McDevitt

Police were steering traffic into a detour. Carole showed her credentials and got waved on. Ahead, at the turnoff to the access road, blinking lights and the white glare of TV lamps spilled onto the highway. Cars and vans were parked on the shoulder on both sides of the two-lane. Chang slowed down and pulled in beside an NBC van.

A cluster of media people had gathered at the access point. An old battered Ford was at the center of attention. She recognized Walker immediately. He had got out of the car and was talking to a deputy. Other police officers were trying without much success to keep the journalists at a distance.

"Set up, Chang," she said, punching in the studio's number on her cellular phone.

"Carole?" said her producer. "I was about to call you."

"We're here."

"Okay. Walker just came down off the mountain. CNN and ABC are already on with it. He's apparently going to make a statement."

Carole was out of the car and on the move. Chang came around the other side, shouldering his gear.

"We're doing the intro now," said the voice from the studio. "Switch to you in twenty seconds."

"Son of a bitch," said Carole, throwing a quick look at her partner. "Chang, you ready?"

They got into the group of journalists, pushed and jostled their way forward until they could manage a decent shot of the proceedings. Walker looked frail and old. The police officers were uncomfortable with the turmoil and losing patience. A woman wearing a U.S. marshal pocket bullion was having an animated conversation with Chief Doutable. Carole was good at lip-reading, and she caught enough of the conversation to understand that she was telling the police chief to let *something* happen.

354

The reporters pushed forward, and the entire scene was awash in bright lights and stark shadows.

The deputy caught a signal from Doutable and backed away. Several hands thrust microphones toward the Ford. How did the Indians feel about being evicted? Would the Sioux fight? Were the Sioux hiding something? Was it true about the Visitor?

"No," he said, "we are not hiding anything." He climbed up onto the hillside, where everyone could see him. "My name is James Walker. I am the chairman of the tribal council."

"Then what's the big secret?" shouted someone in back.

Walker looked puzzled. "There is no secret. We have willingly shared the wilderness world with all who came to look. But the Roundhouse is on *our* land."

The reporters grew quiet.

"It may be," Walker continued, "that the road to the stars crosses this ridge. Some people are disturbed by the discoveries made here. They fear them. And we know that when change comes, no one is more adamant in holding on to the past than those in power. They know change is inevitable, but they would, if they could, parcel it out in measured pieces. Grain for chickens.

"We are told by *your* government," he continued, "that we must leave. If we do not comply, we will be turned out. And those who have the temerity to remain on their own land are threatened with jail. Or worse. I would ask you, if these persons can seize our property because they are afraid, whose property is safe? If they can lay hands on our future, whose future is secure?"

(*Producer's voice*: "Great, Carole. The guy is great! Try to get an exclusive interview when it's over.")

"This will not be the first time we have been called on to defend our land with our blood. But I would speak directly to the President of the United States." Chang moved in. "Mr. President, only you have the power to stop this. The people who will die tonight, on both sides, are innocent. And they are idealistic, or they would not be confronting each other. They are the best that we have, willing to sacrifice themselves for a cause dictated by older men. Stop it while you can."

Tom Lasker's ID had done him no good at the roadblock, and he had been turned away without explanation, just like the hordes of tourists. His first reaction was to use the cellular phone to call Max, but he got only a busy signal, the kind of rasping two-tone that usually indicates a trunk line is down.

He had been listening to the news accounts, and he knew about the ultimatum. It had not seriously hit home until now, however, that there was going to be shooting and that people might get killed.

He hesitated, not knowing what to do, feeling he should talk to someone but not knowing who could help. He called Ginny and told her what was going on. "Come home," she said. "Stay out of it." Moments later she called him back. "One of the people from the reservation is trying to reach you." She gave him a number. "Be careful," she added.

William Hawk picked up on the other end. "Tom," he said. "We need to get a message through to the chairman."

April had been unusually quiet. Max wondered whether she was disappointed in him or whether she was simply frightened. They'd returned to the control module and sat moodily, not talking. The air was heavy, and Max, at least, could not say what was on his mind.

It hurt. "April," he said, "you're sure you want to stay?"

She looked up at him and needed a moment to focus. "Yes," she said. "I feel the same way Adam does. I can't walk out of here and just let them take everything."

"Yeah. Okay." Max got up. "Well, I'm out of here."

She nodded.

"Good luck," he said.

✠ 31 ✠

It is an unbecoming thing to wince before the menacing shot.

—Montaigne, "Of Steadfastness"

As soon as it became apparent the Sioux would not back down, Elizabeth Silvera began listening in on telephone conversations. She was aware of Walker's question to Adam, *How far are you prepared to go?* and of the response. She also understood from his phone conversation with Walter Asquith, the Pulitzer prize-winning writer, that Walker planned some sort of demonstration by outsiders. She had no concrete information. She had listened to other conversations before they shut down communications, intercepts during which the Native Americans reassured their families not that they would be okay but that they could be relied on to defend the birthright. She wondered if they had guessed she was listening and if the remarks were being made specifically for her benefit. And finally she had listened to Max's conversation with the President. Max's refusal to take a stand had elicited her indignation and simultaneously persuaded her that force would be necessary. If the Sioux were going to accept a settlement, that would have been the time to do it.

This was not an assignment she was happy with. Not that she had moral or political reservations. But the situation was explosive, with a lot of risk professionally and relatively little to gain. If she got everything right here, she would simply pass the package on to SOG, which would get the credit. In the meantime, if she screwed up anything at all, it would be her career.

She had officially turned the operation over to SOG during the late afternoon. Horace Gibson, the group commander, had arrived to take charge of things personally. Considering how high-profile the case was, she'd expected no less. Elizabeth had met Gibson once before, and she didn't care much for him. There was a little too much bravado in his manner. Gibson thought highly of himself and made no secret of his opinion that his people were special, the organization's elite. He made Elizabeth feel like a peasant.

On this occasion, though, she could almost feel sorry for him. She knew what his instructions were: take the Roundhouse quickly, to avoid a prolonged media circus; do it without losing anybody; and if possible, do it without hurting any of the Indians.

Good luck.

She knew Horace well enough to conclude that the Indians better look out.

NBC's *Special Edition*, interview of Attorney General Christian Polk by Tom Brokaw

Brokaw: Mr. Polk, we've just watched the plea made by James Walker for restraint and his charge that the government is trying to steal land that belongs to the Sioux. How do you respond to that?

Polk: Tom, we sympathize with Chairman Walker and the Sioux. I would like to make it clear that the action we have taken is, we feel, in everyone's best interest. Let me reiterate that we are not *stealing* the property. We are only asking for oversight.

Brokaw: What precisely does oversight mean, Mr. Polk? Who will actually control operations at the Roundhouse?

Polk: Why, the Sioux, of course. The only reason we will be there is to ensure that— Look, Tom, this is a unique situation. We've never seen anything like this before. We have a duty to see that appropriate safeguards are maintained. We just don't know what we're dealing with, and we owe it to the American people to stay on top of this. There's nothing unreasonable about that.

Brokaw: Exactly what sort of threat worries you?

Polk: The first thing we want to do is to reassure everyone. There have been stories that something came out of the Roundhouse—

Brokaw: You don't really believe that, do you?

Polk: No. I personally do not. But that's not the issue. A lot of people do. And we have to reassure them.

Brokaw: So you plan to take Sioux property by force because some people in North Dakota are getting nervous?

Polk: There are other factors. We don't know what hazards there might be. Disease, for example. That is a primary concern. We have to control these ports.

Brokaw: It appears that the Sioux will not comply with the court order.

Polk: That's not really an option for them.

Brokaw: That might be their call rather than yours. Mr. Polk, are you prepared to use force?

Polk: I'm sure it won't come to that.

Brokaw: But will you use force if you have to?

Polk: We have every confidence this can be settled peacefully.

Brokaw: Thank you, sir.

Polk: Thank *you*, Tom.

Horace Gibson sat in his temporary command post on a hilltop several miles north of Johnson's Ridge, going over the latest pictures from the target area and the weather updates. He'd done his homework on Adam Sky and did not look for any mistakes in the defense. He was also not sure what kind of weapons Sky might be able to deploy.

The Sioux would dig in, using the mounds as cover.

Gibson's preference would have been to drop black smoke on them and follow up with concussion grenades. Blind them, shake them up, and use the choppers to move in before they could regroup. But winds of forty miles per hour were blowing across the top of the escarpment and were expected to worsen during the night. So there would be no smoke to cover an assault. The wind conditions wouldn't help chopper maneuverability, either, but he could manage.

Left to his own devices, Horace would have simply sealed off the area and waited out the defenders. But pressure was coming, he believed, all the way from the White House. *Get it done*.

He didn't like the combat area. The defenses looked out over flat ground with no cover. It was a killing zone.

His most practical tactic was to attack the mounds with

the Blackhawks and try to drive the defenders into the pit. Or sow enough confusion to cover a landing.

Elizabeth Silvera had taken her post, with Chief Doutable and half a dozen police officers armed with rifles, on the escarpment about a quarter-mile west of the top of the access road. The position was exposed, should the Sioux begin shooting, but it offered an excellent view of the defenders across the top of the excavation. The mounds were in shadow, and Sky had erected tarpaulins on a framework of wooden parts to prevent his people from being silhouetted against the glow from the Roundhouse. But it was a clear night and there was a bright moon. A reconnaissance helicopter had been doing occasional sweeps and now hovered over the north side of the escarpment.

Doutable had been relieved to learn that the SOG team would not ask for, and did not want, armed assistance. All they needed from local police was an assurance that no unauthorized persons would wander onto the escarpment. That was shorthand for the media.

Elizabeth knew that when it came, it would be very quick. She'd been through something like this once before with Gibson. She was waiting now for a coded report that would give her the time of the assault and provide any special instructions the commander would have for her. Doutable was saying something that she wasn't really listening to when she became aware of the sound of another aircraft.

It wasn't one of the Blackhawks.

That was strange. There shouldn't have been anyone in the sky over the ridge except marshals.

A gray propeller-driven plane was approaching from the

south. She raised her binoculars. It carried U.S. military markings.

"What the hell's going on?" she muttered to herself, and switched on her link to the helicopter. "Bolt One," she said. "This is Reluctant. We've got an intruder."

"I see him," came the response.

"Warn him away."

"Reluctant, I have been trying to talk to him for about a minute. He does not respond."

The plane was down low and coming fast.

"Please advise, Reluctant."

"Warn him to leave the area or be fired on."

"That's a roger."

The Blackhawk was keeping pace with the gray plane, riding about a thousand feet above it.

"Reluctant, that's an old Avenger," said the helicopter. "World War II fighter." Another pause. "He does not answer."

"Who is it?" she asked. "Is there an ID?"

The helicopter relayed its tail number, which Doutable scribbled down. "Give me a minute," he said. He gave the number to one of the cruisers.

The Avenger was coming in on the deck.

Gibson came on the circuit. "Bolt One," he said. "Fire a warning round."

The Blackhawk fired in front of the vintage aircraft, directly across its line of sight. The Avenger wavered slightly but kept coming.

"It belongs to a guy named Tom Lasker," said Doutable. "The plane's based at Fort Moxie."

"Lasker," she said. "I know him. He's the guy with the boat."

At that moment the Avenger roared over the trenches.

Part of it seemed to fall away. It banked west and started gaining altitude.

"Bolt One," she said, "break off." She turned to Doutable. "Have someone waiting for him when he lands. I think we'll want to talk to him."

"It dropped something," said one of the police officers.

Elizabeth turned her binoculars on the excavation.

"Reluctant, this is Bolt One. The Indians have come out of their hole. They're looking for something."

"Roger."

"There are two of them out front, beyond the ring of ditches. Wait a minute. Wait a minute." He nodded. "Whatever it is, I think they've found it."

Elizabeth watched through her own binoculars while the Sioux retreated back into the crosswork of ditches and mounds. What was so important that Lasker was willing to challenge a Blackhawk?

Max, of course, had recognized the Avenger immediately, and he had watched the drama from his car, cringing, waiting for the helicopter to take Lasker out.

But it had not happened. And now he sat with his engine running, anxious to be away. He was angry, and his conscience was eating at him, digesting him whole. But he had already put his life on the line once for this project, had gone into that goddamn yellow light with no assurance it wouldn't just turn him into a cloud of atoms. Now they were all looking at him as if he were Benedict Arnold. Someone not fit to be seen with.

Well, not all of them. Only April, actually. But that was the one that hurt. She'd still have been sitting on that beach if Max hadn't gone after her.

He sympathized with Adam and the others. But this wasn't *his* fight. If she wanted to throw her life away, that was up to her. *He* had no intention of getting killed over it. None. But the way she had looked at him when he said he was leaving—

Son of a bitch.

He turned on his headlights and started moving slowly toward the access road. He knew the police were over there, and he could assume they were armed and probably a little nervous. That was risk enough for him.

But he saw movement behind him.

Someone waving. Adam.

Max slowed down, circled, and started back.

"Max." Adam came abreast of the car. "Can you do something for us?"

Max squirmed. "What was Tom doing here?" he asked.

Adam held out a piece of paper. "Delivering this."

Max held it close to his map light. It was from William Hawk.

Chairman:

Your people are coming. Two charter flights inbound to Grand Forks at about 11:00 P.M. I am sending escort.

Max looked up. "What's this? Reinforcements?"

"Some people the chairman thinks can stop this."

Max sighed. "I hate to say this, but the chairman's losing it."

"Maybe," said Adam. "But it's all we have. There are twelve or thirteen people coming in on the two flights."

"The problem is," said Max, "that even if they could help, you can't get them here."

"That's right. The roads are blocked."

"So what do you want me to do?"

"Fly them in," said Adam. "Talk to your friends at Blue Jay. Rent a couple of helicopters."

"You're crazy. Blue Jay's not going to fly anybody in *here*. They damned near shot Tom down."

"They're friends of yours," said Adam. "Offer them a lot of money. Make it worth their while."

Max sat staring over the top of his steering wheel at the dark patch of woods that masked the access road. One of the police cruisers had turned on its blinker. Otherwise, nothing was moving.

"I'll do what I can," he said.

Police were waiting for him at the top of the access road. They held him while one of the cars that had been parked out on the escarpment approached and stopped. Elizabeth Silvera. "Nice to see you, Mr. Collingwood. Would you step out of the car, please?"

He complied.

"Is anyone else going to leave?"

"Don't know," he said. "I don't think so."

"How about Cannon?"

"She thinks you people are going to destroy the Roundhouse."

"I take it that's a no."

"That's a no." Max folded his arms, defensively because he had been in the company of people who were challenging duly constituted authority, guiltily because he was abandoning his friends.

"What have they got up there?" she asked, softening her tone, adapting an almost cordial we're-all-in-this-together demeanor.

"Beg pardon?"

"Weapons. What do they have?"

"I don't know. Sidearms. Rifles. They've got rifles. I don't know what else." Strictly speaking, that was the truth. Max did not have the details.

Silvera nodded. "What did the plane drop?" she asked.

Max was ready for the question. "Message from the tribe. To let everyone know they had their support."

"That's it?" she asked.

"That's it. It's a custom. Message of support for the warriors. Goes back hundreds of years."

She never blinked. "Mr. Collingwood, do you have anything to tell us that would help us end this peacefully?"

"Yeah." Max drew himself up to his full height. "Go away. Leave them alone."

"I'm sorry you feel that way." She looked disgusted. "Where are you going to be staying?"

"The Northstar. In Fort Moxie."

"Okay. Stay close. We might want to talk to you again."

"Sure," Max said.

He kept an eye on his rear to see whether he was being followed. The road stayed empty. He debated calling Jake Thoraldson to ask him to get the Lightning ready, but he suspected the conversation would be overheard. Consequently he was delayed a half-hour at the Fort Moxie airport while the plane was brought out and warmed up.

At a little after ten he taxied onto the runway, turned into the wind, and gunned the engines. The twin liquid-cooled Allisons rumbled reassuringly. Jake cleared him for takeoff, a gesture that inevitably contained a hint of absurdity at Fort Moxie, where the pilot was always looking at empty skies. He engaged the throttle, and the old warbird began to move.

Maybe it was the roar of the engines, the wind rushing beneath the nacelles, the geometry of the Lightning. Maybe it was his combat pilot's genes kicking in. Whatever it might have been, his fears drained off as the landing strip fell away. This was the plane that had turned the tide in the Pacific. He looked through the gunsight. The weapons cluster was concentrated in the nose, consisting of a 20-mm cannon and four .50-caliber machine guns. Its firepower, added to the Lightning's ability to exceed four hundred miles per hour, had been irresistible. The Germans had called it *der Gabelschwanz Teufel—the Fork-Tailed Devil.*

The guns were disabled now, but for a wild moment Max wished he had them available.

He was leveling off at nine thousand feet when he saw another plane. It was at about fourteen thousand feet, well to the north. Too far to identify, but it occurred to him he should assume they would be watching.

He was tempted to fly over the Roundhouse, dip his wings, deliver some sign that Adam could trust him. But he knew it would be prudent not to draw anyone's attention.

The other plane was propeller-driven, so he would have no trouble outrunning it. But he couldn't outrun its radar. Still, even if they tracked him into Grand Forks, which they would undoubtedly do, so what? They would lose interest once he was on the ground.

He made a long, casual turn toward the south and goosed the Lightning.

Twenty minutes later he landed at Casper Field and rolled to a stop in front of a series of nondescript terminals. Casper was home to several freight forwarders, a spraying service, and a flying school. And to Blue Jay Air Transport.

He climbed out of the plane almost before it had come to a stop and hurried into the little washed-out yellow building that housed Blue Jay's business offices.

He'd been listening to air traffic control out of Grand Forks, and he knew that one of his charters was already on approach and the other was about thirty minutes out. The Sioux had sent someone to meet the planes, but Max knew *he* was going to have to coordinate things if they were to have any chance of getting Walker's mysterious friends back to the ridge in time to do any good. He found a pay phone and put in a quarter.

Bill Davis sounded as if he'd been in bed. "Say all that again, Max?"

"Got a job for two choppers, about a dozen passengers. And a couple people from the TV station. Say fourteen, fifteen in all."

"When?"

"Tonight."

"I can't get anything out that quickly, Max. I don't even know who's available."

"It's an emergency," said Max. "We'll pay double your rates. And a bonus for the pilots."

"How much?"

"A thousand. Each."

He considered it. "Tell you what I'll do. You say you need *two* aircraft?"

"Yes."

"Okay. Look, I can only get one guy on this kind of short notice. But I'll fly the second chopper myself."

Max thanked him and punched in another number.

"KLMR-TV. If you wish to speak with the advertising department, press one. If . . . "

Max looked at his watch. It was twenty to eleven. He

listened through the litany of instructions, and when the news desk came up, he pushed the appropriate button.

"News desk."

"This is Max Collingwood. One of the people from the Roundhouse. I'd like to speak with the news director."

"Hold one moment, please."

There was a brief silence. Then a familiar baritone was on the line. "Hello. This is Ben Markey. Collingwood, is that really you?"

"Yes. It's really me."

"You're supposed to be on top of the ridge. Are you calling from the ridge?"

"No. Listen, I don't have much time to talk, but I can offer you a hell of a story."

"Okay." Max could hear the man light up over the phone. "Where can we meet?"

Max gave him instructions, hung up, and called the airport tower.

"Operations," said a male voice.

"Duty officer, please." Max was grateful not to have to deal with another automated call-answering system.

"May I tell her who's calling?"

"Max Collingwood. Sundown Aviation."

"Hang on, Mr. Collingwood."

A long delay, during which he was twice assured that the duty officer would be with him presently. Then a familiar voice: "Hello, Max."

Max knew most of the senior air people at Grand Forks. This was Mary Hopkins. She was a former vice president of the Dakota Aviation Association. She was tall, quiet, unassuming, married to an irritating stock brokerage account executive. "Mary," he said into the receiver, "I know you're busy."

"It's okay. What can I do for you?"

"There are two charter flights coming in. One of them must be landing about now. The other is close behind."

"Okay," she said. "I see two."

"I'm going to bring in a couple of choppers from Blue Jay to pick up the passengers. If you could arrange to keep them together and allow a direct transfer, I'd be grateful."

"You want to keep the passengers in the planes until the helicopters get here?"

"Yes. Just park them out somewhere, if you can, where they'll be out of the way, and we'll bring the choppers in right alongside. Okay?"

"Max—"

He knew this violated normal procedure and that she wasn't happy with the idea. "I wouldn't ask, Mary. You know that. But this is important. Lives depend on it."

"This has to do with the business up on the border?"

"Yeah," he said. "You could say that."

"I'll do what I can," she said. "Where can I reach you?"

Bill Davis was three hundred pounds of profit motive and cynicism with a dry sense of humor and four divorces. He had recently suffered a minor heart attack and now had a tendency to live in the past, to talk as if his days were numbered.

His paneled office was filled with pictures of aircraft and pilots. A signed photo of John Wayne guarded the top of a credenza.

"Good to see you, Max," Davis said. "I've got George coming down. Where are we going?" He filled a coffee cup and held it out.

Max took it. "The ridge," he said.

Davis frowned. "Isn't that where they're trying to get the Indians out? National Guard, right?"

"Not the Guard," said Max. "U.S. marshals. They're going to shut the place down tomorrow, and the Sioux don't want to leave."

"Hell, Max, I can't send anyone into that."

"Make it two thousand, Bill."

"Then you *do* expect trouble?"

"No, I don't. I just don't have the time to argue."

Horace did his final reconnaissance at a little after eleven and returned to the command post. His first act was to call Carl.

"This is not good," he said.

"What's the problem, Horace?"

"The wind. Wait one night, Carl. Give us a chance to use the smoke. Otherwise it could be a bloodbath out there. Everything's too exposed."

"Can't do it," said Rossini.

"Son of a bitch, Carl. We can't wait *one* night? Listen!" He held up the receiver so Rossini could hear the wind roar. "What the hell is the big hurry?"

"I'm sorry, Horace," he said. "Get it done before dawn. I don't care what it takes."

"Then I'm going to work over the mounds before I put anybody on the ground. You're going to have a stack of dead Indians in the morning. Is that what you want?"

"Whatever it takes, Horace."

Horace banged the phone down. It missed its cradle and fell into the snow.

"Do not aim to kill," said the chairman, "except as a last resort."

"Why?" objected Little Ghost. "We are going to be in a war."

Walker nodded. "I know. But time's with us. The longer we can delay the decision, the better for us."

They were gathered in a small circle at the edge of the pit. The wind howled against the tarps that shielded them from the glow of the Roundhouse.

"Please explain," said Andrea.

"Help is coming. If we're still here when it arrives, and if the situation by then isn't beyond retrieving, I think we can survive the night. And maybe keep the wilderness."

"But they'll be trying to kill us. Why should we not—"

"Because once we spill blood," he said, "there'll be no stopping it. Keep down. Shoot back. But take no lives. Unless you must."

Adam took Andrea Hawk and George Freewater aside. "I want you two on the flanks," he said. "George, out by the parking lot. Be careful. They'll have a problem. We're going to show them they can't bring helicopters in with impunity. And they can't advance directly on us. So they'll have to try a trick play. Maybe they'll try to bypass us and seize the Roundhouse."

"That wouldn't accomplish anything," said George. "They'd be down in the ditch."

"They'd have the Roundhouse. That would make everything else moot. They might also try an end run." He looked at Andrea. "That would probably mean coming up the face of the cliff. I looked down and I couldn't see anything. But I'd think about trying it if I were on the other side."

"Will there be a signal to open fire?" asked Andrea.

Adam was standing with his face in shadow. "No. Use your judgment. But we want them to fire the first shot."

✠　✠　✠

Grand Forks International Airport is not busy in the sense that O'Hare or Hartsfield is busy. But it services several major airlines and maintains a steady stream of traffic.

The two charter jets were parked on an apron immediately outside the administrative offices at the main terminal. Max circled overhead while the tower directed the Blue Jay helicopters down through a stiff wind.

Max talked to the charter pilots, advising them that he was coordinating the flight and that he wanted to transfer the passengers directly to the helicopters, and to do it as quickly as possible.

They acknowledged, and he got his own instructions from the tower, which vectored him in from the west and, at his request, directed him to a service hangar. He turned the Lightning over to the maintenance people and got a ride in a baggage carrier to the transfer point. When he arrived, several passengers had already climbed into the helicopters. Others were waiting their turn to board. An airport worker was helping load a wheelchair. Ben Markey was there with a cameraman. Max recognized Walter Asquith, who had visited the escarpment and who wanted to do a book about the Roundhouse. One or two of the others looked vaguely familiar, and Max was about to ask for names when he heard his own. He turned and saw William Hawk approaching.

"Thank you for everything you've done, Max," he said.

"My pleasure," said Max. "I hope it works out."

Hawk was tall and broad-shouldered. There was anger in his dark eyes, and Max could easily imagine him on horseback, leading a charge against the Seventh Cavalry.

Bill Davis waved at them from the pilot's seat. "Councilman," he said, raising his voice over the roar of the engines, "we should get moving if you want to be there by midnight."

Hawk looked at Max. "Are you coming, Max?"

"No," he said. And then, weakly, "You'll need the space."

Hawk offered his hand. "Good luck, Max," he said.

It was a curious remark under the circumstances. "And you, Councilman." Ben Markey was already deep in conversation with the passengers, but Hawk was climbing in and the rotors were drowning out everything.

The first chopper lifted off, and someone put a hand on Hawk's shoulder to make sure he was safely inside. Then Davis's aircraft, too, was rising, backlit by the moon.

They arced out over the terminal and started north. Max watched them go. Crazy. They'd be lucky if they didn't all get killed.

Max had done the right thing. He'd set things up, got Walker's people off and moving, and now he could go home and watch it on TV.

The roar of the helicopters faded to a murmur and then gave way to the sound of an incoming jet.

He needed a beer before he went home, but he never drank when he was about to get into a cockpit. Tonight, though, might qualify for an exception. He stood staring at the sky, trying to make up his mind. And he heard the helicopters again.

Coming *back*.

He watched, saw their lights reappear.

Son of a bitch. What now? He hurried inside the terminal, found a phone, and called the tower. Within a minute he had Mary.

"Feds," she said.

✠ 32 ✠

A faithful friend is a strong defense.

—Ecclesiasticus 6:14

Max argued for a while with Bill Davis. He offered more money, a lot more, but Davis wouldn't bite, and Max couldn't blame him. He'd be trading in his license, and probably applying for jail time, if he defied the tower's order to return.

"Isn't there another carrier we can use?" asked William Hawk, his gaze shifting nervously between Max and the passengers, as if they might give up and go away.

"Not that I know of."

"What about you, Max?" said Ben Markey. Markey's ability to blend a kind of lighthearted mockery with rock-hard integrity, the ability which made him the area's foremost anchor, put Max on the defensive. "Don't *you* have an airline?"

"No. Sundown restores and sells antique aircraft. We aren't a carrier."

Hawk was looking at his watch. "Max, there's got to be a way."

Max was sorry he hadn't got into the air quicker. He could have been on his way to Fargo now.

But maybe there *was* an alternative. He picked up a phone and punched in Ceil's number. It rang into an answering machine. He identified himself and waited for her to cut in. When she didn't, he tried the corporate number. Boomer Clavis picked it up. "Thor Air Cargo," he said.

"Boomer, this is Max. Is Ceil there?"

"How ya doin', Max?" he said. "I can give you her number. She's in Florida."

And that was it. "When's she due back?"

"Uh, Wednesday, maybe. They're opening an air museum in Tampa."

Max said nothing.

"Hold on, Max. Let me get her number."

"No. Don't bother. It's not going to do me any good." He stared at the phone, then looked up at the people gathered around him. They were an ordinary-looking group. Twelve men and a woman. Middle-aged, mostly. Could have been traveling to Miami for the weekend and not looked at all out of place.

Their eyes were fixed on him. Max hung up. "Nothing I can do," he said.

A tall, white-haired man suggested they hire some cars.

"They would not let us through," said Hawk. "The only way in is by air."

The woman looked at Max. "Who is Ceil?"

"She owns a C–47. And she's a pilot."

"What's a C–47?" asked Hawk.

"It's a cargo plane. I thought there was a chance she'd be willing to try landing on the escarpment. She's done it before."

One of the visitors was confined to a motorized wheelchair. In a synthesized voice he asked, "Can *you* fly the C–47?"

"Me? No."

"Have you ever flown it?" asked a lean, bearded man in back.

"Yes," said Max. "But I couldn't land it on the top of the ridge."

One of the visitors looked like a retired pro linebacker. He was redheaded, and there was an intensity in his eyes that Max found unsettling. Now those eyes locked on Max. "Why not?" he asked.

"Because there's still snow up there, for one thing. And it's dark."

"Max—your name *is* Max?" said the linebacker.

"Yes."

"You're all we've got, Max. I'm willing to try it if you are." The man looked around at the others, who nodded agreement.

"It's *not* a good idea," said Max.

"Call the Boomer back," said the woman. "And let's get this show on the road."

A voice on the fringe of the group added, "Tell him to put the skis on. And Max, if you need help with the plane, we've got a couple more pilots here."

Reluctantly Max thanked him. He could see no way out, so he allowed himself to be hurried through the terminal and out onto the street, where they commandeered five taxis. He gave the drivers instructions, promised fifty-dollar tips for quick delivery, and climbed into the last taxi himself, with the woman and the linebacker. They lurched away from the curb. "You know," said the woman, "you people don't have this very well organized."

Max looked for a smile but didn't see one.

A few minutes later they were on I–29, barreling south.

The wind blew steadily across the ridge. April was crouched with Will Pipe behind one of the mounds. The chain-link fence that circled the excavation would be taken out first, Pipe was saying. Adam admired her—she was making a blood offering and asking nothing in return. Her presence lent a sense that they were not really alone. He was grateful to her and hoped she would survive the night.

He had formed a line of defense among the mounds, about thirty feet inside the fence, and with his back to the excavation pit. Unfortunately, there would be no retreat. His people could not withdraw into the hole and have any chance of maintaining the fight.

He assumed the marshals would make an effort shortly after midnight to drive them out of their defenses. With luck, the chairman's rescue party would arrive first. For whatever good they could do.

April was cold. She could not bring herself to believe that there might actually be some killing. She was privileged, perhaps, for her world had never contained gunfire. It was the stuff of the network news and lurid thrillers, but not of reality. Not of *her* reality.

"Look," said Pipe.

Three of the cars that had been parked off the access road were moving. Their headlights were off, but it didn't make any difference because the top of the escarpment was flooded with light from the moon. They were keeping a respectful distance. Pipe spoke into his radio.

April felt her stomach tighten. She wanted to be something more than just a bystander. But she could not bring herself to pick up a rifle.

To a degree, she was responsible for the standoff. They had mishandled this, she and Max. They'd been so busy with the discovery itself that they'd lost sight of the political implications. They could have thrown a blanket over everything, kept it quiet. The media and the press had been inclined to laugh, and April should have allowed them to do so until she'd taken time to think out the consequences. But she'd been too busy enjoying the media attention. Calling press conferences. Blab, blab.

Damn.

One of the three cars, a black late-model Chevrolet, had begun to pick up speed. It pulled ahead of the others, came around to the south, swung in a large circle toward them, and nosed up to the security fence. A rear door opened, and the female marshal got out. She was carrying a bullhorn. "Chairman Walker," she said.

Her voice boomed through the instrument.

Walker showed himself, stepping out into the open. "What do you want?"

April looked at her watch. Midnight.

The bullhorn fell to the marshal's side. "Chairman, it's time to leave."

The wind played with Walker's white hair. "No," he said.

"You're under a court order." She came forward to the fence until she could have touched it. "Don't do this."

"You leave me no choice."

Pipe's hand found April's shoulder. "Keep down when the shooting starts. Better, get into the ditch and stay close to the wall. After a while they may hold up and offer a chance to surrender. If they do, show them this and give yourself up. But you will need to do it quickly."

He passed over a large linen handkerchief.

A white flag.

"They're still dug in around the perimeter." The radio operator pressed his earphone close and looked at his commander. "Horace, we are locked and loaded."

Gibson nodded. "Okay," he said. "What's the Rock Team status?"

"They are in place and ready to go."

The plan was simple enough. The weakness of the defenders' position was the fact that they were strung out with a ditch at their backs. If he could drive them *into* the ditch, it was over.

Bolt Two would bomb the chain-link fence that screened the mounds. When the fence was down, they would fire concussion grenades into the Indians' positions and follow up with heavy automatic-weapons fire. One and Three would go in with the ground force while the Rock Team (which was settled in a sheltered area twenty feet below the edge of the cliff) came over the top. With luck, the battle would be over within seconds.

There was a delay while Boomer, Max, and two of the visitors (who introduced themselves as Wally and Scott) finished putting the skis on the C–47. They were on a seldom-used strip behind the National Guard armory. When the aircraft was ready, the passengers hurried out of Sundown's offices and boarded. The cargo hold had benches, but it wasn't very comfortable.

Max, with a heavy heart, watched them disappear inside, one by one. Hawk walked over and stood beside him. "Thank you," he said. "I know you don't want to do this."

"I don't guess anybody does," said Max.

He informed the tower he was headed for Fort Moxie. They gave him clearance as he finished his preflight check.

Scott sat down in the copilot's seat. "Mind?"

"No," said Max. "You fly one of these?"

"I'm just here to watch a pro, Max," he said casually.

Max wondered whether the shooting wouldn't all be over by the time they arrived. He gunned the engines, and the old cargo plane began to move.

As he lifted into the air he was trying to visualize the summit at Johnson's Ridge. He'd probably have to come in from the southwest. The landing space would be short, and the longest run would take him toward the cliff edge. He could angle more toward the north, where he would be pointed at the trees instead of over the side. But that would cut his available space by about sixty yards.

He wished Ceil were here.

The mood in the cargo hold was subdued.

"Maybe that's them," April said, pointing at a lone helicopter.

"I don't think so." Pipe peered through his binoculars. "That thing's got too many guns sticking out of it." He looked at April. "Keep down," he said.

Fear whispered through her.

The helicopter kept its distance, tracking back and forth at a range of about three hundred yards. Adam came in behind them and knelt beside the rocket launcher. "All right, Will. You sure you know how to use it?"

"Yes," he said softly. "But I still think we should take the chopper out."

"No. Stay with the plan."

Pipe grunted disapproval, loaded the weapon, and put it on his shoulder.

"All we're doing," he complained, "is alerting them that we have the launcher."

"That's correct, Will. That's exactly right." Adam's hand squeezed April's shoulder. "We'll be okay," he said.

"Ready," said Pipe.

The chopper, apparently on cue, veered and raced toward the defenses. April saw flashes of light beneath its pods, and Adam pushed her to the ground.

"Fire," Adam said.

The launcher kicked, and the rocket rode a tail of fire out

past the incoming aircraft. Simultaneously a series of explosions ripped the ground in front of her. Metal fragments thunked into the earth, and black smoke blew over them. The helicopter roared overhead, and the distant tattoo of rifle fire began.

A long section of the fence was gone as surely as if it had never existed, replaced by a series of burning craters.

"Everybody all right?" asked Adam.

One by one they answered up.

"Okay," he said. "Now they know for sure that we have the launcher. Let's see if they keep their distance."

"This is an NBC news report."

The sitcom *Angie* just dropped off the screen, and Tom Brokaw appeared standing in front of a display showing the location of Johnson's Ridge. "Firing has been reported in the vicinity of the Roundhouse. We believe that U.S. marshals have begun an effort to seize the structure by force from a group of Sioux who have refused to comply with a court order to abandon the site. Details are sketchy at this hour because of a general news blackout. A press conference is scheduled twenty minutes from now. Meantime, here's what we know. . . ."

"Son of a bitch." Gibson in one of the choppers hit the switch on the phone. "Rock Team, hold off till you hear from me."

Charlie Evans and his two cliffhangers were waiting on a narrow shelf twenty feet below the summit. "Roger," said Charlie.

"It'll be a few minutes." He switched frequencies. "Bolt Three."

"Bolt Three here."

"Follow us down."

Gibson was not going to allow the bastards to blast one of his Blackhawks. He descended in a wooded area on the south and gathered his assault force. He had nine people at his disposal, plus the Rock Team. "Okay, ladies and gentlemen," he said. "We are going to have to do it the hard way."

"They're coming," said Little Ghost. "Pass the word."

Shadows had come out of the woods and were gliding toward them. "Everybody sit tight," said Adam.

The marshals drew closer, moving in a broken line. They were in black and were hard to pick up against the woods, even in the moonlight. Adam waited until they were within about 150 yards. Then he tapped Little Ghost on the shoulder. "*Now,* John," he said. "Keep it high."

Little Ghost fired a half-dozen rounds at the stars. The shadows stopped, waited, and came on again.

"Adam," said Little Ghost, "it's not going to work. If we're going to stop them, we better do it."

Max saw the flashes from about ten miles out. "We're too late," he told Scott.

The radio came alive: "C–47, you are in a restricted air zone."

"Uh, that's a roger," said Max. "I'm lost."

"Suggest you go to two-seven-zero."

"Stay on course," said Scott.

Max frowned. "That's a war up there. We're too late to stop it."

"Maybe not."

Okay, Max thought. In for a nickel . . .

The radar picked up a blip in the north. "Coming for us," said Scott.

Max nodded and tried to look as if he did this kind of thing every day. He snapped on the intercom. "Okay, folks," he told the cargo hold, "we're going to be on the ground in a couple of minutes. Buckle in."

Ahead, the chain of ridges and promontories rose out of the plain. He picked out Johnson's and adjusted course slightly to the south. Visibility was good, and the wind was directly out of the northeast at about forty knots. "Not the best weather," he said.

His copilot nodded. "You'll do fine."

The radio told him in cold tones he was subject to arrest.

Max dropped to two thousand feet, cut speed, and, five miles out, went to approach flaps. The landing area was smaller than he remembered. He saw the Roundhouse and the fires.

An armored helicopter drew alongside. Max looked out his window. A man dressed in black battle fatigues sat in the open door with a rifle in his lap.

The radio burped. "C–47, turn around. You are in violation."

The escarpment was coming up fast. He eased back on the yoke.

A blast of automatic-weapons fire and tracers cut across his nose. "We will fire on you if necessary."

"They're bluffing," said Scott.

Max passed over a swatch of trees, throttled down, and felt the main landing gear touch.

The plane lifted, settled again.

Voices were screaming in his earphones. The tail gear, which was also wearing a ski, made contact.

He cut power. The problem with the ski landing was that there were no brakes available. He couldn't even reverse engines. It was simply a matter of letting the aircraft come to a stop on its own.

The Roundhouse was off on his right. He could hear the stutter of automatic weapons.

"What's at the end of the field?" asked his copilot.

"Another short flight," he said.

The Roundhouse slid by. In back his passengers were silent. Snow hissed beneath the skis.

They passed between the parking lot and a couple of rapidly retreating police cruisers. The cars threw up snow.

Ahead, at the limit of his lights, he was looking at a void.

He thought briefly about gunning the engines to try to get back into the air or yanking the aircraft left to spill it into the trees. But it was really too late to do anything except ride the plane to the end.

The noise in his earphones had ceased.

He hung on.

They bounced over a ripple in the snow.

The void yawned larger. And spread horizon to horizon.

The plane slowed.

And stopped.

A Blackhawk roared past.

Max couldn't see much ground in front. "Everybody stay put," he told the passengers.

"Nice landing, Max," said his copilot.

He glanced through his side window, unbuckled, and looked out the other side. "Plenty of room," he said, sitting back down. He revved the left engine.

"Hey," said Scott, "be careful."

"It's okay," said Max. "This baby'll turn on a dime."

It was true. Max got some protests from the hold, and the voice in his earphones came back, but he brought the aircraft around and taxied toward the Roundhouse.

✠　✠　✠

While Max turned the plane, Gibson recognized his opportunity.

Moments later, the defenders ducked as a barrage of heavy fire came their way. On the left side of the defenses, Andrea saw a grappling hook loop up over the cliff edge and bite into the earth.

"The plane's coming this way," said Gibson's senior deputy. Its lights illuminated the parking lot as it passed and headed in the general direction of Horace's position.

"It damn sure is. What the hell are those fools trying to do?"

His radio operator pressed his headphones to his ears. "Bolt Two requests instructions."

"To do *what?*"

"Shoot, I guess, Horace."

"Goddamn, no. They must all be crazy out there."

The operator was listening again. "The Rock Team's over the top."

Max angled toward the Roundhouse. The night was filled with gunfire.

Asquith's voice came from the back: "Can't we move any faster than this?"

And the linebacker: "This is no time for halfway measures, Max."

Several of the others, in a surprisingly wide range of tones, supported the sentiment. Max throttled up and made directly for the hole in the security fence, for the middle of the cross-fire. Bullets clattered against the fuselage, and he thought how angry Ceil was going to be when she got her plane back. One of the windows blew out.

He wheeled up against a mound of earth, could go no farther. "Okay," he said, cutting the engines.

In back, they were already throwing open the cargo door. Ben Markey's cameraman, a tall, blond kid about twenty years old, knelt in the opening, adjusting his equipment. When he was ready, he turned on the lights. "Okay," he said. "Go."

Ben Markey, who was already talking into his microphone, nodded to Walter Asquith, who had been standing in the doorway. Asquith leaped out of the aircraft into a spray of bullets. One caught him in the leg and another in the chest. He crashed heavily into the snow.

Gibson, horrified, saw the incident from his forward position, saw two other people jump out of the plane and throw themselves across the man on the ground to shield him, saw the open cargo door and the inner cabin filled with more people. He had never witnessed such idiocy. Dumb sons of bitches. He turned to his operator. "Cease fire," he said. And to his senior deputy: "I do not believe this."

He suddenly realized he was on national television. He saw Ben Markey, sprawled on the ground, trying to avoid being shot, but talking into a microphone. He saw the cameraman panning the injured man, the fires and the mounds and the armed people on both sides.

In those few seconds the gunfire trailed off and stopped.

The black government car pulled up. Elizabeth got out on the run. "What the hell's going on here?" she demanded. She saw Asquith and caught her breath. "What happened?"

The passengers were still coming out of the plane, climbing down one by one, some managing it easily, others needing help. Police cars pulled up, lights blinking. The wheelchair came out. "Who are you people?" Elizabeth demanded.

A couple gave names, but Gibson was too far away to hear. She looked in his direction. Horace was thinking how best to handle it: Round these people up, but take advantage of the cease-fire to undercut the position of the Native Americans. He could do it. He knew he could.

"You can see what's happening here," Markey told his microphone. "Walter Asquith, winner of the Pulitzer prize for literature last year, has been shot."

Asquith? thought Gibson. My God. There'll be hell to pay.

The linebacker knelt beside Asquith, trying to stop the bleeding, while a man with a gray beard tried to make him comfortable. "You guys got a medic here anywhere?" the woman demanded as an ambulance pulled up.

Asquith's eyes were glazed, and he died clutching the linebacker's sleeve.

The body was placed in the back of the ambulance. After the vehicle drove away, Gibson came forward and identified himself. "I'll have to ask you people to come with me."

"Why?" asked the man with the beard. He was of about average height, and the cast of his features suggested a mild temper, but he confronted the marshal with barely suppressed rage. "So you can go on with your war?"

Gibson stared back. Nothing was easy anymore.

"Just arrest the whole bunch," said Elizabeth, keeping her voice down.

"Who are you?" Gibson asked the man who had spoken. He had recognized two of the visitors but not this one.

"Stephen Jay Gould," he said, raising his voice to be heard over the wind. The camera moved in, and the spotlight illuminated him for the national audience. "I don't think we're going to cooperate. If the government wants to kill anyone else, it'll have to start with us."

They were beginning to line up now, forming a human buffer between the sides.

"Gould," Ben told the microphone, "is a paleontologist."

The camera panned to a tall, aristocratic figure.

"Charles Curran," Ben said, holding the mike for him. "Theologian."

Curran might have been preparing to discipline a disorderly child. "This is more than a dispute about property rights," he said. "Johnson's Ridge doesn't belong to one government, or even to all governments. It belongs to everybody." He looked directly into the camera. "Tonight, its protectors are under siege. To that degree, we are *all* under siege."

"Arthur M. Schlesinger, Jr. Historian."

Schlesinger's brown eyes flashed behind horn-rimmed glasses. Gibson had a sudden sense of the uselessness of his fire power.

"Scott Carpenter. Astronaut."

Max's copilot. Still looking capable of riding into orbit, he nodded to the invisible audience.

"Gregory Benford. Astrophysicist and novelist."

Benford was of medium height, bearded, wearing an oversized hunting jacket that he'd probably borrowed. He scarcely looked at Gibson. Then he waved the chairman forward. Walker tentatively took his place in the line.

"James Walker. Leader of the Mini Wakan Oyaté. The People of the Spirit Lake."

"Thank you," Walker said, looking left and right.

"Harry Markowitz. Economist."

Markowitz folded his arms in silent defiance.

"Richard Wilbur. Poet."

Wilbur nodded, but his eyes were elsewhere, tracking the geometry between the artifact and the surrounding hills, as if the pattern were familiar, something he recognized.

"David Schramm. Astrophysicist."

The linebacker. He was covered with Asquith's blood.

"Stephen Hawking. Physicist."

Like some of the others, Hawking did not look properly dressed for the climate, as if he had been snatched from doing something else, in a warmer climate, and thrust on a plane. His eyes measured Gibson coldly.

"Walter Schirra. Astronaut."

Brown eyes, square jaw, medium size. Gibson knew Schirra, had read somewhere that he was one of the most gregarious and good-humored of the astronauts. But there was no sign of easy congeniality today.

"Ursula K. Le Guin. Novelist."

She stood staring at the place where Asquith had fallen. She too was stained with his blood.

"And Carl Sagan. Astronomer."

Like the others, Sagan seemed angry, frustrated, his signature optimism jolted by events. "Walter Asquith," he said, "was also with us on this journey. Walter was a poet."

"You know," said Gibson, in a low, dangerous voice, "you people are not above the law."

"Sometimes the law is stupid," said Markowitz.

April Cannon appeared and took her place between Schirra and Hawking.

Gibson was already formulating what he was going to say to his superiors.

✠ 33 ✠

Our song will enter
That distant land. . . .

—Southern Paiute poem

They spent the evening camped on the other side of the port, along the shore of the unnamed sea. Sagan and Schramm lay with their heads propped on backpacks looking up at strange constellations; Carpenter, Wilbur, Hawking, Benford, and Schirra sat by a dying fire, talking little, listening to the murmur of the tide, feeling, perhaps, what people have always felt when they've been washed up on an unknown coast. LeGuin, Curran, and Walker had tossed off their shoes and walked out into the water, where they wondered what lay on the other side. Schlesinger, Gould, and Markowitz were comparing notes with April on the transportation system that had brought them here, and what its adaptation to local use might mean. "The end of the city," said Markowitz.

Gould was not so sure. "Cities have a social utility, if only as places to get away from," he suggested.

Max stood off to one side, intimidated, until April noticed and handed him a Coke, bringing him within the circle of friends. "I don't know whether we thanked you," she said. "None of this would have happened without you."

Markowitz laughed and put an arm around him. "Yes, Max," he said. "Like it or not, you got us here. Whatever happens from this point on, *you* are responsible."

"The real question," Sagan said later, when it had grown cool and they'd all moved close to the fire, "is, where do we go from here?"

"How do you mean?" asked April.

"I think he means," said Wilbur, "that the government has a point. And I believe he's right."

"I agree," said Schirra. "If we exploit the Roundhouse, we move completely outside human experience. For one thing, we're going to have to have a whole new type of economy. Wouldn't you say, Harry?"

Markowitz nodded. "Oh, yes," he said. "But we can prepare for it. Adapt to it." He smiled and pointed out to sea. "The future lies that way."

"We," said Hawking, speaking through his electronics, "have incurred a responsibility. After all, we took it upon ourselves to make a decision today. I don't see how we can back away now."

The air moved. The long shoreline curved beneath the stars.

"But there are risks," said Walker.

Curran nodded. "The risks are proportionately high, as are the fears." He grinned. "We may have a lot to answer for."

"We have nothing to fear," said Schramm.

"Stephen is right," Schlesinger said. "We're looking at a new world. New worlds are always hard on old ideas."

Benford opened a box of marshmallows, stuck one on the end of a stick, and put it over the flame. "Are we saying that *we* should lead the charge?"

"I think you have to," said Max.

Several faces turned in his direction. They looked, he thought, not uncomfortable with the prospect. LeGuin poked at the fire. It crackled, and a cloud of sparks rose into the night. "It seems arrogant," she said.

Schramm opened two beers and passed one to Benford. "Of course it is. But I think we might need a little arrogance here."

"We might not be around to help," said Curran. "I'm not sure yet, but I think we committed a federal offense out there last night."

Sagan smiled. "I don't think we need worry. Matt Taylor's going to need all the help he can get."

"Yeah," said April. "I'd really like to help the President. He almost got us killed."

"He was in a box," said Schlesinger. "Right now everyone in the world may be in a box, and we've helped put them there."

"I agree," said Hawking. "And I think we should begin to consider how to get them out."

Benford nodded. "For a start, we need some positive PR."

"Precisely," said the chairman, who had seen a demonstration that day of the power of public relations.

"Maybe a TV show," said April. "Let people know what this place really is. What it can mean."

"And what the risks are," suggested Carpenter. "We need to be honest. Speaking of which—" He looked at Walker. "What about the Sioux? Are you willing to help?"

All eyes turned toward the tribal chairman. "I think we will insist that this world not be turned into a second North

America. And we will control the use of the port to that end. Beyond that, yes, we will be proud to help."

The Horsehead Nebula was in the northern sky, out over the sea. The illusion that it was an approaching storm was very strong.

"We'll have our hands full," said Schirra.

They looked at the stars, listened to the wind coming off the sea, felt the warmth of the fire on their faces. "I wish we could all have made it," said LeGuin.

Wilbur nodded. His eyes were lost in shadow. "I have Asquith's notes on this project."

"Enough to publish?" asked Hawking.

"Oh, yes." Wilbur reached behind him for a jacket and pulled it around his shoulders. "And it's pretty good stuff. Maybe, in the end, he'll outlive us all."

✠ EPILOGUE ✠

April Cannon watched her duffel bag disappear in a blaze of light. Her seven companions (one of whom was her retired boss, Harvey Keck) were making last-minute checks of equipment.

She turned to Max. "You're sure you don't want to come?" She was lovely in the green-tinged light.

"No," he said. "I don't like surprises, and I think you're going to find a lot of them out there."

She touched his arm. "We'll be careful."

They were planning on exploring the links to the Eden terminus. The expedition had an ample supply of food and water. They carried pressure suits and oxygen masks and contamination test kits and spare parts and a wide array of sensing equipment. If everything went well, they would be back in two weeks with a wealth of detail about the worlds beyond Eden. (For the time being, at least, the Maze was being left alone.)

"Max," she asked, "what are *you* going to do? Buy an island in the Bahamas and retire?"

He grinned. "I'm going to try to track down our visitor."

She shivered. "It seems to be gone now," she said. "I'd let it be."

"I think we have an obligation to try to find it."

"An obligation to whom?"

"I'm not sure. Maybe to the creature. I have a certain fondness for it."

"It might be dangerous."

"Maybe. But we know it has a sense of humor. And it rescues kids. I'd like very much to talk with it."

Harvey signaled her. Ready to go.

"Be careful, Max," she said.

"Sure." He was having a little trouble with his voice. "You too. Come back, okay?"

"Count on it." She moved suddenly, unexpectedly, into his arms, warm and yielding, and turned her face up. He kissed her, long and deep and wet.

✠ AUTHOR NOTE ✠

Lake Agassiz existed. I've taken a liberty or two with the shoreline, but other than that I've tried not to assault the facts unduly. Anyone who cares to may fly over the western limits of the valley of the Red River of the North, up near the Canadian border, and the ancient coast will be quite visible.